INSPECTION

INSPECTION

A NOVEL

JOSH MALERMAN

DEL REY / NEW YORK

Published in the United States by Del Rey, an imprint of Random House, a division of Penguin Random House LLC, New York.

DEL REY and the HOUSE colophon are registered trademarks of Penguin Random House LLC.

Hardback ISBN 978-1-5247-9699-0
Ebook ISBN 978-1-5247-9700-3

Printed in the United States of America on acid-free paper

randomhousebooks.com

2 4 6 8 9 7 5 3

First Edition

Title-page and part-title-page images:
copyright © iStock.com/AGrigorjeva

Book design by Victoria Wong

For Allison
The artist, the athlete, the model, the masks
The spirit I seek when I reach for the flask

INSPECTION

PART ONE

THE ALPHABET BOYS

Good Morning at the Parenthood!

No boy had ever failed an Inspection.

For this, J felt no anxiety as the steel door creaked open before him, as the faces of the Parenthood looked out, as the Inspectors stood against the far wall, each with a hand on the magnifying glasses hooked to their belts. J had done this every morning of his life, every morning he could remember, and, despite Q's theories on *likelihoods* and *probabilities* (his idea that eventually someone must fail in order to justify a lifetime of Inspections), J felt no doubt, no dread, no fear.

"Enter, J," Collins called. Collins, the stuffiest, oldest, burliest Inspector of all. The man smelled of old textbooks. His belly hung so far over his belt D joked he kept an Alphabet Boy hidden in there. *That's where we come from,* D had said. But all the Alphabet Boys knew they came from the Orchard, having grown on the Living Trees.

"Come on, then," Collins said. It was a wonder any words at all made it through the man's bushy brown mustache.

J knew the Inspector did not speak for himself.

D.A.D. must've given the signal it was time to begin.

To the snickers of L, D, and Q behind him, J entered and removed his pajamas, folding them and placing them in a neat pile upon the steel end table by the Check-Up room door. As the door was closing behind J, D called, "Shoulda showered, J!" And J pointed at him, the Alphabet Boys' gesture that meant, *You're a jerk, brother.*

The door locked into place, his clothes nicely piled, J stepped to the pair of rubber footprints on the cold steel floor. Winter was close, arriving perhaps as soon as tomorrow. And while J enjoyed the Effigy Meet as much as his brothers, he liked to keep the cold outside. The Check-Up room was as frigid as any he knew in the Turret.

"Turn," Inspector Collins said. He and Jeffrey observed from a distance, always the first step of the morning's Inspection. The dogs breathed heavy behind the glass door beyond the men. J turned to his left. He heard the leather of D.A.D.'s red jacket stretching. The man, as of yet out of sight, must have crossed his arms or sat back in his chair.

Winter outside the Turret could be brutal. Some years were worse than others. J, nearing his thirteenth birthday along with his twenty-three brothers, had experienced twelve winters. And with each one, Professor Gulch warned the boys about depression. The sense of loneliness that came from being stuck inside a ten-story tower, when the Orchard and the Yard froze over, when even the pines looked too cold to survive.

Hysteria, J thought. He shook his head, trying to roll the idea out his ear. It was a word he didn't like anywhere inside his head. As if the four syllables had the same properties as Rotts and Moldus, Vees and Placasores. The very diseases the Inspectors searched him for now.

"Turn."

Collins again. His gruff voice part and parcel of the Check-Up room. Like the sound of clacking dishes in the cafeteria. Or the choral voices of his brothers in the Body Hall.

"Cold," J said, turning his back to the Inspectors, facing now the locked door.

It was often chilly in the Check-Up room; unseen breezes, as if the solid-steel walls were only an illusion, and the distorted reflections unstable drawings on the wind. J imagined a slit somewhere, a crack in those walls, allowing pre-winter inside. It was similar, J thought, to the veterinarian's office in Lawrence Luxley's book *Dogs and Dog Days*. The brilliant leisure writer had described the poor animals' reactions so well:

> Unwelcoming, cold, it was as though Doctor Grand had intentionally made it so, so that the dogs understood the severity of their visits. And still, despite the inhospitable environs, the dogs understood that the room was good for them. That their lives depended on these regular visits. Some of them were even able to suppress their basest instincts . . . the ones that told them to run.

J had memorized all of Lawrence Luxley's books. Many of the Alphabet Boys had.

"Turn."

J did as he was told. Always had. The routine of the Inspections was as ingrained in his being as chewing before swallowing.

And with this third turn, he faced D.A.D.

A thrill ran through him, as it always had, twelve years running, to see D.A.D. for the first time in the day.

The bright-red jacket and pants were like a warm fire in the cold Check-Up room. Or the sun coming up. "Did you sleep well, J?"

D.A.D.'s voice. Always direct, always athletic. J wasn't the only Alphabet Boy who equated the man's voice with strength. Comfort. Security. Knowledge.

"I actually did not," J said, his twelve-year-old voice an octave deeper than it was only a year ago. "I dreamt something terrible."

"Is that right?" D.A.D.'s hazel eyes shone above his black beard, his hair black, too. J had black hair. Just like his D.A.D. "I'm intrigued. Tell me all about it."

"Turn," Collins said. And J turned to face the Inspectors and the dogs all over again.

No longer facing D.A.D., the color red like a nosebleed out of the corner of his eye now, J recounted his unconscious struggle. He'd been lost in a Yard four hundred times the size of the one he enjoyed every day. He described the horror of not being able to find his way back to the Turret.

"Lost?" D.A.D. echoed. The obvious interest in his voice was as clear to J as the subtle sound of his leather gloves folding around his pencil.

Yes, J told him, yes, he'd felt lost in the dream. He'd somehow strayed too far from the Turret and the Parenthood within. He couldn't remember how exactly—the actual pines framing the Yard were not present in this dream. But he was certainly very anxious to get back. He could hear his floor mates Q, D, and L calling from a distance but could not see the orange bricks of the tower. He couldn't make out the iron spires that framed the roof's ledge like a lonely bottom row of teeth. Teeth J and the other Alphabet Boys had looked through many nights, having found the nerve to sneak up to the roof. Nor could he see the tallest of the spires, the single iron tooth that pointed to the sky like a fang. Gone were the finite acres of the Yard, the expanse of green lawn between himself and the Turret. So were the reflections in the many elongated windows of the many floors. In their stead was endless green grass.

And fog.

"Well, winter *is* upon us," D.A.D. said. His voice was control. Always. Direction. Solution. Order. "Couldn't even see the fang, hmm? No sign of the Parenthood at all. No sign of *home*."

J thought of the yellow door on the roof, visible all the way from the Yard below. He thought of the solid orange bricks and how, on a summer day, the Turret resembled a sunrise.

"No," he said, shaking his head, looking to the silent faces of the Inspectors, who quietly fingered the magnifying glasses at their belts. J understood now, as a twelve-year-old boy, something he hadn't at eleven: The Inspections didn't begin when the Inspectors used their glasses. It began the second you walked through the door.

"You must have been so scared," D.A.D. continued. His voice was fatherhood. Administration. Always. "But, tell me, did you eventually *find* the Turret before waking?"

J was quiet a moment. He scratched at his right elbow with his left hand. He yawned a second time.

Hysteria, he thought again. He actually made fists, as if to knock the thought out of his head. Professor Gulch taught psychology and often stressed the many ways a boy's mind might turn on itself: mania, attention deficit, persecution, dissociation from reality, depression, and hysteria. For J, it had all sounded like distant impossibilities. Conditions to be studied for the purpose of study alone. Certainly J wasn't afraid of one day experiencing these states of mind himself. Yet here he was . . . twelve years old . . . and how else could he explain the new, unknown feelings he'd been having of late? What would Gulch call the sense of isolation, of being incomplete, when he looked out across the Yard, toward the entrance to the many rows of the Orchard? To where the Living Trees grew?

The boy recalled his childhood as though through a glass with residue of milk upon it. Unable to answer the simple question: Where do I come from?

Another Lawrence Luxley line. A real zinger, as Q would say.

But no, J thought, there in the Check-Up room. He wasn't trying to answer that question at all. No boy had ever determined which of the cherry trees in the Orchard were the ones they had grown on. And as far as J knew, they were fine with that.

Weren't they?

"No," J finally said. "I never found my way home." He heard the pencil against paper again, could easily imagine D.A.D.'s bright science eyes reading the words he wrote.

Like all the Alphabet Boys, J felt honored whenever D.A.D. noted what he said.

"And when you woke?" D.A.D. said. He didn't need to finish his sentence. It was clear what he was asking for.

"I thought it was real. I thought I was still out there. Like I'd woken in the Yard, on my bed. I looked up, must have seen the ceiling, but I mistook it for more of that fog. It took me a minute to understand I was just in my bedroom." He paused. Imagined D.A.D. stroking his black beard with a gloved hand. "This all happened moments ago, of course, as the call for Inspection woke me."

"Of course," D.A.D. said. "Now tell me," he began, and J knew the question he was about to be asked, before D.A.D. asked it. "Do you have a theory on what prompted this dream?"

While J had experienced a wide range of emotions in this room before, he wasn't prepared for the one he felt then.

Fear.

And where had it come from? Surely he knew this question was coming. Had he not had time to prepare for it? Was that it? Or was it something Q would call "deeper"?

Of course J knew the right answer to D.A.D.'s question. But for the first time in his life, he didn't feel like telling the truth.

The shock of this realization didn't strike him as hard as the one that immediately followed: a sense that he had decided to lie before entering this room and had simply not told himself about it.

Why? Why lie?

Because, just prior to going to bed the night before, long after his studies were done, J had seen someone crouched behind Mister Tree, the lone willow that denoted the end of the Yard and the beginning of the Orchard. It was a figure, he believed. Perhaps it was the way certain branches reached down to the forest floor as others united across it, but in J's mind's eye, the sight he'd seen was a person.

Crouched.

By Mister Tree.

At the time, J thought it was A or Z. He couldn't say why.

And maybe that was good enough reason to lie, J told himself. D.A.D. and the Inspectors would think he was crazy for suggesting such a thing!

A dead brother hiding behind a tree at night.

As if!

He looked from Jeffrey to Collins and thought maybe the two Inspectors could detect the hidden story. Jeffrey adjusted his cap. Collins the gold sash that ran from over his shoulder to his waist. J looked to their belts, as if that glass could penetrate his very skin, could determine the purity of his heart. Even the shepherds started breathing heavy, and one, Max, tilted his head to the side, the way dogs do when they hear a curious sound.

Hysteria. J didn't want to sound crazy. He didn't want to *be* crazy. It was branches and shadows and nothing more. Surely.

Yet, lying *was* a betrayal of sorts. J knew that. Perhaps, as kids, he and D had fibbed about who spilled the cherry juice on the hall carpet. Maybe once or twice, as a toddler, he'd shaken his head no when asked if he had gone to the bathroom in his pants. But these brief (and harmless, J believed, despite what lying could lead to) fabrications were easily washed clean with a single slap of that red-leathered hand. D.A.D. was very good at getting the real story out of his boys, as if he owned unseen shovels that always dug for the truth.

"J?"

J thought of Lawrence Luxley's book about soldiers, *Great Horses.* Thought about one soldier in particular, a general named Sam. Sam, Q had pointed out, dressed much like the Inspectors did. A gray wool uniform that always looked too warm, no matter that the temperature seemed to gradually lower during an Inspection. A gray kepi. A gold sash and a brown belt. Black boots. All throughout *Great Horses,* Sam felt a similar feeling to the one J had now: Sam had information he wasn't sure he should tell his troops. Luxley did a masterful job of highlighting this, a near twenty-page interior monologue where Sam weighed lying and lies and the right and wrong time to use them. In the end, he'd determined that no time was a good one and that his troops deserved to know the truth, even if it hurt them. But J read something deeper into that monologue than simply the merits of honesty: General Sam was scared. Not scared in the way the Parenthood had lovingly taught the Alphabet Boys to be afraid—that is, *of* themselves and what they were capable of doing *to* themselves if they did not adhere to the laws of the Turret. But rather . . . scared *for* himself.

"Why?' he asked out loud. Both Inspectors tilted their heads like the dog had just done.

"What's that?" D.A.D. asked.

Again, Professor Gulch's lectures on psychology rose up like birds in J's suddenly troubled mind.

Sam, J knew, was torn. J felt the same way, exposed beneath the bright fluorescent lights of the Check-Up room. After all, the harsh illumination showed every crevasse in the faces of the Inspectors, lines that told the boys how old these men truly were even if the sun in the Yard could not. And the reverse held true for the boys. Their youth was never as obvious as when they removed their pajamas and folded them in a pile on the end table by the door. A boy could see much more of his body in here than when he was in the shower . . . revelations that often alarmed him. Holding out his arm, looking down at his belly, lifting a knee, a boy could almost make out the very tunnel-and-bridge system of veins and arteries traveling beneath his skin. A pimple, normal in the hall light, could be Placasores in the Check-Up room. The light hairs on the arms looked sewn into the skin. Knuckles and toes resembled old weathered leather. Belly buttons looked like holes. Fingernails like dead wood.

And sometimes J felt like he could see even more than the unflattering details of his body. Sometimes it felt like he could see motivations in the Check-Up room, fast fleeting glimpses of the truth, whatever that might be.

"J," D.A.D. repeated. His voice was impatience. As loving as he was to his twenty-four boys, D.A.D. was without question the most impatient man within the Turret walls. "Come now. Out with it. You have a theory for what prompted this dream."

J recoiled at the sudden volume of his voice, as if the man had silently transported across the cold floor, his lips less than an inch from J's ear. *"Tell me."*

It was true; J indeed had a theory for D.A.D. It's what the Alphabet Boys were raised to do.

Think.

But J was thinking of A or Z, impossibly mobile, crouched and unmoving.

Tell him, J thought. But a deeper voice argued. One that sounded like it belonged to a wise brother.

A dead one?

"I'm thinking," J said. "I want to articulate this the right way."

He should've woken Q last night is what he should have done. He'd considered doing it, of course. The boys on Floor 8 had long crept into one another's rooms when a particularly powerful storm came through. Or a nightmare of equal measure. J had knocked on Q's door as recently as a month ago, feeling sick and hoping Q had some soup remaining from dinner. But last night, despite wanting confirmation, he remained by his large window overlooking the Yard, a window almost as wide as the wall. He knew Q would have something intelligent to say, would perhaps even be able to prove the form as an unfortunate combination of branches, leaves, and moonlight. Because it *was* probable that what J had seen was no more than a combination of inert, non-sentient pieces. And yet . . . J felt knowledge coming from those woods.

J felt life. Or something like it.

Felt like you were being watched is what it was.

"I think it's because of the coming floor shift," J said. "I've grown up with D and L and Q. To be moved, in the shuffle . . . I don't know. I agree that it's a good thing for the Parenthood to do, to promote fresh experiences, to forge new bonds, but it's also a little . . ."

J felt cold leather upon his shoulder.

"A little like being lost?" D.A.D. asked. Gently, D.A.D. turned J to face him. The bulb hung directly over the man's head, and parts of his face were obscured by shadow. J thought how D.A.D.'s entire face looked to be covered in hair, as if the shadows cast were actually his beard growing, rising up to his shining eyes, climbing higher yet to his thick, fur-like pompadour.

"Yes." J swallowed. "A lot like being lost." He glanced past D.A.D., to the notepaper upon the steel desk. There was a lot of activity on the page. Many notes.

The Inspection begins, J thought again, *the moment you walk through the door.*

D.A.D. did not nod. He did not smile. He simply stared. It felt, to J, as if the man were using those shovels indeed, searching J's mind for a better dream-prompt than the coming floor shift.

Then D.A.D.'s face changed, a little bit. Both eyes squinted and the right side of his mouth lifted. Just enough to suggest warmth.

"I get it," D.A.D. said. "And I'm sure I'll run into more stories like yours today, as we make our morning Inspections." He did not pat J on the shoulder and then walk back to his desk. He did not say anything else on the topic at all. Instead, he remained, staring. "I've just had a wonderful idea," he said. "How about if I manufacture a means by which you can tell me your thoughts, your feelings, directly. Something we can share, just you and I. A notebook perhaps. You take notes and . . . deliver them to me. Why, we could be pen pals in that way."

There was never a feeling so bright as being singled out by D.A.D.

"That would be . . . really nice," J said.

"It would, yes. Excellent."

Yet, as D.A.D. continued to stare, continued to study, the usual list of horrifying diseases crossed J's mind. The reason, the boys had long been told, for the Inspections in the first place.

Vees. Rotts. Placasores.

Was D.A.D. looking for these? And could he spot them in J's eyes? Could he spot them in a notebook, too?

"Gentlemen," D.A.D. said. He snapped his gloved fingers. A

sound that was almost as familiar as the word *Inspection* itself, as it came shrill through the floor's one steel-meshed speaker in the hall.

Collins and Jeffrey removed their magnifying glasses and advanced. D.A.D. retreated, but not all the way to his desk. J, turning back to face the Inspectors, could feel D.A.D. crowding him still, standing close behind with his arms crossed, his leather gloves gripping the sleeves of his red jacket. Both Collins and Jeffrey looked to D.A.D. with the same expression J imagined himself to be wearing. A tick past confusion. A few ticks shy of fear.

D.A.D. had never watched an Inspection from so close.

Why this one?

Hysteria, J thought, and decided it was the last time he was going to think it. It was only Mister Tree's low-hanging branches. Natural as cherries in the Orchard. And a dead brother crouching at midnight was . . . was . . . *hysterical.*

No. He was hiding nothing because there was nothing to hide.

"Go on," D.A.D. said, his voice like flowing water over J's shoulder. That water became a wave, and in that wave J imagined a figure crouched behind Mister Tree. "I want to make sure J understands that, in light of his bad dream, he *is* in the care of the Parenthood and that the Parenthood will always be here to protect him. By way of Inspection." The Inspectors held their magnifying glasses up to J's naked body. D.A.D. continued to talk. Close. Too close. "I want you to know, J, that if something like what happened in your dream should ever occur in waking life . . . impossible as that scenario is . . . you needn't worry about finding your way back to the Turret."

"Lift," Collins said. J lifted both arms and the Inspectors brought the magnifying glasses to his armpits.

"If ever you stray so far, J, my J," D.A.D. said, "the Parenthood will find *you.*"

THE BURT REPORT: NOVEMBER 1, 2019

To Be Read upon Waking

I'll cut right to it: If it's order Richard cherishes most in what he himself has dubbed "the Delicate Years," then this is simply not the time to shuffle the boys' bedrooms. The simple take is this: Richard's right—at age twelve the boys are treading very close to experiencing a degree of sexuality unparalleled thus far in their lives. It's a phase that each of us adults knows well. And do we remember how vivid everything became a year or two past twelve? How frightening and exciting at once? Most important, how emotional? (NOTE: Richard, I realize you loathe when I address you directly in my reports, but I cannot underscore this point enough: You must try to recall your own blossoming, for there is nothing quite as potent as male sexuality in bloom. Now multiply that by 24.) I would not be surprised to discover, reading today's Inspection reports, that many of the boys are already expressing anxiety with the shuffle. Some might express anger. Some might even lie. My rationale for including the latter is not to instill fear into Richard and it is certainly not with a mind to belittle him, but rather . . . I think it's true. Teenagers lie because teenagers aren't yet aware that their warring emotions are natural. The Alphabet Boys are knocking on teenage's door. And in an environment like the Parenthood, they don't even have the example, usually set a year or two prior . . . by girls.

One of the many difficulties in keeping the knowledge of the existence of women from them. But, admittedly, one we have been prepared for.

Now, Richard's logic for instituting the room shuffle at this time is sound. Rather than wander the halls of the Parenthood confused and restless, the boys might blame their growing anxiety on the move itself, therefore supplying them with an easily avoided focal point, by which they can carry on with their studies as Richard contends they will. This logic makes sense, yes, but only stands as a placeholder and eventually will fade out. And when the uneasiness with the shuffle does fade out . . . what then will the boys blame their sudden emotions on? I know Richard well enough to believe he has a second distraction planned . . . and a third . . . and what must be an entire deck of cards, already arranged, to be flipped, out into the light, new worries, new concerns, until the boys become visibly comfortable with the fresh feelings within them.

The Inspection reports will reveal when that day comes. These are the Delicate Years, indeed.

But if I'm going to admonish Richard for his use of distractions in what must be a futile effort in the end, I must be able to contribute to the conversation. I must be able to provide an alternate solution to how we, the Parenthood, deal with this sexual revolution (make no mistake, Richard; there will be a revolution waging in each and every one of our boys. Bloodshed on their own private battlefields). Here, then, are my five solutions:

1) Encourage the boys further in the arts. Of course we cannot reveal to them the nature of procreation. That's fine; as the Constitution of the Parenthood clearly states, we are not in the business of creating biologists, and while genius can wear many coats, the Alphabet Boys are being raised to become the world's greatest engineers, scientists, and mathematicians. ARTICLE ONE of the CONSTITUTION OF THE PARENTHOOD: GENIUS IS DISTRACTED BY THE OPPOSITE SEX. Richard's entire experiment balances upon this initial article, the fountainhead of the Parenthood at large. So while other boys their age, or a couple of years older, spend two-thirds of their waking life attempting to court women (and/or simply impress them), the Alphabet Boys will be working three times as hard on the aforementioned subjects. And yet . . . there must be an outlet. The arts could provide this. I do not think the leisure books penned by Lawrence Luxley are capable of satisfying this need. The arts, good arts, encouraging arts, can act as a more refined placeholder, a bucket, if you will, to catch the boys' wayward sexuality as it comes pouring out their ears and eyes. Make no mistake, the boys will be changing, in paramount ways, to degrees not experienced in the Parenthood thus far.

X is a fine artist. G has shown signs. To me, Voices is simply not enough. As magnificent as that choir has become.

Painting an abstract *picture, singing a* non sequitur *song ... these may placate the unfathomable, focal-pointless feelings they will experience.*

As always, more to come on this at a later date.

2) Attempt to influence their dreams. Subliminal hints throughout the Parenthood might cause the boys to dream of specific things, calming things, visions and images that could take the place of a sexuality they intentionally (on our part) know nothing about. I'll provide one example (but we can certainly discuss this in a much bigger way in person): Hang color photos of rolling hills or desert landscapes outside the door of the bedroom belonging to the most popular boy on each floor of the Turret. That is to say: Whichever room the boys have a tendency to congregate in most often, hang a landscape that resembles something of a naked body. Perhaps this tiny gift (on our part) will assuage (momentarily) the growing need each of them will be experiencing.

As is the case with all these posits: More on this at a later date.

3) Encourage the boys to increase their athletic endeavors. We do this already, but perhaps not to the degree we will need to. It is well understood (and well documented, of course) that Richard would prefer the boys to spend no more than 10 percent of their days in physical pursuit, but the Delicate Years not only announce the coming of an emotional deluge; the boys will need a physical outlet. Why not order a new athletic decree: ONE LAP OF THE CHERRY ORCHARD, which constitutes a 3.1-mile experience, the exact distance of the fabled 5K, which boys their age are no doubt running in other parts of the world. If this idea doesn't suit

Richard's tastes, then I suggest purchasing treadmills and installing them in each of the boys' bedrooms; who knows at what time of night they'll feel the need to burn off some steam. My professional guess is ANY. ANY time of night. And any time of day.

4) Limit the physical portion of the Inspection and increase the emotional query. As I've stated above, the boys have much to gain through addressing the abstract feelings they will be (already are!) experiencing, and whether they make complete sense of their "new selves" doesn't matter. As we adults already know: There is no such thing as "knowing yourself," not wholly, but the attempts to do so along the way certainly ease the pain.

5) Reconsider Article Sixteen of the Constitution of the Parenthood in which Richard (forcibly, this is true) included the rule that states that, under no circumstances, no matter how trying the Delicate Years prove to be, will the Alphabet Boys undergo any form of castration. And yet . . . we've already lost A and Z to much more gruesome ends. Might it be time to consider removing the sexuality Richard so dreads is coming? NOTE: It's a year or two away. Plan now.

In summation, Richard and the Parenthood would be well served to either nurture the coming barrage of sexuality through abstraction or to (pardon) nip it off at the bud. It is my professional opinion that a series of distractions (i.e., the floor shift) will only compress the issue, increasing the boys' curiosity, their thirst for answers, until their behavior resembles nothing like we've seen before, or until they break the cardinal rules of the Parenthood and all of Richard's dalliance and jurisprudence is lost.

Genius may be distracted by the opposite sex, but sexuality itself is not so easily distracted.

(Thank you for your time, Richard, and I look forward to speaking with you directly when next we meet in the Glasgow Tunnel.)

The Body Hall before Breakfast

Just before breakfast, the boys were informed D.A.D. was going to make a speech. This, of course, would take place in the Body Hall, named so, J assumed, because of how many bodies they fit into the high-ceilinged, echoey, wood-paneled concert hall whenever D.A.D. had something important to say.

All of them. All of the bodies. From the Alphabet Boys to the Inspectors, Professor Gulch to the cooks. Even Lawrence Luxley himself, always a highlight for J and the others to see in person. The nurses, the cleaners, the health aides, and the plumbers.

The Parenthood.

Speech, the word, like *Inspection,* had changed over the years. It invoked a much different feeling now than it had when the boys were just children and would, presumably, spark something else years from now. When the boys were kids, D.A.D.'s speeches meant hardly anything at all; J mostly recalled the back of other boys' heads, the back of their benches, and the dark sonorous syllables of D.A.D.'s words echoing off the walls that seemed to reach the sky. In those days, it took a simple glance across the hall to D or F and it was all J could do to stifle a bout of uncontrollable laughter.

But things had changed.

RICHARD UNDERSTOOD THIS more than anyone. He had planned for it.

It matters not, an early Burt Report stated, *whether the boys take in what Richard says. The point is to instill a sense of wonder, a plan that is no doubt working, based upon the sincerely awed visages observing him as he delivers his speeches.*

The Alphabet Boys had not been taught God. For Richard, obedience trumped religion.

This morning, the Inspections over, Richard held the day's Burt Report in one hand, a glass of scotch in the other. He read half of the first sentence his personal psychiatrist had penned one more time:

I'll cut right to it: If it's order Richard cherishes most in what he himself has dubbed "the Delicate Years"—

He set the papers upon his desk. Despite the light snowfall outside his first-floor window, he felt warm. He rose from his desk and stepped to the full-sized mirror on the back of his front door.

"You look good," he said. "Hardly the parent of twenty-four twelve-year-old boys."

The number was once twenty-six and, having flipped through the report, he'd seen Burt had mentioned A and Z, despite Richard's personal orders not to.

. . . we've already lost A and Z to much more gruesome ends . . .

He removed his red coat, exposing a simple tank top beneath. The muscles in his shoulders and arms looked strong beneath the soft overhead light. His beard as dark as misinformation.

In the beginning, following the successful launch of the Parenthood, Richard was very aware that he had to fill the tower with a profound sense of character. It was his duty to deliver the philosophy of the Parenthood. His duty to make good on all that he claimed the place could be. In those days, it wasn't uncommon for him to feel the pressure of the Inspectors he'd hired, simple convicts only a year prior, to *feel* them and the cooks and the teachers and the academic-book writers, ex-cons all, watching him as he gave his speeches to the (then) twenty-six toddlers in the Body Hall. The Alphabet Boys, Burt had come to call them (a name Richard, as their D.A.D., was rather fond of). A name for each letter of the alphabet.

A

B

C . . .

Yes, in those days Richard gave his speeches for the benefit of the staff, whether he directed his voice at them or not. It was exciting indeed when, five years into the experiment, Richard first spotted comprehension in the eyes of his boys, knowledge transferred, from the pulpit to P, from the speech to each.

And now . . . The Delicate Years were close. No longer could Richard come at the boys subconsciously, through feel, a vague but powerful sense of rules and why not to break them. With the Delicate Years came the full attention of discerning boys. Intelligent boys. Boys who could, and would, now analyze each and every word Richard used.

He smiled in the mirror. It wasn't the first instance of his boys breaking stereotype: In the world beyond the Parenthood, teenagers *stopped* listening to their parents.

Richard flexed his aging biceps, frowned at their appearance in the glass, and put his jacket back on. He'd read the Burt Report later. The staff psychiatrist broke more rules on one page of paper than other staff were permitted over a decade.

Addressing Richard directly. Mentioning A and Z.

He left his quarters and was greeted by two guards in plain-clothes outside his door. Both armed. Richard recognized the awe in their eyes—as if he were a celebrity, the pastor in their church.

He still had them, he knew. Twelve years in.

"Just get up there and spread some excitement, right?" Richard said for their ears as they followed him up the black-tiled walkway to the Body Hall. "Show them it's okay for a man to be overwhelmed by his passions, dangerous as some may be. The time of radiant men has arrived." Here Richard paused and turned to face Bobby, the thin-haired guard who once stole cars and spent three years in jail for theft. Sometimes Richard wondered if the staff hadn't simply traded drugs and drink, incarceration, for the Parenthood. "God is sweating, Bobby. Can you feel it?"

Beyond the glass walls of the hall, snow fell. Richard stepped to it and looked out upon the Yard. In the now-hazy distance, the pines stood guard.

"It's time to usher in the new father," he said. "And his new sons."

Greatness, Richard once told a former guard, with one hand on the shoulder of the man's plaid short-sleeved wholesome shirt, just before sending him to the Corner, *is not pretty to look at. Study the faces of the world's biggest thinkers and you'll note an optimistic dismay. Exhaustion. May this be the last thing you ever learn, Brad: Exhaustion isn't brought about by sitting still. You gotta move to get it. And motion will give you those worry lines, that thinning hair, that shell-shocked glaze over your once-bright eyes. Tell me, Brad, which would you rather have? A simple, easily read face or the bloody knuckles of a man who has knocked on his inner sanctum's door?*

The guard Brad had experienced doors locking on him before. Four years in Jackson for assault. But he'd never seen anything like the Corner.

"Welcome to the Parenthood," Richard said now, still watching the early-morning snow fall through the hall glass. The sudden swell of choral voices, Alphabet Boys singing in the Body Hall, broke his reverie. In blond Bobby's eyes he saw the dark side of the Parenthood, the closing of the Corner door. Richard thought maybe he could hear the door creaking.

Richard smiled. It was not the Corner at all but rather Gordon emerging from his own quarters on the first floor. The Parenthood's chief assistant to D.A.D. looked as wonderfully infallible as he always did. His black hair like a shining singular piece, the face and hair of a plastic toy soldier in a thousand-dollar suit.

"Richard," Gordon said. "Did you read the Burt Report?"

"Some."

"Well, I have a *lot* to say about the five suggested alternatives to the floor shift. And seriously, where does Burt get the nerve? I'm sorry the two boys were named."

"A and Z," Richard said. He was quiet a beat. "And here I've just said their names again."

The six-part harmony of Voices seemed to emerge from one holy throat. A minor chord as sad as the death of their brothers A and Z.

Spoiled boys. Spoiled rotten.

Richard closed his eyes. He turned his back on the falling flakes and walked toward the Body Hall, toward the sound of his boys singing.

"Yes," Gordon agreed, writing Richard's words down on a clipboard. "But you shouldn't have to think about them just prior to delivering a speech. It was egregious, as Burt often is."

"Have I changed, Gordon?" Richard asked, his eyes open again, his black boots clacking against the black tiles. Ahead, the last of the boys—H, in all black—could be seen hurrying through the Body Hall doors.

"Changed how, sir?"

"Do I value now what I valued then?"

"You've remained staunch in your vision, sir."

"I have. And yet . . ."

"The Burt Report is getting to you. That's all."

"I fear, Gordon."

From the Body Hall, the voices rose, swelled to a weeping peak. Richard paused at the door. He eyed the alternating choir, the six boys who sang today. In their black slacks and black turtlenecks only their faces shone, floating visages hovering in the shadows under the arches of the Body Hall. The echo of their song added ghosts to their small number.

Richard relished the sight. The Parenthood choir, Voices. The other boys, too, dressed in black, seated in the pews. The white carpet of the aisle. The shadowed podium on the stage. The staff lined up against the walls like watchers.

Or perhaps like the victims of a firing squad.

Richard spotted Warren Bratt, sloppy and overweight, slouched and frowning.

"What do you fear?" Gordon asked.

The Body Hall lights reflected off Bratt's glasses, and Richard couldn't tell if the cynical author was looking at him or not.

"Surprises," Richard said.

One deep breath and he entered the hall. Gordon followed.

As Richard walked the white carpet, his red jacket and slacks like spilt blood upon it, he was engulfed in the morbid tones of Voices, today the boys from Floor 8 with F and W accompanying. Despite Richard's total ban of religion in the Parenthood, the boys sang Barber's *Agnus Dei*. Aesthetic gibberish to them all; they had no way of knowing Latin.

His boys. His Alphabet Boys.

Oh, how they stared. Flat admiration in their eyes. Even those who sang: J and D, L and Q, F and W. As their voices rose to the Mural of Ambition upon the Body Hall's high ceiling, they did so in one unified chord, seemingly adding dimension to the image of the shirtless man raising the boulder with his mind. The boys in black, the boys in the pews, some whispering, some elbowing, all fixated on the man in red leather, a moving wound now upon the white carpet toward the stage. As Richard climbed the steps, as Gordon and the guards shuffled to the sides of the stage to join the other staff, many of the boys inhaled deeply. They'd been with him only moments ago at their individual Inspections, yet seeing their D.A.D. at the podium in the Body Hall was a sight each and every time. Looking right, Richard smiled Warren Bratt's way, showing nothing of his opinion of the unkempt, balding author's particularly rumpled appearance. Then Richard signaled the boys of Voices to cease singing, and their final chord rang out long after they took his cue.

The boys of Voices took their seats.

Richard leaned toward the mic till he felt the cold metal touch his beard.

He delivered his speech.

"BOYS! I won't take up too much of your time. I expect you're hungry and can smell breakfast from where you sit. I thank you, each of you, for congregating on such short notice. These Body Hall events are, as you well know, rare enough that my calling them must mean something or must mean, at the very least, I've got something to get off my chest."

Richard paused. He'd opened with "plain speak." Gordon's suggestion, many years ago: *Relax them with something casual, Richard, then Trojan-horse the real message in.*

"First I'd like to congratulate you all on some of the best Inspections we've had in years. Your frankness, your honesty, and your transparency are valued above all things. You've brought a tear to your D.A.D.'s eyes."

"We love you, D.A.D.!"

F called it out. Funny F. Richard smiled and held up an open palm to quiet the rumbling the boy had inspired.

"Thank you, F. I love you, too. I love all of you boys and I feel particularly proud of you today." He looked to J directly. J's eyes were partially hidden by his black bangs. Richard could barely make out the innocent spheres that had looked to him for everything in this life. "But I wouldn't be honest with myself if I claimed that it was only through the Inspections that I've concluded you are all, indeed, on the right path in life. I've observed you boys very closely, perhaps in ways you don't even know." Here, E and O looked to one another and Richard saw hope in their eyes. *Has D.A.D. been watching us? Isn't that exciting?* "Why, before Inspection this very morning I overheard a wonderful conversation brewing between two of you regarding a possible alternative to gasoline, and I couldn't help but smile. My boys. My boys! Oh, how I enjoy eavesdropping as two of my boys employ the powers of their blooming intellect, toying with the concepts of cures, alternatives, of process and progress, the same. Do you see? Are you able to recognize the virtue of such an exchange, no doubt considered flippant by the two participants, and how much more meaningful it was than the subject matter boys your age *could* be engaged in?"

Richard inhaled. That last line was what Burt called a *thin-icer.* Possibly too close to the truth of things. But Richard didn't think so. His boys knew as much as he wanted them to know. And who cared how thin the ice was when the truth was twice frozen so far below?

"Can you believe we've all reached the point we have? It seems like yesterday little Y was asking . . . why?" Some laughter from the boys. "And now? Now I ask *him.* Why? And he might just tell me." The laughter gave way to awe. It usually did. "We've accomplished so much, yet we have so very far to go! And, boys, my beautiful boys, this is what troubles me, this is what has brought me to call upon you . . . today."

Richard thought of the losses mentioned in the morning's Burt Report. A and Z. The bookends of the Alphabet Boys. A coincidence (of all the boys to lose, those two?) that nearly tore Richard's stomach lining out with worry. It took many hours with the staff doctors, many days in the bowels of the Turret, the boiler thrumming near, the sound of two dozen toddlers a floor above, for Richard to be convinced of the probability, the *likelihood,* that two boys of twenty-six must meet an unhappy end.

The fact that he was responsible for those ends didn't factor into his thinking.

A and Z had both seen women.

A and Z had been spoiled rotten.

A and Z had been sent to the Corner.

"I'm going to tell you boys a secret." Richard paused for effect. It seemed to work. "Long before you reached the age you are now, I had already dubbed these days . . . *the Recasting Years*. Just as you fine-tune your visions in the Effigy Meet, so will you recast yourselves here, in the Turret. Why? Why would I consider this age any different from any other? Why would I consider this era any more notable than your budding baby youth, when you couldn't even lift your own heads? I'll tell you why: Here . . ." The Delicate Years to the staff. The Recasting Years to the boys. "You have now officially begun the process of cutting your father-strings, becoming men of your own." He paused, allowing for the gravity of this to sink in. The fear of being untied, too. "Observing you in the Yard and the Orchard. Observing you at mealtime. Reading over your reports and listening to your reactions to the latest Luxley novel. Your opinions are as sophisticated as mine. The thoughts you casually cast aside are as revealing as those you deem important. Your Inspections prove it. Boys! My boys! You are coming into your own!"

A and Z. A and Z. The bookends are what keep the books standing. But the bookends had been taken away.

Richard adjusted the collar of his coat.

"This is how it goes when it goes right, boys." The boys in black. Some in turtlenecks and slacks, others in blazers and button-downs. But Richard spotted a dot of white. As he spoke, his eyes traveled to the small spot of color: T's undershirt showing between the buttons of his shirt. Another omen? Like the coincidence of A and Z? "The mind takes its time, in youth, before it starts acting on its own ideas. Can you remember doing everything your brothers did? Do you recall the days when you would invariably spend the night with your floor mates? Almost incapable of taking some time alone, or simply not wanting to? You boys were inseparable. Why, there were times we had to physically pry you apart and place you back in your own rooms. And look at you now! You have individual

interests. Individual theories. You've discovered the beauty of intellectual property. The gratifying essence, the root of real *genius*. You
know I am right! Just as those early days were important for the
bonds that were built and for the confidence you gained in seeing
your ideas and actions approved by your brothers, these new days,
now, this molting, has a fresh purpose of its own. Today can be
considered tomorrow for how quickly you are growing! Your opinions are yours! They are not mine! Do you see? I taught you when
you were small. But you are almost as big as I!"

Had he established an undeniable sense of fatherhood? Or were
the boys, brighter than any boys in the world, instinctively aware
that he was not blood? That he was not genes?

That he was not *father*?

"I wish I could reach out to each of you with my mind alone;
you'd understand how much I value the time you have before you,
you'd see the great open expanse of an infinite Yard that needs
great care. For any idea you have in these forthcoming years is
worth noting, is worth writing down, is worth talking about with
your floor mates or taking a short trip to another floor to partake
in discussion with boys you don't see as often. You might even be
inspired to take a longer trip to my very quarters. I cannot stress
this point enough, how available I am to you during these years,
how interested I am in the smallest thought that may occur to you.
Your trivialities are my life's work."

Many boys exchanged shocked glances. An invite from D.A.D.
to his quarters? This was a big day, indeed.

Richard felt sweat dripping beneath the tank top under his
jacket. He relished it. It meant he was working. It meant he was
present. It meant he was burning with the things he'd said. Burning
in front of the boys.

"You look as though you know what I speak of already. I see
some of you are blushing. And do you know *why* the words I say
are sinking in? Do you?" He paused. Tried not to look at the spot

of white exposed at T's chest. Tried not to think of omens. "It's because what I say is the truth! And every one of you values the truth. A change is upon you! And here, you knew it already. You didn't need me to tell you that your most recent thoughts are the most fascinating thoughts you've ever had. After all, you're experiencing them on your own." Then, suddenly, with no segue, "You will find a fresh notebook upon your beds following breakfast. It is blue. I encourage you to write these new thoughts down. The erasers have already been removed from your pens and pencils. I do not want to miss a *moment* of this, the Recasting Years." Richard paused. He had them. Rapt. His boys. "Write it all down. Every word. Express your strangest thoughts. Nothing would please your D.A.D. more than to be presented with full blue notebooks, overflowing with your concerns and ambitions, the secrets you keep. Do you understand? I can see by your nodding heads that you do. And so I will leave you with this: Hide nothing. For as your intellects have grown, so has the space in which to hide. From me. From your D.A.D. And who among you would do that? Who here would hide what they know their D.A.D. prizes so deeply?"

"Nobody!" S called. More laughter from the boys. This time charged with excitement.

Richard held up an open hand.

"Now," he said. The boys shifted in their seats because they knew what was coming next. D.A.D. always closed his speeches the same way. D.A.D. thrummed his fingers on the podium, a drumroll of sorts. All at once the Body Hall erupted into two simple words, as the boys cried out exuberantly with their D.A.D. *"Let's eat!"*

Richard acknowledged the choir. Voices. The six boys rose, took their places in the shadows again.

J SAID TO D, "I thought the notebook was for me only. D.A.D. told me it was for me."

"What?"

But they didn't have time to discuss this. And despite J's obvious concern, he and the other five boys began *Miserere mei, Deus* together.

The other Alphabet Boys made for the Body Hall doors.

RICHARD STEPPED FROM the podium. The staff made to leave, too, but Warren Bratt was easy to catch up with.

"Lawrence," Richard said, calling Bratt by his nom de plume lest a boy was in earshot. "How hungry are you?"

Bratt turned to face him, and all of Richard's concerns with the author of the boys' leisure books were increased. Warren Bratt was a priggish, stuffy, self-centered former punk who once fancied himself a fine writer. Ten years as Lawrence Luxley had done much to squash the snobbery, but Richard was learning that, as Burt once said, you could only tie an artist's hands together for so long before he began creating with his feet.

Warren's leisure-book ideas had grown disturbingly original. Not a good thing at all.

"Pretty hungry," Warren said.

"That's fine. Gordon will meet you in your office after breakfast."

"Why?"

Richard did not feign friendliness.

"I think it important that, as the boys' tastes change, so do the books they enjoy."

Warren nodded. "I know that, Richard. But I'd like to—"

"Good. Then you won't mind a chat." He eyed Warren from head to foot. "And wash your shirt. The sweat stains make it look like you're working too hard. As if you're being forced to write something you don't want to write." As he stepped by Bratt, guards in tow, he added, "The boys worship Lawrence Luxley. Please, show them how a genius dresses."

The Alphabet Boys Eat

Seated six a table at four large round tops, most of the Alphabet Boys appeared charged by D.A.D.'s speech in the Body Hall. F, funny F, joked as freely as if the Parenthood had outlawed studying for the day. His large front teeth looked especially white in contrast to his black button-down shirt and the black blazer that hung over his seat back. J and D had long, privately, joked that F looked like a "living cartoon." They watched him talk, now, as they once smiled at drawings scribbled into the margins of their textbooks.

"Hey, W," F said. "Don't eat my breakfast today. I know you're gonna want to and I know you're gonna ask for my leftovers, but there simply won't be any. So the only way you're gonna get at my food is by eating your way through my stomach." He paused, feigned seriousness with his overweight friend. "I shouldn't have given you that idea, huh."

J eyed the two boys. F and W were very close. They'd shared a floor with P and T their whole lives. And would J be sharing a floor with any of them when the day of the floor shift came? And how many years would it be that way?

"And what's with *you*?" F asked, pointing two fingers directly at J. "You look like you just got sent to the Corner."

"Oh, come now," L said. Conservative, proper L.

F snorted. "Oh, stop it, L," he said. "It's good to talk about scary things. Makes them less so. But I'm not gonna let J here get off the hook just because you don't like the way I speak." He smiled at J. Eyes wide. It was F's way: exaggeration.

"Nothing's wrong," J said. But it was clear something was.

"*Is* something the matter?" Q asked. Q's glasses magnified his eyes as the Inspectors' glasses might.

"No . . . it's just . . ."

"Ah-*ha*!" F said. "I knew it! I told you! Am I good, or am I good?" He nudged W, and W nodded a yes. "Come on, then, J. Out with it."

J thought fast. He couldn't and wouldn't tell them that he'd hidden information in the morning's Inspection. He would not look hysterical in front of his brothers any more than he would the Parenthood.

"The notebooks," J said. And as the words left his mouth, he understood that he was more upset about it than he'd realized.

"And what about them?" F asked, his big teeth wrinkling his lower lip.

"Well, in my Inspection this morning, D.A.D. told me he had an idea, just for me. He mentioned a notebook. Something I could write in. Fill . . . just for him."

W smiled and his fat cheeks turned a rosy shade of red. "You mean this one?" He pulled one out from under the table. A large black *W* was printed on its cover.

"You sneak!" F said. "You already went up to your room and nabbed it!"

"I move well for a large boy, F."

The friends laughed heartily. Then W turned his focus on J. Like Q, W had especially intelligent eyes. Quiet as he was, he often gave off the impression that he knew something the other boys did not. But whereas Q's intelligence seemed to flow from an inquisitive place, W's was more rooted in the Constitution of the Parenthood. D.A.D. himself had said W would make an excellent lawyer one day.

"Either way, what you're saying isn't true," W said. J felt a quiet jolt. Had W just suggested J hid something in his Inspection?

But no. He had not.

"What do you mean?" J asked.

W hid the notebook back under the table. "Three days ago, in Professor Kinney's class, K's calculator stopped working. Kinney sent me to the office to fetch him a new one."

"No doubt to encourage a little exercise, friend," F poked.

W waved his brother off. "While I was there?" He leaned back in his chair, crossed his arms. "I saw a stack of twenty-four blue notebooks, each with one of our names printed bold upon its cover."

"I don't follow," L said.

"You never do," F said.

"What W is saying," Q kindly said, "is that D.A.D. couldn't have told J he had an idea planned just for him, when three days ago he'd already carried out the same idea for us all."

Silence at the table. The voices of the other boys in the cafeteria filled the space.

They all looked to J for some sort of rebuttal. But J was at a loss for words. D.A.D. *had* told him he'd thought of the notebook just for him. And the way he'd said it . . . like he'd just thought of it . . .

Suddenly, as if a fan had been turned on in a very hot room, J felt some of his own guilt cool off. But the cool air brought cold.

Had J and D.A.D. lied to one another on the same day?

It was almost too frightening to imagine.

"You must've misunderstood him," L said. "Simple as that."

"But I didn't."

"Poor J," F said. "Thought he had a little special attention and, in the end, he did not."

"Obviously you're not suggesting D.A.D. lied to you, J," Q said.

J thought of the Corner. What little he knew of it. A door in the basement of the tower. A basement none of the boys knew how to get to.

"I didn't say he *lied*," J said.

"Of course you didn't," Q said. "That's the silliest thing I've ever heard."

"But you *are* saying he got something wrong," W added. "And that's perhaps just as egregious."

Before J could defend himself, the bell rang and the cooks appeared with trays of waffles, eggs, fruits, and vegetables. As each boy was served, Q spoke of the merits of fruit in the morning and F pretended to hide his food from W. But J didn't feel hungry anymore.

J was thinking about lies.

The train of thought was so profound that he found himself replaying exactly what D.A.D. had said in the Check-Up room. *I've just had a wonderful idea. How about if I manufacture a means by which you can tell me your thoughts, your feelings, directly. Something we can share, just you and I. A notebook perhaps. You take notes and . . . deliver them to me. Why, we could be pen pals in that way.*

Not quite a lie after all. Technically, D.A.D. hadn't said it was just for him.

Yet, *just you and I . . .*

Surely J had it wrong. A word here, a word there, and the meaning of a thing could change so much. Luxley talked about that in one of his books. J couldn't tell if he felt relief at the idea of D.A.D. blurring the truth or if it scared him more deeply than the idea of that vague door in the basement. Was that door below him now? Below the very chair in which he sat?

"Eat up, J," F said. "Or W is gonna leap across the table."

"I just might," W said. The way he said it, J couldn't help but feel like W was angry with him. As if the large boy was reminding him that he'd implied something wrong. Terribly wrong.

J poked at his food until he ate it. Until he realized, for the first time in his young life, that it was possible to carry on, to eat and to sleep, to talk and perhaps to even study, as the world around him . . . changed.

"Heck of a speech," F said. "Luxley must have written it."

"Luxley doesn't write the speeches," D said.

"Oh? How do you know that?" J asked.

D shrugged. "You can tell. They don't have the same energy."

F flailed his hands in the air. "Would you listen to you two? One implies D.A.D. lied to him and the other says Lawrence Luxley has more energy than our father! Maybe the coming floor shift is a good thing. You guys could use splitting up."

He laughed, but J and D looked at one another across the table.

"I didn't say he lied," J reiterated. "Don't even say something like that. I'm sure I just . . ." He paused. "I had it wrong. He didn't say what I thought he said."

"No kidding!" L said. "Now, can we move on?"

They did. J ate to the rhythm of the other boys discussing Lawrence Luxley and Professors Gulch and Kinney. Yellow Ball and Film Night. He ate to the uneven beat of his own thoughts as well, as his own words played out—*I didn't say he lied, I didn't say he lied*—at odds with the equally rhythmic rebuttal:

But I think he might have.

Warren Bratt and Lawrence Luxley

Richard could do everything in his power to make the basement more comfortable for Warren, but in the end it would still be a basement. And the truth was, Richard *had*. He'd ordered the carpenters to swap out the carpet, hang better pictures on the walls, renovate the storage rooms, realign the shelves, and muffle the boiler, repaint the doors, install a new toilet. Hell, Richard had even sent him flowers. They stood now in murky water upon Warren's writing desk, equidistant between Gordon and Warren, as the writer received his weekly earful on how to write a book from a man who certainly didn't know how.

"Richard isn't asking for anything from your soul, Warren. I think you know that." Gordon wore his trademark fine suit. The way he sat half upon Warren's desk drove him insane. "He's not interested in the tangle of emotion and epiphany that no doubt swirls in your belly. To be brutally honest with you, Warren, he's not interested in your artistry at all."

Warren, hefty and sweating, standing beside his chair, tried to maintain a look of professional ambiguity. But it was hard. Gordon spoke to him on Richard's behalf like he spoke to all the Parenthood staff: as if Warren Bratt, a.k.a. Lawrence Luxley, were a child. Younger somehow than even the boys. "If you ever find that you are blocked, just remind yourself that he's not looking for the great American novel. He's not even looking for the great Antarctic novel. He's looking for a *book*. A bad book will do. In fact, a bad book will do better than a good one. You know this. You've written twenty-nine of them already."

"Thank you, Gordon. Thank you very much."

For a decade, Warren had considered these meetings to be the most difficult part of his job. But recently something much worse had come up.

The Guilts, he'd called it.

It was a dangerous emotion for a staff member of the Parenthood to experience. He could hardly admit to himself what it was for. But really, there was no hiding it, as the source operated above him in the many floors of the Turret, day in, day out.

Guilt, yes, for how they were raising these boys.

Shut up, Warren thought now, Gordon so close. He half-imagined an Inspector bringing a magnifying glass to his ear, proclaiming him *unclean*.

The Guilts.

The feeling was only a splinter now, but not long ago it had only been a sliver.

Gordon smiled and Warren felt the familiar rush of rage in his chest, his blood, his bones. Gordon had a way of smiling that suggested you agreed with him in the end, no matter how ridiculous a thing he had proposed. And Warren, like the rest of the Parenthood, complied. Smiled back. Beyond the white door of Warren's basement office, the subterranean halls of the Parenthood wound like catacombs. And while the boiler had been quieted some, Richard had no plans to turn down the volume of the Corner.

"What are you thinking for the next book?" The way Gordon asked it was nothing like Warren's old pals, the Writing Gangsters, used to ask it at Don Don's pub in Milwaukee. In those days, Warren's equally idealistic cohorts had to blow their purple-dyed bangs from their eyes before they could look into his, usually flexing a tattoo or two for good measure. And if ever they asked after a book idea, it was with genuine artistic concern. Oh, how Warren Bratt missed his pretentious, holier-than-thou, degenerate former friends.

But those days were ten years past. And Warren's gut wasn't the only thing that had grown in that time. The Alphabet Boys were almost teenagers now. He'd watched them grow up in real time. Knowing what they knew. And what they didn't.

The Guilts, indeed.

"I'm not sure yet," he said purposefully. It felt good to make the corporate suck-up squirm. Corner hum or not, once a punk always a poker, and Warren Bratt had to stick it to Gordon anytime he could. Of course he had an idea for the next book. He had one thousand ideas for the next one thousand books. Because Richard, the Alphabet Boys' magnanimous D.A.D., wasn't looking for, as Gordon just said, a work of art. Most decidedly not. Richard wanted supermarket slop. The kind of books that Warren's aunts used to slurp up on the beaches of the Wisconsin Dells. The kind of books that showed half-naked men clutching half-naked women, their lust as clearly stated as their loins.

Except . . . no women in *these* books. Oh no.

"Let's do this," Gordon began. Always an idea for the next book. Always similar to the last one. "Give us something about a man who washes windows." He snapped his fingers. Warren knew very well where this was going. The plots of the leisure books were more formulaic than the romance novels he wished he was writing instead.

Has it come to that? Warren asked himself.

But no. Not quite that. And though Warren wasn't able to examine this feeling in whole, as Gordon sat staring at him from across his writing desk, he understood it was *something* like that. Something like wanting to write the worst thing he'd ever written, if only it meant not writing more of the same.

"Right now," Gordon said. "Give the window washer a name."

Warren didn't have to think hard. He had a long list of trite masculine names.

"Jerry."

"Great. Jerry it is. And what does Jerry do?"

"You said yourself he washes windows."

"Where? What building?"

Warren wanted to grab Gordon's smug face by the perfectly shaved chin.

"How about the Turret."

"Great. Yes. The very building we're in. So?"

"So?"

"So what happens in your next book? No women, of course."

"Gordon—"

"We could all use a gentle reminder. The boys have reached the Delicate Years, after all. Their fresh needs will be . . . in the air. Let's be careful what we breathe, Bratt."

Warren felt cold fingers up and down his arms. What was Gordon actually after down here? Had Richard grown . . . paranoid? Was it possible that, after all this time, Richard had begun questioning the foundation of his darling experiment?

That's all you, buddy, Warren thought. *Alllll you.*

The Guilts.

Indeed.

"Stop it," Warren said, not meaning to. The office lights exposed his thinning curly hair, anxious eyes behind his black-rimmed glasses, and a belly the Writing Gangsters would've thrown pencils at.

Oh, how he missed those friends.

"Tell me more about this window washer."

Warren was glad for the return of the subject.

"Okay. One day, while washing the windows of the Turret—"

"Yes."

"Jerry sees a naked blonde bent over a writer's desk."

"Warren." The temperature in Gordon's eyes dropped to none.

"While washing the windows of the Turret, Jerry sees something curious happen inside one of the boys' bedrooms."

"Now I'm interested. Very."

"He sees one of the boys cheating at Boats and—"

"Not Boats. Don't want them analyzing that particular game. How about Panhandle?"

"Panhandle. And—"

"This is very good."

"—and first he finishes his job—"

"Of course, of course."

"—and when he gets back down to the ground, he either goes to the head of the Parenthood and informs him of what he saw or he approaches the boy himself."

Gordon frowned. The angles of his face worked in such accord that it looked, to Warren, as if he were a puppet made of Parenthood wood.

"Hmmm. The problem with approaching the boy himself is that we'd be empowering the window washer. As a profession."

"I'm not so sure about that."

"Oh?"

Warren brought a stubby hand to his collar. He tugged on it. It always felt as if the temperature in the office increased incrementally for the duration of his meetings with Gordon. This story (Warren had a hard time calling it a story, calling it anything other than propaganda) was no different from any other leisure book he had written. Yet Gordon nitpicked.

An editor in hell, Warren thought. But it wasn't funny. And when did jokes like these cease to be funny? When had Warren started feeling this way? Hadn't he bought in, years ago, when they paid him his first check?

"The boys are young enough that they'll eventually substitute window washing with the fields of study Richard's hoping they're drawn to. For Christ's sake, Gordon. Do they have a choice?"

Gordon clucked his tongue. Warren stopped talking. He knew he'd come close to saying something he shouldn't have. A statement like that might reveal the Guilts.

"We're not raising *the right thing to do,* Warren. We're raising the most enlightened, undistracted minds in the history of mankind."

Gordon rose, got up off the desk. He stood a full five inches taller than Warren. But Warren didn't attempt to correct his slouch. Let the corporate slave own the room. Warren didn't want it anymore.

"So tell me," Gordon said. "Is this idea artistic to you? Is this the sort of thing your younger self would have thought fit to write?"

"No. Not even close."

He thought of Gordon's voice on an answering machine, echoing in a shitty apartment, so long ago. He thought of the Writing Gangsters. How they would recoil at what he'd become. How they might kill him, for his own sake.

"You see, then? If ever you find yourself blocked, call for me and we'll have another little chat. Richard would very much like to see this window-washer book done as quickly as possible. But you are, of course, the writer."

"I wasn't blocked."

"I didn't say you were."

"I'll write it."

Of course he would. He always did. And the money in his bank account swelled.

But, then, so did this new feeling. It used to be he could push the young men from his mind. But the young men weren't so young anymore.

"Good." Gordon crossed the stuffy room. His black loafers were silent on the plush carpet Richard had ordered installed not six months back. At the door he turned to face Warren once more. "Now go write a bad book, Warren. For the boys. For the Parenthood. For Richard. For *you*."

As Gordon slipped out of the office, Warren could hear the hum of the Corner from down the cobblestoned hall. He heard Gordon's shoes, too, clacking a serf's march. And when the office door clicked closed again, the sounds ceased, mostly, and Warren was left with the shitty vision of a banal window washer teaching a young man one of life's many morals. But, of course, a lying fable.

Warren Bratt the cool, Warren Bratt the skeptic, Warren Bratt the Cocky from Milwaukee, had fallen as far from artistic grace as he could.

He slouched his way into his chair, his sneakers dragging on that same carpet. And as he sat down to write, to work, to pretend to be a writer, an artist, a man, he tried very hard to shove from his mind the thoughts and feelings that had worked so hard to squeeze their way in.

He tried not to think about the way the Alphabet Boys had ogled him during the morning's speech. Christ, they looked at him like he was a celebrity.

The Guilts.

Warren opened a desk drawer and pulled forth a fresh yellow legal pad. He lifted a blue pen from the desk and brought it to the paper.

He wrote. He wrote a lot. As if each page, each word, each letter, played a small part in staving off those dangerous new feelings. For if Warren Bratt were to speak of them, even once, or if he were, as Lawrence Luxley, to slip one nugget of truth, even clandestinely, into any page of any book, why, God forbid . . .

. . . he'd be sent to the Corner.

Like A had been.

Like Z, too.

Outside the office, the Corner hummed.

Warren sat back quick in his chair. He breathed deep, intentionally, attempting to calm down.

He shouldn't be thinking this way. Oh no. He shouldn't even be considering it at all.

"STOP."

He hadn't yelled it, but it was certainly firm. Yet, rather than

listen to his own wise admonishment, he opened his desk drawer
again and eyed an untouched white legal pad that sat, uncluttered,
unbent, to the right.

Richard, he thought, *don't make me do it.*

But would it be Richard who was making him do it? Or were
the words Warren imagined filling those white pages all his own . . .

He slammed the drawer. Caught a finger in it and yelped.

All of Lawrence Luxley's books had to be submitted on yellow
legal pads. It had been that way since Book 1. And so . . .

"So stop thinking about the white pad," he said.

He flipped the bird to his closed office door.

Fuck you, Richard.

He couldn't have phrased it any better if he'd written it in black
Sharpie in a bathroom at Don Don's in Milwaukee.

He wrote. He wrote a lot. And as the yellow pages were filled,
in rapid, uncaring succession, Warren imagined a stack of white
beside them, growing at the same rate.

It was a downright scary place to be: writing the book he should
be writing, while imagining the one he shouldn't.

After ten pages about the window washer, he opened the drawer
again. The white pages shone like a spotlight. His desk the stage on
which he wanted to perform.

He closed the drawer. Lest someone in the basement hall open
his office door. Lest the bright white of those pages creep out under
that door, illuminate the winding halls, reach the Corner.

What was he thinking of doing? Really? *What?*

But Warren didn't want to answer that. Couldn't begin to. And
as he tried to eliminate the images of the boys, now twelve, from
his mind, he found it wasn't any easier replacing them with his old
writing friends.

So who, then? Who to think of when thinking of the present
was as troubling as the past?

Warren stopped writing. Stared at the desk as though it were a
stage after all.

He looked to the door.

Then, sweating, opened the drawer.

He thought of the incinerator square down the hall, embedded in the stones. He could always torch whatever he wrote.

Yes. But could he ever burn the idea to write it?

At the Window Overlooking the Yard

Overly full and lazy, the four boys ignored their studies for an hour and sat by the window in J's living room. Many years ago they had determined it was the Floor 8 window with the best view of the Yard. D and L sat on the couch near one another, L with his legs crossed as D leaned forward on his bony knees. D was the skinniest of all the Alphabet Boys, and compared to W, he was downright skeletal. His hair, long and black, was tucked behind both ears, in direct contrast to L's curly brown mop, which shadowed his ears and gave the impression that he was never quite listening to what the other boys had to say.

Q and J sat upon the window's ledge. Q not only scored the highest on every engineer exam and mathematical quiz, but he also had what D.A.D. once called *itness,* a term the other boys good-naturedly teased him about, until they realized they agreed with D.A.D. completely. A lot of the Alphabet Boys were smart, very smart, they knew, but Q's particular brand of intelligence appeared effortless.

"I think I speak for us all," L said, finally broaching the topic, "when I say I knew exactly what he was referring to."

D knew what D.A.D. was referring to, too.

"I didn't like it," D said.

"No? What was there not to like?" L asked.

"It sounded to me like D.A.D. is getting . . . nervous."

The boys shifted uncomfortably.

"Nervous?" J asked. "About what?"

"You heard him," D said. "All that garbage about us coming into our own . . . as if we weren't there already."

"Garbage!" L said. "Goodness. First J accuses him of lying and now you're calling his speech garbage. Times are certainly changing! Maybe he has a right to be nervous!"

"I didn't say he lied," J said again. But his voice came out quieter than he'd meant for it to.

"Well, where does he think we've been?" D went on. "Sometimes I think he doesn't know a thing about us."

L lifted his blue notebook. He wrote something down. "He will, D, so long as we write our thoughts down."

D frowned.

"But what if I don't *want* to do that? What if I want to keep my thoughts"—his hair swung down in front of his eyes—"to myself?"

"D," Q said, shaking his head no. "What a strange thing to say." He opened his blue notebook and set his eraserless pen to the paper. "Have you felt this way before?"

D looked to the notebook, then to J. In that moment J wondered why D had looked to him. Did he know J was feeling the same way? At breakfast, J hadn't outright called D.A.D. a liar. But still, he had insinuated *something*.

"You going to Inspect me, Q?" D asked. "That notebook is for *your* thoughts. Not mine."

Q smiled.

"But what of my reaction to your thoughts? That's certainly my jurisdiction."

D flailed his hands and fell back into the couch.

"Whatever. Go ahead. Write all about me."

J looked out the window, across the manicured acres of the Yard to the wall of pines that signified the boundaries of his world. He thought of the shape he'd seen crouched there. He almost spoke of it.

"Wild as his words may have been," he said, "they articulated a feeling I gotta admit I've been having."

"And what's that?" L asked.

J turned to face the others. "I feel . . . new."

"Yes." Q said. His glasses slipped to the end of his nose. "Me, too."

"Really?" D asked. "Because I don't feel new at all. I feel like my old wonderful self. And to be honest, I'd like to stay that way."

"Scared of change?" L asked.

"Not scared, nitwit. Happy. Already content. Sorry if I'm the only one in this room who doesn't mind being the boy he's always been."

"Is this about the shuffle?" Q asked. "Because I'll agree with you there. Who wants to change rooms? Not me. And yet . . ."

"And yet," D mocked. "Always *and yet* with you."

Q held up his pen. "And yet . . . change is good. It must be natural. Otherwise, why would D.A.D. spend so much time thinking about it? Obviously he has. So one can only surmise that, there being no option *but* to change, D.A.D. is graciously preparing us for our internal growth with a little external one. That's balance, boys. Homeostasis."

J turned to him. "What have *you* been thinking?"

"Me?" Q asked.

"Yeah. You said, *Me, too,* a minute ago."

Q pondered this. The shadow of the snowflakes falling outside the window made brief, ever-changing patterns on his face.

"I've been thinking of locating the Living Trees, for one."

The four boys were quiet. J felt words trying to squirm their way up his throat. A vague description of a figure. The way the branches and leaves met in the moonlight. The ghost of a dead brother. Or a hysterical vision at midnight.

"Then you should write about that in your journal," L finally said, breaking the loaded silence.

"Right," Q said. "I plan to."

"This conversation is weighing on me," D said.

"Why?" J wanted to know.

"I mean . . . come on! Listen to us. *Are* we changing? I sincerely hope not."

L smiled, leaned over, and patted D on the shoulder.

"Right before our very eyes."

Another block of silence. J thought of the morning's Inspection. The fact that he wasn't entirely honest with D.A.D.

"And if you feel like keeping secrets," L said to D, "you should write *that* down, too."

"But first," Q said, wiggling his eyebrows, "tell *us* what those secrets are."

The boys laughed, but there was some nervousness to it. J heard it in his own voice, too.

"While it's true that some thoughts are probably best kept until we really understand them," Q said, more seriously now, "we don't want to ignore the Recasting Years, either."

"*Recasting*," D echoed. "So now it's just . . . official. We heard the phrase this morning and now it's just . . . recasting."

"Well, of *course*," L laughed condescendingly. "That's how it goes! D.A.D. said so."

"But what does that mean?" J asked suddenly. He got down from the window ledge and stood before his brothers on the couch.

"What does *what* mean?" L asked. "And don't fly into that lying bit again."

"D.A.D. said so and so it is," J said. "But who told *him*?"

Q laughed. He wrote something down in his notebook.

"D.A.D. is older than us, J," he said. "More experienced. All it means is that D.A.D. knows more than we do and for him to organize a speech must mean *something*. I don't claim to know all the answers, but I do believe we were warned of something today."

"And what'll happen to us if we *don't* write everything down?" J asked. "What then?"

Q shrugged. "We'll have to ask him."

"Oh, come out with it!" D said. He tossed his blue notebook to the carpet. "Just tell us what's on your mind, J. If you're not saying he lied today, you're still trying to say *something*."

J paused. He hadn't realized how obvious he was being.

"I think . . . I think I have a disease."

His brothers looked justifiably surprised.

"What sort?" Q asked, hopping down from the ledge.

"I . . . don't know," J said. "But I don't think it's physical. Or . . . I think it's invisible."

"Location!" L said. "J! You *definitely* need to speak to D.A.D. about *that*!"

J shook his head. "But I don't *want* to do that! And I *don't* think Location is what they say it is."

The others were confused.

"What do you mean?" D asked.

"Are you saying the Parenthood is lying to us, J?" L asked. "Again?"

J could feel his face turning red. He wished it wasn't.

"Listen, guys," he said. "Whatever is going on—this . . . feeling— if it's Location or if it's not, it feels . . . *good*."

He looked to D, and D averted his eyes.

"Please," Q said, "go on." He spoke like D.A.D. himself, conducting an Inspection. "Tell us what feels good about this confusing, complex, and *invisible* condition you have."

"Okay," J said. He stepped to the window and brought a finger to the condensation. "Here's the Turret." He drew a tower. "And here's a boy." He drew a boy with long, funny hair. Nobody laughed. "And just like Q said, he wants to locate the Living Trees, the things that birthed us. . . ." He drew a question mark far from the tower. "I'm wondering what's beyond ourselves."

"Our minds," Q clarified.

"Yes! Our minds. I feel as though . . ." J looked to the ceiling, then out the window. "I feel as though someone is splitting the pines up here." He pointed to his head. "And through them, I'm seeing something new. Only . . . only . . ."

"Only you don't know what it is yet," Q said. "That's *exactly* the kind of thing you ought to write down. D.A.D. will adore that."

"This is all making me uncomfortable," L said. He got up off the couch. "And I don't want to talk about it anymore." He walked to the door. "I'm off to study. If you guys find yourselves talking about less dangerous things, please let me know. Also, you, J." He pointed two fingers at J. "You need to talk to D.A.D. right away about any . . . invisible problem you're having!"

Then L was out of the room. The door closed behind him.

Q rolled his eyes and said, "L has never been much of a trail-blazer. If our talks are getting too advanced for him, well . . . maybe he'll like his new floor mates better."

"Ugh," D said. "Sounds *awful.*"

"I'm worried that it'll show in the next Inspection," J said. "No-body's ever failed an Inspection before."

"*Failed* an Inspection?" Q echoed. "Don't you think you're being a little . . . hasty? You're experiencing new thoughts, just like D.A.D. told us we would. He told us so *today.* Seriously, don't give yourself nightmares over it."

J looked at him quickly, his eyes wide.

"Nightmares," he said. "I've . . . I've . . ."

He almost told him, almost told them both. The figure behind Mister Tree.

"Why don't we take a walk through the Orchard?" Q asked, obviously changing the subject for J's sake. "A nice snowy walk might do us some good."

"Maybe you'll find the Living Trees," D said.

Q shrugged.

"You're humoring me, but . . . maybe. Maybe I will. Maybe *we* will. Either way, I'm putting it in the notebook. And don't worry so much, D. Truly. *Change is good.* I imagine it might even be fun."

"A walk sounds good," J said. "You in, D?"

D looked to the notebook on the floor.

"Sure, but I'm not bringing that with me. It already feels like an invader. Like it can read my mind."

The boys knew he was referencing Luxley's *The Invaders*, the story of a quiet staff member of the Parenthood who clearly wanted what was worst for the boys.

"It's supposed to," Q said, crossing the room. "That's exactly what it's supposed to do." He opened the door. "I'll grab my coat, be right back."

Then Q was out the door and J and D were left alone. J went to the front closet and removed his blue-plaid winter coat with the lamb's fur collar. He'd got it as a gift from D.A.D. All the Alphabet Boys had received the same for their communal birthday, January 1.

"We're growing," J said, trying to limit the new, frightening feeling.

"Think so? I don't."

"Oh, come on. I don't know how much of this I can handle in one day."

"I think that, whatever we're feeling, it's going to go on for a lot longer than one day," D said.

J looked to him. It was clear to them both that they'd shared something over the course of the post-breakfast conversation.

"In any event," J said, opening the door, "D.A.D. may as well have been speaking directly to me. He knows something new is happening inside of us."

"Sure," D said, following J into the hall. Above them, the silver Inspection speaker stood inert, not to be heard from again until tomorrow morning, when a new day's Inspection would be announced. "But one thing about it is bothering me."

"What's that?" J asked.

"The feeling that D.A.D. wanted us to talk about these very things upon returning to our rooms."

"What do you mean? Why does that bother you?"

D took J by the arm, stopped him in the hall. Behind them, the Check-Up door reflected the dull overhead lights.

"He's always a step ahead of us. Always. Like he knows we're worried before we have anything to worry about. Like he knows we're laughing before a joke has been told. And doesn't that bother you? Is everything so . . . preordained? Are we so obvious? It bothers me. I want to have my own thoughts, J. Is that so wrong? And I'm certainly not going to do *that* by writing them all down in that little blue book."

"This one?" Q had snuck up behind them. He held D's notebook between two fingers.

"Hey!" D said. "I left that in J's room! How'd you—"

Q slapped him on the shoulder.

"I'm stealthy. I'm fast. You know that. Now go get your coat, nitwit, and let's take a walk. L, too. And if you feel like writing anything down? Do it. And if you don't? Write that down, too."

Richard

T he windows of Richard's first-floor quarters acted as a two-way mirror, but not in the traditional way. Rather, to those standing outside, the Yard was reflected in the glass, but a hint of a large photograph of an empty apartment could be seen behind it. For this, none of the Alphabet Boys ever saw their D.A.D. as he stood watching from within, often wearing nothing more than a bathrobe. Today, as he watched Q, J, D, and L tramp across the snowy Yard, headed for the Orchard, he wore the tank top that he'd sweated through while giving his speech. He'd sweated more since then, after receiving Gordon's report on his meeting with Warren Bratt.

He doesn't believe in the Parenthood like he used to.

Did he ever . . . used to?

He certainly believed in the money he was making from it.

And now?

Now I'm unsure.

Bad word for the Parenthood.

And how did Gordon know this? What brought him to this conclusion?

He didn't sit down for the entire meeting.

And?

That's what you do when you want to appear big, big as you can be. You stand. You stand, too, when you're close to walking.

Richard watched the boys happily crossing the whitening grass, wearing their newest winter coats.

Almost teenagers now.

Growing up.

Soon to be men.

The Delicate Years.

"You've got to clothe your kids," Richard said, alone in his quarters. "You've got to feed them, too. And"—he reached a hand to the glass and cupped the boys, as if their distant smaller forms could fit easily into his palm—"you've got to make sure they're telling the truth."

As the four boys grew even smaller, walking the long border of pines, Richard's mind traveled back to the Basic Years. It was a flaw of his, he admitted, that he'd long considered the past with a raven's eye but often assumed the present was in working order. He knew he had the Inspections to blame. The daily reports that his boys were clean, the daily reminders that things were going according to plan. Had he always leaned too hard on the Inspections? Put too much stock in them? Could they tell him . . . everything?

They certainly reaffirmed for him the most important thing: the lack of knowledge in the boys . . . the absolutely vacant and seemingly endless acreage of once-loud distractions, the earth now scorched of . . .

. . . woman.

Soft string music played from his antique hi-fi radio, loud enough to mingle with the sound of the winter wind outside and the faint ripple of the Corner below. Richard thought back, not searching, not looking for any mistake now, just back to images of the boys as toddlers and their incredible potential.

In those days, he'd believed he could tell which boys were more apt to shine. Which would develop into the scientists and engineers his experiment promised. But he was never exactly right. And these slight errors in his predictions worried him mercilessly.

One incident from the Basic Years caused him particular concern now: a routine patrol he'd conducted himself one evening, his black boots echoing off the brand-new, shiny floors, the distant clink of dishes in the kitchen. He'd looked to his watch that night and frowned. The rules of the Parenthood had been drilled into the minds of the money-hungry staff, mostly ex-cons happy for the clandestine gig. Yet . . . someone was up. In a place they weren't supposed to be. Perhaps sneaking a snack? The kitchen had long since been shut down; dinner was many hours over. He quickened his pace to the beat of an increasingly angry inner monologue—preemptive chastising of the dishwashers and cooks.

The tower's décor was different then, over a decade ago, and the halls were only partially lit, by English tavern lanterns Richard had foolishly insisted upon. The black-painted doors of the storage and equipment rooms unfortunately resembled open doors (another mistake on Richard's part), and Richard turned to look at each one, expecting a face to look back, someone who knew more than he did about who was making that racket in the kitchen. Someone who knew the mistakes that Richard had made and the mistakes he would make down the road. Someone who saw, in whole, the failures of the Parenthood long before they came to be.

Now, in his quarters, Richard wondered if he'd lost the paranoia he'd possessed in those early days. And he wondered, too, if he should find it soon.

Paranoia, Burt once said, *is probably the only thing that's going to make this experiment a success.*

He remembered . . .

He'd taken the glass walkway to the Body Hall, through its doors, and arrived at the kitchen's swivel doors, pausing to compose himself. If he were seen fretting, especially in those early years, who among the staff would still believe in him?

This was paramount then, as it was now: Pay the staff enough money to make them happy, but in the end they had to buy in. Had to think they believed in the Parenthood on their own.

Outside the kitchen that night, he polished the top button of his coat.

He entered.

C, hardly more than a baby, was alone on the kitchen floor, his back to the door, lifting plates from the open drying rack and stacking them on the floor to his right.

Richard stepped back into the shadows created by the wheeled plate racks and watched the small black boy in diapers carry out his task. He didn't know if he should smile or scream. The boy's methodology was beyond impressive.

Richard noted the resolve with which the boy studied the greater kitchen, possibly eyeing what else he could arrange. C was expressing key personality traits. Fearlessness: He'd crawled here alone. Productiveness: He'd completed a task. Ambition: He was looking for more to do. Imitation: He'd seen the dishwashers stacking the very same plates.

And free will, to boot. Richard felt proud as a parent.

But there was something terrible about it, too.

If C, as a baby, could so genuinely surprise him . . . what might happen when he grew up?

Enjoy this, for fuck's sake, Richard thought. *Enjoy the first signs that your experiment is working.*

But how could he? C had made it out of his crib and into the kitchen. What would stop him, or any of the Alphabet Boys, from one day . . . going anywhere they pleased?

Anywhere at all?

Now, his nose to the cold glass of his quarters' window, Richard stared far, to where the pines gave way to an open snowy path. Beyond that, Q, J, D, and L were walking through the Orchard.

Right?

"Spoiled," Richard said aloud. But, no, not that. None of his boys were spoiled. And the two that had gone bad had been taken care of.

There was only one solution to *spoiled.*

Yes, Richard's last line of defense. His ultimate deterrent for staff and boy alike. Just thinking the name of the room calmed him, reminded him that, if ever a boy learned of the existence of women, the Corner was there to be opened.

Paranoia . . .

He remembered . . .

Richard stepped out from the shadows of the plate racks and approached the boy.

C, hearing his D.A.D., looked up at him.

Richard smiled then as Richard smiled now, the sweet sounds of the cellos lubricating his nerves.

Study my face, C, for if ever your curiosity leads you astray, it will be this face that weeps, these lips that send you to the Corner.

He picked C up and brought the boy's nose close to his own.

You've made your father very proud tonight.

But he wondered if the boy could detect his lie. He wondered if all the Alphabet Boys would one day detect his many lies. . . .

But paranoia, Burt had also said, *will be the Parenthood's undoing in the end.*

Now Richard made a fist and pounded the glass. He gave it one solid thwack and stepped from the snowy sight of the Yard.

He crossed his quarters, past his large oak desk, went to the bar, and quickly fixed a gin martini.

Burt had also suggested a dry tower. But Richard downed it in two swallows. Energized, he turned to face the windows again, the weather, the world he'd created.

Oh, the Basic Years were *such* beautiful days!

In Richard's memory, the early epoch glowed. The illumination in the halls of the Parenthood was softer. The elevators ran quieter. The faces of the boys were the faces of the future. Richard's vision had come to life.

Genius Is Distracted by the Opposite Sex

So what do you do?

Cast the opposite sex out.

And . . .

. . . watch . . .

. . . the . . .

. . . genius . . .

. . . sprout.

Do you remember what progress smelled like, Richard? It was as sweet as childhood, yeah?

Yeah.

Do you smell it still?

He fixed himself a second drink, let the alcohol do its job, and recalled the Basic Years.

We could live forever like this! he used to think. As he fell asleep. As he woke. *Forever perfect.*

Forevolution.

He poured a third drink, could hear Burt advising him to make the Turret dry. No booze around the boys, four of who were no doubt stretching their legs, taking a break between studies, bonding, exploring, growing.

Q, D, L, and J.

Richard carried the drink to the window. Drinking this heavily often led to evaluating his boys, his prized possessions, his masterpiece. And in doing so, two names, two letters, an omen he wanted desperately to avoid, invariably came up. As though someone other than himself had stolen two especially shimmering trophies from the case.

A and Z.

Richard closed his eyes. Wobbling a bit before the glass, he focused on the music, found balance there. The deep tubas mimicked the shadows in the basement that pooled by the Corner's door. The flutes cried out like children behind it.

A had gone to the Corner.

Richard had sent him.

He opened his eyes to see that the snow had increased outside. He thought maybe he saw the form of the four boys, perhaps just one of them, walking the line of pines.

But no. Only the branches, swaying in the growing wind.

A was the first to die. A was the first letter of the alphabet. How terribly fitting. The perfectly lit match to set a paranoid man's paper mind aflame . . .

The boys would die, one by one, following A, in suit, in order, B, C, D, E . . .

Richard laughed. It was harsh, nervous laughter, which grated against the gorgeous music that no longer carried a tune for him.

The Delicate Years . . .

No. The other boys were still here. The other boys hadn't died, and no, they *wouldn't*. So long as they weren't spoiled. Spoiled rotten. And wasn't that all there was to it? The experiment held so long as the Parenthood's singular, irrefutable law was upheld.

A man spends all his time building something, Burt once wrote, *and that object becomes his everything. His reward, yes, but his panic, his horror, too.*

Of course, A hadn't *done* anything wrong. A hadn't done anything at all.

F's mother did.

A recalcitrant whore. A weeping, second-guessing *woman*. A fool who let her heart best her mind until she broke the deal she'd made with the Parenthood.

She'd shown up.

Here.

At the Turret.

Richard had been out in the Yard that day, the very same expanse of grass he overlooked now, his third martini sloppily dripping gin to the floor. He'd overseen the disassembly of the enormous Glasgow Plexiglas crib. The boys had outgrown it. The carpenters (ex-cons, all) were carrying the pieces back to the tower when

Richard's placid, proud mood was interrupted by a sound he hadn't heard in a very long time.

A piercing shriek. A falsetto of pain.

A woman.

She looked terrible, stumbling by the tower's first-floor windows. A cuckoo wretch. Her clothes hung from her body as though she'd escaped from a hospital and had come running . . . running here . . .

The carpenters were upon her before Richard could speak. But Richard spoke.

Cover her mouth, he said calmly, crossing the Yard, already seeing the Corner door closing on her like a coffin lid.

The sky felt too big above him. The windows of the Turret too clean. Sudden sweat soaked the edges of his hair and beads dripped down to his black beard, blue in the summer sun.

At first, upon reaching her, he said nothing. He only stared into her heartbroken eyes: a mother who'd realized how much motherhood meant to her after all. Later that night, one carpenter told another he thought Richard was going to bite her. But Richard didn't bite her. He did worse.

Go to the Corner, he'd said to her. As if she knew what that room was. As if she had any idea about the door in the basement of the building that harbored her son, the boy she'd come to retrieve. *YOU GO TO THE CORNER RIGHT NOW!*

The carpenters had made to move, to drag her inside, when Gordon, always present, always a witness, gasped so audibly it rivaled the mother's lunatic shriek.

Already knowing what was wrong, what had caused his assistant to cry out, but not yet wanting to believe it, Richard turned to where Gordon was pointing a shaking manicured finger.

A boy stood with his face and hands pressed to the first-floor hall glass.

He was looking right at them.

Right at her.

Her.

"It's A," Gordon said, trembling.

A at the window. F's mother in the clutches of the carpenters.

Richard felt the strength flow from his legs. But he did not fall.

Parenthood law was the one and only.

You can't raise a truly blind man who has already seen the sky.

He'll remember . . . he'll remember . . . he'll always remember . . . and he'll ask about her . . . her . . . HER.

Richard walked past the carpenters, past the mother who had unknowingly sentenced somebody else's son.

He entered the tower.

He went to the boy and knelt.

He held A's face in his fingers.

The woman you saw, he said, *has spoiled you rotten.*

The Corner.

The only room in the Parenthood the boys were raised to fear. A place that existed before even their nurseries were complete. Somewhere in the basement maze not far from where Lawrence Luxley wrote the books they loved; a door at the end of a cobblestone basement corridor; the place where the noises of the night were made.

Over the years, Richard had noted small rips at the shoulders of the uniforms worn by his staff. He knew the fabric had been torn on the stones across the hall from the Corner, as the ex-cons attempted to stay as far away as they could.

The Corner.

An appellation that seemed to reach out into the hall. A door with fingers. And reach.

The Corner.

Where A and F's mother went.

Together.

"That's enough," Richard said now, draining his third martini. "Time to—"

But his sentiment was cut short at the sight of the four boys returning from the Orchard. Snow had painted the shoulders of their new coats white. Their smiles underscored the laughter he heard through the glass, through the snow, through the distance.

Richard smiled, too. Four of his boys, *his* boys, twelve years old now, returning from a break in their studies. But as they continued to laugh, as they carried on in the way he'd once envisioned they would . . . as Q, D, L, and J presented the perfectly proud picture of all that Richard imagined they could be, he felt something sour spinning in his gut. A loose screw in his heart.

"What are you laughing at?" he asked them, clinking his glass quietly against the window, in rhythm with his words. "Be . . . good . . . boys . . . now. Tell your D.A.D. . . . *what are you laughing at?*"

And the boys, reaching the Yard, only saw the snowfall reflected in the glass of the quarters belonging to their D.A.D., a new winter upon them.

In the Orchard

On their walk, the boys talked about many things. But J's mind continued to return to the discrepancy between what D.A.D. had told him in the Inspection and what he'd said during his speech.

Why did it matter so much? Plenty of Alphabet Boys had slipped up, forgotten something said, put something a different way, or simply intentionally delivered a small harmless lie. J had done it himself. With the cherry juice on the carpet. Or how about the thousand times he'd pretended to understand a joke just because the others obviously did? Was that a lie? And if one of those boys had asked him to explain what was so funny about the very joke they were laughing at, how would he have responded? Would he have been caught in a lie?

"T got in trouble," L said. "Wore white at the speech."

"This morning?" Q asked.

"How do you hear about these things so fast?" D asked. "It's like you're one of the bricks in the Turret walls."

"Why did he wear white?" J asked.

The snow fell soft upon their coat shoulders, their collars, their hair. As they reached Mister Tree, J felt something like a tether coming loose. A leash unlatched. He thought of the dogs in the Inspection. He hardly remembered he'd asked a question.

But he looked, too. Looked to see if anyone was crouched behind the tree.

"Must have been tired," L said. "I can't imagine he was protesting a speech!"

L laughed the way he did whenever the absurdity of defying the Parenthood came up. The snow settled so uniformly upon his curly hair that he looked aged, playing the part of an old man on the stage of the tower theater.

"It's possible he did protest," Q said. "As D.A.D. told us today, things are changing."

They'd reached the rows now, Mister Tree being no more (or less) than a greeter, a solitary outlier between Yard and Orchard. The boys paused. Somewhere out there in the rows of cherry trees were the trees they'd grown upon. The Living Trees D.A.D. had plucked them from twelve years ago.

After a glance at the way the snow fell upon the uniform branches, the boys commenced walking.

"Maybe he just likes white," D said. "You don't have to call it a protest just because he likes white."

"Well," L said, obviously trying to change the subject. "There's plenty of white out here!" He held his open palms to the sky. "Maybe he should come outside!"

They had entered the first row of cherry trees, the branches of one nearly touching the next. For the first time in his life, J thought it looked like a fence.

He recalled the days when he and D played hide-and-seek in the Orchard. When they'd look for the Living Trees, too. No boy knew which ones they were. And the Parenthood said it was up to them to find out.

"What was his punishment?" D asked.

L scoffed. "How should I know?"

"You know everything else!"

"Well, I don't know the answer to *that*. But I can guess." Their shoes crunched the fresh snow and grass. Out here, walking the rows of the Orchard, things were less manicured than they were in the Yard. The boys had no doubt that D.A.D. intentionally left it so. A chance for his boys to explore, to feel less tethered to the Turret.

"Probably lost this year's Film Night privilege," Q said. "Which is a shame, because I've heard good things about it."

"What have you heard?" D asked.

"C told me it's the best one yet."

"Oh, what does C know."

"Film Night would be a fairly large punishment," L said. "And yet . . . T should know better. Wearing white to a speech!"

"An oversight," D reiterated. J heard the frustration in his voice. But J's mind was still elsewhere. Still stuck between two places, like Mister Tree between the Orchard and the Yard; between what D.A.D. said in the Check-Up room today and what he'd said on-stage in the Body Hall.

They'd reached halfway down the first row of trees, the horizon obscured by a mist of fine snow. The cold wind tousled their hair, and Q bundled himself tighter in his coat. He wiped the fog off his glasses, too.

"It's official, then," D said.

"What is?" L asked.

"Q cleaned his glasses. Winter is here."

Every year, the first snowfall announced the coming Effigy Meet, when the twenty-four Alphabet Boys competed for the best ice sculpture, as judged by the Parenthood. J hadn't ever come close to winning, but he didn't mind. The Effigy Meet encouraged crea-tion itself, construction, the angles and necessary math. Tempera-ture and sustainability. When considering the annual event, J couldn't help thinking of the many rooms of the one building he knew so well. The Turret that grew smaller behind them.

"What do you think the Corner looks like?" J surprised himself by asking. He looked over his shoulder—they all did—for fear that the legendary basement door might have followed them outside, was perhaps suspended between the rows of cherry trees.

"Come on!" L said. "T isn't going to the Corner for a white shirt, J! My goodness, you're acting strange today."

"I'm not saying he will," J said. "I'm just wondering. What do you think the Corner looks like?"

"We know what it looks like," Q said. "It's just a door."

"How do you know that?" D asked. Again, J felt a bond between himself and D. He wasn't sure he liked it. It seemed easier to hide dangerous thoughts when you were the only one having them.

"Because I've been told so," Q said. J heard rare embarrassment in Q's voice. Q was, after all, the one who typically questioned things. "Why are you asking, J?"

J lifted his hand to a leafless tree branch, made to break off a piece, thought better of it.

He stopped walking.

"Aren't you interested in where A and Z went?"

The other three stopped walking, too. D turned to face J, interest in his eyes. Q pulled out his notebook and wrote in it. L bent at the waist, planting his hands on his knees.

"I think all this walking is limiting the oxygen to your brain," L said. "And the cold is freezing what remains."

"Don't you wonder, L?" J asked.

L rose to his full height again. "No. I don't. The Corner. So?"

"Where *exactly* do you think they went? What do you think is on the other side of that door?"

L made to speak but stopped.

"I imagine it's like the Nursery," Q said. "The same place we were raised, we die."

"Come on!" L said. "Lies and death! I've had just about enough of this!"

"What do you mean?" J asked.

But Q only shrugged. "I don't know. I'm working on it. Here's a new thought: We were made out here in the Orchard. So maybe this is where . . . we die."

They were quiet. But J wanted more. "And how do we die? What happens to us? Who . . ."

"Who takes away our life?" Q asked. "That's easy. The Parenthood. Who else? It's part of their responsibility. To see us all the way through birth to death."

"And how do they know when it's time?"

"When we're spoiled," L said. He said it like he was bored. "You know, guys, you're making me very excited for the floor shift. I think I need new boys to talk to. Boys who talk about better things!"

Subtle movement on the nearest tree caught D's eye.

"Look," he said. "Fighting Bugs."

It was one of the many things the Alphabet Boys hoped to see in the Orchard. Rarely was a bug found inside the tower and never two at once. Certainly no two like the two small red ones they observed up close, one mounted upon the back of the other.

Fighting Bugs.

"They're angry," L said. "And they picked a perfectly fine day to have it out!"

Coat shoulder to coat shoulder, the boys observed the tiny bugs, red with black spots, struggle upon the bark of the cherry tree. They watched for a long time.

"Who do you think will win?" D asked. But the boys knew better. Nobody had ever seen a Fighting Bug win its fight. Rather, these two, like all the others, would simply go their separate ways when it was over.

"I suppose they're something like us," Q said.

"How so?" D asked.

"Well, they jockey for position. Speak their minds. Argue about it. Go their own ways."

They sallied forth and talked this way, this subject and others, until they reached the first turn. Three-quarters of a mile later, the second. The snowfall got heavier. Q, L, and D discussed the number of trees, their height, and how they'd grown. They searched for the

Living Trees. Examined many up close. Perhaps a new boy could be found growing on one? By the time they reached the end of the Orchard, Mister Tree in sight again, J was deep within a hole of his own thinking. He imagined a Living Tree at one end of a basement hall, the Corner at the other. He imagined being plucked from the former and stepping into the latter. He imagined being born and dying. Like A and Z.

As they passed Mister Tree, he said, "I'm going to find the Corner. And I'm going to look inside."

The others stopped walking.

"Okay," Q said. "Now I'm starting to agree with L. You sure you're all right?"

"Yes."

"But you'd like to go look at the Corner?"

"I wanna know what's in there," J said.

Only D remained silent. L and Q discussed the anti-Parenthood (and just plain silly) qualities of J's remark.

"Why don't you just climb the tower spires and leap to your death?" L asked. "It'd be an equally satisfying end."

Tired of arguing and exhausted by the day's bizarre subjects, the four boys went quiet. D and J looked to the ground. Q and L to the snow that fell to it.

"The Recasting Years," Q finally said. "D.A.D. knew something was coming. And here it is. It was very wise of him to tell us so."

Slowly, the boys traipsed back into the Yard.

"If you really wanna know what the Corner looks like," L said, "go stand in one."

Even J had to laugh at this. As they passed D.A.D.'s first-floor window, as they saw themselves and the pretty snow reflected in the glass, all four floor mates giggled about J standing in a Corner, any old corner, as if it could possibly emulate the horror they could hear humming, all day in the Turret, from below.

It felt good to laugh. Especially for J. And hearing Q's high laughter and L's bellowing belly laugh served to root J again, even if momentarily, to the foundation of the Parenthood. And, despite these new thoughts, foreign and overwhelming, he felt safe. He felt protected. He felt warm.

But D's laughter didn't last long, and J noticed.

As Q and L walked ahead, D turned to look at J, and J intentionally did not look back. He knew that a simple exchange of unspoken questions would be enough to uproot him all over again.

So when L asked, "Do you think D.A.D. is watching us from in there?" and Q answered, "I think he's picking his nose," J laughed with his brothers, as if the laughter might stave off the thoughts he'd been having, might block their way, laughter versus thought, like two Fighting Bugs in his head, stopping it all from multiplying.

Warren Writes

Warren set the yellow legal pad aside and removed the white one from his desk.

And that was all there was to it.

He looked to his office door. It was locked, he'd locked it himself, but that didn't make him feel any safer. He'd written every Luxley book on yellow legal pads before delivering them to the typesetters and printers down the cobblestoned hall of the Parenthood basement, where the pages went from Warren's chicken scrawl to the semiprofessional look they adopted by the time they ended up in the hands of the Alphabet Boys.

But the white pad . . .

Warren hadn't used the white pad since he was a . . . a . . .

Fledgling wasn't the right word, and Warren would've been pissed if he'd heard someone else use it. *Fledgling* suggested he didn't know how to write. Even back then. *Chick, greenhorn, rookie, novice, tenderfoot.* Everybody in Milwaukee could take those words and shove 'em up their ass. Warren *liked* how he wrote. He always had. He liked *what* he wrote, thank you, and writing, for Warren, had never had anything to do with money. Nothing to do with toasting vodka in a big-city publishing house. Nothing to do with seeing his novels printed with a professional, glossy Modern Library cover that featured a wise photo of himself readers couldn't help but look at every time they encountered another well-crafted sentence.

"Nope," Warren said, tapping his pencil against the white pages on his desk. Beyond his office, the boiler hummed. Or maybe it was the Corner. "I was never in it for the money."

Yet . . . here he was, so much richer than his former colleagues, the Writing Gangsters, his Milwaukee crew of pretentious, self-absorbed . . .

"Artists, my ass," Warren said. He looked to the door again. Still locked. He eyed the white pad. He thought of the Alphabet Boys, twelve years old now, and wow how time flies when you're having a terrible time.

He tried, really tried, to imagine not knowing what a woman was.

"It's criminal," he said. But that much was obvious. And certainly not the worst of it. *Agreeing* to be a part of it, ah, now, *that* was something. The other staff needed the gig—hell, the other staff were like born-again drug addicts, offered the chance of a lifetime by a man who looked like God to them now. Richard had made wealthy men of them all. Made hidden men of them all, too.

But what was Warren's excuse? No criminal record. No real *reason* to disappear. To drop out. To hide. Why oh why had he agreed to work here and why oh why had it taken him so long to realize how terrible that decision had been?

Warren was stuck when he met Richard. Yes. He had no illusions about that now.

Oh, how good a drink sounded.

Drinking had never been a social event for the Cocky from Milwaukee. Beer and booze weren't *fun*. Rather, they were physical locations, places he went looking for new ideas, bridges between existing ideas, channels he had no access to when sober. When Warren left his crummy apartment and walked into a liquor store, he didn't consider himself to be scratching an itch. Rather, he saw the bottles as doors, with so many potential stories behind them.

"Remember *Detective Bratt*?" Warren asked himself, allowing a small sad smile to crawl up his lips. "You used to pretend you were hunting ideas. Holy shit, Detective Bratt. Private Eyesore."

He thumbed the white pad's top page. So much potential there, he thought. Any story . . . any story at all . . .

"Okay," Warren said, pushing his chair from the desk. "Enough." He got up as though prepared to do something specific but only paced the office instead. At the black leather couch he paused, then plopped down, only to get right back up. He adjusted his fogging glasses. Ran his chubby fingers over his big belly. Thought he could smell his own fear.

He thought of the Writing Gangsters, too. Tried not to imagine what they would say now if they'd read the books he'd made so much money from. The shitty Lawrence Luxley adventure stories that always (always!) followed the same arc, the same themes, and certainly featured the same gender over and over and over and over and over and . . .

Warren glanced at the white pad on the desk. From across the office it looked something like bright evidence. White fire. Like he might want to run and put the legal pad out.

He heard something in the hall, boots on the stone floor.

There were no words on that white pad, but if Richard were to try the door, find it locked, unlock it with his own key, and *see* that pad . . . why . . . wouldn't he know what was going through Warren's mind? Wouldn't he be able to see the shame-inspired story as it slid down Warren's arms, bringing his fingers to move as if they were already writing the book?

"Book?" Warren whispered to himself. "What book?"

The steps got quieter as they passed his office door. Or maybe they just stopped outside it? No, no. They were gone now. Warren imagined the printers, the pair of ex-cons down the hall who ran off the pamphlets, the textbooks, the announcements, the letters, the report cards, and (yes) all of Lawrence Luxley's terrible, artless books.

"The Writing Gangsters would lynch you," he said, half-stammering, walking slowly back to his desk, his eyes on the clean white pad. "They'd call you a fraud, a forger, a sellout." He staved off slim tears. "And they'd be right."

Oh, how high and mighty he'd been in Milwaukee, despite the drinking, despite being bone broke . . . back when the offer of a lifetime came to him by way of a phone call.

"But whose life?" Warren asked himself, still staring at the blank white cover page. "This isn't your life."

Oh, but it was.

I'll tell you how to write, he used to stammer in his gruff and short way, speaking blunt to the rest of the Gangsters. *You got the way you write and you got the way you* want *to write. And then you got what you think is too crazy for you to be writing. What you need to do is embarrass yourself . . . get crazy. In the end the embarrassing shit is what you wanted to be writing all along.*

Oh, so full of soul. So full of *art.*

So full of shit.

The Gangsters ate it up. *Warren's gothic minions,* an ex-girlfriend had called them. His personal fan club. The only people in all of Wisconsin who'd brave a winter storm to go listen to a drunk Warren Bratt define what real writing was. He looked the part, too, and certainly drank it. The stocky, angry author going on about the heart of art and the purpose of a good book. Books were his religion, he'd said. His Jesus, his God. His maker.

But despite his claims that he wasn't interested in money, he sure believed he was worth a lot of it.

Countless rows in Don Don's. So many fights with the Gangsters. Always always always about money.

Always.

"You were a pig," he told himself now. "Fucking Christ, Bratt. You were a pig."

A stuck pig, no less. Perfectly fixed for a visit from Richard.

Warren used to tell anybody in earshot how much he was

worth. How much a sentence of his was worth. How much even a conversation about how much he was worth was worth. Once he asked a fellow Gangster for payment, for having been sanctified with Warren's advice.

"You used to call yourself a *seer*," he said now, finally lowering himself into his writing chair. He had no recollection of picking the pencil up, but there it was. Between his fingers. "Oh God. How fucking embarrassing."

Why now? Why realize this *now*? Was it the natural arc of an asshole? An inevitable day of retribution?

Or was it the look of adulthood in the eyes of the Alphabet Boys? The moment when he could no longer say, *Well, what do kids know anyway.*

He tried to slink back into the hollows of his own smoky parlors, his troubled mind, the rooms he'd occupied for so long, making his role at the Parenthood bearable. But he couldn't find them anymore. Like the Nursery that once harbored twenty-six cribs, those rooms had been cemented over.

"What have you done?"

He looked up, actually expecting to see someone else standing on the other side of his desk. Surely it wasn't *his* voice he'd heard ask the question? Surely he didn't sound like that? And there was simply no way the man who asked that question was the same one who had agreed to write books for two dozen boys gaslighted and locked into an experiment of ungodly dynamics . . .

. . . for life.

He felt something unnatural move in his gut. As if a very bad thing had gotten inside him and there was no way to get it out. No surgery to remove the barbarity he'd been a part of.

The Parenthood was no longer bearable. On any level and in any way. That was certain now.

"Oh fuck," he said. "You're gonna do it, aren't you?" It wasn't a motivational thing to say. It didn't feel good at all.

It scared him to death.

He looked to the office door, perhaps considering unlocking it. Putting the white pages away.

But he knew he'd just passed that option, as if it were a deep-space mile marker, one Warren saw as he floated, without gravity, beyond it.

The Gangsters had warned him about his obsession with money. Bald Bill O'Brien said it would grow on him like mold. One day it would swallow his art. And the next day it would swallow *him*. Warren denied it all. Punched O'Brien for saying so. Broke up with Trish Newton for saying the same thing.

When the Cocky from Milwaukee got rolling about money, it was like standing inches from a lit Civil War cannon, and there wasn't much one could do but duck.

The top page of the white legal pad looked lit, too.

Ready to blow.

Warren told them the art was in an untouchable place, that that wasn't what he meant when he said he was worth something, when he drunkenly charged his friends for wisdom. Money was not something to be afraid of. Not something to avoid. And he proved it, too, or thought he did; with his first published story, he used the sweet reward to buy the Gangsters a round at Don Don's.

But the night didn't go the way Warren wanted it to.

"Urges" appeared in a punk magazine, *The Hips and Lips Trip,* and when the Gangsters actually *read* the work he'd gotten published, they had a lot to say.

What are you gonna write next, Bratt? A fuckin' western?

This was Arlene, the pockmarked cigarette-smoking blimp that Warren could hardly stand to look at let alone accept a critique from.

You don't like it? Warren told Arlene, his eyes two slits of pompous paid-writer. *You know what you call a guy who puts pen to paper and doesn't get paid? A camper. Dear Mom, I'm so sad and lonely . . . and broke. Please send money so I can buy a goddamn drink. Fuck you, Arlene. I'm a professional now.*

But if getting paid to write constituted "professional," Warren Bratt was much closer than he realized.

On a warm summer evening, home alone, wearing only his underwear and seated at the typewriter upon his kitchen table, Warren received a phone call. Assuming it was one of the Gangsters calling, he didn't answer. He'd already begun typing when the answering machine announced it was no friend. No magazine, either. The crackly little speaker delivered a voice Warren didn't recognize at all.

Warren, hello. My name is Gordon Fink.

Warren cocked an ear toward the machine.

We're very big fans of your story and we have an opportunity for you. A job, if you will. A career in writing.

Was this how it worked, then? Finally make enough money to buy a round and it all starts rolling in from there? In the mind situated beneath his thinning hair and behind his wrinkled brow, Warren imagined more money slipping in through the vents, stopping up the toilet, falling like snow outside.

Whoever Gordon Fink was, his voice sounded like he had more money than the editors of *Hips*.

It's my employer's preference that I do not leave our number, but I will try again soon.

CLICK.

When the phone rang again, an hour later, Warren leapt from the kitchen table, his troll's body moving faster than it had in years.

"Warren Bratt here."

Static popped at the other end. Sounded like the guy was calling from Aruba.

"Can you meet us tomorrow evening, Mr. Bratt?"

The word *scam* crossed Warren's mind.

"I don't know. I've got shit to do. Another story."

"I don't mean to make light of your plans, but this is a significant offer."

Warren took in the dimensions of his crappy apartment. He saw men's magazines scattered on the lumpy wood floor. He saw an unmade bed illuminated by the light of a crappy television set. He saw empty pizza boxes and no whiskey. No wine. No women.

No wonder.

"I can make it," he said. "What time? Where?"

"That'll do for now. Thank you, Mr. Bratt."

The man hung up.

Warren lowered the phone from his ear and stared at it. A shiver parachuted down his neck, landing somewhere on his back. The call had felt more like a death threat than a writing opportunity.

That'll do for now. Thank you.

Scam, he thought. He hung up.

A prick who bought *Hips* got his number from the publisher and lived for pranking writers. That's what it was and all it could be. But later, much later, Warren struggled to fall asleep, beset with images of Gordon Fink sneaking into his apartment through holes in the water-damaged ceiling. A scam. A prank. A kook.

When he woke the next morning, he had to consider the reality of those dreams. A folded note upon his chest forced him to.

He leapt from his bed and searched every cupboard and closet in the cramped apartment. The front door was locked. Had it been all night? The windows still down. The alley below was empty. The note read:

7 P.M.
The Brewer
313

Warren shook his head and laughed harder than he'd laughed in weeks. Gordon Fink and his boss were out of their fucking minds if they thought he was going to show up to a hotel like the Brewer *now*. After a call like that and a note like this.

Phoning the police was more like it.

But he didn't do that. And he didn't tell the Writing Gangsters about it, either. No. Rather, Warren spent the afternoon seated at his kitchen table, rereading the note, replaying the original answering-machine message, over and over again.

Thing was, the money in Gordon Fink's voice really *did* sound genuine. It was as if it were made of the sounds of checks being signed, handshakes over legitimate book deals, the respectful greetings of familiar bank tellers and hosts seating him at what they knew to be his favorite tables.

By six-thirty, Warren was dressed. He told himself he was just going to the bar. Don Don's. And he believed it. He'd do some research. Find a new story. Detective Bratt. Maybe in a bottle of whiskey. Maybe gin.

He tied his boots, ran a handful of water across his face, and made to leave. But as he reached for the doorknob, he saw that the note was still in his hand.

Nope, he thought, stepping out his front door and locking it for the last time.

"It was never about the money," Warren said now, seated at his desk in his basement office of the Parenthood. The Corner crooned.

But it was. Always.

Then, with enough sweat on his face to consider it a shower, he brought the tip of his pencil to the white pad. He looked to the yellow pad beside it, relegated to the far corner of his desk. He read the title page of the book he'd already begun.

The Window Washer
By Lawrence Luxley

He turned his attention to the white pad and wrote, for the first time since showing up at the Brewer Hotel and agreeing to a job, a second title page.

Needs
(a novel of reality and what's real)
By Warren Bratt

He did not look to the office door. And once he started writing, really writing, he forgot the Luxley book was there beside him at all. And for the first time in more than a decade, Warren Bratt felt like a *writer*, a man with a story to tell.

While the themes, the meat, and the message would be unrecognizable to a Luxley fan, the intended audience remained the same.

The Alphabet Boys. Growing up.

With new feelings to address.

Now. Today.

With needs.

J

J slept.

He'd wrapped up his day's studies, reread close to forty pages in Luxley's most recent book, and put himself to bed. But it wasn't easy.

He tossed and turned, the blanket long discarded to the carpeted floor, the single sheet suddenly too hot even with the window open halfway.

He didn't dream often, but he did this night, and because he was in and out of sleep, the dream meshed with his reality, and the result was a strange, uneasy sensation of finding himself living in an approximate world, one he couldn't trust. Reality . . . or not?

At the height of the difficult night, a boy called to him from outside his bedroom window. Not from the Yard below, but from right outside the glass. Because J lived on the eighth floor (and surely nobody could float that high), he knew he was dreaming. Yes. But the knowledge somehow wasn't strong enough and came without as much confidence as he'd have liked. At the window there was, indeed, a boy. He wore one-piece spotted pajamas like all the Alphabet Boys once wore, and his bare feet looked red from the winter air.

J sat up.

"A?" he asked. A because, while it was many years ago, J retained some memory of the brothers they'd lost.

"J!" A called back, his voice like the sound the steady heat made coming out of the vents. "Get out of bed, J! Go into the pines!"

J decided no. No, he would not go into the woods. He would not leave the tower in this cold, the first of winter, and search the same woods in which he'd seen a person crouched the night before.

Or had he?

"I didn't see anyone," J said. But talking only made it worse. "It was a tree!"

A shook his head. Snowflakes rose from his hair. Or perhaps it was dust.

"Not a tree!"

J got up and went to the window. The cold air there outfought the heat from his bedroom. It felt good against his naked chest.

"You were sent to the Corner," J said, unexpected tears accompanying his sleepy voice. "You were spoiled rotten. D.A.D. said so!"

A wintry mist passed over A, and his eyes flashed green and his skin crinkled, too. Then the mist passed, and J saw the young boy again, still hovering so high above the Yard. Red-faced and alive.

Or not?

"Go into the pines, J. Someone is waiting for you there. Someone you want to meet!"

J looked down to the trees lining the Yard and saw a second figure standing in the middle of the white expanse. At first, he thought it was Q. The glasses fooled him. But the figure was too young to be Q, wore no coat, and the clothes he did wear were the very sort J wore himself as a six-year-old boy.

"Z!" J cried out. Below, the boy pointed to the woods. When he spoke, his voice sounded impossibly close, as though his lips stretched high into the winter sky.

"You want to see who's in the woods. You want to meet him."

A descended, as though lowered by stage wire strung to the Turret spires. J had seen a trick like that in the tower theater. When B played a bird.

A landed softly near Z. The long-dead brothers held hands.

"Z!" J called into the open cold. "You were spoiled rotten, too!"

Mist rose from the Yard, like blue smoke. Behind it Z's eyes flashed green, his skin cracked and parted, revealing dark bones and tissue beneath.

Dirt on his hands and feet.

Then A seemed to glide to the border of the pines. J couldn't see where his bare feet met the lawn. And as A moved away from the tower, his head turned slowly, impossibly back, until it was at a hundred-and-eighty-degree angle to the way it should be.

He looked up at J.

"Right here," A said. "Right here!"

J climbed up onto his window ledge, opened it fully, and stood, gripping the sides of the frame. Something inside him said he could fly if he really wanted to. Just like A. Just a leap from the Turret window and he'd glide across the Yard, meeting up with his dead brothers at the pines.

Instead, J quickly got down from the ledge and closed the window. The sounds of the waking winter were cut off, and J hurried to the far side of his bedroom. There he turned his face to the wall and shook his head no. No, he hadn't seen A and Z. No, there was nobody waiting for him in the woods. No, there wasn't—

Tapping, and J turned to see A at the window again.

"No!" J called out. "You're trying to spoil me, too!"

A looked through the glass, to the hallway leading to the bathroom in J's quarters. J looked, too. He saw Z standing in the dark.

"Go down to the Yard," Z said. "You want to meet him."

J stood flat to the wall. His legs were paper, it seemed, perhaps the pages of a blue notebook not yet filled.

Half-dressed, shirtless, and barefoot, J sprang for his front door, opened it, and scurried out into the hall. The floor was silent. The silver speaker that announced Inspections reflected the dim hall overheads.

J hurried to D's door. He knocked.

"D," he said. "Let me in!"

A sound from behind him, his own rooms, and J looked back to see his door slowly opening. He didn't wait to see what might come out. Instead, he ran to the far end of the hall, opposite the Check-Up door, to the one marked STAIRS. No way he was taking the elevator at this time of night. No way he was risking waking D.A.D. and the staff, the Inspectors, Lawrence Luxley, *anybody* who might stop him, ask him what he was doing.

Inspect him.

Why not, J? he asked himself, racing down the stairs, barefoot still, two concrete steps at a time. *Why not tell D.A.D. about the figure in the woods and now . . . now . . .*

"Now *what*?" he asked, out of breath, already two floors down. "The ghosts of A and Z? Not real!" He shook his head as he descended, no no no, not true, no ghosts, some kind of rotten half dream, an impossible marriage of day and night.

Four floors down and his movements echoed loud enough to wake anyone struggling to sleep. But J pressed on, until he reached the first-floor door and exploded out into the black-tiled hall. There he paused, listening for the Parenthood.

Nobody there. Nobody came.

J had only been alone on the first floor at night a handful of times in his life. The Body Hall's oak doors were closed. The kitchen's main doors, too. Offices J had never entered. Broom closets. The locker room that led to the pool. The staff bathroom.

He ran for the hall of windows, where he'd be able to look out upon the Yard.

Why, J? Why aren't you running from *the Yard? Don't you wanna go* away *from the Yard? As far as you can go?*

NO!

Why, J?

BECAUSE I WANT TO KNOW WHAT I SAW BY MISTER TREE!

This last rebuttal emboldened him. It was true: Impossible visions of dead brothers or not, J *had* seen someone. Someone crouched. Someone looking up to his very own window.

Dream or not, this admission felt like a big one.

At the glass, J looked. There was no sign of either brother out there. Only the white wind, blowing up frost from the freezing lawn of the enormous Yard.

J waited. He watched. He looked. He looked closely. And he saw . . .

Perhaps, yes, maybe, yes, a shape that didn't belong.

Below him, a sudden crashing caused him to recoil from the glass, to look down to his bare feet. D.A.D.'s quarters were down the hall to the right. But that sound had come from the basement.

What do you think the Corner looks like?

J looked through the glass again, to the shape of Mister Tree. Someone?

It's A and Z. They want you to join them. They were sent to the Corner and now they're rotting in the pines. You saw your dead brothers, J. You saw—

But it just didn't feel true. No. And for the first time since hearing the tapping on his glass, J understood clearly that he was awake now.

Downstairs. Alone.

"Someone you want to see," J whispered, his nose to the cold glass.

He thought of Luxley's book *Folks and Folklore,* and he thought of the myth of a boy who drank some water, found it to be the best water he'd ever drunk, and then drank so much he drowned. It'd frightened J when he'd read it.

Death from quenching a thirst.

It's how J felt now. Thirsty for knowledge.

Another rattle from below, and J did not take his eyes off Mister Tree. Rather, he thought of what disease he might catch out there, what might show in the morning's Inspection.

Placasores, he thought. *Vees. Rotts.*

But what did any of the Alphabet Boys actually know about these diseases? J recalled all he knew in full.

And he discovered he knew nothing more than that those diseases were more likely to be contracted in the pines.

Nothing from the textbooks. Nothing from Luxley's books, either. The Alphabet Boys had simply always *known* these diseases were very bad. And all they had to do was break one of the Parenthood's rules to catch one.

He thought of his own trips to the Parenthood infirmary. The sad way Doctor Previns used to look J over. As if the man was deeply troubled. Deeply sad. J had always assumed it was because he feared what he might find on J's person. But now . . .

The shape in the woods moved, just enough, and J gasped.

A shape for sure.

Are you okay, Doctor Previns?

Aren't I supposed to ask you that, J?

It was always like that in the infirmary. Sure, Doctor Previns examined the boys with the same cold precision of the Inspectors and their magnifying glasses and their eventual declaration of

CLEAN.

But there was no joy in the way Previns said it. And Previns had been gone many years now. Where did he go? Did he go the way of A and Z? Was he sent to the—

A third coughing rattle from under his bare feet, and J kept his eyes on Mister Tree. He thought of A and Z sent below.

Spoiled rotten, D.A.D. said.

It's just a door, Q had said in the Orchard. But Q knew better than that. Q knew J was asking what happened to a boy inside.

Was it Location they searched for in the Inspections? Or was it Vees? The names had changed so many times over the years, and the explanations didn't stay the same for very long. The boys never asked for one.

Why not?

D.A.D. hardly explained anything at all. What he did say he said in passing, casually, as if suggesting a game of Boats.

Excellent Inspection, J. No signs of Moldus at all.

I'm glad to hear you don't have Rotts.

No Vees, J. And that, *my boy, is a good thing.*

Oh, J knew the Inspections were for his own good. He knew the Parenthood was doing all it could to protect him and the others from unfathomably dangerous things. He *loved* them for it. He loved them for getting him through the years when he was too small to protect himself, too little to follow the rules.

Moldus, Rotts, Vees, Placasores, Vegicks.

Location.

J studied the shape in the woods.

His mind, however, the track he was on, couldn't be stopped. He thought back to the infirmary, back to the Check-Up room, back to the thousands of Inspections he'd endured.

Was it all some sort of test? Was Location the kind of thing a boy could *fail*? Was he *supposed* to encounter Rotts in the woods and eventually overcome it on his lonesome own?

And if he didn't, if he failed?

Exactly what would happen if any of the many diseases with the changing names were discovered on him?

No boy had ever failed an Inspection. Not even A and Z.

"So why do Inspections scare you?"

The adult tone of his voice scared him even more than his thoughts, and J looked over his shoulder, half-expecting to see a full-grown man. D.A.D., perhaps, with the answers. Always, D.A.D. over the shoulders of the Alphabet Boys.

But J was alone. Alone with this new voice. A voice that sounded smarter than he believed himself to be.

J almost wanted to see A and Z again, through the glass, as if, in death, they might explain things to him. Luxley had written about a ghost once, the first time any of the Alphabet Boys had ever been exposed to the idea at all. In Luxley's book, a man died and returned from the dead to instruct a young boy on the right way to live. To study, to focus, to make progress in whatever field he chose to devote his life. But, despite the daunting message, it was the concept of the ghost that shocked J most.

J looked to the pines and was surprised to see the branches and leaves in great detail. The Yard was no longer shadowed with snowfall but rather a blinding, glossing white.

"Oh no," J said, feeling the unstoppable pinpricks of horror. "The sun."

J had no idea how long he'd been standing at the window on the first floor and certainly no idea when he'd woken from his dream of A and Z. But the sun was coming up and that meant that, sooner rather than later, the tinny voice from the silver speaker on the eighth-floor hall would announce the day's Inspection.

Would they catch this on him? Would they find it on his person, the fact that he'd spent the night staring out into the pines that bordered the Yard?

A door clicked open down the black-tiled hall, in the direction of D.A.D.'s quarters.

J ran. Quiet as he could, he ran to the door marked STAIRS and then took them up again, realizing at the fourth floor that he was less afraid of the vision of the dead boys he'd seen tonight than he was of the living grown men who might be patrolling the first floor already. Inspectors. Staff. D.A.D. And by the time J reached the still partially open door to his quarters and slipped inside, his mind was full of madness: the infirmary, Luxley's books, the names of the many diseases, the Inspectors with their magnifying glasses held close to his naked body, and the endless questions D.A.D. asked in the Check-Up room every morning of every day of J's suddenly confusing life.

He got into bed fast.

And he realized, too, pulling the covers to his nose, that, despite the fact that two of his brothers had been spoiled rotten and that he'd dreamed of their festering forms, he'd never been so scared in his life as he was just then. Scared to hear the voice in the hall.

Scared of the coming Inspection.

Warren Learns the Printing Press

Half-dazed, the fingertips of his right hand blistered bad, his shirt stained with sweat and cold coffee, Warren walked the dark halls of the basement, headed places he shouldn't go.

His mind was moving a mile a minute, hadn't moved this fast in years. *Years.* In fact, Warren couldn't remember a writing experience quite like the one he'd had overnight. How many pages did he write? He'd gone through a legal pad and a half, no doubt about that, a seventy-five-page handwritten cannon blast that even smelled a bit like gunpowder. Holy shit it felt good. So good that he wished he was in Milwaukee, could phone up the Gangsters, tell 'em all to come down to Don Don's, boy did he have a story to tell.

"Seventy-five pages?"

He wanted to smile but his face hurt from keeping a straight one all day, all night, and into the morning, as the sounds of the Parenthood waking slowly dribbled into his office. The truth was, the smile he searched for wasn't a happy one anyway, hardly even proud. But seventy-five pages was a quarter of a book. This book. And how many pages did he need? Wouldn't one suffice? One page with a detailed, vivid, living, breathing . . .

. . . woman?

Oh, if he were to bump into Richard now. If, turning the corner ahead, Richard were to suddenly pop out of the shadows, his beard rendered snake-hole black by the bright red of his gaudy ever-present jacket and gloves. He'd most likely place one of those hands squarely on Warren's shoulder and say, *Why the sudden interest in the printing press, Warren?*

"Who said anything about the pressroom?" Warren said out loud, his voice bizarrely hoarse, as if he'd recorded himself reading seventy-five pages rather than writing them.

"Warren Bratt," a voice spoke. Warren turned to face it quick. "I was beginning to think you didn't like us."

Warren shook his head no, prepared to lie if he had to, *no no no, I haven't begun writing a book I shouldn't be writing. No no, I wasn't intentionally heading for the printing press.*

But here he was all the same.

It was the printer Mark who spoke to him. The lithe man emerged from the smoke and shadows within the cramped space and extended a hand. Warren took it.

"You remember Clarence, doncha, Warren?" Mark thumbed toward a man hunched by the press. "The grumpiest man in the Parenthood. Be nice, Clarence."

"I remember Clarence." Warren's voice again. Hoarse. As if some part of him had slept and was just waking as the rest of him wrote that book.

"What brings you to this side of the basement?" Mark asked.

"Fresh air."

Mark laughed. Clarence eyed Warren from behind the machine he was fixing.

"Figured I can relate to you two more than most," Warren said, attempting to make something of this meeting. The very something he'd come here for, whether he'd admitted it to himself or not. "The kitchen is a fucking maze to me, and good luck squeezing an ounce of entertainment out of accounting."

Mark laughed again.

"We're actually setting today's news right now," Mark said, wiping ink on his jeans. "Why don't you come see how it's done?"

Warren eyed the man as if Mark had just announced to the whole Parenthood his intent.

Richard, Warren could hear the wiry, greasy man saying, *Warren stopped by. Pretty interested in the printing press. What do you think inspired him?*

Warren felt like it was all over him. A broken egg.

Intrigue.

"Clarence won't tell you himself, but it took all morning just to fix a smudge on page eighty-five of the new science book. Got it set, anyway."

Clarence grunted. Warren watched as he traded out one wrench for another.

He heard a bootheel in the hall.

Richard?

Are you happy, Warren?

Do you like the Parenthood, Warren?

What are you doing over here, Warren?

An Inspector tipped his hat to Warren as he passed. It wasn't Richard. But it was close.

"Come on in," Mark said. He even motioned with his hand the way drug dealers do with their marks. The way people do when you shouldn't follow them. *This way.* Warren followed him. "The paper's easy," Mark said, preparing the ink. "But a Luxley book takes about half the day."

"More 'n that," Clarence grumbled.

Half the day.

"I'm always a hassle," Warren said. "One way or another."

"Aren't we all?" Mark said, smiling.

"How many hours is half the day?" Warren asked.

It made him nervous, asking questions directly rather than waiting for the information to be offered up.

"A good seven hours," Mark said.

"More 'n that," Clarence said, swapping wrenches again.

Mark stepped to where the templates of the news lay spread upon a transparent tabletop. Warren stepped farther into the room. Whether he looked too interested or not, he needed to see this part.

Mercifully, Mark was a show-off.

"Say this was your book," Mark began.

Yeah, let's say it was one of my books.

"We don't need to set every page, but we damn well need to eyeball 'em. Things get stuck all the time. Pages are off a centimeter and the whole thing is shit-city. You've probably noticed inconsistencies yourself. It's the best we can do, using this old heap."

"It's a good machine," Clarence said.

"Sure," Mark said. "When we're running the news, it's a beauty queen. But dammit if those Luxley books don't make us mean."

Warren watched everything. Every movement Mark made. He counted the steps of the process, one, two, three, and wished he was able to write them down. Instead, he experienced it like he would a story. Chapters. And tried to retain them the same way.

"What are you fixing?" Warren asked Clarence.

"What Clarence is trying so valiantly to adjust," Mark said, "is the actual ink vat. Fucker gets clogged all the time. And unless you feel like writing out all thirty copies on your own, Clarence has got to keep it going. Can't have the news without ink, can you?"

Mark crossed the room, stopping at what looked like big towel-dryer rolls. He nicked his shoulder on the string of the room's hanging lightbulb and it swung. Warren thought of an interrogation.

"The pages run through these twice," Mark said. "Once on the way in and once to help dry the ink. But if we've got the rollers too tight we can smudge the pages, and if we've got them too loose we can end up with the words overlapping on the page above and below it. It's a delicate business, but I suppose you got your own problems to deal with, Warren."

A delicate business. The Delicate Years.

Warren wished Mark would stop saying his name.

Who came to visit you today?

Warren.

Who did you show the printing press to today?

Warren.

Who was sweating and looked like he might try to bring down the Parenthood today?

Warren.

Warren pointed to his own head.

"All my problems are up here," he said.

Mark smiled. "I like that! And that's why you're the writer. You do got a way with words."

"A lot of words," Clarence muttered.

Mark pointed to the pages of the news, spread out on the table.

"Have you ever seen one of your books laid out like this?"

"No. Didn't know it happened like this."

"I imagine it'd be like seeing what the human body looks like for the first time, under all that skin."

Warren watched him closely.

"The editor, Jim, gives it to us this way. After he's typed out your chicken scratch. Technically we could run copies of your rough drafts, but who'd read that?"

Yeah, Warren thought. *Who, indeed?*

Mark went on, "We set it, of course, but we get every page separated, one-sided, formatted just this way. I'd explain to you why, but we'd be here till lunch. Come here, this will interest you."

Mark flipped a switch on the side of the table and both their faces were lit from below. It worried Warren, being this far into the room. Looked less like a man stopping by and more like one staying.

"Now, you've got to keep the pages within these borders or not only will some words get axed from the final pressing but you'll clog the whole thing and it'll take Clarence all day to pull the pages out. Trust me. We've done it before. Just don't bring up *Allan Prime* if you don't want to make Clarence crazy."

"I had no idea there'd been an issue with that book," Warren said.

Clarence peered around the machine.

"Nobody told you the work we had to do on that one?" Mark asked.

"Nobody."

Clarence huffed and got back to work.

"It's really pretty neat," Mark said. "You line them up like so, and when the machine's running, you flip the green switch and send the pages through and your book comes out like a book. Bound, I mean. It's no cakewalk. Grumpy Clarence here would run me through the rollers if he heard me say it was."

Chapters. Warren felt like he'd retained the info as if given to him in chapters. He badly wanted to get back to his office and write it down.

He looked to the wall clock.

"You gotta get back?" Mark asked.

"I should."

"Breakfast?"

"I should."

What you should do is sleep. What you should not do is write another seventy-five pages of a book that will get you killed.

"Jeez-o-pizza pie," Mark said. "I probably talked your ear off and here you are just taking a stroll before breakfast."

"Oh, it was cool," Warren said. Then, "It's nice to see other people have just as much bullshit to deal with as I do."

Mark nodded. Clarence looked up from the ink vat.

Nobody said, *Hey, know what? This is fucking insane, us working in a place where we're hiding the knowledge of women from twenty-four boys who we call the Alphabet Boys. This is FUCKING CRIMINALLY INSANE.*

Warren headed for the door. It seemed to get farther away the closer he got.

"Stop by anytime," Mark said. "And good luck with this." He pointed to his head like Warren had earlier.

Warren half-smiled and nodded. Just a couple of coworkers talking shop around the watercooler. Nothing insane here. Nothing at all.

When Warren stepped out of the printing room, he looked both ways down the dark stone corridor. To his right, about a hundred feet away, a red arrow glistened. It had been painted long before Warren arrived at the Parenthood, but he knew what it was. The one hallway in all the Parenthood that only Richard was allowed to walk.

The Glasgow Tunnel.

For reasons Warren couldn't articulate, that red arrow scared him as deeply as the Corner door.

Heading back to his office, keeping the chapters fresh in his mind, he heard another set of bootheels on the stone floor. A flock of red-leather birds took flight in his imagination, and he realized he had no good excuse prepared.

He thought of the Corner. The Alphabet Boys had reached the Delicate Years, that stupid appellation Richard couldn't stop using. Warren had never seen Richard quite this . . .

. . . piqued.

You've been a bad boy, Warren Bratt. Go sit in the Corner.

And every thought of the Corner came with an image of its door opening . . . just for him.

You're spoiled, Warren. Spoiled rotten.

The bootheels again, closer.

Warren slipped into a closet, a tool room, he couldn't be sure. And it wasn't until he was fully inside, the door closed, that he realized how terrible the decision had been.

Not having a prepared excuse for wandering the basement was one thing, but being caught hiding was suicide.

Worth the money, Bratt? It was Arlene's voice. Arlene from the Writing Gangsters. *Worth making money in a world you can't leave?*

No, Warren thought. *No, it's not.* He closed his eyes and imagined the title page of the book he'd written seventy-five scorching pages for.

Needs
(a novel of reality and what's real)

Working at the Parenthood, every waking (and sleeping) moment came with a bit of fear. But Warren hadn't been this scared in a long time.

Nobody's gonna open the door. Calm down. It would be too . . . too . . . too fucking terrible. CALM DOWN.

The boots were very close now. Warren heard them as if he wore them himself.

Clack-clack, clack-clack.

He flattened himself to the wall. Almost knocked something over in the process. He tried to keep the chapters quiet in his mind, his knowledge of the printing press like an autopsy of a still-living hyena, messy and loud.

Looks like you could print a book all by your lonesome little self, couldn't you now, Warren?

The boots stopped outside the closet door, an inch of wood away. Warren could hear dust under one heel.

He balled up a fist. He understood clearly that he was prepared to murder whoever opened that door.

The doorknob turned.

"Dan!"

Warren leaned forward at the sound of a name. His fist up and ready in the dark.

"Dan, hurry up! We've got about four minutes here!"

Dan. Who's Dan?

Maybe you should pay more attention to your coworkers, Warren. Maybe you shoulda made some friends.

"One second!" Dan hollered back. "I'm grabbing some TP!"

Warren held his breath. Other boots. The first voice much closer now.

"That isn't a TP closet. Come on, let's get this done."

"I gotta get *this* done first."

A sigh. Movement. Boots on the stony ground.

"That door there," the first voice instructed.

A door opening. A different door. Movement. Boots. Gravel. A door closing. A different door.

"Thanks. Prick."

A pause. Silence.

The men walked away in tandem, their boots and voices fading through the cobblestone hallways of the Parenthood's basement.

Warren stayed inside the closet another ninety seconds, then he quickly slipped out. He hurried, electric, back to his office. Saw nobody on the way.

Once inside, he sat at his desk and simply breathed. Slowly. In and out. Out and in.

After a few minutes he wrote down what he'd learned about the printing press. Wrote it in code on a bookmark. All that he could remember.

He thought of his Luxley books. The many he'd written for the Parenthood. He imagined the pages spread out on the table like Mark showed him. Pages that brought him so much money he could be anywhere in the world he wanted to. Just five more years of this. Fifteen in whole. The contract. Then . . . paradise. Whatever that meant to Warren.

But how to wait when you can . . . no longer . . . wait? The Luxley books. Pages that meant as little to him as they did to the pair of mismatched mechanics who bound them into a book. Books the twenty-four boys above would talk about over meals, talk about by the windows of their rooms, think about as they slept, and (oh merciless God) even use as examples for how to live their lives.

When he was done writing down what he'd learned, he crumpled the bookmark up and tossed it into the garbage can. It made a soft thud when it landed upon the other trash, and Warren imagined the ripple effect of their landing, the way they must have infinitesimally touched the seventy-five pages there at the bottom of the same can. Thinking of those pages encouraged him, brought him the first sliver of peace he'd felt in many years, despite the horrors they implied. Simply put, *Needs* was the greatest thing Warren Bratt had ever written.

And he was only getting started.

PART TWO

NEEDS

THE BURT REPORT: DECEMBER 1, 2019

To Be Read upon Waking

Entering the Delicate Years Carefully

So, we're nearing "The Delicate Years." But here's the thing: They don't exist. At least not in the way Richard assumes they do. The boys' inevitable sexuality is not, as far as I can surmise, what worries Richard, though, of course, the platform that birthed the Parenthood would suggest that it is. Richard knows as well as any of us that sexuality is a locomotive, an unstoppable force that's going to come in through the window if it's not allowed through the front door. His real concern is something much more frightening:

The evolution of the boys' PERSONALITIES.

Is it a coincidence that a man's worldview solidifies as he grows hair under his arms? As he discovers what his body is for? The obvious connection between the two (body and mind) is the unseen thread that forces the well-being of one to be entirely dependent upon the other. Body and mind. The body develops; there is nothing one can do about it and there is nothing one should do about it. The danger, in Richard's case, is that the mind will grow in direct proportion, making the thoughts and insights the boys carry with them as strange to us (the staff) as M's sudden height or L's ability to grow a mustache. In a word: unrecognizable. And if Richard cannot recognize the thought pattern and behavior of his boys, how is he to 1) predict their potentiality, 2) make use of all the data he's compiled in the past, 3) fully comprehend exactly what a boy means when he poses a question or theory that is apparently irreconcilable with the boy Richard knows him to be, and 4) guard against the very thing the Parenthood was founded upon? I have no doubt in Richard's intelligence, of course; I have no reason to think he'd ordinarily have trouble keeping up with the development of his boys; but in this case, extreme as it is, the mind of a boy may change seemingly overnight; F could suddenly withdraw, suggesting something akin to depression when he is actually just applying his proclivity for situational comedy to more-serious matters. Q, having mastered Boats, could give up the game out of boredom. Naturally, yes, but it might come off as some sort of rebellion. R could channel his anger into an astonishing, focused drive, a drive we might mistake for even more anger, us being the conditioned ones here. In other words, the transformation, if not noted, could make it seem like the whole Turret has gone pell-mell. That all the precautions Richard took a decade and a half ago have gotten loose now, shaken, so that the tower itself might fall. The change in behavior of twenty-four young men will be felt in every room, every floor, like the spreading of heavy air, filling the Body Hall to the roof, spoiling the kitchen, contaminating even our offices and bedrooms, choking us in our sleep. The "years" Richard has prepared himself for have less to do with the increased chances of things falling apart and more to do with his subconscious knowledge that one day the boys' moods and personalities (as we know them) will be out of our control.

This is the natural side effect of toxic masculinity. A sexist platform must be partially built out of fear . . . and one day that fear, like the boys' sexuality, will sneak out that window if not let out through that door.

Excluding a true epiphany or something tragic enough to alter a boy's persona inorganically, the transformation the boys are enduring is without question the most significant personality overhaul any boy would experience over the course of a lifetime. For twelve years, B has been kind. He could go mean in a month. These new personalities could seemingly be installed overnight, resembling something close to possession. There may be no warning signs. No red flags. This, of course, goes against everything the In-

*spections stand for: Richard, for all his wanting the boys to aston-
ish him, loathes surprises.*

*The days have come in which we may not recognize those we
love.*

Those we study, too.

*Imagine the headaches that come from raising a boy in the "or-
dinary" sense. But here? At the Parenthood? Those headaches
could crack the skull. For what we oppress in the Alphabet Boys
must come out. Some of them won't even open that window before
going through it.*

Mind the broken glass, Parenthood.

*How will Richard steel himself from being swept up in the cha-
otic mood? How will he avoid burning eyes from the sight of his
unrecognizable sons? (I apologize for the prose, Richard, but some
subjects are more moving than others.)*

*How is Richard going to change in step with the changing of his
wards?*

*Blooming sexuality has its own rules, rules the Parenthood sim-
ply cannot enforce. How are we going to talk to them about it?
Directly? Truthfully? We're not. As a result, the boys will probably
have difficulty letting go of their younger selves (in that they aren't
making a clean break, the break we all made, into legitimate and
isolated adulthood; in other words, sexuality defines ages and eras,
separates the child from the man). It's the ghost of the boys' past
that will haunt Richard first. And the forms they will take in the
future are unknown. Once so familiar, Richard will overhear them
laughing at jokes he does not understand, suggesting theories he
cannot comprehend. Perhaps pointing out things about him, Richard, that he hadn't even noticed himself.*

*Is there anything more frightening than two dozen strangers
you are sure you once knew?*

*What was once dormant in G may rise. The phrase O learns
today may be his mantra tomorrow.*

The meek traits may inherit the boy.

Scary thought: What if these new traits include a thirst to see the world beyond the pines? Surely one out of twenty-four will get curious. . . .

We've all been shocked at how close to organized religion Q's thoughts have come. But can a modern boy invent God the same way cavemen once did? Will God turn out the same? And is Q a modern boy? Are any of them? Q is a theologian's fantasy. But what if Q were to impress this thought upon his peers? What if Q begins preaching, instilling spirituality into his brothers, demanding they cross the pines and venture out together in search of meaning?

Scenarios like these are not unlikely, Parenthood.

As a child, I knew a boy named Roger Doll, who was very good with science. He won many awards in school. His instructors applauded him and universities offered scholarships. Years later, I encountered a mutual friend who, over drinks, asked if I'd heard that Roger Doll had dropped out of college. He'd found God and was running a ministry now, all his own.

Roger Doll changed, greatly, not long after his own Delicate Years.

We all did.

Our minds are smarter than we are. This, of course, results in enormous sadness, depression, mania, and more. Once this is accepted, fully in whole, the changes our peers undergo enhance our appreciation of the elaboration of the mind. I did not write Roger's actions off as desperation. Roger as a God-fearing man was the same to me as Roger the dedicated follower of facts. One part of him was simply lying in wait when I knew him.

Be warned: The boys will behave like strangers. It is up to us to accept the new people they become.

Richard's boys, I'm afraid, are growing up.

. . .

NOT HAVING QUITE finished reading the pages, Richard reached for the black telephone on his desk.

"Gordon."

"Richard."

"Please inform Burt that I'm excited for the changes detailed in the newest report. I do not fear them."

Richard hung up and read again.

Richard is obviously concerned with the amount of energy a man puts into courting women, energy that could be put to studying, to attaining expertise. But what really frightens him is what mature sexuality naturally implies: The boys will be men and, for this, Richard will lose much of the control he exudes over us all.

In my professional opinion, the boys are as well adjusted as they could be, given their unique circumstances. They are almost teenagers, after all. The problem inherent in this is obvious: Teenagers lie to their parents. Teenagers should lie to their parents. It's part of developing their private worlds and keeping those worlds private for as long as they can.

Will the boys feel as comfortable expressing their coming, inevitable moods? Will they hide things from us? Will they suspect that we've hidden things from them?

The point of these reports, of course, is to give an expert opinion on the psychological state of the Parenthood and its main components (in this case, D.A.D. and the Alphabet Boys). The simple answer, the overall assessment, is clear:

Things are going according to plan. But things are going to change. And I fear the Parenthood's plan doesn't account for that.

The boys are happy.

The boys are healthy.

The boys are brilliant.

But the boys will hardly be boys for much longer. And men are much more difficult to control.

CLOSING THOUGHT: *Boys aren't the only people who go through changes. Men do, too. And so, while the Delicate Years demand we pay extra-close attention to the Alphabet Boys' every whim (the blue notebook has proven somewhat effective, and Boats of course, always), we may want to keep our eye on the staff as well. I'm not suggesting Richard needs to enforce sudden room checks, sending Inspectors into the accounting offices, snooping for signs of insubordination. But with a change so big, the change in the boys, the entire Parenthood must change with them.*

Warren at Work

*T*he Guilts.

That's what Richard ought to have been inspecting for. The GUILTS. Of all the things to contract . . .

See Warren walk. See Warren walk the halls of the basement. See Warren wipe his slippery hands on his increasingly stained button-down shirt. See Warren unraveling. See Warren freeing himself. See Warren pushing back.

See Warren writing.

See Warren putting his life in danger. Real danger.

Cowered over a white legal pad, Warren Bratt was in the midst of another word marathon, pumping out two books at once, one for the Parenthood, one for himself, one for the Parenthood, one for himself, one for the—

Bootheels outside his office door, and Warren furiously slid the white pad onto his lap, eyes wide and fixed on the doorknob. He could feel the sweat drip from his thinning hair to his ears.

Things change things change people change things change people change things change I don't have time to think about how things change people change I'm writing people change I'm writing things change I'm writing two fucking books at once.

Who was outside his office door? And, more important, who was he inside his office?

People change.

Things had changed, indeed. The once-flippant antisocial self-aggrandizing author rose from his desk chair and waited. Listened for those boots. Hadn't heard them pass yet.

You'll write your way out of this.

But that phrase fell horribly flat in light of what his imagination could conjure: the door exploding inward, a pair of Parenthood ex-cons entering, grabbing him by the shirt, Richard emerging from the dust in the hall.

What do you think about writing in the Corner for a change, Warren?

Still, he tried to hang on to the concept. Writing his way out of this. The ink of the words rising, creating a set of stairs that could lead him out of the basement to the first-floor hall. There the words from the white pad might become a skateboard, a boat on wheels, anything to carry him out of the Parenthood, across the Yard, through the pines.

Get out of here. Get out of the state. Get out of the country. Get anywhere, but just write enough words to *get* there.

Warren, once so pompous, once so *above* the daily rules and riddles of the Parenthood, didn't move. He kept his eye on that knob. Someone was in the hall. There was no doubt of this.

What's the matter, Warren? Going soft?

Gone. Yes.

Suddenly you care about the Alphabet Boys? Suddenly you care about their education?

Warren recalled Richard, a little drunk, confiding in him the reason he'd hired him: *You care about nobody but yourself, Warren Bratt. You are guilt-free.*

And now, the Guilts.

People change.

Warren couldn't look the boys in the eye at this morning's breakfast. Couldn't wait to get out of the cafeteria. Did anybody else feel this way? Any of the teachers, the cooks, the Inspectors?

Mutiny.

That was one of the words he wasn't allowed to include in his books.

He stepped out from behind his desk at last, quietly took the carpet toward the door. Stopped halfway. It struck him that if the door were to open he wouldn't have an explanation for what he was doing, standing in the middle of his office. He looked to the coffee-maker on the counter. Looked to his desk. Thought of the white paper on the chair there. Thought of the yellow pages, too. Can't write the white without the yellow. Gotta have the yellow to show them, to show them a book, to say, *Hey, yes, I've been writing, writing a book, what of it?*

Silence from the hall.

Who goes there?

His mouth half-open; he didn't know he was baring his teeth.

Slow, he went to the door. If it opened now he'd simply say he was on his way out, out into the hall, out for some fresh—

Fresh what, Warren?

He could almost hear Richard say it. Could hear the condescension in the man's vexatious voice.

His ear to the wood, Warren heard the boiler, hissing, and beyond it, the rumble of the Corner.

He opened the door.

"Hello?"

His voice sounded very small out there in the hall. Like the voice of someone afraid to answer their phone, afraid of the news it might bring.

The hall was empty and Warren frowned. It was one thing to have decided to go against the Parenthood. It was another to live in complete, abject horror of that decision.

Yet . . .

"That's where you're at, asshole. Utter horror."

He shut the door, returned to his desk.

Instantly he got back to work, the pencil moving slower at first, a word or two, half the idea, the small bones of the story connecting.

In a way, writing this book, this terribly dangerous book, was like teaching himself to write all over again. Like he was reading the book he was writing, wishing he could write just like it. At times, it moved quicker than Warren could speak. The feeling then the idea, the bones then the flesh. The letters then the words.

Oh, how these particular words thrilled him. Almost as much as the vision of the Alphabet Boys reading them, their faces scrunched with confusion, their gasps, their voices as they spoke of it with one another.

So many questions. Big ones. Like how to explain the characters the author called *women.*

Warren finished a page, got up, set the pad on his chair, and went to the small office refrigerator. He removed a carton of milk and drank straight from the lip. He heard another soft click from the hall and turned.

Gordon was standing silent in the open doorway.

Warren looked to his chair. From here, the seat was hidden by the desk. The pages upon it, unseen. Just.

"Mind if I come in?" Gordon asked.

Warren took another swig of milk, wanting the extra beat of time.

"You don't knock, Gordon? Richard never taught you that?"

Gordon smiled. "I gotta say, Warren, at this hour, you gave me a little scare yourself. Worried you might have collapsed in here. It's not like you to work so hard."

Warren looked to the clock. Midnight. How?

Gordon stepped inside and shut the door behind him. He walked straight to the desk. Warren did, too. And because he was closer, Warren got there first. He sat upon the white pad on his chair. Gordon flipped through the yellow pages on his desk.

"Is this it?"

"Don't touch those."

"Seriously? Have you always been so protective of your work?"

"Just don't want your notes."

"You must feel awfully strong about this one." Gordon craned his neck, read the title. "*The Window Washer*. Ah, to the point. You always work this late? I ask in earnest. In all our time together I'm not sure I've ever gotten to know your . . . process."

"You usually walk basement halls looking for children's books this late at night, Gordon?"

Gordon looked up quick. Warren counted four, five meanings in the glance.

"Well," Gordon said, "there's no reason to be sassy. I'm as curious as the Alphabet Boys. You know I'm a huge fan of Luxley."

Warren took it to mean Gordon was a fan of anybody but Warren Bratt.

"Be my guest," Warren said. "But I won't tell you how it ends. Even when you beg."

Gordon lifted the yellow pages. Warren tried not to move, tried not to ruffle the white ones beneath him.

"You write so small," Gordon said. "It's awful for your eyes, and it's no wonder you squint like you do."

Gordon's back to him, Warren slowly slid open the top drawer of his desk. He gripped a fresh, sharp pencil the way he would a knife.

Gordon read a paragraph, looked over his shoulder.

"Relax," he said. "I'm no editor."

Warren felt like he had no gravity to hold him in place. Like he might suddenly float to the ceiling, revealing the second book on his chair. He thought of the Corner. Imagined Inspectors rushing in now, taking hold of him, thanking Gordon for keeping him occupied.

He gripped the pencil harder.

"Wow," Gordon said, nodding. "This is very good, Warren."

Warren watched him, his face bathed in shadow.

The pencil broke. He broke it.

"I *love* it, Warren." Gordon set the pages down on the desk. "*As he washed the windows he wiped clean his past*. How in the *world* did you come up with that?"

"Don't you know that's the worst thing you can ask a writer?"

Gordon clucked his tongue. "Oh yes. You are an *arteest*, after all."

"Haven't been that in a long time."

Gordon smiled, and in the smile Warren saw that the man had found what he'd come looking for: self-loathing in the writer.

"I'll tell Richard all about it," he said. "He'll be happy to know how hard you've been working on this book."

"No harder than any other."

"No? That's not what we've been told."

"Told?"

"No." Gordon shook his head slow. "People hear scribbling through your office door all night. Odd hours, they say." He paused, stared long.

Warren made a show of scoffing. Felt like he was acting. He was.

"I'd like to get back to work now."

"By all means."

Gordon tapped the desk once with a clean fingertip. As if to tag it like cattle. As if those Inspectors were coming for the desk soon. And the writer who sat at it.

Gordon left, closing the door behind him.

Warren slunk deep into his chair, heard the irreverent pages crinkle under his ass.

What are you doing? he asked himself. *Seriously. What are you doing?*

An eye on the office door, he pulled the white pages halfway out from under him, then tucked them back again. He would address them soon. In a minute maybe. But he needed that minute, a solid minute or two. To think this over. To think about what he was doing. To think about the danger he was putting himself in. There was still time to put a stop to this. There was still time to do right by himself. After all, what did he owe the Alphabet Boys? Weren't they tragedies either way? What could *he* do to change that?

He looked to his desk and saw a droplet of blood there. His hand; he hadn't noticed the pencil had cut into his hand as it snapped.

Warren held open his palm, inspected the thin line of blood there.

In its way, the wound felt as good and as bad as writing *Needs* did. Bad because the blood was like a signal, a light, an alarm: *DOWN HERE! A MAN BARING HIS SOUL! BLOOD AND SWEAT! COME GET HIM! COME TAKE HIM TO THE COOOOOOORNER!*

But good, too.

Yes.

Good because the split skin signified a crack in the Parenthood.

Things had begun to unravel. People had begun to bleed. Begun to change.

And whether or not the Alphabet Boys were tragic beyond repair, wasn't Warren more interested in slicing the Parenthood open? And wasn't it sliced open already?

And who was Warren Bratt, lowly writer . . . to stop the flow of blood?

Black Math

Professor Hall wrote with especially squeaky chalk as the eight Alphabet Boys sat quiet, absorbing the day's lesson. But only seven of them were truly engaged, as J struggled to focus on the morning following yet another night of seeing a figure crouched by Mister Tree. He hadn't told D.A.D. or the Inspectors about it, hadn't found either the strength or even the motivation, despite the fact that the longer he kept it hidden, the more trying the experience was becoming.

"In the end," Professor Hall said, his back to the class still, "the answer is the same. But what a *difficult* way of getting there this route has become!"

E raised his hand just as Hall smiled over his shoulder. The teacher called on the boy, and J looked out the window to the pines at the far side of the Yard. The white expanse between the Turret and the tall trees looked welcoming. All it would take was a single lunge out the first-floor window, and the momentum, the slide, ought to take him all the way to the border and the name of the stranger who lurked there.

Was he there now? Was *anyone* there, ever, at all?

J leaned toward the window, squinting. The way the sun hit them, the leafless trees looked almost branchless, but the space between them was hazy at best. J leaned closer.

Was someone there?

"Get off me, J!"

J saw that his hand was planted firmly on G's shoulder. The latter boy struggled to remove it.

"What are you *doing*?"

"Nothing!" J sat up quick. He looked to Professor Hall, but it was too late. The teacher, along with the rest of the class, was staring at him.

"Yard dreams?" Hall asked. He fingered the chalk, making it disappear in his palm, reappear again.

"Yes," J said. "Sorry. I was . . . I was thinking about . . ."

"About the Effigy Meet, of course," Hall said. He smiled smug and nodded. "But that isn't here yet, certainly not today, and we can't have you boys distracted by games or they're not doing what they're designed to do. Can anybody tell me what they're designed to do?"

"We're not ten-year-olds," F said. He only half-laughed, but it was half-laughing at a professor; the other boys felt it in full.

"Okay, F," Hall said. "Go on, then, tell me."

F shrugged. "Obviously it's a systems check."

"Oh? In what way?" Hall smiled the way professors did when they believed they knew something a boy did not.

The partial smile left F's face. A rare serious expression replaced it. "It's the Parenthood's way of seeing how far we've come. How advanced we are." He looked around the classroom. Nobody spoke. "What?" he asked. "That's obvious, isn't it?"

Professor Hall responded, "That makes it all sound a bit clinical, don't you think, F?"

F shook his head. "No. I don't think so at all. I think it sounds like the truth."

The teacher set his chalk on the blackboard sill and wiped his palms together. A white cloud rose up. "The Effigy Meet is supposed to be *fun*. A challenge. Is it neither of those things to you anymore?"

"What is this?" F asked, turning a bit red. "An Inspection?"

The other boys murmured. J watched F close. The boys had, of course, rebelled in the past. They'd each been escorted out of a class for disruptive behavior before. But most of those cases were many years ago now. And the way F was speaking, it was as if the boys were on the same level as the professor. As if the boys had the answers to the questions now.

Professor Hall was not pleased.

"How dare you," he said, expressing hurt and disappointment in those few words. "And how do you think D.A.D. would feel if he heard you'd disrespected your daily Inspections?"

"What? I didn't do that!"

"But you did, F. You most definitely did." Professor Hall made a show of stepping to his desk and writing something down. Done, he looked up to F again, his eyes flat and cold. "Do you have any idea how valuable the Inspections are for you? Do you have any *idea* how safe they keep you?" The boys sat very still. Not a word from one. What would come next? "How would you like the Parenthood to abandon you, F?"

"What?"

"You heard me." Louder now. "How would you feel if the Parenthood and all its staff simply . . . left you here alone? Who would write your books? Who would teach your classes? Cook your food? Who would get your movies and fix your Boats boards and sew your clothes and *teach you*?"

"Professor Hall—"

"I am *not* finished." He stepped out from behind his desk, stepped to the blackboard, and took the chalk again. With the sleeve of his plaid button-down, he erased the formula he'd written. He drew a tall rectangle. "Can you tell me what this is, F? Can any of you boys tell me what this is?"

The boys studied the simple shape for a long time.

"Nobody? How about now." Professor Hall drew a small circle about halfway up the rectangle's right side. "Anybody?"

Nobody. Almost.

"It's a door," E finally said.

"Yes," Professor Hall said. "Of course it's a door. But not just any. What is behind this particular door, boys?"

J knew the answer but didn't want to say so out loud.

"*Anybody?*" Professor Hall was yelling now. For no specific reason, J imagined the man had seen something outside as well. No. Not that. He imagined the man had something deeper than this classroom on his mind. Thicker than the pines. "No," the man said. "Of course you don't." He brought his hand hard to the board. The chalk squawked with each line of each letter. He wrote:

THE CORNER

There was no audible gasp from the Alphabet Boys. Rather, the inverse happened. The silence somehow deepened. As if all the power in the Turret had been cut with the last letter, the *R,* the very name of the boy who sat stunned in the first seat of the far right row. And in that moment, each of the boys imagined the Corner below them, just as they'd imagined it all their lives.

For R it was complete darkness.

For E, walls of needles.

For F, a piercing sound, mist, then . . . nothing.

And for J . . .

J looked out the window again, having seen movement out of the corner of his eye. He squinted at the pines.

Someone there?

Hall tapped the chalk in the space between himself and the boys. Knocking, it seemed, on an unseen door. "None of you have ever *been* to the Corner before." He paused. He looked each boy in the eye. "Dishonor the Parenthood again and you will. All of you. You will."

The buzzer on Professor Hall's desk went off. Class was over. But nobody moved. Nobody even slid their papers into their folders. Eight Alphabet Boys, their black turtlenecks flat to the backs of their chairs.

"Go on," Professor Hall finally said. As though he was disgusted. "Leave."

J was the last to exit the room. As he did, he looked back, once, to the blackboard, and to Professor Hall who sat at his desk, staring ahead at the empty chairs. He, too, wore an expression of warring emotions. Of inner turmoil. J thought of D.A.D.'s speech from a month ago. About change. About the blue notebooks.

J walked quick across the classroom to Professor Hall and said, "F knows better, Professor Hall. We all do."

But when the teacher looked up at him, J didn't see in his eyes what he imagined he'd see. Compassion. Or understanding.

"Do you?" Hall asked. And the defeat in the man's eyes was equal to the pain in his voice. J recognized both as the qualities of a man who had begun questioning.

Everything.

The Floor Shift

The harrowing day had come. At the morning's Inspections, the boys were instructed to pack all their belongings; they would be changing floors. J, Q, L, and D were not unique in how the news made them feel; the entire Parenthood was unbalanced. L, having delivered the floor notebooks to the office on the first floor, returned to tell the others that he'd heard "crying in the halls." His current floor mates didn't doubt it. Sitting around J's living room, they all felt like crying as well.

"It's not right," D said. "We've spent a decade on Floor Eight. How would D.A.D. feel if we moved his office to the roof?"

"Not likely," L said. His support of the floor shift had bothered the others for some time. Now it had become unbearable.

"Can you at least *pretend* you recognize this as a significant event?" J asked.

"But I do! Of course I do. Only I, unlike you, think it's for the best."

"Shut up," D said.

"Really? You wanna hate me over it? Listen, D . . . listen all of you: This is life. This is what we've been taught life *is*. Growing, changing, branching out. Do you want to stay on the eighth floor forever?"

Without hesitation the other three responded with a unified "YES!"

L shook his head. His curly hair bobbed like a wig.

"That's the silliest thing I've ever heard. And you all know it is."

"Yeah?" D said. "Well, maybe that's because you were never really part of this floor, L. Maybe it's because you've always been the outsider up here."

Some silence. But Q addressed it before it became something worse.

"Oh, come, L. D is just flustered about the shift. We all are." D made to say something, but a look from Q kept him quiet. L wasn't satisfied yet.

"No no," he said. "Please, D. *Go on.*"

"Guys," J said. "If you wanna fight—"

"You never agree with us on anything," D said, digging in. "You've intentionally taken the 'other side' for years now. We noticed it a long time ago, and every time you do it, it's as clear as day! You constantly contradict yourself in the name of always contradicting *us*. Yes, L. You are a contrarian. And you know what? Sometimes it's nice to be around someone who sees the world the same way we do."

L looked to the other boys. Again, Q tried to squelch the moment.

"How about a game of Boats?" he asked.

Then L dug in. "So I find a lot of your theories to be juvenile, D. Even bordering on conspiratorial. My goodness, sometimes you sound as if you think the Parenthood is out to get us!" L laughed, harsh. "You *do* realize we can't exist without them, don't you? You do realize that D.A.D. has taken care of us and taught us literally everything we know, *don't you?*"

D brushed his black hair from his eyes. "That's *exactly* what worries me, L. What you just said. And the only thing worse than receiving all your information from one source is believing it entirely."

L gasped. "Exactly what *are* you saying? As if there's another source to get it from! You sound . . . insane!"

"Yes, D," Q said. "What are you saying?"

J and D met eyes. Again. The still-unspoken bond. Two Alphabet Boys who had begun questioning the Parenthood that raised them. In that moment, J decided to tell D about the figure outside. How he'd hid it from D.A.D. in the Inspections.

D stood up. He paced to the window and back. "Let's play Boats," he said.

"No way," L said. "Tell us what you mean first."

"I'm not saying anything," he said. But he was. "And I wanna play Boats. Okay?"

Silence. Finally Q went and got the boards from J's closet. He set them on the living room table. Arranged the chairs on opposite sides. Two games for four boys. One on one.

"Me versus D," Q said, smiling. "J and L." The boys took their seats. "And when we're done? We'll finally pack our stuff." He removed the plastic boats from the boxes. He plugged the boards into the floor beneath the table. All four boys placed the nodes on their necks and forearms. Their chests and wrists.

Q took the line switches, turned on the games.

The painted waves of each board began to ebb and flow, rise and crash. The white surf looked like it could spill over onto the table but never quite did. The variations of blue alternately calmed and overwhelmed the boys: The apparent depth was always a bit uneasy to fathom. As little ones, each of the Alphabet Boys had looked under the tables they played upon, sure to see more water, flowing, getting darker, the deeper it went. But, of course, there never was any. An optical illusion, a source of endless fascination.

Boats.

The plastic crafts bobbed on the waves. The boys felt a slight current of electricity, dual in nature; the current calmed, the current concerned. D closed his eyes. L closed his eyes. Q smiled at J, and J knew it was because Q had quieted the bad feelings, the argument, before D had said anything irrevocable. Yet J wanted to hear it. And a part of him wanted L to have heard it, too. The dimensions of his room on the eighth floor were no different from the dimensions of the room he'd be moving to, mere hours from now, down on the third floor. He'd have another window overlooking the Yard, a lucky break, as most boys were placed in new corners of their floors. And how long would they remain in their new rooms? How long would J share a floor with G, F, and X? D.A.D. didn't seem to know, as the boys had asked him throughout their daily Inspections. The best D.A.D. offered was, *Time will tell*. Well, J thought now, it always did and it always does. But what else might time tell?

"Look!" L said, wide-eyed, staring at his boat upon the board, watching the small piece rock upon rough waters. One of the two of them wasn't feeling at ease. It was their job, and the object of the game, to expose which one it was.

But J knew he was a goner in this particular game of Boats. Q was a master at it for being more "emotionally composed" than his fellow Alphabet Boys. D.A.D. had long praised him for his "natural proclivity" with the game. And the others couldn't deny it. Nobody "beat" Q at Boats. Yet that was half the fun of playing him. As if Q were a machine, the game itself, a benchmark by which the other boys could measure their own progress. And it was Q who suggested the game most often. Not because he was a superior player, but because he knew the real merits of the game: the always soothing resolve of confronting troubled waters head-on.

J stared long at the waves crashing against the boundaries of the board between himself and L. L always looked something like a stuffed doll when he played. His big curly hair and wide eyes hadn't changed much since they were little boys. For that, J felt a sudden deep longing for the days when he and L, D, and Q, would race one another out in the eighth-floor hall. When they played hide-and-seek with all four of their doors open, anywhere but the Check-Up room fair game. J had strong memories of himself and L laughing, crying, eating, studying, discussing, debating, hoping, espousing, choosing, wanting, and growing up.

"Look!" L said.

J was looking. He saw waves reach heights he'd never seen before. One appeared to come close to his face, and J actually moved out of the way to avoid it. L laughed. Of course it was only more illusion. But oh how real Boats felt!

J thought of the Parenthood. The Turret. The Inspections.

He thought of illusions.

"My goodness," L said. "Quite a tumultuous day on the water! My notebook is going to be full of theories on *this*."

"It's the floor shift," J lied. "Nothing more."

L shrugged, his eyes still on the board. "Might be. *Might* be. But I'm gonna have to write it—"

"It's the floor shift," J said again. The waters turned dark blue upon the board. J's boat was leaning so far to its side he could almost make out the entire bottom.

"Okay, that might be *your* take, but—"

"IT'S THE FLOOR SHIFT, YOU IDIOT!"

J tore the nodes from his body and hurled the board from the table. Because it was still connected to L, it swung back and cracked against the table legs.

The world seemed to go white for J. Then black. And as the details of his room (no longer . . . his room no longer) returned, J saw that Q and D were staring at him.

"Oh, you're gonna *get* it," L said, rising and removing the nodes. "What is *wrong* with you, J?" L stormed toward the door. "Nice living with you," he said. "You . . . you *fool*."

When he'd gone, Q and D removed their nodes as well.

"Shaky game of Boats?" Q asked. He and D had been locked into one of their own.

J shrugged, but he was as red-faced as L had been. "I guess we don't have to pretend to relate to L anymore."

Q smiled softly. "We're just growing up is all. This is change. And change is scary."

"Change in what?" J asked, still piqued. "Change in exactly what?"

Q considered this. "If perspective is everything and our perspectives are changing, then I suppose this is change in . . . everything." Q sat quiet a beat before getting up. "All right," he said. "Don't worry about L. I'll talk to him. You should, too. But for now?" He looked sadly around the room. "Now we pack."

Once Q was gone, J turned to D. "I've seen someone hiding behind Mister Tree," he said.

"What?"

"I've seen someone out there and I want to know who it is."

D looked to the window. He did something J wasn't expecting him to do at all. He smiled. "Well . . . why didn't you say so? Let's go see who it is. Tomorrow night."

J stared back, stunned.

"Really?"

"Why not? You're sure you saw someone?"

"Maybe."

D seemed to study his one-word response. "*Maybe* is good enough for me. And you know what?"

"What?"

"You've finally given me something to look forward to today." He winked. "Thank you."

D left. And as J packed his belongings and prepared himself, mentally, for living five floors closer to the ground, he thought how good it was to be able to speak to someone. Someone he'd shared his whole life with.

But should it feel so strange? he thought. So strange to speak the truth?

And stranger yet: Should it be such a relief to *feel* it, the truth, in the room with him? Within the confines of the Turret . . . should the truth feel so rare?

Needs

The fuel burned steady, mocking the pace at which he worked. The Alphabet Boys themselves might've said there couldn't be enough gas to support the endless run of energy. But the Alphabet Boys had yet to know passion.

Oh, two books, such different stories, such different souls! One the result of another man's delusion, the other all the author's own.

White heat. Felt like white heat emanating from the pages.

Warren wondered if the pace had gotten . . . dangerous.

It'd been a while since he'd stopped for water. Food was a distant annoyance. To get up and go to the sink wasn't possible at the moment. The cold sweat, the muscle pain, the headache, the wrist that felt made of wood (Pinocchio was made of wood! Pinocchio had to learn to stop lying, too!), the madness of plumbing his own gutted depths.

Gotta write them both. Gotta look the part while being something else.

And finishing them together was, for Warren, the greatest trick he could pull on the Parenthood.

I finished the new book, Richard. Truly.

Warren hadn't had a session this good in years.

Warren hadn't had a session this good in . . . ever.

When was the last time he felt the current of the rushing words? When was the last time he *could not stop*?

He sneered as he wrote; he smiled as he wrote—incongruous

visages for incongruous tales. Flames cooked his skull for one book and were put out by the other. But even the bad book added to the accomplishment, the session, the feat. Periods of time passed in which he watched his fingers moving, pen to paper, writing, pen to paper, writing, across the page. The motion was silly. It made him laugh. Hyena laugh. Witch cackle. Surely these hands could not be his own?

So fluid, so forceful, so unbelievably assured.

Could they be? His own?

As he approached (cannon shot) the two finales, he wondered how many words might he get done today. Fifteen thousand? Twenty? Twenty-five?

He didn't know. Didn't care to know.

Half of it meant so much, the other so little. And the movement of his hand across the page was all that mattered.

After a while his hand looked like a plastic boat, bobbing on the white waters of the page.

And wasn't that what Boats was, in truth? Wasn't it, in essence, the same as what Warren did now?

The truth?

When the muscles in his writing wrist cramped, Warren massaged it with his other hand. And when his right hand froze, he wrote with his left. One book was laughter. The other a scream.

"Fuck the money."

Ooh, did it feel *good* to say *that*.

No money. No more.

On the run now. Very soon. Running. On the.

He'd written so many words they seemed to no longer fit on the pages. They floated about his office, settling in the corners, at the coffee machine, on the couch.

Look! It was the window washer himself! Dunking his rags in fresh water!

And look! By the refrigerator! The Titan of the Turret! The Party of the Parenthood!

Woman.

Oh, to write a woman again. Oh, to simply *describe* her.

Every *she* tasted like steak.

But the desk against his belly felt like the tip of a bayonet.

Write, Bratt. And do not stop till you're done.

He bobbed his head to the uneven rhythms of the opposite books.

How different a single word was, appearing in one story, then the other:

The window washer must do good work.

We knew lying would work.

Shame.

The Parenthood.

The boys.

Fear, too. Fear of that same Parenthood and the humming from down the hall.

But Warren didn't slow down. Warren couldn't. Wouldn't. No.

He shook out his right hand as he wrote with his left. Shook out his left as he wrote with his right. Felt like his back would crack if he were to get up too fast. He was killing himself at his desk. Didn't mind it at all.

Warren had never been so *alive.*

Do you look like you're dying? Or do you look like you've just been born?

Both at once. Both at once. *The Window Washer* and *Needs.*

He was minutes away now, ma-ma-minutes away.

The everyday terrible sounds of the basement continued beyond his office door. The angry boiler, boots in the hall, the swelling of what thrived in the Corner. Warren feared it all, but he did not falter. It was all a reminder, a slap of his cheek, a voice demanding he

FINISH FINISH FINISH

then go.

Yes, go. That would have to be next. *Go* had to follow the delivery of the books.

But go where?

Did it matter so long as it was go?

Because of the legitimate purge he was experiencing, Warren thought of his friends. The Writing Gang. Dana the Dude. Arlene the Asshole. He imagined them watching from the other side of his desk.

Were they alive still? It'd been ten years. Did they still write? Did they still roll their eyes? Did they harbor hatred for the way he'd turned his back on them? Did they know that, despite so much writing, he hadn't *written* anything in ten years?

Warren laughed, and his laugh mingled with the death-cough of the Corner. Dana and Arlene, still wearing those angry expressions, arms crossed, *disappointed* in Warren Bratt.

Maybe they were dead?

Warren, Dana's corpse might say. *Why not write on your money? You got a lot of bills for paper now.*

Warren laughed, shamed and proud both, the sound of the pen to paper unflagging.

You two died of Art, he thought, raging. *But would you, could you, write a book in a place where nobody looked? Would you, could you, tell the truth? To a tower of boys without any proof?*

Warren wrote. One book. The other. One book. The other.

What are you writing, Warren? Arlene might ask. *A check?*

"I'm writing the *best* thing I've ever written, you pretentious fucks. Now leave me alone!"

Wait. Quiet. Hadn't Gordon said people heard scribbling in his office?

What else had people heard?

He was close now. So close. So so so so so so—

This doesn't absolve you, Warren. Dana. Still proud. Still righteous. *Just because you're facing the truth now doesn't mean you didn't turn your back on it then.*

"GET OUT OF MY OFFICE!"

Bootheels in the hall. Warren didn't care. Not this time. This time Warren wrote.

One book. The other. One.

The other.

One.

What happens, Warren wondered (and wrote it, too, wrote the thought into the one book, not the other), when a man feels so much guilt that he must perform self-surgery, must remove it from his body? And what does that man do with it once it's gone? And what does he do with the empty space?

Warren wanted Richard to read *Needs*. Oh, how he wanted Richard to read it. Oh, how he wanted the man in the red jacket to *see* red.

GET ME WARREN BRATT!

One page to go in each. Oh my.

One page to go in each.

Oh.

My.

Richard. The Corner. Deliver the books and go. Who the fuck cared about the Corner right now?

Half a page in *The Window Washer* . . . half a page to go. The electricity was blinding. Felt like madness. True, uneven, unstable madness. As if the colors of the carpet were rising from the floor, filling the air between himself and the door. Like he was surrounded by bright yellow light, hot light, light he could feel, the spirits of A and Z, the spirits of all those mothers and fathers, the ones who agreed to give up their boys in the name of

"MONEY!" Warren cried out. Then he cried tears. Why finish *The Window Washer* at all? Was he so institutionalized that he felt he must? Still? Did he doubt his own escape after delivering the boys the real book, the real good book?

Did he doubt he would deliver it at all?

As he wrote THE END on *The Window Washer* and shoved the stack of yellow pages off his desk.

They sailed like jaundice to his office floor.

Made more room for the white.

He sat back, eyes wide, hardly able to comprehend his own scribbling (he actually cared deeply for penmanship throughout the process, as the book for the boys would be copies . . . printing-press clones of the very draft he was so so so close to wrapping), hardly able to bring his pen to the paper, aware that YES this was it YES this was the greatest YES this was the greatest work of art Warren Bratt had ever done.

And it was . . .

THE END

Needs

Done.

The boiler went quiet. No noise came from the Corner.

He reread the final words.

Because women do not distract. They inspire.

He pulled the title page from beneath the pile.

Needs

(a novel of reality and what's real)

By Warren Bratt

"Dana, Arlene," he said. "Feast your eyes."

But his own eyes welled up. There was no sense of having righted a wrong as he crossed the finish line. No lessening of the guilt.

He imagined the Writing Gangsters reaching for the manu-script, flipping through its pages.

It's good, Dana said.

It's really good, Arlene said.

Warren looked up and saw nobody in his office. Saw how empty the office was.

He slouched. Felt an emptiness within him expanding.

Whatever he experienced upon wrapping *Needs,* it was much heavier, much colder, than what the Writing Gangsters used to call Post-Write-'em Depression.

Warren felt as if he had nothing. Not a thing in the world but this one shiny object. And even it was not enough.

The Guilts. For ever agreeing to be in a position that would lead him to writing this book at all.

But, forgiven or not, he had two things to do.

Deliver the book.

And GO.

Did he have the strength to do them?

Both palms on the desk, he pushed off from the wood and fell to his knees by his chair. He hadn't planned on collapsing.

He felt the desk against his belly, though it no longer was. And his wrists were cramped as though still holding a pen. He wept, contorted yet in the posture of the writer.

He didn't want to let that posture go.

Then, coming to, Warren did get up. He went to the kitchen and removed his briefcase from the counter. He brought it to his desk and carefully placed both manuscripts inside.

The job was done. And there was no point in waiting now.

He dried his face and neck with a towel. He changed his clothes. He did not glance about his office before leaving. This would be his last time standing in this room, breathing the thick air.

Yet, absolved or not, it would forever be the room in which he molted.

He turned off his desk lamp, took his briefcase by the handle, and stepped out into the hall. No guards. No Inspectors. No D.A.D. Not yet.

Warren's sneakers made no sound at all. He was grateful for that. Had someone rounded the hall ahead, Warren would've killed him on the spot.

He did not allow himself to imagine exactly who he might encounter. That no longer mattered. Despite the emptiness inside him, the zenith of expression was alive within him. He did not slouch, that uniquely Warren Bratt troll-walk that long irked his colleagues and once fooled him into thinking he had power in this place.

Today he walked upright. His head held high. And the walk went quick, perhaps too quick, as the door to the editor's office appeared suddenly by his side. He stepped in, removed *The Window Washer* from the case, and set it on the unoccupied desk with a note.

Here you go, Jim. Tear it apart.

~WB

When Warren left the room, it struck him how unnecessary this move actually was. There was no doubt now as to the next step he would take. He did not need the security of having written the book for the Parenthood, proof if Richard should come asking. In fact, *The Window Washer* was the only thing remaining that could stop him from doing what he should. What he must.

Without it, what did he have to show for his marathon session of late? How else to answer any inquiry as to the source of the scribbling heard from the hall?

He looked back to the office he'd just left. Then he entered it again, took his book and his note from the desk, carried them with him.

He didn't want to be able to answer those questions anymore.

Down the hall, heading in a direction he had no business going, toward the printers' once again, Warren paused at the incinerator square. Without hesitation, he pulled the door open, felt the brief heat, and tossed his book and note inside.

For the first time since experiencing the Guilts, he felt a fragment of absolution.

But not enough. No no. And now he was balancing very high without a net.

He continued to the printing room, Mark's and Clarence's infinitesimal claim on the world.

He was shaking when he reached the door.

Why'd you come here, Warren?

I got another book.

Why'd you come here last time?

Taking a walk.

Why do you got another book?

Because I got two this time.

Why do you got two this time?

Because one is a lie. But in this case, two is not.

But there was nobody inside.

The Parenthood was asleep. But everybody?

Could take seven hours or more. That's what Mark and Clarence had said. Told him. Taught him.

Warren entered.

He opened the briefcase and removed the manuscript, lining up the pages on the table.

He'd make twenty-four copies of the handwritten novel. One for each of the boys. He didn't want one for himself. *Needs*, to him, was more a painting than a book.

Let someone else hang it in their home.

The pages in place, he set the gears in motion and watched as the first words of the most meaningful thing he'd ever done began to duplicate, like the phony viruses the boys so feared.

It took four and a half hours. And not a minute of it was nice.

Not scared to die. But scared of dying before delivering the books to the boys.

The boys would (*MUST*) wake to the mysterious paperbacks, like a note announcing a speech, in their bedrooms.

Some of them would begin to flip the pages. Some would begin to read.

About the real world.

About real life.

About women.

Could've killed him, Warren, he thought. *Could've just tore Richard's intestines right out of him.*

Warren smiled sadly. That's exactly what he was doing.

The room smelled of motors pushed past their breaking point. The room smelled of fact.

All done, he put the copies in a box. He carried the box out of the printing room. At the Corner he did not speed up and he did not slow down. He only walked. And walked. One turn. Then another. Eventually his eyes were firmly locked on a door marked STAIRS. The stairs led, of course, up. Up to the first floor. Up to the many floors above it, too.

He scaled the steps. As the Parenthood slept, Warren began the process of waking it up. And as the marked door closed behind him, his overwhelmed mind imagined, momentarily, that it was the door to the Corner.

But by the time Richard demanded his head, Warren Bratt would be so far from the tower he might not know the way back.

And the boys? Where will they be, Warren? Isn't this a death sentence for them? Knowledge? Spoiling them . . . rotten?

The questions came muffled. He wouldn't allow himself to hear them.

"The truth," he said, climbing the steps. "They deserve the truth."

He imagined each Alphabet Boy in a cage; twenty-four boys behind bars painted to blend in with the rest of the world.

He reached the first-floor door.

He pushed it open with his shoe.

And he stepped through.

Carrying keys for the locks, delivering reality in a box.

"A Monster in My Rooms"

J and D did not search the pines for the figure the next night. They'd planned to. They wanted to. They were excited to. But then they woke to find a strange book in their rooms, a thing so mysterious it washed their calendars clean.

With the book was a note from D.A.D. ordering them *not* to discuss it with anyone, even himself, until they were done.

Baffling, indeed.

"Inspection!"

J woke to the word after only two and a half hours of sleep. He'd been up all night, staring out the third-floor window, unable to come to grips with the new view. After all, the third floor was five stories closer than the eighth, and whatever J had seen lurking last night was that much closer, too.

He heard G, F, and X out in the hall. His new floor mates no doubt already standing in line, discussing their studies, the floor shift, breakfast, who knew. J longed for the voices of D, Q, and L. Yes, even L, who, as D rightly pointed out, was always a thorn in the others' sides. It was astonishing to J how palpable the feeling of loss was. As if the other boys had been connected to him physically, as if D.A.D. had removed more than just proximity in the shift.

J sat up.

"I'm late," he said, rubbing his eyes until the boxes with all his clothes and books, supplies and tools, came into focus. His bedroom was a mess. And while he knew his new floor mates had unpacked their belongings before going to bed (he'd heard them and seen their open doors), J hadn't been able to bring himself to do it. He just didn't want to. It was more than just resisting change; J was struggling with the idea of seeing this change as permanent. There was nothing about the new rooms that felt like they were his own. They may have looked similar but they smelled different. Felt different, too.

And that new view.

Upon a stack of boxes just beyond the foot of his bed, J saw a pile of white papers, bound, in the form of a haphazard journal or poorly constructed textbook. He didn't think it'd been there the night before, but the Parenthood was no stranger to slipping notes overnight, and J assumed this was something like that.

Pretty big note, though.

He got out of bed.

"INSPECTION!"

J had a little time. Very little. G, F, or X would go first, giving him precious minutes to brush his teeth, comb his hair, shake the uneasy and alien feeling from his shoulders. He crossed his new bedroom and read the cover page of the stack of white paper.

Needs

Just below this word, the note from D.A.D.

"Needs, indeeds," J said, hurrying to the bathroom. He grabbed his toothbrush, put toothpaste on it, then sat down to pee and brush his teeth at once. As he did, he eyed the messily bound papers on the pile of boxes through the open door.

A knock on his outer door caused him to leap from the toilet, flush it, then spit out the toothpaste into the sink.

"Coming! I'm sorry!"

J splashed some water on his face, tore into his bedroom, and realized he was still wearing his clothes from the day before. Hadn't changed into his pajamas to go to sleep.

J quickly took off his clothes and put the pajamas on. Feigned sleep.

Just as he'd finished, the door opened. X peered in.

"You're late," he said.

"I know." J felt a pang of resentment. This new floor mate telling him what to do. That job ought to be Q's.

"Well," X said, his blue eyes and blond hair so different from Q's, "come on, then."

J nodded and made for the door, passing the papers again.

Needs

Did it say *novel*?

Still walking, he looked back over his shoulder. Couldn't read the title page from the door. Didn't matter. He'd read it when he got back from the Inspection and, besides, he was sure D.A.D. would mention whatever it was in the Check-Up room.

Outside in the hall, X and G waited by the metal Check-Up door.

"Sorry," J said. "I didn't sleep well."

"Neither did I," G said. "Thought there was a monster in my rooms."

"A what?" X asked.

"I heard someone in my room last night. Moving around. And I think I may have even seen him."

"What did he look like?" J asked.

X and G eyed him as if J had exposed something. Had he?

"Stubby. Wide. I don't know."

"You don't know," X echoed, as though to flatten the conversation before it rose any higher.

"Who had your room before you?" J asked.

"I," G said.

"It was probably him, then," J said, thinking of the lurker in the pines. Thinking of the fact that he still hadn't told D.A.D. about it.

"Don't worry," X said.

"I'm not *worried*," G said. "But I didn't like it, either. It's bad enough we had to change rooms, but I can't even sleep in peace in this one."

"Had to be the delivery of that new book," X said.

J looked to his front door, then back to the boys. "New book," he echoed. "Luxley."

"Not Luxley," X said.

"Warren Bratt," G said.

They both looked to the Check-Up door. J sensed they were hiding something. The name *Warren Bratt* sounded as exotic as the mental illnesses discussed in psychology.

"What's up?" he asked.

"The note," G said. He was very close to whispering.

"I saw it," J said.

"Yeah, well, let's not talk about it, then."

They didn't. They didn't talk about anything at all for a minute or more.

J thought of the name they'd said.

Who in the world was Warren Bratt?

"New floors, new floor mates," G said. "How do they expect me to get any sleep around here?"

X laughed. "They know you'll be fine is how. And if you really can't handle it, which of course you *can,* just write about it in your notebook."

J felt a drop in his belly. This conversation again. Only new floor mates now. He didn't want to write anything down in the blue notebook. Not one word.

He thought of the poorly bound book in his bedroom. Looked like a notebook, too.

Warren Bratt.

J knew the book hadn't been delivered overnight. He'd been awake all night, peering out the window, tossing and turning, feeling entirely confused and out of place.

The Parenthood must have dropped it off early this morning, perhaps minutes before the call for Inspection.

"But you can't write about the new book in your notebook," X reminded them. "Not until you've read it all."

"Enough about it," G said. "Not another word."

The Check-Up door opened and F walked out, big teeth and messy hair. He yawned and winked at J.

"You always late?" he asked.

"No," J said. "Only on the mornings when our lives are turned upside down."

Effigy Meet

J had no time to read the new book following the morning's Inspection and breakfast. In the cafeteria, the Parenthood announced the coming of an enormous storm. The Alphabet Boys knew what this meant.

Today would be the Effigy Meet.

As J put on his gloves and hat, a blizzard began. It was a profound way to spend the first proper day in his new rooms, and as the pines looked larger from the third floor, so did the snow.

Across the hall, X, G, and F discussed what they were going to build. The Effigy Meet was the annual contest to determine which Alphabet Boy could carve the most original sculpture out of ice. D.A.D. awarded first place to the boy who showed the least derivation in his work. And while each year the twenty-three runners-up momentarily despaired, all respected the winner.

Another look at the snowfall and J opted to wear his long underwear beneath his black slacks that were also beneath his snow pants. Mobility was important in the Yard, but not as much as stamina, and any boy who thought of going back inside the Turret was not going to make it to the finish line, the judgment, at sundown.

J hadn't considered what he was going to build. Hadn't been thinking of it at all. His mind was on the pines, notebooks, and lies. This, he knew, put him at a disadvantage: If you wanted to win the

Effigy Meet, you had to be prepared. Q, for example, mapped out his ideas in a series of drawings taped to his living room walls. L made blueprints. In past years even D discussed what he'd like to create and why.

It wasn't just the floor shuffle, for J. It wasn't just hiding something from the Parenthood.

He'd been questioning everything.

And the uneven stack of pages he'd left behind in his rooms, the new book by a new writer, sounded like a good place to start looking for answers, a response to the emotional bell that had begun tolling.

He'd reread the accompanying note before heading for the Yard:

Boys—Consider this book a new challenge. Be discreet. Experience the words on your own. Which boy can go the longest without discussing its contents with another? Which of you can resist speaking to me about it? Try. In fact, I forbid you to speak of it at all, with anyone, including me, until you have reached its end. I think you'll discover it to be a refreshing and insightful way to read a book. Perhaps the way all books were meant to be read.

D.A.D.

The mystery of it was unbearable.

"J!"

Outside under the snowfall, J turned to see Q's unmistakable glasses adorning an otherwise completely covered face.

"The Effigy Meet," Q said. "And the perfect storm for it."

"How are your new rooms?" J asked.

"Just like the old ones. Only without you to talk to. In other words . . . it sucks. Do you know what you're going to build?"

J attempted to play the part of a boy engaged in the event. He stomped on the ice beneath the falling snow. Looked to the icicles hanging from the branches of the pines. But in the end he couldn't lie. Not to Q. Never could. "I have *no* idea what I'm going to do."

Q laughed. "Well, as you know, some of the greatest designs *have* been made on the spur of the moment. Don't worry about it. But at the same time . . . think fast."

"What are you gonna do?"

"Little ol' me? I'm thinking of . . . a ladder."

"A ladder? Hey, that sounds neat."

"Indeed. A ladder of ice. How much weight will it support? And much more interesting: How high will it go?"

"You'll probably win."

"Oh, you never know. *You* might win yourself. Idea or not. In fact, I'm a little jealous. A clean slate has always been my favorite way to start something." He looked up to the falling flakes. "And now I'm off. Good luck, J. I can't wait to see what you come up with."

Q nearly vanished into the wind-curtain of falling snow, joining other vague blurs in the Yard.

Like ghosts, J thought. As indeterminate as the shape he'd seen lurking by Mister Tree at night.

Ahead, a taller figure emerged from the wall of mist and snow. J, bundled, idealess, watched him come.

D.A.D.

Without a hat or scarf, his exposed face was pink above his red jacket and gloves.

"J," he said. "You're standing still as a statue. Nothing in mind?"

J stared up into the eyes of the man who, for so long, had been the rock by which J navigated. The rudder and the root.

"In mind?"

"For the Effigy Meet!" D.A.D. fanned a hand toward the other boys, his gloved fingers tipped with frost. Then he brought one of those red fingers to his lips. "Wait," he said. "Don't tell me. *Surprise* me."

J thought how similar it was—what D.A.D. just said and what he'd written on page one of the strange new book in his bedroom.

"I will," J said.

"Thatta boy, J. Set your imagination free, but make sure it's backed up by all you've learned here."

All you've learned here.

Was there anywhere else to go?

"Thank you, D.A.D.," J said, already stepping into the white folds of the storm. "I will."

RICHARD WATCHED HIM go.

He watched them all.

His boys.

The Effigy Meet was as indicative of where the Alphabet Boys were at as any exam or sport they partook in. Richard had long prided himself on the idea: Wait for the first brutal storm of the season and see what the boys can do with it.

Molding nature.

How sweet the sound.

In a way, the Effigy Meet resembled the science fairs of Richard's youth. But those minor contests always took place in gymnasiums, hotel conference centers, the library. Here, at the Turret in winter, the Yard was majestic. The minds of the boys, with only snow and ice for palettes, created some of the most astonishing accomplishments of their young lives. In winters prior, Richard had walked through perfectly crafted tunnels of ice; ridden in mobile, wheeled sleighs of snow; and even eaten dinner upon a frozen table. The spirit of the event was palpable, and often the boys assisted one another. They worked in tandem, creating frozen pulleys to raise bricks of snow, white wheelbarrows to cart blocks of ice. C once attempted to re-create the Turret itself, a project that proved too ambitious but one D.A.D. very much admired. The Effigy Meet was a busy day for the Parenthood, indeed, as Richard documented every and all conversations, theories, plans, and achievements.

Every winter's first brutal storm had become Richard's annual way of marking the practical/impractical progress of his boys. How high would they think? How wide? And what skills would they employ to make these dreams come true?

Richard had thought high. He'd thought wide, too.

The Parenthood itself was his eternal contribution to the Effigy Meet. A thing he'd built from frigid emotions, so close to freezing. A boundless ideal, a law of nature . . . from scratch. Did the Alphabet Boys have this degree of ambition within them? And did they have the gall to pursue it? Some of the ice contributions, year in year out, were simple. Some were quite serious. Some were silly and some were spectacular.

But did any of them . . . reinvent natural law, as he had?

Richard shook snow from his beard and hair. He had to be patient, he knew; they were only twelve years old. Where had Richard been at twelve?

"Distracted," he said. He spit in the snow.

This thought, not voiced often, was much too serious for the day. Richard let it vanish into the snowy mist, where it might freeze and break into unexamined pieces.

His boys had no idea how powerful they could be. How focused. The Effigy Meet was meant to reveal their deepest psychologies . . . not his own.

The Effigy Meet, Burt told Richard, represented the communal understanding of life (creation, by their own hands) and death (even the most spectacular sculptures eventually became puddles). Richard, Burt said, relished this, for it forced the boys to consider their own mortality. Their genius, Richard believed, would inspire the boys to figure out a way to prolong it. Immortality by way of eliminating distractions. For, if a man has no one else to live for but himself, might he not spend his life combating death?

At the Parenthood, snow was good for serious thinking.

Never were the boys as curious about the *meaning of existence* as they were in the winter. Burt found this fact endlessly fascinating. The Alphabet Boys expressed as much self-analysis as men living in the hub of a big city, surrounded by thousands to bounce themselves off, myriad *ways of life,* various styles and moods. It was senseless to Burt, impossible to think that the homogenized world of the boys could harvest the same results as those of a child from Detroit, Chicago, Los Angeles. Yet annually the winter Inspections showed the boys contemplating metaphysics as complex as that which Richard himself had devoted his life to. More complex in some cases. The emotional questionnaires procured odd answers and fresh questions of their own, ranging from what it meant to be embarrassed to determining the finite number of heartbeats a man has in his lifetime.

Death was a striking topic when discussed by boys who knew nothing of being born.

All this in mind, always, Richard watched them now, his boys, working, carving, creating. But he couldn't quite stop his train of thought.

Richard knew there were recent whispers among the boys, attempts at trying to understand the purpose of the Parenthood. He equated this with their changing philosophies and expected some degree of tumult and even mutiny along the way. His (now legendary among his staff) absolute dismissal of video cameras, while counterintuitive to his end goal, was proving more right by the year. The boys didn't need to be *spied* on. The boys needed to be trained to come clean with their transgressions, their concerns, their worries. For was there really the possibility of a boy being spoiled so long as the Parenthood stood guard over the grounds?

The boys ought not to be watched but watched *over.*

Here, observing this year's Effigy Meet, watching the boys cleaving and cutting, the chips of ice collecting like beliefs at their winter boots, Richard felt as confident as the storm.

Hands ever-folded behind his back, his hair white now with winter, he strolled the Yard like a general, the specter lieutenant, his black boots crunching the packed snow, leaving evidence of his having been there, having observed the work of his boys. His boys! Oh, how the air felt *crisp* against his skin! How the sound of the ice picks danced ballet in his ears! The *click click click* of so many doors opening! So many minds unlocked!

A curtain of sleet caused him to shield his face, and when he opened his eyes again, Y came storming through the snowfall upon a carriage of ice. W and F pulled him, sled dogs for the moment. Tandem. Teamwork.

His boys.

Richard called to them, encouraging them to ride, ride, ride *into* the winter.

And never from it.

G worked hard on a road, wide enough to circle the tower, level enough to carry Y's coach.

S sat upon the early-draft stages of a rocking chair.

P polished a mirror of ice.

"Excellent work!" Richard hollered. *"Excellent work!"*

X seemed to be working on a stage. What for? Richard would have to wait and see.

I built a room. Four walls and two doors. What for? He'd see.

Q had begun a ladder.

What for?

"Will you help me test how much it holds?" Q asked him. "It could certainly use a dry run."

Richard eyed the seven rungs, the top leaning flush against the Turret bricks.

"I'd love to," he said.

He climbed Q's ladder, finding a perfectly solid base with the first rung. His implicit trust, his faith in Q's precision and practicality, moved him, and soon Richard was standing above the Yard, looking down upon his pupils, his sons, his boys. A full story high, the wind cut even deeper.

String music flowed from the Turret speakers above him. His boys in perpetual motion below.

"And it's going to go even higher!" Q called, cupping his mouth against the distance and snow.

"I believe you!" D.A.D. called back. "I believe you could reach the roof!"

After climbing down, Richard continued his Zen trek through the spectacle in snow, applauding each boy he came to.

"This is wonderful, P! Wonderful stuff!"

L had built a cold pendulum of ice. D.A.D. knew well the craftsmanship necessary for executing this task, yet, in the midst of a true storm, the boy had done it single-handedly.

Richard continued, shoulders straight, hands clasped behind his back. Hair bone white. A waltz through his own winter parade.

B showed him the likeness of a man whose frozen organs could be removed, the torso swiveling on ice hinges.

N paved a patio deck for Richard's quarters.

Still a few steps from D, Richard paused. D, of course, had shown irregular signs in his recent Inspections. Suggestions, Burt claimed, of a boy about to revolt. And here the boy had carved a door of ice into the ground. Down to the knob. As if he might open it and descend into the earth.

Or beneath the Turret.

A simple design?

A thing to make?

A way out?

"Tell me, D. To where does this door lead?"

D did not hesitate when he said, "The Corner. As I've always imagined it to look."

For the first time today, Richard was surprised.

"And why have you decided to make *that*?"

D weighed his words. "I don't know. Maybe because I feel that, if I build it here, outside, I'll never actually see it . . . in there."

D.A.D. placed a hand upon D's shoulder. "Let's call it a door to the future," he said. "And let's hope that you do see it . . . in there, out here, always."

He held D's gaze as falling flakes passed between them.

"I like that," D said. Were those tears in his eyes? And what for? What feelings had the boy been keeping in? "A door to the future."

A COLD SMILE and D.A.D. continued. D watched him go. And when he looked down at the door again, when he tried, sincerely, to see it the way D.A.D. had described it, he could not. For, no matter what angle he adopted, no matter how hard he tried to smooth over the cracks and splinters he'd added, the door refused to have anything to do with the future.

"Unless that future is . . ." D began. But he did not say *the Corner.*

Time Enough at Last

J hadn't got the feeling entirely back in his fingers yet. So the book felt a little odd in his hands.

Back in his rooms now. His body thawing out. That book open before his eyes. The warmth of the bedroom, the comfortable black couch beneath him, the snow falling outside.

Page 1.

Needs

Written by a man named Warren Bratt (what a name).

This was much better than unpacking.

The tip of Q's ladder leaned against the glass of his living room window, and J felt as if it was his good friend, his brother's way of making contact, even with the floors between them.

J read.

From the very first line, the book felt different from any Luxley book J had ever read. It was, in a word, forceful. He wasn't sure if he liked that. Lawrence Luxley painted gorgeous pictures of the Orchard and the Yard, the tower and its many floors. But this man Bratt was talking about a place called . . . *Milwaukee?*

It sounded silly. Too silly. A completely imaginary place the author referred to as a "city." There were many towers in Milwaukee. Too many to comprehend.

J closed the book.

The wind outside took the ladder, then set it against the glass again. J spun quick at the sound of the tap, half-expecting to see Q at his window.

The wind. The storm. Still going.

He got up off the couch and went to the glass, looked down to the many sculptures below. The Turret lights illuminated the scene and J was able to see details, from this angle, that he hadn't been able to when down in the Yard.

He looked back to the couch. To the book.

"Milwaukee," he said. He shook his head. Whatever this book was, it wasn't very good. It made him feel . . . weird. Almost as if the one or two pages had actually scared him.

A second strong wind lifted the ladder and set it back again. Tap. Sounded like knuckles.

J looked to the pines. Saw nobody there.

"City," he said. Again, the idea of so many towers (*and how many boys, then, huh? How many boys in so many towers, Mr. Bratt!*) overwhelmed him. He looked to the book. He went to it.

Sitting up now, he opened to where he'd left off.

Milwaukee. City. Bar. Cars. Cigars. Alcohol. Some of the words in the book J knew. But he'd never seen them used this way. One word that particularly stuck out, that chilled him, was:

Alley.

More specifically, J read about men discussing something in an *alley*. From what he could gather, they were standing between two towers, surrounded by trash bins. Warren Bratt wrote a lot about the smell of trash. The smell of machine exhaust. The smell of the *city*.

It didn't sound like a good place to be. J looked to his bedroom door. Should he and his floor mates get together and talk about this? Like . . . *right now?*

But no. The note. D.A.D. had expressly told them *not* to discuss the book until they were done. J was discovering how hard that was going to be.

He closed the book. He got up. Despite the cruel cold outside, his rooms felt hot. Too hot. He took the small hall to the bathroom and washed his hands. His face. He wanted to feel the cool water. Needed a change, any change. That book . . .

He looked down the hall to the couch.

"That book is *not* right," he said.

He thought of D.A.D. and the blue notebooks. Thought of a lot of things. The new feelings he'd been having. The new ideas and fears. Was this book some sort of experiment? Surely D.A.D. would eventually be asking him and his brothers about it in the coming Inspections. What questions might he have?

"You gotta finish it first," he said.

But *could* J finish a book like this one? Would he make it through it? Leaning against the sink, as though trying to get as far from the book as possible while still keeping his eye on it, J didn't think he could.

When the wind took Q's ladder again, then set it back, J yelped with genuine fright.

Milwaukee. Alley. Trash.

He hurried back to the couch. He thought about Q. Q would read it. All of it. And he'd have a hundred brilliant things to say.

"Don't be so scared! It's just a book!"

He tried to laugh about it. Tried.

What did D think of it? What did L think? J was sure of one thing: L wasn't going to talk about it until he was done, because the Parenthood had told him not to. But D? D might. D might say something on purpose just to break the rule.

D had also carved the Corner door out of ice. Certainly a topic of gossip among the Alphabet Boys.

J went to the window and eyed the sculptures below. Y's carriage. I's one-room home. D's door.

J was worried about D. The Corner. Why? Why had D decided to make *that*?

He looked to Mister Tree. To Q's ladder.

Back on the couch, he picked the book up and started reading where he'd left off. He had half a mind to skim it, if only to spare himself the weird feelings it gave him. Already. Yet, J had to admit, whatever Bratt was doing, it was effective. Here he was, scared to open a book! Never before had J experienced that kind of power with a pile of pages. Oh, Luxley knew how to thrill. No doubt about *that*. And the textbooks could be daunting . . . but this. *This* was different. This was as if someone was in the room with him. Like Mr. Bratt was crouched behind the couch, listening to J as he read, waiting to pop out, to grab him, to say, *DID IT WORK? DID I SCARE YOU?*

Yes, J thought. *Already.*

He read on. Read about a man who drank so much *whiskey* that he was on his hands and knees in the *alley,* throwing up blood. He read about another who watched people walking in the street below his *studio apartment.* The man had bad thoughts about these people. Very bad. He read about another man who had bad thoughts about himself. Very bad.

But the man who interested J most was the one named Robert, who sought *inspiration in the form of a person, someone with whom he might build something deeper than a basement with. Someone to love. Someone to tell the truth to.*

J looked to the ceiling.

Someone to tell the truth to.

It all sounded so strange, so foreign, so utterly creative.
He read on.
Seemingly against his own will, he started liking it. Partly. Like

when one man punched another in the face and blood sprayed out like *he'd sneezed red.* Or like when one man stepped in a *puddle of puke.*

It was all completely incredible. Every word. There wasn't a familiar sentence in the book.

Outside, the wind howled what sounded like an actual word, and J watched the ladder settle against the glass again. He had a sudden shocking vision of Q's creation smashing the glass, allowing the bad weather in.

And more.

Like Milwaukee. Maybe Milwaukee would get into his rooms.

He imagined the characters of Bratt's book entering through the broken window. The men with *pockmarked faces, red boozer noses,* and *sad watery eyes.* Slack skin and frowns. Bad breath and greasy hair.

Each Bratt grotesquerie filing into his rooms. Crowding him on the couch, forcing him to drink *gin.* To talk loud. To confess.

Confess what? What did the man Robert want to confess?

Needs

What a terrible title for this book! What was Warren Bratt thinking? Using such a title while describing everything a boy *didn't* need!

The thought made J smile. As if, by way of dismissing it, he'd somehow gotten the joke. As if, by seeing how ridiculous it was, he somehow understood what Warren Bratt was trying to *say.*

But did he? Could he or any of his brothers ever understand this book?

He read on.

Robert was walking down one of the *many streets of Milwaukee* when he saw someone (*a slim figure, long hair, sunglasses*) enter a *corner bar.* J could hardy keep up with all the made-up stuff, the imagery, the names of the places, and the way Warren Bratt wrote about it all as if the reader, J, was supposed to get it without an ounce of explanation.

Gibberish.

But what interesting gibberish it was.

After a very long internal monologue in which Robert wondered if the man he saw walking into the bar might be the one he could *confess to,* Robert entered the bar, too. J wondered if D had read this far. Q, L, X, anybody. Had any of the Alphabet Boys read this far? Had any already finished this book?

The thought made him surprisingly jealous. Like when J had to use the bathroom while the movie was playing on Film Night and he'd missed a scene that D or Q later cited as one they liked.

What did Q think of Robert? What did Q think of the *neighborhood bar*? And had he already read far enough along to know what happened to Robert when he entered the place?

J read on.

The description of the bar was so *Bratt.* Smoke and vomit. Stale air and whispers. Round cushioned seats called *booths.* Stools lined up at a long wooden counter (also called a *bar,* odd to J). Mirrors and bottles. Lights, but not the bright kind apparently, as Bratt's description was very dim, gloomy, dark. Music played, but Bratt didn't describe it the way J knew music to be. J thought of the violins and drums, cellos and flutes, that came through the speakers in the halls of the Turret during school hours. D.A.D. said it was all in the name of *enhanced study,* but J didn't think there was any studying going on in this neighborhood bar in Milwaukee. There were a lot of men inside (*at least three people to a booth and sometimes two to a stool*), but there was no mention of any books. In fact, it was more like an unsettling combination of the Body Hall and the cafeteria; everybody was either making a speech or drinking ... *something.* And what exactly were they drinking? That was hard to say.

Bratt kept using the term *booze,* and his description of how it smelled (*something rancid, something sweet*) had J thinking he'd smelled it before on D.A.D. On the few occasions D.A.D. was, as Q said, *not himself.* L once suggested D.A.D. had endured mild cases of Vees through the years, moments when he smelled like someone else.

Or maybe, J thought now, what they'd smelled was booze.

J was getting excited. The bar, dismal as it was, sounded like an adventure. As if the shadowed booths harbored entire worlds where anything was possible so long as you felt it, spoke it, drank it.

"This book," J said, "is *good.*"

He looked to the shadows of his new living room, where the light did not reach. Did similar adventures await him there?

J didn't think so.

Professor Willis, professor of psychics, often discussed art with the Alphabet Boys. He stressed how necessary the imagination was to a big thinker, no matter what that thinker wanted to do with his mind. He spoke of the music D.A.D. loved and Lawrence Luxley's books. But other things, too. Willis talked about the art in the sky, in the pines framing the Yard, the Yard itself. He told the boys that it was important to slow down, to notice the craftsmanship in the bricks of the Turret, the spires upon its roof. He said the Orchard was an excellent place to experience *living art,* the rows of cherry trees, one facing another, like an endless reflection, but which was real and which the mirror?

Professor Willis said that was art. J liked that.

The art in J's everyday life. The art in the couch he lay upon. The clothes he wore. The book he read.

Oh, it wasn't hard discovering it in the book. The book was dripping with it, as if Warren Bratt, this totally new and unknown author, had accidentally dropped his pages into a vat of great meaning, the kind of *deeper instinct* that Q often talked about over Boats.

J read on.

Robert slowly walked toward the wooden counter, where so
many men drank the liquid J had smelled on D.A.D.'s breath on the
days D.A.D. seemed *unlike himself*. But Robert seemed fixated on
one man, the lithe one who wore his hair long (J thought of the
pictures of the Alphabet Boys as toddlers, back when some of them
wore their hair to their chins). J noticed something. Warren hadn't
called the man a *man* yet. He kept saying *person*, in a way that had
J questioning what exactly was sitting at the bar, tapping painted
fingernails against the wood.

A monster?

The wind took Q's ladder again and set it back hard against the
glass. J actually gasped. But he didn't stop reading. Didn't look
away from the book. Robert was halfway across the bar now. Passing men in booths who *sneered and leered*, who laughed so deeply
they coughed. Smoke rose from these same booths and from the
shadows at the corners of the bar, creating a mist, not unlike the
storm outside J's window.

The person's face at the bar was entirely obscured by hair and
shadows. Those nails kept clacking the wood. It drank.

J was scared to see his face.

*A stranger, of course, but not for long. A person Robert had to
speak to, had to meet, no matter what deflating rejection might be
returned. No matter what feelings of inadequacy he might walk
away from the experience with. Because, as Robert knew, there was
legitimate power seated there at the bar. A power Robert had been
covering up for many years.*

How entirely weird, J thought, the way Warren Bratt described
people! Luxley always started with a man and a task. In *Another
Tower,* Jacob set out to build . . . another tower . . . brick by brick.
On his own. And did he succeed? You bet he did. And Jonathan
Ford harvested the entire Orchard *on his own* in Luxley's *Orchard
Plans.* See? Even the titles made sense with the stories being told!

But this book?

"He's got a lot of nerve," J said, struggling to focus on the words, trying (and failing) to resist the incredible energy that poured forth from the pages. In his nearly thirteen years of life, J had never experienced anything like it. It was impossible to ignore. In the same way it would be impossible to ignore an Inspector standing inside his living room, reading the same pages over his shoulder.

J shivered. The storm increased outside. Had it gotten colder within?

He read on. He simply had no choice. Because whether or not Warren Bratt wrote as well or plotted as well or knew how to tell a story as well as Lawrence Luxley just didn't . . . didn't . . .

"MATTER!" J cried out.

It didn't matter! A book, J suddenly believed, didn't *have* to tell any story at all.

"Freedom," J said.

The word resonated in a way it never had before.

Warren Bratt, J realized, was, to use a Q phrase, *disrupting his mind*.

And he liked it.

He read on.

Robert reached the bar. Okay. He hadn't said anything to the person he'd followed inside. Okay. He ordered a drink.

Okay.

He needed a minute to think, Bratt wrote. *What he was going to say and how he was going to say it. Though it was all he'd thought about on his way to the city, he still wasn't exactly sure how to word his confession.*

Robert ordered a *vodka*. The word sounded an awful lot like Vees to J, and he shuddered at the idea of consciously ordering a disease. Would the Inspectors be able to check for vodka in the Check-Up room? J looked to his arms, to the fingers that held the book. Did he see vodka there?

Robert drank. The man who gave him the drink nodded and Robert nodded back, and J steeled himself because, however Bratt had done it, he'd made it clear as day that the moment he'd been building toward had arrived.

Robert wiped his lips dry with the back of his hand. But he was surprised to find his lips were already dry, despite the drink. He was nervous. Not because he didn't know what to say or how to say it anymore but because it had been a long time. Too long. And any man will tell you that time plays a very important part in the game. The man you are when you meet someone and who they are then in return. But sometimes, prepared or not, scared or not, a man simply has to pivot, to face the person next to him, to face himself in her.

"Her," J said. He scrunched his brow.

Her.

A typo. Of course. A funny one at that.

So Robert turned and saw he was not alone in his idea. She had turned, too.

She. Bratt was getting sloppy. An extra *S.*

The woman.

"The woman," J echoed.

He set the book on the couch and got up. Outside, the wind seemed to have settled into a consistent humming moan. A soundtrack, it seemed, for the story.

He looked up to the ceiling. As if through the floors he might see which of his brothers had just read the word *woman*, too.

Woman.

Kind of like *man*. But more.

At the window, his palms to the glass, J laughed at the absurdity, the gall of this author Warren Bratt. The man simply made up words! On the spot, it seemed. One minute the thing at the bar was a person. The next? A woman.

Typos.

Mistakes.

Or . . .

J headed for the kitchen. He had to do something other than read. Drink some juice. Eat a chip. Anything.

But halfway there he cut for the couch and grabbed the book again.

> *"I saw you walk in," Robert said. "And I had to follow you."*
>
> *"Yeah?" the woman said.*

Woman. Again. It was incredible, truly, the way Warren Bratt made his own rules as he went along.

"Ha!"

> *"I know it's not the sanest thing to say to a woman the moment you meet her, but it's the truth. And the truth matters more to me these days than anything else."*
>
> *"That's a good thing," the woman said. "But I'd have to know you a lot better than I do before I believe that."*
>
> *"Well, that's just what I want us to do. To get to know one another. A lot better." Then, with real despera-*

tion in his voice, "Listen, there's a place in the middle of nowhere. A place I worked at for far too long. It's a tower in the woods, so far deep that nobody could find it unless they set out to do just that. It was a terrible place, conducting an experiment of the worst kind. And I was a part of it. I let it go on! Until today." He paused, not for effect but to catch his breath, to allow his heart to settle into a beat he could live with. "Today I decided to start telling the truth. To myself. To the world. To those boys."

J's eyebrows met in an almost comical expression of confusion. But he didn't feel funny.

Where was Warren Bratt going with this?

"Their whole lives were a lie! So many lies! Can you imagine the guilt of looking young men in the face, every day, pretending that the world they live in, the reality you helped create, is the truth?"

The bartender slid Robert a second drink without him asking. Robert didn't acknowledge the gesture other than lifting the glass to his lips.

"I don't think I want to get to know you," the woman said.

"No," Robert said. "I wouldn't, either. But you must listen to me. For if ever you've met a desperate man, you've never met one as desperate as me."

"Go on," the woman said.

Robert turned to face her in full. Took in the shape of her eyes. The gentle slope of her small nose. Her high cheekbones, her long black hair. It made no difference if this woman was "pretty" or not. They all were, Robert understood clearly. Every single woman on the planet was beautiful.

"I have no choice but to go on," he said. At last he sat

on the stool beside her. "We created a false reality, built entirely of misinformation. If this sounds dramatic, if this, too, sounds like a lie, that's only because you didn't live it."

"Why would you take part in such a thing?"

Her voice. So different from the voices he'd heard for a decade.

"Money!" he said. "What else?" He slammed a fist on the bar, rattling the glasses. The woman reached out, placed a hand on his coat shoulder.

"It's okay," she said. "You're contrite. You're troubled. Imagine those who were in your position and are not."

"I am. They're all I can think about. Them and . . . the boys."

J didn't like how Robert said *the boys*. It was almost . . . too relatable. Here Warren had changed gears too quick. Yes. From absurdity to . . . things too real.

"Tell me," the woman said. "What exactly did you do?"

She did not look away as tears rose at the bottom of Robert's eyes. She removed her hand from his shoulder as those same tears rolled down his face.

What had he done? she wondered. But she knew now that whatever it was, it was very bad indeed.

"We raised them without the knowledge of women. We pretended women didn't exist. All in the name of genius." This last word came out like a cough. Like it was the most disgusting word in all of language. "All at the behest of a madman we—

J threw the book across the room. It smacked against the wall and fell with a thud to the floor. He expected to hear three more thwacks from up and down the hall. More from above and below, as the other Alphabet Boys tossed their books in turn. Surely nobody was going to finish this. What was the Parenthood thinking, giving them this to read? It was awful! Just . . . *terrible!*

J got up and paced his living room. Warren Bratt was an awful man who wrote about awful things. He made up his own world, his own words! And he didn't care one bit what a reader might think of them!

Not one bit!

J slammed his hands against the glass. Hadn't even realized he was by the window. The ladder rattled and the wind howled and down below, at the base of the partially lit pines, he saw the silhouette of a crouched figure.

He recoiled from the glass.

The figure!

Angry, confused, but emboldened by the book as well, J picked up his winter clothes from the living room floor and got dressed all over again.

"That's it," he said. "No more sneaking around!"

There was a line in the book that flat-out haunted him, the words that finished the sentence he'd thrown against the wall.

"That's *it!*" he said again, tying his boots in a rush. Put on his gloves and hat.

The window opened easily and the cold air felt surprisingly good. He gripped Q's ladder.

He'd watched his brother climb it earlier in the day. All the boys saw it. They cheered when Q turned at the top, the third floor, and raised his fists to the snowy sky.

J swung a leg out the window, onto the first rung. He moved fast. Breathed fast. He looked over his shoulder, to the base of the pines. Couldn't make the figure out with the snow in his eyes. Both boots on the ice, he descended. The warring emotions propelled his muscles, bones, heart, and head. He couldn't see straight, hear straight, think straight. It made no difference if it was night or day.

Warm or cold. All sense had been shaken by that blasted book and the words that finished that cruel sentence that haunted him, yes, scared him too deep.

Down in the Yard, J looked once to the first-floor windows, then walked toward Mister Tree. He weaved between the ice sculptures, evidence of the incandescent minds of his brothers, the Alphabet Boys. He didn't pause to examine them, didn't think of his brothers by name. Details were difficult to discern: words, letters, names, ideas, feelings. It was all a rash (INSPECTION!) of overwhelming emotions that came together in a storm of their own, swirling dark colors, black winds of why.

J carried that fiery fear with him to the tree. A feeling so hot it denied the winter.

Built entirely of misinformation . . .

"*No!*" J growled, punching his gloved hands together.

There was nobody behind Mister Tree. He turned to face the pines. Where the floodlights reached their limit, J squinted into the woods. "*Show yourself!*" he cried. And the words of that last sentence he'd read sprang up, as if they were what had been hiding in the pines all along.

"*SHOW YOURSELF!*"

But nothing stirred. And nothing showed.

J stepped into the pines, cracking frozen sticks with his winter boots.

Those words . . . that sentence . . .

All at the behest of a madman we—

"Show yourself, dammit! Be . . ." The word evaded him. But he found it. "Be *contrite*!"

All at the behest of a madman we called—

Movement in the snow behind him and J whirled, fast. Nothing in the pines, no, but something in the Yard, yes.

The silhouette of a burly man. His features blackened, being lit from behind.

"J," the man said.

"Who are you?" J asked. *"Who are you?"*

The man took a step closer and J saw it was Inspector Collins. His mustache white with winter.

"You need to go inside," Collins said. "Now."

J looked to the pines, then back to Collins.

All at the behest of a madman we called—

"I'm . . . I'm sorry," J said.

"Come on. Inside. Now."

Inspector Collins held out a gloved hand for J to take. But J only stared at it, thinking of the *woman's* hand upon Robert's shoulder in a bar in Milwaukee.

"I . . . I . . ."

He couldn't speak. Couldn't move.

So Collins moved him himself. He took J by the shoulders and forced him toward the Turret. J let him take him but shook his head no, thinking over and over the words that had confused him even more than *she, her,* and *woman:*

All at the behest of a madman we called D.A.D.

Free Swim/The Pool

Richard, wearing his red bathing suit and cap, sat in the stone-bleacher balcony, overlooking the boys as they enjoyed Free Swim. But perhaps *enjoyed* was the wrong word today, as each of them appeared to be completely on edge—*freaked out,* as Burt would say. Richard believed this was because of the incident with J the night before. J had been caught walking in the pines framing the Yard. Not the worst thing for a boy to be caught doing but certainly alarming. Especially his reason for being out there.

I'm just curious how far they go.

How far they go.

Burt had long warned Richard that this moment would come, and the staff psychiatrist, upon hearing of J's excursion, expressed surprise that it'd taken this long. Richard understood. Curiosity was not only to be encouraged, it was absolutely necessary to his eventual goal. What sort of scientists, what sort of thinkers, would his boys be if they were taught not to look, listen, and search?

Still, something about the way J said it . . . And Collins reported a *palpable fear* in the young man's eyes. It was enough for Richard to order J quarantined for the day. He wanted to look into this further. Had to.

Yet to allow it to rule the Parenthood would be foolish. Yes, let the other boys know J was caught. Yes, scare them some with J's mild punishment. But in the end, Burt was right: Boys will be boys.

And perhaps J's midnight sojourn wasn't as troubling as it first sounded.

Time would tell.

After teaching the remaining Alphabet Boys the butterfly stroke, an hour's worth of dedicated instruction, Richard had retired to the stone bleachers, a towel draped over his own wet shoulders. Quietly, so as not to miss a word they said, he climbed the steel rungs to the observation deck and settled into a seat near the railing. It felt good to get in the water. Felt good to teach. Felt good, too, to observe his boys from above, as none of them knew he was still in the facility.

The profound, all-encompassing appellation THE PARENTHOOD decorated the front bricks of the balcony in vivid blue and white. Like the name of their team. Which, of course, it was. Richard couldn't see the letters from where he sat, and the words felt further from his reach than he felt comfortable with.

Something was afoot here.

Sure, J had been caught in the pines. Yes, the boys knew he was being questioned as they swam. But it simply wasn't enough of an event to cause such ... *distance* in their eyes. To a boy, they appeared to be thinking of something far from the pool, something none of them spoke openly about at the morning's Inspection and certainly not during their swim lesson, with their D.A.D. present.

Were they hiding something? Did it have something to do with J? If so, what?

Richard watched them carefully, swimming below. Their voices and their splashes echoed high off the white brick walls.

Spying on the boys was often more revealing than the Inspections.

It was true the boys, like all near-teenagers, could be deceitful and, yes, they were growing up fast, but Richard had never prized their innocence like he did now. To him, it was clear the experiment was working; any toddler had the strength to carry the weight of his purity, but in the real world most lost sight of it by thirteen.

The boys were right there. Right there. Yet . . . so different from boys in the real world. So different from who Richard had been himself.

Still, a side effect of such chastity was how obvious a blemish was; they'd been polite with him today. Too rigid perhaps. Already, now, they seemed looser, unaware of the shadow he cast.

He wanted to tell them to stop. Stop growing. Stop growing *up*.

You are perfect, he longed to tell them. *You are blameless. Your perspective is as pure as that of the caveman, who knows nothing beyond his daily tasks, but your intellect surpasses my own.*

Stop growing out from under his control.

Richard held his head in his hands and massaged his temples. He'd been doing this a lot lately. He attempted to allow his mind passage, over water and sky, empty, uncluttered fields. But it was ever so hard to remain calm; the Parenthood was always one event from toppling.

"Come on, E!" R howled. "To the lip!"

Free Swim always ended with a handful of the Alphabet Boys congregating by the lip of the shallow end. Some were already there. D leaned against the steel railing of the shallow steps, his arms crossed, his eyes affirming a ponderous state of mind. Q floated nearby.

Richard continued to massage his temples.

Q spoke.

"Strange night," he said.

D agreed, yes, strange indeed. R and E joined them. L, too. All agreed. Strange night.

Had J's midnight stroll affected them so deeply?

"I've never read anything like it," Q went on. "None of us have."

Burt had long given the boys the benefit of the doubt, explicitly underscoring the fact that they were always only aging. *There is no such thing as an unnatural occurrence,* Burt once wrote, *if a natural being makes it happen.* But the mood in the pool bothered Richard deeply.

So had the morning Inspections.

Thing was, they were *too* good. Too clean. As if the boys had mutually agreed to keep a secret.

Don't get paranoid, Burt wrote more than once. *You'll see secrets in everything they say.*

"It scared me," L said. "Really really scared me."

In a world such as the Parenthood, how was a secret possible? Who would have taught them to lie?

"I think that was the point," Q said. "To scare us. To get us thinking in a new way."

None of the boys looked to the balcony. Did this suggest preoccupation?

What exactly was on their minds?

"Hang on," L said. "Has everybody read it? To the end?"

Richard did not move. Snake-like still in the balcony shadows. Read what?

"If anybody has, don't spoil it for me," Q said.

Spoil what?

The boys seemed to intentionally talk about something else. An effort to change the subject. They brought up their studies. L discussed the density of the water they stood in. Q and U discussed Boats. The game, U contested, was supposed to be played as freely as the mind thinks, complete with tangents, second-guessing, and self-doubt. But there was a catch.

"But by virtue of it being a game, and therefore having *rules,*" he said, "Boats is incomplete and doesn't do what it professes to."

Q couldn't disagree more. He believed Boats was perfectly crafted.

"No two people play Boats the same way," he said. "Therefore, it succeeds. There are rules to our communally agreed-upon reality, too."

In this way, Q suggested, Boats was a better representation of *reality* than the one U hoped for. U countered again, citing that the rules of their agreed-upon reality were self-inflicted and therefore could change at any moment.

"But your mind isn't as free as you think it is," Q said. "You would come to the same rules, every time, every day."

Richard breathed a semi-sigh of relief. The boys were talking Boats. And they sounded well beyond their years while doing so.

They must have been discussing a Luxley earlier. Oh, how the boys loved their leisure books.

Do you remember when you hired Burt? he thought. *Do you remember why? You wanted somebody to check you. To remind you of your priorities. To ensure you didn't get drunk on progress. But here you are, distrustful of your own boys. Who is checking you now? They're discussing topics far superior to those you discussed at their age, yet here you are, searching for a problem, determined to find something wrong. Burt would tell you there was nothing to fear. Yet you fear. So did you hire Burt because it would look* like you wanted to remain honest through all of this?

Or did you actually want to remain true?

He had no desire to examine himself in the balcony. He should feel good, should feel *great*. About the progress of things. About the way his boys talked. And the things they talked about.

"The book," D said. "Can we please talk about the book?"

"When everybody's read it," Q said.

But that didn't stop D from talking. "Warren Bratt writes like a person who needs to say something. I guess reading it has made me feel the same."

Richard exhaled and smiled. He gripped the balcony rail and rose. Good God, how close was he to thinking there was a conspiracy in the Turret when, in the end, all the boys had been referring to was a leisure book?

Adjusting the towel on his shoulders, he took the stone steps to the balcony exit. He was quiet about it. No need to alert the boys they'd been watched. No need to make them feel violated in any way. He took the steps down to the first floor. His sandaled feet clopped on the cool black tiles as winter continued beyond the hall windows. At the door to his quarters, he paused. He removed his swim cap.

A drink? Why not. A celebratory gin to acknowledge the progress of his boys. Oh, how worried he'd been. How *suspicious*.

J had taken a walk. So what? Long live J.

The telephone rang on the other side of his door. Richard entered and answered it.

"He's not saying any more than what he first told us," Gordon said.

"Do you believe him?"

"Do *I*, Richard? Well, yes, I suppose I do."

Richard hung up. He went to the bar and fixed a gin martini. Already drunk on the intellectual momentum of his boys, he recounted some of the key things he'd overheard them say in the water.

Boats is unrealistic in this way.

The water we stand in asks nothing physical in return. It only makes room.

The job is dependent entirely upon the tools. The Yard will always only look as good as the tools.

There was more. So much more. Richard stood in the semi-darkness, stirring the drink, relishing the calming sound. Like the arms and legs of the Alphabet Boys through the water of the pool.

Oh, the Alphabet Boys. Oh, the things they say . . .

—whole idea of a swimming pool is fascinating because—
—wood doesn't burn unless we ask it to—
—a good idea but also flawed—
—because one boy's motivation for enjoying a film might—
—his book . . . his book . . . his book—
—careful not to spill it on the way to the Turret—
—doesn't matter how you enter it, once you are submerged—
—his book—

Who was it that had enjoyed Warren's book so deeply? Was it D?

Yes, D had said, *Warren Bratt writes like a person who needs to say something. I guess reading it has made me feel the same.*

Good ol' Warren Bratt. How many books had he written for the Parenthood now? Close to thirty? A fine career by any standards, one that would make any writer in the real world proud. Only this was even better. No matter how sullen or stodgy, cynical or insane Warren Bratt might be, he was contributing to the single greatest experiment in the history of mankind.

In a rare moment of sentimentality, Richard picked up the phone again.

"Go get me Warren," he said. Then he hung up.

Warren, Warren, Warren. Might not be writing the sort of books he wanted to, but Richard would bet on the leisure books being a lot better than anything Warren would've worked out back home.

Richard laughed. Not because it was so easy to poke fun at Warren Bratt, but because the overweight troll with the bad posture (*Quasimodo in the basement,* he'd dubbed him for Gordon's pleasure) had no idea how much Richard had done for him. How much he'd supported the arts after all.

Would Warren like a drink, too? Yes. Maybe he would. Maybe Richard should share a drink with the Parenthood's prized writer and tell him, *Yes yes, good job, the boys love you, Warren. They love you so.*

At the bar, inspired, fixing the second drink, he again replayed a handful of highlights, words and ideas expressed by his boys when they believed themselves to be unwatched.

> —*we're made up of so much water we might swim in our-selves!*
> —*could we make a film of our own? Starring . . . us?*
> —*I've counted the Turret bricks and there are many more than that—*

—Warren Bratt writes like a person who needs to say some-
thing. I guess reading it has made me feel the same.

Richard looked over his shoulder to the phone. Maybe it was
the gin, but he felt a brief wave of sickness. Something deeper than
the need to throw up. It passed. But its echo remained.

Something one of his boys said had worried him after all?
Maybe.

"Nope," he said. "Today we celebrate."

But, stirring the second drink, he didn't feel like celebrating was
the right thing to do. Not quite. No.

Why not?

—we're made up of so much water we might swim in our-
selves!
—could we make a film of our own? Starring . . . us?
—I've counted the Turret bricks and there are many more than
that—
—Warren Bratt writes like a person who needs to say some-
thing. I guess reading it has made me feel the same.

Warren, Warren, Warren. Always made him feel a little sickly,
Richard supposed. Maybe he should call off the drink.

—whole idea of a swimming pool is fascinating because—
—wood doesn't burn unless we ask it to—
—a good idea but also flawed—
—because one boy's motivation for enjoying a film might—
—Warren Bratt writes like a person who needs to say some-
thing. I guess reading it has made me feel the same.

Warren who lived so well here. Warren who'd written more in
the basement than he ever would've in Wisconsin. Warren who, as

Lawrence Luxley, had written himself into the annals of literary history. If only for what he'd been a part of.

"Lawrence Luxley," Richard said, absently lifting the second drink to his lips, as if it were fixed for him. "Lawrence . . . Luxley . . ."

The name sounded so fresh. As if he hadn't spoken it in a long time. As if he hadn't thought it, either.

—*we're made up of so much water we might swim in ourselves!*

—*could we make a film of our own? Starring . . . us?*

—*I've counted the Turret bricks and there are many more than that—*

—*Warren Bratt writes like a person who needs to say something. I guess reading it has made me feel the same.*

But no. No no. The boys (D? Yes, D) hadn't said *that*. He'd said *Lawrence Luxley* writes like a person who needs—

Richard dropped the drink. The glass exploded at his sandaled feet. A shard cut his ankle, and the blood made a trail from the bar to his desk as he dove for the telephone there.

"*Lock down*," Richard said. Hardly able to believe his own words.

"Richard?"

"*LOCK DOWN THIS MINUTE!*"

"Richard . . . what . . . what's happened?"

"The boys, Gordon. The boys used his name. His real name."

"Richard, I don't understand."

"*THE BOYS REFERRED TO HIM AS WARREN BRATT!*" Richard couldn't focus on anything in the room. The desk, the mirrors, the bar. All of it was a sudden cold blur of winter come inside. "Did you get him for me? DID YOU?"

"Warren?"

"WHERE IS HE?"

"Richard . . ." But Richard knew what words were coming next. Before they came. And as Gordon spoke them, he gripped the phone until it cracked. "He's not in his rooms. He's not in his office. Richard, we don't *know* where Warren is."

Richard did not hang up. Rather, the phone fell in pieces to the desk.

MINUTES LATER, AS the Alphabet Boys walked the first-floor hall, having left the pool behind, their many conversations about many exciting subjects were shorn to pieces, blackened, then burned by the power of a single word they had never heard spoken after seven o'clock in the morning. Each boy came to a stop because of it. And nobody responded. All only stared at the silver speaker, rattling high in the wall, from the volume, the heat, the anger inherent in the voice that pronounced the word in a way it had never been said before.

"INSPECTION!"

Lockdown

He started crying. He'd never seen D.A.D. this way before. The boy was scared. And the worst part of it, the absolute most grueling part of being in the Check-Up room midday for the first time in his life, was that the Inspectors Collins and Jeffrey looked scared, too. . . .

. . . "HOW MANY PAGES did you read, Q? I heard you talking about it in the pool. If you lie to me, you will be sent to the Corner this instant. How many pages?"

Behind his large glasses, Q studied D.A.D.'s crazed face. Sweat drained from D.A.D.'s black hairline all the way to his dark beard, as if the man were an irrigation system, and the sweat, the horror, the anger, were keeping him alive.

Q could barely find his voice.

"Thirty," he finally said.

"Thirty," D.A.D. echoed. He'd been pacing since Q walked in, and by the look of him he'd been pacing in every other Inspection, too. The Alphabet Boys were lined up outside the first-floor Check-Up room. All but J. D.A.D. stepped to the steel table and eyed the stack of poorly bound white pages there. "Thirty is a very round number, Q. Very round. I'll ask you again . . ."

"Thirty," Q said. "On the button."

He was telling the truth, but when D.A.D. turned to face him *again, it didn't look like it mattered. It didn't feel like truth mattered anymore at all. . . .*

. . . D.A.D. HAD T by the neck against one of the Check-Up room's steel walls. He did not see his distorted reflection in the steel, but the Inspectors did. His eyes were made enormous by the metal, his open mouth a black nest of desperation. His skin looked to be made of stone and his black hair rose like burnt wood to the ceiling.

The dogs barked hysteria behind the glass.

"HOW MANY PAGES, T? HOW MANY PAGES DID YOU READ?" . . .

. . . W STARTED CRYING in line outside the Check-Up room door. The sounds that were coming from within were unfathomable. D.A.D. was yelling loud enough that his voice should be broken. But it wasn't. He went on.

And on.

"He didn't write the note," X said, farther up the line. More than one boy shushed him immediately. But X had to finish his thought. "He wasn't the one who wrote the note that came with the book." . . .

. . . L TRIED NOT to look at D.A.D. It was so hard to look right at him. D.A.D. didn't resemble D.A.D. Not at all. Not anymore. He'd become a monster. The kind of thing he used to be afraid of under his bed, down the hall to the bathroom, in the bathtub behind the curtain. An approximation of D.A.D. That's what it was. This man in the Check-Up room, no longer wearing the red jacket or gloves (they were long discarded on the steel floor, by the rubber-soled mats), this man was not D.A.D. This man was Vees. This man was Rotts. This man was disease.

And this man had asked him a question. A question L was un-

able to answer. Not because he didn't know the answer but because he couldn't find the saliva in his mouth to speak.

"What new words did you learn, L?"

It was like no question L had ever been asked before. Certainly not by D.A.D. Not by anybody. Never. No. Never. The way he asked it, the look in this man's eyes, the glare in the eyes of this approximation of D.A.D., it was as if D.A.D. didn't know who L was. Or like L hadn't ever known the real D.A.D.

The Corner, L thought. Did D.A.D. say something about the Corner?

Then D.A.D. was walking toward him in such a way that L thought the man was going to strike him. Strike him! And L found his voice at last.

"Milwaukee," he said, shaking, rooted to the floor as if his soles had been glued.

D.A.D. stopped. He stared at L's lips as if L had allowed Rotts to pour forth. L could tell D.A.D. had heard the word before. But that didn't change the dumb slack-jawed look of the man. As if hearing the word from L's mouth had hurt him deeply, had done something terrible to his mind. . . .

. . . "Bar," N said. "Neighborhood bar. Horny. Alley. Milwaukee." . . .

. . . "Cab," P said. "Cabdriver. Milwaukee. Bar. Whiskey."

"What else?" D.A.D. asked. But he hadn't really asked it. It was more like a snake made of letters had slid over his teeth.

"America," P said. "And the U.S. of A." . . .

. . . "I haven't read it at all," B said. "Not one word. I'm sorry. I was studying. I was—"

"Not one word?"

D.A.D. was standing against the glass door that kept the dogs in.

"I'm sorry, D.A.D. I just hadn't had time yet."

D.A.D. studied the boy in complete silence for two excruciating minutes. Long enough for Collins and Jeffrey to steal a sideways glance before quickly looking ahead again, fearful lest Richard threaten them with the Corner next. . . .

. . . "I DIDN'T LIKE it," E said. "It scared me."

"What did. What part."

No question marks at the end of D.A.D.'s questions. Just flat remarks spoken in a voice E did not recognize at all.

"I only made it a page deep. I just didn't like the voice."

"What voice."

D.A.D. looked terrible. Pale. Sweating. Tired. He sat in a chair not two feet from the boy, his bare arms crossed over the chair back.

"You know," E said. "The author's voice."

Something distant sparkled in D.A.D.'s eyes. "You mean . . . you didn't appreciate the artistry?"

"No. I didn't."

For a flash-beat it appeared that D.A.D. was himself again: strong, intelligent, in control. Then the old him was gone, replaced once again by someone whose eyes betrayed the possibility that the mind behind them had cracked. . . .

. . . "I DIDN'T ENTER the bar, no," Q struggled to say. "I just didn't make it that far."

D.A.D. was kneeling above the boy. Q was on his back. Blood dripped from his split lip.

D.A.D. had punched him. It was all Q could think, on repeat.

D.A.D. punched me. . . .

. . . "ENTER THE BAR?" S asked. "Do you mean to ask if Robert entered the bar?"

D.A.D. was upon him so fast that S almost laughed, thinking

the madman rushing toward him must be kidding. Must be coming to show kindness, jocularity, affection.

But that's not what happened. Before S could raise his arms to protect himself, before he could duck, D.A.D. had him by the back of the neck and was pressing his head against the rubber-soled mats.

"Did you enter the bar?"

S couldn't speak, his lips mashed against the rubber.

"Rich—" Collins began, but D.A.D. looked up at him so quick that his glare seemed to cut the word in half.

"Tell me, S," D.A.D. said. "Tell us."

"No," S finally got out. "I didn't enter the bar."

"Why not?"

S was crying. All the Alphabet Boys had cried today. Every one so far.

"I was too scared to see the person up close."

"What person?"

"The person Robert entered the bar to talk to."

"Why were you scared?"

S cried. Tears pooled on the mat where the soles of his naked feet should be.

"I didn't want to know what Robert wanted to confess."

D.A.D. let him go. S rolled onto his side.

"Is that okay?" S asked. "Am I going to . . . the Corner?"

Part of S, the majority, expected D.A.D. to smile, to plant a hand on his shoulder, to laugh and to say, Don't worry, S, of course not the Corner, why would you be sent to the Corner, this is all a misunderstanding and you'll see, very soon, how sensible it truly is, how much sense it really makes.

But D.A.D. didn't do that. Instead, he stared back at S questioningly . . . as if he were saying, I don't know . . . are you? . . .

. . . "How far did you get into the book, J?"

J, who had spent the morning quarantined from the other boys, who had been sent for, who had been marched down the first-floor hall past the other twenty-three Alphabet Boys, hadn't heard the shouts from within the Check-Up room. But he saw the faces of his brothers. Saw the fear and heard the silence. Saw the blood on more than one of them. Felt a horror swirling in his gut greater than what he'd felt last night upon being found by Collins in the Yard. And he knew that no matter what D.A.D. asked him beyond the metal door, he was not to tell him about Warren Bratt's book. Not because of the note on page 1 that D.A.D. himself had signed, but because what he'd read in the book resonated more with J than anything D.A.D. had ever taught him.

"Page one," J said. "Your note. No further."

D.A.D. stared at him, studied him in a way J had only seen in the faces of the dogs. Like if he smelled something he shouldn't smell, the man might suddenly bite him.

"Page one," D.A.D. echoed. "And why did you climb the ladder down to the Yard, J?"

J did not look to Inspector Collins. He knew very well that no-body was going to help him here but himself.

"I wanted to see how far the trees go."

"That's what you told us last night. What you told us this morning."

"Yes, well . . ."

"I don't like that, J."

"Why not?"

"Because you tell it the same way every time."

J still did not look to the Inspectors. Not to the salivating dogs behind the glass, either.

"Let them out," D.A.D. said.

Jeffrey unlatched the door. The dogs came forth. They smelled J's hands. His legs. His feet.

In that moment J told himself it didn't matter. None of this. Let the dogs say he was lying.

A boy, he thought, has needs.

But the dogs tired of him and trotted back to the Inspectors.

Collins and Jeffrey remained ice-sculpture still and seemed to melt with sweat.

D.A.D. only stared from across the Check-Up room. J thought his eyes might crack. Like eyes made of ice, too . . .

. . . "I READ THE whole thing," D said. "Every single word."

Collins audibly groaned. D.A.D. exhaled as though he'd found proof, at last, of the affair he'd so long suspected, the lie he hadn't wanted to be true, but the lie he'd wanted so desperately to prove.

"Every word," D.A.D. echoed. Loss in his eyes. Pain. A door, too. One D had re-created in the Yard.

The Corner.

"Yes."

"And why? Why did you read an entire book in one sitting? Was it so . . . good?"

D smiled. "Because it's the best book I've ever read," he said. "Because it's the most honest thing I've ever heard." He paused, eyeing the floor as though looking through it, as though seeing the Corner itself. "Because, D.A.D. . . . ." A tear fell from his eye, splashing upon the rubber mat, just like the rubber mats he'd stood upon barefoot and naked, every morning of his life. "Because finally . . . it sounded like a truth."

Panic

The Body Hall. Richard in black at the pulpit. Black slacks, black coat, black gloves. Black hair, black beard, black eyes. Black voice.

Black words.

Almost the entire staff in attendance. Every cook. Both accountants. The men who ran the printing press. Almost all the Alphabet Boys, too.

No Warren Bratt and the men hired to bring him back.

No D.

"Panic," Richard said, his voice still hoarse from the Inspections but infused with the righteousness that follows a threatened vision.

Prior to entering the Body Hall, as the horrified Alphabet Boys were shuttled into the pews by the staff, Richard had gone to the basement. Past the printing press, Richard eyed the red arrow and letters painted on the cobblestone wall: GLASGOW TUNNEL. RICHARD ONLY.

The letters of his name looked paltry at first glance, as if he'd overlooked the design, as if he'd overlooked every single aspect and element of the Parenthood, as if he'd gotten lazy, as if he'd destroyed his dream, as if he'd—

"FUCK!"

He'd slammed a gloved hand against the stone and turned at the arrow, entering the pitch-black of his private tunnel.

"Panic," Richard repeated, gripping the podium now. No sing-

ing before this speech. No Voices. "I've always hated the word. For more reasons than we have time for, but allow me to scratch the surface."

His voice echoed off the high ceiling the same way his boots had echoed off the tunnel below moments before.

The same way another pair of boots had echoed coming toward him down that same tunnel.

"It implies, of course, that one has lost control. That one has let the world get the best of him. But do you have any idea how unhealthy serenity is? Do you have any idea how much damage it can do?" He paused, wild-eyed. "I don't mind worry. Worry is very, very good. The problem, boys . . ." The word *boys* made him feel temporarily dizzy. Still his? Still his boys? "The problem is when worry becomes panic. For panic is a bad boy. Spoiled all the way through."

Ahead, in the dark tunnel, a light had come on. By its illumination, Richard could make out the Plexiglas wall at the tunnel's center point. The shape of a figure standing very still on the other side. Richard knew the disappointed posture well.

"Panic!" Richard yelled now, so loud that all twenty-three Alphabet Boys in black recoiled at the static breakup of the PA. "What do *you* see when you hear the word? Do you see bricks falling from the Turret like I do? Do you see the spires falling point first into the Yard?"

In the tunnel, he did not speak till he reached the Plexiglas. And even then he did not speak first.

How many are spoiled? the shadowed figure on the other side of the glass wall asked.

One read the entire book.

Then . . . silence. Not because even losing one was terrible, but because it was clear Richard did not yet know the answer to the question.

"What year is it?" he asked now, his voice booming in the Body Hall. "How far have we traveled into the future, a future we once glimpsed? There are great builders, inventors, thinkers behind us.

And did they not experience panic, too? And should we expect the same to destroy *us*? Why? Why should we be punished by the same thing that propelled so many before us? We have history to warn us, to show us how *not* to behave, what not to do, how to avoid panic. Yet . . . here we are. Trying so hard to gain control again. Trying to put bricks back into a falling wall."

Do you believe the others? the figure had asked. Through the Plexiglas wall, the voice sounded tinny, small, young. But Richard knew better. The explosive force inherent in those syllables was strong enough to topple the tower.

I don't know.

Shouldn't you? Shouldn't you know your boys better than you know anything in the world?

"Between my own foolish youth and the lives of people I've known, I've learned that panic *steals*. Panic scars. Once a man feels panic, he will never again face a challenge without some amount of fear. Once a man has known true hot fright, he will forget the fixed face of security. Because panic, *real panic,* is a state of mind that is larger than the thinker. It shrinks the thinker. It makes the thinker small! And once a man discovers something bigger than himself, he must be awed by it. And what is awe if not reverence? And what is reverence if not respect? And what is respect if not adherence to the laws of that which you respect? Oh, boys. I cannot say we must not panic, because we already have. And in doing so, we have seen the face of fear. But I wonder . . . does this face teach us something? Can we *learn* from it? Can we determine when a face like it might come again? Can we predict similar faces?"

I know my boys.

But you can't tell who is lying?

No. I cannot.

The figure on the other side of the Plexiglas pondered this. Richard waited.

Have you considered—static accompanied the words through

the small speaker—*that a fictional woman is not the same thing as a real one?*

Richard was surprised by the question.

Of course I haven't. Once a boy has knowledge of a woman in any way, any form, the experiment is void.

Is it, though? Would a snake fail to achieve its potential if it was simply shown a drawing of a mongoose?

"Whether we set out to break the rules intentionally or we do not, once a rule is broken it cannot be glued back together. You did not ask for this book. Yet each of you could sense that it wasn't right . . . wasn't something you should possess. I cannot fault those of you who moved slow through its pages, despite believing it to be diseased. I cannot blame you boys for turning pages the way you might turn corners in this very building, to see what is making the sound down the hall. But I can punish those who did not see the disgusting essence therein. And certainly those who celebrated it.

"D has confessed he's read the entire book. It remains to be determined if D is spoiled rotten."

But what of the words her *and* woman? Richard asked through the glass wall in the tunnel.

Gibberish. To them. But take D away. Weigh what to do. D's disappearance will reestablish your grip on the Turret. Do you understand?

Of course.

Can you do it?

Of course.

"D told me the truth, and I did the same in return. He described the book, and his thirst for more, in great detail. I asked him, if given the option, knowing what he knows now, knowing that the Parenthood had been deceived, would he read it again? D told me he would. I do not blame him for his curiosity. But I can punish him for his heartless mutiny. He described the book as *better than any dinner, better than any shower, better than any sleep.* I asked him why he would read the book again if given the option, and he told me, *There are things we have to do, even if you told us not to.*"

Carry on, then, Richard. And through the Inspections you will discover who else may be hiding something. If there is more to hide. Let's hope the book is all they've encountered.

Is there any question?

"Are any of you spoiled? Any boy in this room?" Richard paused. For effect and nothing besides. He eyed the boys in black. His boys. Yes. Still his boys. Scared to immobility. Their eyes as wide as the biggest cherries in the Orchard.

"Have you told me the truth about this book? All of you? I leave you with a warning." Richard leaned closer to the microphone, the whiskers of his black beard tickling the mesh head like spider legs. He scanned the young faces. Saw dried blood on Q's lip. Saw horror in L's face. Incredulity on J's. "If something spoils in the Turret, the Parenthood *will* smell it. And nobody has a better sense of smell than your D.A.D." Another pause. "If you've lied to me today, you will be punished. You will be sent to the Corner. Where you will join your dead brothers, A and Z."

A communal gasp from the Alphabet Boys. As if D.A.D. had released Placasores into the Body Hall.

"We will know if you've lied. No matter where you keep that truth in your mind, no matter how deep you bury it. The Parenthood will know if you've lied."

Don't we have a more pressing matter? the figure on the other side of the Plexiglas said.

What could be more pressing than the sanctity of the boys, my boys?

Silence from the other half of the Glasgow Tunnel. Strong enough to hear.

You must find Warren Bratt. Before he tells.

I'm on it. Of course. I've sent—

Before he tells the world.

It Came from the Land of Snow

J lay in bed, staring at the ceiling, thinking of D.

D was in quarantine. The day after he himself had been. And for what? For having read a book. J had read much more than he'd admitted. Did that make him potentially spoiled rotten, too? What would happen to D? Would D be sent to the Corner? J didn't feel any different. Did it feel any different to be spoiled rotten? Did it matter?

At all?

The idea of D being sent to the Corner was unfathomable. Both A and Z were sent to the Corner at such a young age that the rest of the Alphabet Boys were hardly capable of processing what it meant. But now, at age twelve, they'd had years to imagine what the Corner was like, years to solidify their idea of the boogeyman, years to become permanently afraid.

J sat up. D.A.D.'s spontaneous speech was horrifying. There was no better word to describe it. The man's voice sounded different. He *looked* different. Like a stranger had taken D.A.D.'s place. A man who had been hiding in the Turret for a long time, waiting for his opportunity to emerge.

He had emerged.

Q had been hit. T and S assaulted.

J got out of bed and took the carpeted hall to the living room. Q's ladder had been taken down the night before, the Parenthood's way of ensuring J didn't take another midnight stroll. Why not? No book and now . . . no walk, either.

He checked his reflection in the window overlooking the Yard. No sores. No scratches. No rash. No changes at all.

Shouldn't the Inspectors have been able to see that J had read more than he said he did? Shouldn't D.A.D. have seen it? What did *spoiled rotten* mean, then, if they couldn't?

J took the hall back to his bedroom. He lay down and tried to sleep, even succeeded for ten minutes. He was emotionally exhausted from the day. He did not dream, though Q once said that everybody dreams and sometimes they just don't remember them. Q bled today. Outside J's bedroom window, the wind sighed, then sobbed; the icy branches of the pines crackled. The ice sculptures in the Yard creaked as they were tested.

It sounded like music down there. A very cold song. Possibly one Warren Bratt would've known how to describe.

J got out of bed again, feeling more than a little crazed. More than a little afraid.

The carpet was warm against his feet, contrasting with the world outside his window. In the bathroom it was even warmer, the space being smaller than his bedroom. J basked in the heat rising from the vent. He thought of a person seated at a bar in Milwaukee. Thought of a man named Robert needing to confess something to that person.

Her.

Nonsense. Made-up words.

The relief of peeing was welcome, as though all the bad feelings and fears flowed from him and splashed into the toilet.

He could almost make out D.A.D.'s speech swirling below.

Finished, J stepped to the sink and washed his hands. A palm print, his own, on the mirror glass reminded him of the handprints he, D, Q, and L made as toddlers in the snowy Yard in winters past. He imagined his younger self now. He spoke to him.

J? Where are you? Have you grown up? Have you changed?

Let's do the things we used to do, when we trusted the Parenthood and looked to D.A.D. for guidance. Can you find that place again, J? Can you find me? Where are you?

He dried his hands and stepped from the mirror. Outside the bathroom, the wind beyond the window was much louder. He'd heard this song many times, last winter and the winter before, but now it sounded like it might accompany Warren Bratt's Robert as he confessed to the *woman* at the bar.

We created a false reality, built entirely of misinformation . . .

J was surprised to find he was standing in the hall, staring at a picture of himself as a baby, in the arms of D.A.D.

How innocent J looked. How easy to fool.

"Don't do that," he told himself. "Stop thinking like that."

But what other way was there to think? The Parenthood had lost its collective mind over a book. The author of which D.A.D., in the frightening pop Inspection, had referred to as a *fucking troll.*

In one of Luxley's books, a troll granted a boy three wishes.

From the hole in your face to the one in my ear, three wishes you'll speak and three wishes I'll hear!

J felt a momentary wave of stability. Luxley's books were still a place he could go to without wondering *why.*

In this way, fiction, for J, had become more trustworthy than fact.

Three wishes. From the hole in J's mouth to the one in Warren's ear.

First, I want your book back.

Are you sure?

Yes.

Are you sure?

Yes.

Okay.

Secondly, I'd like to know what D.A.D. is so afraid of.

Are you sure? The truth is frightening.

Yes.

Okay.

And thirdly . . . I'd like to meet you.

Are you sure?

The reflection of J's face in the glass overlapped the image of his face as a baby.

Oh, how things had changed.

There was no knowledge in the face of that baby. No suspicion at all.

He tore himself from the photo.

Oh, D.A.D.'s voice today. In the first-floor Check-Up room. Blood on his knuckles. In the Body Hall, too.

The sound a man makes when the one thing that could unravel his life's work shows up at his rooms, knocks on his door.

Someone was knocking on J's door.

J stopped at the entrance to the living room. Stared across to the door. Who? Who was here so late at night?

A second knock, more forceful than the first, told him it was not the door. It was coming from the wide window to his right.

J looked.

Someone was gripping the top of Q's ladder with one hand, knocking on the glass with the other. Someone had placed Q's ladder back up against the window.

"Oh!" J cried, stepping back into the hall, out of view again. He couldn't breathe right, couldn't find the strength to stop his legs from shaking.

More knocking. J thought of the long hair he'd seen blown by the winter wind. The pale skin. The small fist that knocked on the glass.

A voice now, added to the cold song.

"Please! I need help!"

It spoke. It spoke! And its voice was like none J knew.

"Who . . ." He repeated the word many times, still out of view.

"Please! Hurry!"

J flattened himself to the hall wall. He shook his head no. No, whatever this was would go away. No. He was not going to look at the person at his window again.

But after another desperate knock, J peered around the corner.

What he saw at the glass chilled him colder than the ice of the ladder it'd used to reach him.

Long hair, yes. A skinny body, yes. Small hands.

Wide eyes. An unhappy face. Lips in a square, teeth bared.

What kind of boy was this?

The kind that Robert followed into a neighborhood bar in Milwaukee.

"*Go away!*" J shouted.

But the thing knocked again.

"*Please!*"

J couldn't comprehend what he was hearing. The Turret lights that lit the sculptures below lit the thing at his window, too. And the face that spoke to him was like no face J had ever seen.

"Go away!" he cried again.

The wind wailed, the Turret creaked, and the person outside trembled for balance on the ladder.

It's one thing to read about it in a book, J thought. *But to* see *it . . .*

But what did that mean? *Who* was this?

Was it death? Was it disease?

"J!" the person said. "LET ME IN!"

J. It knew his name.

spoiled rotten spoiled rotten you're going to be spoiled rotten

Feeling as though nothing was real anymore, that he knew nothing at all, J stepped fully out of the hall and approached the living room window.

"Hurry," the person said.

J hurried.

"Open the window, please! I'm so cold."

J went to the glass. The window did not shatter upon him. The person did not break it.

Placasores did not come screeching into his room.

J unlocked the latch.

He thought of Robert walking into that neighborhood bar. He thought of Robert confessing.

We created a false reality, built entirely of misinforma-tion . . .

Why would you take part in such a thing?

J held the side of the window, still too afraid to open it, to let in the storm, to let in the . . .

"Her," he said. But he wished he hadn't.

"Please."

"She."

Shivering, crying. "Let me in."

"Woman."

"I can tell you the truth about the Parenthood." Smart eyes. Kind eyes. "The Turret. The Corner. Your D.A.D. I have those answers."

The words from the book crawled up J's throat like the many-legged bugs in the Orchard. Crawled all over his mind. Threatened to drive him mad.

"Please," it said.

J opened the window.

And the person who so resembled Warren Bratt's mystery in Milwaukee, the long-haired *thing* at the bar, at his window, at the threshold of his sanity, climbed in.

A woman lowered herself into his living room.

And into his life.

PART THREE

K

The World as It Looks
Whizzing Past You

It wasn't only that K liked to draw, it was that she showed an incredible propensity for the craft at a very young age. At four years old, her rendering of the Turret was so precise that Inspector Krantz had thought it was a photo and brought it to Marilyn, concerned that someone had been photographing the Parenthood. Marilyn, having seen K's work before, wasn't fooled for long. But there was a beat, an unhappy jolt of fear she hadn't felt in many years, as Krantz held the drawing up from across the room and said, *What do we do about this?*

Marilyn—M.O.M. to her girls—did not show her prized Inspector the fear she felt inside. Rather, she sat stoic and said in a steady voice, *K. My K.*

Photos of the towers were not allowed. Neither were photos of the acres of pines that separated the two towers. No evidence, she and Richard had agreed upon from the start. No photos, no videos, no tape recorders. If someone were to discover what was going on here in the deep woods of northern Michigan, it would not be by any errant proof the Parenthood had overlooked. It would have to be word against word. Theirs against them.

The long-married couple believed that their denials, bolstered by their money, would be louder in the end.

These were the thoughts that rose in Marilyn's mind as Krantz waddled across her office and handed her the image that had looked so fabulously realistic from across the room. But up close, she recognized the tiny inconsistencies that marked it as a drawing after all. And there was only one Letter Girl in the Parenthood who could pull that off.

Marilyn smiled, not only because it was often easy to thwart Krantz's concerns, but because one of her girls was indeed showing early signs that the experiment was going to be an unparalleled success.

How many children in the *real world* could draw like this? More so, how many four-year-olds actually had the capability but were lacking the tutelage to do so?

The real world was a constant waste of potential.

K HAD BECOME so fond of drawing that by six she was allowed alone time in the Yard, as B and V picked teams for soccer or Yellow Ball, as F and L ran races from the tower to the far end of the cherry Orchard. Yes, K got some exercise in by way of long walks through that same Orchard, but M.O.M. knew that wasn't quite enough. If K chose to sit and draw her sisters in the Yard, she would have to take the stairs to her seventh-floor room, a floor she shared with B, V, and Y. She'd take them at least twice a day. The elevator was firmly denied her.

At first, the agreement felt odd, of course, as K told B she'd see her downstairs for breakfast, but K quickly became aware of how much downtime there was in a day at the Parenthood. Yes, breakfast started at eight A.M., but when did it *really* start? How much time did the Letter Girls spend discussing their dreams and studies before the actual food was brought out? This was true of every event, daily or otherwise, from Film Night to Free Swim, story time to class.

The only thing a girl absolutely had to be on time for was the Inspections.

K didn't miss a thing. And by age eight she was rather fond of the daily up and down. On the way down, she liked imagining how her day would go, and later, on the way up again, she enjoyed comparing those morning thoughts with how the day actually went. Rarely did they mirror one another.

This was, in effect, K's first reward for dedicating herself to art. More would come.

Drawing pictures distinguished her from her sisters, not only physically (by way of stairs), but it provided her with a unique identity: No other Letter Girl took to drawing, took to art, like K. For this, she was asked by all her sisters and even some Inspectors to draw their likeness. As gifts. As presents. Inside the Turret, outside in the Yard. By sun during the day, lanternlight at night. Until the walls of K's bedroom were covered with her own drawings, photo-realistic renderings of each of the Letter Girls and the faces of the Parenthood staff watching over her as she fell contentedly to sleep.

All but M.O.M., who had kindly asked that her face not be drawn. Ever.

K complied, as all the girls complied with everything M.O.M. and the Parenthood decreed. All but one. One unfortunate seven-year-old girl who had been spoiled rotten and sent to the Corner.

J.

K had been particularly fond of her drawing of J and felt great sorrow while removing the tape and taking it down from her bedroom wall. It had hung there for over a year, the drawing having been done in the Yard when the girls were both six, and the space it left behind was glaring, as if it were a frightening facsimile of the Corner door itself.

Am I easy to draw? J had asked, seated on a wicker chair near the boundary of lush pines. A spring wind tousled the girl's hair. K had tucked it back behind J's ear many times that day.

Nobody is easy to draw, K said. *But I especially enjoy the challenge you present.*

J frowned. *I hadn't thought of myself like that. A challenge.*

When she took the drawing down, when the Parenthood told her she had to, K saw that she had captured more than just J in the drawing. She'd also captured the look of someone with a secret. To answer J's original question much later, K thought that J was, indeed, difficult to draw after all. Most girls wore their thoughts at the front of their eyes, but J's were kept much deeper in her head. And the day K folded the drawing of her sister, now gone, was the day she realized her own potential: She was able to capture not only the surface details, the angles and shading, of those she shared the world with, but what lived inside each of them, too.

Maybe that was why M.O.M. refused to be drawn.

By the time K was ten, the routine of the Yard (in all seasons) included her seated upon a wicker chair, drawing photo-realistic pictures of her sisters, the arms of the chair, the grass, her own fingers, her own knees, her snow boots, snowstorms, and the unfathomably inventive sculptures her sisters created during the Effigy Meet.

Including B's brilliant slide.

In the winter of their tenth year, B built a slide that wrapped around the entire Turret, with just enough declination to uniformly run from a third-floor window—O's living room—to the Yard below. The Letter Girls took turns riding it without the use of their hands, their feet, or even a push. K, like everybody else, was very excited to experience it. She stood in line as M took her turn, then L, then U, until, having been sufficiently riled by the seemingly endless screams of her sisters, K stepped to the window and climbed upon B's creation herself. She lay flat on her back, arms folded as her sister advised, legs straight ahead, her boots pressed to the sides, waiting for the word to go.

You're gonna love it, B said, justifiably proud. *And don't forget your number one sister made this thing.*

How could I forget, K said, her eyes on the winter sky, *with you around to tell me?*

It was frightening being outside a Turret window, three stories high.

After a characteristic theatrical pause, B said, *Go,* K brought her boots together, and go she went.

She moved much faster than she thought she would. And the slide walls felt too short. The rush was something close to scary as she zipped toward the first turn, where the ice wrapped around the Turret bricks. It didn't look wide enough to hold her. K, like her sisters before her, screamed, sure that she was going to go straight off the edge and drop to the hard-packed snow. Instead, she took the turn with enough velocity to give the sensation of being shot from a cannon (something a girl named Susan had done in the most recent Judith Nancy book, *A Circus in the Yard*) before settling in again between the icy walls and the cold smooth groove B had designed so well. Sisters cheered from every window she passed. And by the time her scream dissipated into the frosty sky, K had taken a second turn, putting her on the opposite side of the tower from where she'd started, on the backside, where she saw an Inspector high up in a leafless tree, pulling aside the branches of another, reaching for a mitten shot there by a catapult of ice. K didn't realize it at the time, but while eyeing the Inspector, she saw, through the split pines, a spire showing among the many barren treetops. A spire not unlike the one that crowned the very Turret she traveled around so quickly.

K wouldn't know she'd seen this until much later, when the mysterious spire showed up in her art.

But first, the end of the slide, as it took her at last to the snowy Yard, as her sisters were there to greet her, and as M.O.M., dressed in her formfitting red snowsuit, her black hair peppered with flakes, knelt down to her, reached out a hand to help her up, and said, *Maybe you can draw the world as it looked whizzing past you.*

THE BURT REPORT: JULY 1, 2018

To Be Read upon Waking

The Letter Girls are eleven years old now.

Please, take a moment to let that sink in.

More than a decade has passed since you and Richard hatched the mutual plan for an unprecedented experiment in which boys and girls would be raised without the knowledge of each other's existence. Broad, bold, and (some would certainly say) controversial. Nevertheless, here we stand, eleven years deep.

And what have we learned?

First, Marilyn, I thank you for allowing me to address you directly in my monthly reports, a thing your husband still does not permit. One can only assume it is because either 1) he is attempting to sustain a veil of scientific research or 2) it makes him uncomfortable reading about his own faults and foibles. NOTE: It is my job to provide legitimate analysis of you both. I say that in the event Richard argues my termination upon reading the lines above.

For me, it is much easier speaking directly to you. Feels more like a conversation. Or, perhaps, like my opinion is not peripheral but rather examined head-on.

But enough about me.

The Letter Girls . . . the Letter Girls . . .

Eleven now and far superior to their real world counterparts, or as you like to call the rest of the planet: Distraction. It's no surprise that the girls are far ahead of the Alphabet Boys in almost every calculable subject, but perhaps this is something to examine a beat further, for isn't part of the Parenthood's philosophy based upon the concept that boys are out to impress girls from a very young age and therefore more concerned with how they are perceived than with what they actually are? Yet here are the boys, lagging behind the girls again. Just like on Planet Distraction. Some things, Marilyn, are simply biological, and it would behoove us to remember that.

K is possibly the most exceptional of all the kids combined (boys and girls) in that her scores completely dwarf the others'. But while Q on the boys' side stands out for his interesting combination of the scientific with the spiritual, K seems as though she were plucked yesterday from Planet Distraction: Even her figures of speech suggest a worldly upbringing—e.g., don't give me that, whatever's clever, *and* what's up? *And while these words are clichés around, say, Detroit, they are most decidedly not here at the Parenthood. So while Q begins to contemplate a spiritual force behind all of existence, as Q begins to invent God, K is busy inventing clichés, figures of speech that, had she been born at a different time and under much different circumstances, might, like Dickens, have changed the lexicon of the world.*

K is almost oddly in touch with the human condition, what is interesting to her fellow Letter Girls, what is interesting to us, the staff. Some of this is easy for us to take for granted, as we've all grown up with the things she says, the things she likes, the things she draws. But we must remember to ask ourselves (and constantly at that): Who taught her these things?

The answer? Nobody. In this fashion, K is prized in an almost inverted way: Here the Parenthood had hoped to develop a completely fresh way of thinking by eradicating the influence of the outside world, but instead we find ourselves with a Letter Girl who is re-creating *that outside world. And how fascinating is that? What's more astonishing, given the world we've created: a genius scientist or someone who could fit right into the world we've denied them? We've stressed art as an outlet for sexuality, a vent for the overheated studies in math and science, a mild form of entertainment . . . and K has made it the centerpiece of her life. QUESTION: Is K transcending the Parenthood in this way? A meta-child, if you will? My professional opinion is that it's too early to tell.*

We're about two years away from Richard and your Delicate Years *and are very aware of how drastically the girls and boys might change. For all we now know, K may disavow her artistic prowess and turn her full attention to physics. But I wonder . . . would this make you happy, Marilyn?*

Or sad?

And then there's the matter of K's recent drawings. Oh yes . . . her fixation of the past six months: the endless drawings of the pines and the One Tree.

We've discussed the One Tree enough times to give it a name— the treetop that more resembles the top spire of the boys' tower than it does any pine in the forest. Because K is such a realist (and phenomenally so), how can we not question her about the slightly different look of that spire in comparison to the trees surrounding it?

Well, we have. In numerous Inspections you, Marilyn, have interrogated the girl as to the meaning of this One Tree, as it's shown up in forty-four drawings by my latest calculation. And her response has not wavered from the start: It's only a tree. *And perhaps her response last week was the most telling of all (and maybe should mark the moment in which we start believing her):* Maybe it looks a little different because I'm a little different. Maybe that tree is me.

Artistic, certainly, but unlike K. Again, K is a realist, and if there's one thing we know about artistically minded people, even when their work changes, the subconscious root of it seems to stay the same. I can't help but imagine an interpretation *of a treetop driving the young girl crazy as she stares at it, knowing that it's not how it actually looks. So, for all that, we question her. We get nowhere. Maybe there's nowhere to get? But there is more we can, and have, done.*

We've brought her outside into the Yard and asked her to point out where the One Tree might be. We've stood in the Yard our-

selves, holding up K's drawings, comparing them with the tops of the pines, lining up her reality with ours, until we felt confident we knew where her One Tree stood. And do you know what we found? We found it stood exactly where the boys' tower should be. But while that should be the end of the story, it's not. Why? Because we have yet to find an angle by which we can see the boys' tower from any place in the Yard. We've stood in the many windows of the Turret's backside and done the same. And still . . . no sign of the tower. NOTE: Of course there's no sign of the tower; that's Parenthood 101. Yet K seems to have seen it.

Or has she? Is it possible our outlook, what we see, has been so influenced by what we've built? Here we think it's so clear that the girl must have seen the tip-top of the boys' tower, but there is no visual evidence to support this. The only theory I can come up with is the possibility that someone was in the pines one day (had to be day, not night), possibly retrieving something from the trees, possibly pulled them aside to form an opening of sorts . . .

But this is all too perfect a storm, and my professional opinion is that we trust the girl and call ourselves fortunate that she's simply drawing something that looks like a spire rather than the face of a boy.

Brings up interesting questions, doesn't it, Marilyn? Is a child spoiled if he or she sees a drawing of the opposite sex? Hears a quote from the opposite sex? Reads a book that features a member of the opposite sex? The way we've raised these kids, wouldn't the opposite sex be the equivalent of a unicorn or a hobgoblin on Planet Distraction? Wouldn't the features be so foreign, so outrageous, as to be (safely) fiction?

But it isn't only the fact that K may have seen the top of the boys' tower (terrible as that thought may make you feel); it's that K might not be telling us the truth when she claims the consistent oddity in all her drawings is only a tree. Because seeing is one thing, but lying is clearly another. Yet, by way of Boats, we know K to be as honest a kid as any raised by the Parenthood. We worry because you and Richard both have indoctrinated us with the need to worry, to question, to constantly Inspect our kids.

You have asked that, with this report, I offer my official/professional stance on the K situation. My vote. It is rare that you or Richard ask for so specified a report, and it is also inherently impossible for me to do so, for my first duty at the Parenthood is to always analyze both you and Richard, including responding with WHY I think you'd ask for a report based solely on one Letter Girl's series of semi-concerning drawings.

So allow me to do my job first:

K poses an existential threat. And just as her personality is difficult to accept, given what we've taught her, how we've taught her to be, and how she's turned out on her own, the threat she poses is also worthy of a philosophical discussion. Did she see the boys' tower? Has she dreamed it? Has she invented for herself a mirror-image tower of the very one she lives in, situated in the only topography she knows beyond the Yard—that is, deep in the pines? Is K, an artist, attempting to create a fictional version of the tower not unlike the ones presented in the Judith Nancy books she adores? If so, is this not something to celebrate? Please refrain from considering me the liberal voice in your otherwise very conservative choir; K's creativity is something to be studied, for what other place on Planet Distraction harbors an eleven-year-old girl capable of inventing the real world by way of her imagination? Perhaps a child in the Yukon Territories. Perhaps a child raised in a cave that we've never heard of. But we have heard of K. And my professional opinion is that you and Richard have nothing to worry about. None of us do. K isn't drawing men and she's certainly not talking about them. Here we have a wildly bright young female who has discovered, for herself, a place beyond the Parenthood, beyond the pines.

K cherishes both her imagination and her ability to re-create the real world as she knows it. Her photo-realistic renderings do not imply she is incapable of thinking for herself. Rather, it's the op-

posite; K has the legitimate soul of an artist, and whether you paint pitch-perfect landscapes or three-eyed women with twelve arms, the artist is ultimately moved by the imagination.

Which brings me to my vote, the thing you asked for in the first place.

I don't think K consciously saw the top of the boys' tower. I also don't think she has lied in her Inspections. And while the latter would matter, I don't think the former does. But there's one thing about this situation that concerns me, a question I'm sure you have asked yourself many times throughout:

Whether K saw a spire or has invented a second tower in the way fantastical artists/authors do, we must keep an eye on her.

Why?

Well, what if our little eleven-year-old girl decides to visit the place, imagined or not?

While I am in no way suggesting K is spoiled rotten (not even close), I am aware of how quickly word might spread if she were to seek (then find!) the boys' tower and report back to her brilliant (and very loud) friend B. The Parenthood, of course, would topple, as the variables in the experiment were compromised.

So there you have it, Marilyn. My vote is to simply . . . watch her closely. And please, for my own sanity, and for the integrity of my specified job as underscored in my contract with the Parenthood, allow the next report to be my usual mundane musings on the inner workings of both yours and Richard's minds . . . I'm much more comfortable in there than I am deciding the fate of a girl.

Barbara Burt
The Parenthood

Bad Decisions, Always, with B

"**B**ecause they're always asking me about it. That's why."

K and B sat cross-legged, the game of Boats between them but not plugged in, no nodes connected to their bodies. The blue waters did not rage with the emotions expressed by the Letter Girls. Their individual boats were in no danger. B fingered the line switch, as she'd been doing for many minutes. She was ready to play, but K had halted that with this unexpected conversation.

"What do you mean they keep asking you about it? About what?" B said. She had a way of asking questions that forced a friend to tell the truth. K loved that about her. B was as straightforward as any Letter Girl in the Parenthood.

"Well, it's like this." K reached across the carpet for one of her drawings. She brought it back, placed it upon the Boats board. "I've been drawing the pines a lot lately."

"You don't say."

"Stop it. What can I do? I'm interested in them. There's something"—she leaned forward, eyed her own work—"fascinating about the treetops."

B studied the picture.

"Okay. So?"

"So . . . what?"

"So what is M.O.M. asking you about?"

"Right here," K said, bringing her finger over the drawing. "Wait—" She stopped herself. "First, do you see it?"

B scrunched her face the way she did when she was concentrating. An exaggerated emotion. Classic B.

"No," she said at last. "I don't see a thing. Treetops, yes. Anything else? No."

K brought her finger down at last.

"Right there. You see?" She moved her finger enough to reveal the one errant treetop. The one peak in all those peaks that looked just different enough.

B shook her head. "Nope. Still don't see it. Is this like some kind of art game? An optical illusion?"

"Well, yes. In a way it is." She turned the drawing so that it faced herself. "If you look close, you'll see the smallest tethers of bark, frayed edges, at the tip of every treetop but one. See?"

B studied. K saw a light come on in her best friend's eyes. "Yeah! I see it." The light went out. "So? So what's the big deal about a mistake?"

K shook her head. "Well, that's what caught their attention. I don't make mistakes. Not like this. I've been drawing what I saw out there."

"Out . . . there?"

"Yes. I don't know when, but I saw something and I've drawn it ever since. And believe me, M.O.M. would *love* to know when and how I saw it." She looked to the drawing. "I hardly realized it was in there myself until the Parenthood pointed it out. Now I see it's in every one." She stretched out sideways and plucked a few pieces of paper from the stack on the carpet. "You know me, B. I draw exactly what I see. I just assumed this particular treetop was . . . different. Look."

One by one, K showed B the lone barkless tip of the pine in each drawing.

"Okay. I see it. Weird. What does M.O.M. think it is?"

"I don't know," K said. She looked to the door. To the windows. She knew that B recognized she was trying to keep a secret.

"What's up, K? You're scaring me."

It was true that the humor had left K's room. B obviously felt it go.

K got up, paced her room, came back, and knelt before the board. "The first time M.O.M. asked me about it, she and Krantz exchanged a glance. A knowing glance."

"Ol' eagle eye," B said. "Nothing gets past my K."

"Not much anyway."

"And so . . ."

"So it struck me as weird." She shrugged. "Weird enough to wonder *why* they were so concerned with this . . . treetop."

The two girls looked down at the top drawing together.

"So," B said. "This is why you're feeling suspicious. They keep asking you about it. Like you said. Hmm."

"At every Inspection. And I wouldn't say I'm *suspicious*. Just . . . it's interesting, isn't it?"

B shrugged, too. "Yes. And so . . ."

"So . . ."

B shook her head. "No, K."

"Why not?"

"I mean . . . I don't . . . just *no*."

"B, hear me out."

"No!"

"It's probably just something we're not supposed to see until we're older." K held out her hands, palms up, as if to say, *No big deal, right?*

Even devoid of an expression, B looked exaggerated. Even her stoic look was overly so.

She got up and went to the door. K didn't ask where she was going. She knew B was going to her own rooms, that there she would read a Judith Nancy book and that she wouldn't be able to stop thinking of that one different treetop. Just like K couldn't. Just like M.O.M. couldn't.

"Okay," B said, turning to face K again. "Okay. Sure. Let's do it."

"Really?" K got up and went to her. B held out her hands as though warding off a hug.

"Don't get so excited. It's probably a tall stick in the ground. Marks some kind of spot. A toilet."

"A toilet?"

"Well, who knows!"

They laughed.

"You really wanna do it?" K asked. "You know we can get in trouble. And we'll definitely have to tell M.O.M. in the Inspection that follows."

"Yes," B said. "Why not? If your photographic memory captured something interesting, why *shouldn't* we act like we're in a Judith Nancy book and check it out? What are we if we're not . . . adventurous?"

"Exactly," K said. Then, more serious, "Thanks, B."

"Of course." B opened the door. "Tomorrow," she said.

"Tomorrow's Film Night."

"So? I'd rather make our own film."

"Wow," K said. But before she could say any more, B was out into the hall, the door closed behind her.

K walked back to the unplugged Boats board on the carpet. Still standing, she eyed the drawings at her feet.

Tomorrow, she thought. Then she looked out the window, to the pines, and thought the word again, one more time, before thinking it again, one more time.

Tomorrow

Film Night in the Body Hall was an annual highlight for the Letter Girls. When spring finally gave way to summer, most of the girls' first thought was of the coming Film Night, the one time of the year they experienced moving pictures on a screen. Z suspected the films were written by none other than Judith Nancy, a theory that spread rapidly and was never denied by M.O.M. Nancy was legendary among the girls for her adventure stories that featured Letter Girls all grown up, overcoming obstacles and distractions in the name of achieving their goals. K's favorite Nancy book was one titled *In the Evening*, in which Marla Haynes dedicates herself to long hours of study after her sisters have gone to sleep and in doing so cures all her sisters (and herself!) of a disease. But the plot of this particular book wasn't what resonated so wildly with K and the others; rather, the book was written so well it was breathtaking, with a voice that seemed to whisper directly into their ears.

Did Judith Nancy write the summer films the Letter Girls pined for all year? M.O.M. wasn't telling, and that was just fine with K. Mystery, she'd come to believe, could be a character all its own.

Nancy or not, Film Night was magic.

And on this night, it was the exact variety of distraction K and B were counting on.

On no other day of the year did the Letter Girls sit unified in the dark, their twenty-five little bodies unseen in the pews. More than one girl fell asleep each year (inexplicably, G simply didn't care for the films at all), and no Inspector or staff, writer or M.O.M., had ever emerged from the sidelines to wake them. B, who had suggested *tomorrow* the evening before, was well aware of the opportunity afforded the two girls on Film Night. Two hours of darkness, two hours in which M.O.M. would assume the duo were seated with the others, two hours that ought to be enough to reach the odd treetop in K's drawings, determine what it was, and get back before their absence was noted. And if they *did* get caught, the punishment surely wouldn't be too much; they were conducting an Inspection of their own, after all.

They were dressed for the Body Hall, both in their black slacks and black turtleneck shirts, standing outside K's rooms. Luckily, neither was slated for Voices that day.

"Let's go over the plan," B said.

"Yes."

They walked to the end of the seventh floor, opposite the Check-Up room door where they'd endured Inspections every morning of their lives. Here, K opened the door to the stairs and said, "We check in like we would any year."

"Yep. We check in."

They entered the stairwell. The door closed behind them.

"We wait for the lights to go out."

"Yep. The lights."

As their shoes clacked in the stairwell, K tapped B on the shoulder, signaling for her to stop. They both looked over the railing. B looked up, K down. They couldn't have Inspectors Krantz or Rivers overhearing them. That would certainly derail their adventure. Eyeing the lower stairs, K imagined M.O.M., her dark glasses and dark hair blending into the shadows, looking back up to her.

Let's talk about this One Tree, K . . . and this plan of yours, too.

But the girls were alone.

"We need to sneak out before the movie begins, when the Body Hall is as dark as it's going to get, the moment the lights go out," K said. They walked in tandem, hand in hand, down the stairs.

"Right," B said. "And the only door that won't give us away is the kitchen."

"Because dinner has been served. Nobody will be in there."

"And no lights."

"Yes. That's it."

They paused at the door to the first floor.

"You ready, then?" K asked.

"Ready to investigate the only mistake you've ever made in a drawing?" B looked to the door. They heard other Letter Girls in the hall. Enthusiastic voices and the patter of so many shoes. The choir had already begun.

"Yes. I'm ready."

Each placed a palm upon the door, smiled, and pushed it open.

All of their sisters were preoccupied with the movie as they rushed toward the Body Hall doors. Most spoke as they moved. Would it be better than last year's? Would it be their new favorite film of all time? The anticipation was palpable, and both K and B experienced dips of self-doubt, wanting badly to see the movie themselves. Surely M.O.M. would ask them about it at tomorrow's Inspection; Film Night was always a Check-Up room topic the following morning. But neither said as much to the other. It was their way: independence wherever they could find it. And both felt like they were starring in a movie of their own, after all, or a Judith Nancy book called, perhaps, *Sleuths* or *Getting to the Bottom of It*.

"Hello, K," E said. E, who was as proper in speech and appearance as any Letter Girl would never want to be. "Hello, B."

There had long been tension between conservative E and funny B. K nodded, her mind too distant to smile at that tension now.

"You excited for Film Night?" B asked cordially.

E adjusted the hem of her black turtleneck, adjusted her black slacks. She smiled the way only E could: She had information about the movie. "I happen to know the"—she looked both ways for effect before whispering the last word—"*title.*"

"Oh?" K asked. "Well . . . what is it?"

"Take your seats, girls."

K and B both froze, as M.O.M. had seemingly materialized out of nowhere, passing them before entering the hall, walking the center aisle toward the steps, the podium, and the screen. She smiled as she passed, but K caught something else, something that almost brought her to call the night's mission off.

M.O.M. had winked at her.

Probably it was meant to acknowledge the excitement of the evening, but K couldn't help thinking it meant something else.

K, dear, tell us if you could: What's the meaning behind this one treetop, this one here, with no bark?

"*Ugly,*" E said. Then she crossed her arms and smiled, waiting for K and B to respond. "Girls? Did you hear me?"

But neither really had. Or, rather, distantly.

"Ugly what?" B asked. K noted the defensiveness in her best friend's voice. As if E were suggesting their plan was . . . ugly.

"That's the name of the *movie,* dingbats," E said, shaking her head. "What's wrong with you two tonight?"

Again K considered calling it off. First the wink from M.O.M., now a sister suggesting something was wrong.

But B lit up. "Oh! That's a *fantastic* title! And really leaves you wondering!"

"Doesn't it?" E asked. "Fortunately I hardly relate to the word." She looked to the other Letter Girls filing into the pews. Then followed them.

With the lush harmonies of Voices so soothing, K and B took the center aisle and slid down the length of a pew as far as they could, wanting to get close to the black kitchen doors.

But they had to step over Q on the way.

"Mind if we pass you?" K asked.

Q's pale face seemed to float above her black clothes and the shadows in the Body Hall. K knew that particular face well; Q's frown had been preserved in a drawing on K's bedroom wall for a few years now.

"Why would I mind?"

"Oh, it's just a nice thing to say," B said.

"Sit wherever you'd like."

"That we will."

The girls stepped over Q's outstretched legs and slid at last into their seats. The kitchen doors, out of range of the podium spotlights, looked to K like a black hole in the wall. A tunnel. She thought of the only other tunnel she'd ever heard of in her life. The Glasgow Tunnel below the Turret. And the Corner one had to pass to get there.

"Okay," B said. "You ready?"

K thought of the Corner. She couldn't help it. Her idea of it, anyway. Shapes behind the door M.O.M. had long ago described as the one place no Letter Girl ever wanted to go.

It would take a very bad girl to be sent to the Corner. One who'd been spoiled rotten.

K imagined herself rotting from the inside out.

Even Voices couldn't calm this image down.

"Yes," she said. But there was trepidation in her voice.

"We don't have to," B whispered. "We could just stay put and watch the movie. Sounds like fun, doesn't it?"

K tried to smile but couldn't quite find it. The plan sounded like a good one the night before. But now? Now B sounded as nervous as she did. K had no doubt her sister was imagining her own version of that same wooden door.

"No," K said. "When the lights go off, before the movie starts. Like we planned. Let's just . . ." But fear had built up within her. Real fear. Enough of it to give her pause.

"Know what?" B said. "It's okay. We're gonna be fine."

They looked down the length of the pew at the same time, looked to Q, whose long brown hair hung in front of her face. All the Letter Girls had tried to get to know Q better. The staff included. Nobody more so than M.O.M. But some girls, K had learned, simply didn't want to be known.

Onstage, a minor squawk of feedback brought the girls to sit up straighter, to focus on M.O.M. at the podium.

"My girls," M.O.M. began, her voice equal measures tender and direct. Always. The girls of Voices concluded on a bright augmented chord. "Welcome to Film Night at the Parenthood." The Letter Girls cheered, their voices electric, resonating off the high Body Hall walls. K and B included. "I won't say much now, as I've no mind to stall what you've been eagerly awaiting for months. But I do have a few things to point out first."

K found herself mesmerized as ever by M.O.M.'s tone of voice, her posture, her lithe build, and the way her black hair framed the angles of her face. M.O.M.'s eyes were obscured by her ever-present dark glasses, giving her a sense of heightened acuity; M.O.M. was, it appeared, *all-seeing*.

K shifted uncomfortably in the pew. B leaned close and whispered, "Forget it. We'll stay. What were we thinking anyway? Who cares about a treetop with no bark? What was wrong with us?"

K nodded but had not yet given in. She knew this was important, *not giving in*. She and B could alternate their yeses and nos, but if they were to say no at the same time, the mission would be off.

As M.O.M.'s voice traveled throughout the Body Hall, K found herself swept up in the perfect pitch, the calming tone, the voice of the woman who had guided the Letter Girls all their lives. It was M.O.M. who, long ago, informed the girls that there was such a thing as girls with nobody to care for them. Girls who starved to death in the halls of other towers. Girls who unknowingly took the stairs to the basement of these other towers, to the Corner itself, where, with no one to tell them otherwise, they opened the door.

Years ago, before our time, some less fortunate girls let it out.

It, *M.O.M.?*

Oh yes. And it took a long, long time to put it back in the Corner again.

K adjusted the neck of her turtleneck.

"K?" B asked.

K turned to her in the semidarkness. "It sounded so fun last night."

"It did."

M.O.M. discussed the weekly activities. Athletics in the Yard. A change in diet. The coming exams.

"It still does," K said. But her voice said otherwise.

"Does it?"

K tried employing a trick sunny Y had taught them less than a year ago.

You can fool yourself into being happy. It's true. When you don't feel like smiling . . . do it anyway. And guess what? You start to feel happy!

At the time she'd said it, both B and K rolled their eyes. Y was easy to poke fun at. Yet here they were, in a moment of big decision, doing just what their impossibly optimistic floor mate taught them to do.

And it was working.

"Yeah," K said. "Fun. Just . . . slip out through those doors . . ."

"Out through the kitchen."

"Yes. Through the kitchen and out the garbage door and out into the Yard . . ."

"Out into the Yard."

"Yes. And from there to the pines and then into the pines . . ."

"Then into the pines we go."

"Yes. We go."

M.O.M. had stopped speaking. To K it looked momentarily like she was eyeing her directly, like M.O.M. had paused to stare at K and B. Like she was about to say, *What's all this about the kitchen doors, the Yard, and the pines?*

Instead, she said, "Now, for your viewing pleasure, the Parenthood presents . . . *Ugly.*"

The Letter Girls went crazy. P and F got up and clapped. Smiling smartly, M.O.M. stepped from the podium, to the far side of the stage, where she vanished into the black shadows.

And the lights went out.

K knew she and B had maybe fifteen seconds to move. The projector would come alive no later than that. The room would be filled with the light of the titles, the word *UGLY* in a font larger than any the girls saw all year. She and B would be as obvious as a cherry stain on the carpet of her bedroom.

K moved first. Then B did, too. They slunk along the pew, crouched, then darted quickly across the small space between pew and kitchen doors. At the doors they slowed, until each had a palm against the wood.

Silent, they entered the kitchen. The doors swung to behind them.

B put a hand on K's shoulder, put her other hand over her own mouth. K heard B's stifled laughter as the Body Hall lit up through the kitchen doors' small circle windows. Just in time, then.

The girls watched the titles for a few seconds before stepping deeper into the kitchen. They moved slowly but deliberately, never stopping to look back, to think twice. B knocked her hip against a steel sink just as a cymbal crash erupted from the Body Hall, followed by the first line of dialogue in the new movie.

"Where are you, Franny?" It was the voice of an older woman. *"Are you* hiding *again?"*

"Here," K said. They'd reached the back door. The handle, K thought, felt too big, much bigger than the stairwell. She paused.

"What is it?" B asked.

"I don't know. What if there's an alarm?"

A younger voice cried out from the screen in the Body Hall. *"But, Mom! I'm soooooo ugly!"*

The Letter Girls erupted.

"Maybe we go through the first-floor hall," B said. "Take the front door."

It sounded too dangerous to K. Inspectors on patrol.

"Why is the handle so big?" she asked.

"No idea, but maybe you shouldn't—"

K opened the door.

No alarm. No sound at all.

"What's the worst that can happen?" K asked. "Lose a leisure book? Eat alone?"

"Quarantine," a third voice said from the kitchen darkness.

K and B gripped each other's hands.

M.O.M.

But no. A Letter Girl stepped into the scant moonlight let in through the open door to the Yard.

"Q?" B asked.

"Sorry," Q said. "I actually couldn't resist following you. What you were talking about sounded so much more fun than the movie."

"Q," K said. "You shouldn't come with us."

"Why not?" Q asked, stepping past them, stepping outside. "What's the worst that can happen, right?" Under the moon she looked somehow more at home. Less the antisocial Letter Girl and more a part of nature. "But you gotta tell me what we're going to look for," Q said. "Otherwise I'm just a blind tagalong."

K and B exchanged glances. What to do?

"Fine," K said.

"K drew a picture of the pines," B said.

"Many pictures."

"And in all of them there's one treetop that isn't like the others."

Q frowned. "Really? That's what we're missing Film Night for? A weird tree? Okay."

"Well," B said. "It's more than that. K never draws a mistake."

Q nodded. "I know that. So?"

"And so . . ." B closed the kitchen door quietly behind her. As it snapped shut, so did the voice of the mother in the movie playing in the Body Hall. "If it's not a tree . . . what is it?"

"Ah," Q said. She split her frizzy brown bangs, exposing more of her face. "It's a storage shed."

"No," B said. "Too tall. Why would a storage shed need a spire?"

"A spire?" Q asked. She looked up the length of the Turret. They all did.

"Come on," K said. "We can guess as we go."

And they went. K, B, and Q, leaving the tower behind, growing increasingly excited with each step toward the trees. More anxious, too, as none had ever done what they were doing. No Letter Girl had ever ventured into the pines without some sort of chaperone, an Inspector, a teacher. K couldn't deny that she was afraid. Thrilled, yes, interested, of course, but what was she hoping to find?

"It's an electrical pole," Q said.

"No," B said. "The Parenthood wouldn't be secretive about an electrical pole."

"Secretive? Hang on."

Q stopped walking.

"Are we going to get in trouble for this?" she asked. "Like . . . real trouble?"

B opened her mouth, ready to say no. Instead, she shrugged. "We might. We don't know."

Q seemed to think about this. She didn't look back to the Turret but rather vanished into her hair, as if she had private curtains to deliberate behind. She emerged again with a partial smile. "Okay," she finally said.

"Okay," B echoed. "That was . . . weird."

They continued deeper until, behind them, the Turret was obscured by so many trunks, so much brown and green, that the bricks and glass were visible the same way the cafeteria was when viewed through the tongs of a fork.

"It's a marker, then," Q said. "For buried treasure."

"That would be great," B said. "We'd be heroes at the Parent-hood."

"Straight out of a Judith Nancy book," K said.

"But no," B went on, pulling aside a particularly long branch. "No buried treasure out here. Why mark it so high? Why not just an X on the ground?"

"It's a finger," Q said. The other girls stopped.

"A *finger*?" K asked. They waited.

Q smiled, her teeth showing white through her hanging hair and the shadows of the trees. "A really long finger sticking up from the ground. A dead body in there."

K and B looked at one another. B giggled first. Then K. Then they both broke out in full laughter, a half mile from the tower, the Parenthood, their world. It felt good to laugh. It felt great. K and B both placed a hand on each other's shoulders at the same time. Then Q joined them, a slight hiccup of a laugh at first, until K and B heard the girl's full laugh for the first time in their lives. It was high and wild, pocked with snorts, and it soared to the top of the pines, as if it might eye the errant treetop for them, like the peri-scope used by Karen in Judith Nancy's thrilling book, *Look Up, Look Out, Look In*. Q's laughter, or more so her willingness to let loose, was the final piece the other two needed to feel assured that the decision they'd made was a good one. For what was more memorable? A movie called *Ugly* or the beautiful sound of an otherwise-shy girl laughing from her belly to her chest to the sky?

THEY CONTINUED. FASTER. Guided by B's compass. And while some stretches were darker than others, most were illumined by the moon. Only twice did they have to pause, hold hands, and head forth as one, emboldened by the chain they made. They discovered that the spaces between the trees were wide enough to fit two at a time, a trick of the eye as, from the Yard, the long tract of forest looked nearly impenetrable. And as they went, each carried a simi-

larly vague idea of a tall brown pole stuck in the ground, a meaningless thing perhaps, a bald and barren tree at best. K started to
believe that it wasn't *what* they'd find but the finding of it that
mattered. According to her watch, they'd been gone only fifteen
minutes. Another hour and a half of Film Night back home.

Maybe they'd even catch the end.

"How far do you think it is?" Q asked.

"We don't know," B said. "But we can guess." She stopped in a
particularly bright shaft of moonlight filling a particularly open
pool of forest. She removed a folded piece of paper from the back
pocket of her black slacks.

"You brought one of my drawings," K said.

"Of course I did." The three girls huddled together, B holding
the drawing out before them. "Based upon its width and height we
ought to be able to determine its distance."

"But we don't know what it is," Q said. "It could be something
very wide that looks very thin from so far away."

"True. But let's say, for argument's sake, that it's the width of a
tree."

"But we don't know if that's accurate."

"We don't. But it's something. And Professor Huggins always
says that—"

"A little something is better than a lot of nothing," K and Q said
at once.

"Right. So let's study this drawing. And let's consider the mystery object. To scale."

They took ten minutes to do so. Despite their awareness of the
inaccuracies of their method, they determined the thing to be between three and four miles away. If they moved at an average of
fifteen minutes per mile (slowed by the trees; no straight line out
there), they might have enough time to determine what it was, turn
back, and slip inside the Body Hall just as *Ugly* was ending.

"But we gotta keep moving," B said. "No more calculations.
And we won't be able to stay long with it, whatever it is."

"And if we haven't reached it after forty-five minutes of traveling, then we just turn around," K said.

None of them liked this idea, but K was right. They couldn't risk missing the return to the Body Hall. They could, of course, tell M.O.M. they were in the Orchard, they were in their rooms, anything other than the truth, but none of them felt comfortable with outright lying.

Not yet.

"Why wouldn't we just tell her we wanted to figure it out?" Q asked. "I think M.O.M. would be happy to hear that some of her Letter Girls would rather solve problems than watch a film in the dark."

"Totally," B said.

"Probably," K said, thinking of the interest M.O.M. and the Inspectors showed in her drawings. She almost said, *But I just don't like the way they looked at each other. I don't like the way they keep asking me about the drawings without telling me why.*

But she didn't.

A half hour deep, the sky had brightened, the moon higher than when they'd set out. The girls no longer talked, as the clock they'd set at their last stop proved too thought-consuming to think of anything else. Each in turn imagined the movie playing out in the Body Hall, the arc of the story, as it crested past the first quarter and headed toward the first third, the moment in which they'd better locate their mystery object or turn around, defeated. K and B compared compasses as the summer night sky warmed them, causing both to sweat, both to breathe hard from the constant ducking and pulling branches aside.

Then, as if she hadn't actually expected them to find anything, B gasped.

"What?" Q asked. But she didn't have to wait for an answer. B was pointing ahead.

"Lights," K said.

Not from the moon.

The three girls looked at one another and, without discussing it, used the nearest trees as cover. Whatever they were expecting to find so far out in the pines, it was not something with lights.

"This certainly changes our guesses," Q said.

B looked to K, and in that moment both felt a seed rattle somewhere inside their bodies; perhaps this experience had the potential to grow into something bigger than either had planned on.

K considered turning around. For the betterment of her sisters. Before she got them into something she hadn't meant to at all.

"Wait a second," she said.

"What?" B asked. "We don't have time."

"What if what we discover is something we shouldn't find? What if M.O.M. is worried about what she saw in my drawings because she knows it's unsafe? For us."

"Worried?" Q repeated. "You never said she was worried."

"We did, too," B said. Then, "Well, we said she was *interested*. Wasn't that close enough?"

"No," Q said.

"Okay," K said. "Right now we're out here in the pines. That's all that matters. And if we turn around *right now* we might be avoiding something . . ."

"Something what?" Q asked.

"I don't know. Something we don't want in our lives."

The three looked toward the hazy light that seemed to emerge like fog from the coming pines. Like snowy frost on the eve of the Effigy Meet.

"Well," B said, stepping ahead. "I for one would like to get to the bottom of this."

"Me, too," Q said. "I'm not sure I could turn back now."

"Our own movie," B said. "Let's see how it ends."

"Our own movie?" K said, relieved that her sisters weren't scared enough to stop. "What would you call it? That feels like an important question right now."

Q said, "I'd call it *Three Letter Girls and a Discovery.*"

"And does it have a happy ending?" B asked.

But her sisters didn't answer.

The needles were loud under their boots. The branches loud as they pulled them aside.

And the closer they got to the source of the lights, the more the light resembled night in the Yard back home. The floodlights K had tried to dull for so many years, drawing the drapes of her bedroom window before bed.

A few more steps and the light was strong enough to fill the spaces between all the trees, so that it looked to K like the pines broke up the light rather than the other way around. Behind her, B and Q moved steady.

But K saw it first.

The One Tree.

The different treetop.

The spire.

She stopped and pointed, but B spoke first.

"Oh wow. That's it."

"That's it," K echoed.

"Well, it's definitely not a bald treetop," Q said. "It's a spire."

"Like the one on the Turret," B said.

"Exactly the same," Q said.

"Come on," B said. "We don't have much time."

"How much?" K asked.

B checked her watch. "Five minutes?"

"Really?"

"If we wanna be safe. Yes."

K advanced first. B and Q followed. Q tapped B on the shoulder. "I don't know if this is a good idea," she said.

"What do you mean?" B asked. K was getting farther ahead. Her form was cut by the light, then made impossibly slim, before she vanished into the remaining trees that separated them from whatever held the spire.

"If this is something we should know about, M.O.M. would've told us."

"Well, of course! We've been saying that the whole time."

They moved fast then, trying to catch up to K, unable to turn away no matter what sort of eleventh-hour admonishment they felt. They couldn't hear K moving anymore and found out why, as B ran into her best friend's back, knocking K out onto a grassy open field. B, stumbling, almost fell after her. Instead, she found her balance and, halfway to standing up, was frozen by the sight of the brick tower rising up, up, up, to the spire so high above them.

"Um, K?"

K was on the ground, on her stomach, also looking up. Not just at the bricks that made up this edifice, that made this a replica of the tower they left behind, the one they had to return to now (*now!*), but at the windows lit up along the tower's side. And at the girls who moved about within them.

By the time K rose, B and Q were beside her. All three edged back to the border of the pines.

"This is just like the Yard," Q said, acknowledging the field of open grass that was all that separated them from the second tower they'd ever seen in their lives.

But K and B weren't listening to her. And they didn't take their eyes from those windows.

"Those . . . girls," B said.

K didn't know how to process it any more than B did. Had they gotten turned around? Was this their home?

"I don't understand," Q said. And simple as it was, the few words explained perfectly how they all felt.

No, K knew. This was not home.

It was hard to make sense of the short hair, the shirtless girls with flat chests, bony shoulders and necks.

"Look!" B said.

A large woman entered the glass hall on the first floor. Her stomach hung over her belt. Attached to that belt was a magnifying glass.

"She's dressed like an Inspector."

Only this one had hair on her face. And moved like no woman the girls had ever seen move.

She slouched like an ogre from Judith Nancy's *Odds and Ends*, plodding along the glass hall.

"This isn't good," B said. "We have to go now. We have to go tell M.O.M. *right now.*"

"Hang on," K said, still staring, unable to pull herself away. The disappointment at having left Film Night was erased entirely by the scene they beheld. The thrill of moving pictures eclipsed by a hidden reality, nonfiction, so close to their own.

"B?" K asked, still staring at the windows. At the huge Inspector lumbering on the other side of the glass.

But B knew no more than she did.

"I don't feel good about this," Q said. "At all."

The big Inspector paused at a drinking fountain, bent at the waist to use it.

Through a window two floors up, K saw two naked backs in the light of a lit living room. Beyond them, a shirtless girl with short hair was talking. Above them, the next floor up, another girl with short hair passed by the glass, carrying a stack of books.

It looks just like ours, K thought. Down to the details. Yet it was nightmarishly unlike home. As if the Letter Girls had returned after all, having traveled in a circle that changed them.

Changed everything.

"We have to go," B said again. "We just . . . *right now, K.*"

K turned quick on her sisters. "Promise me," she said. "Promise me we don't tell M.O.M. Not yet."

"*What?*" B asked.

"What are you talking about, K?" Q asked.

K didn't know exactly. But what she felt, this overwhelming

sense of having woken up to a second dream, wasn't made up entirely of revulsion and fear.

There was interest there, too. Interest in this second reality. In the distortion of her own.

"I just wanna process this," K said. "I just wanna think for one second before we run back and tell M.O.M. about something we know nothing about."

B studied her sister. Her best friend. "You're scaring me, K."

"I'm sorry. Just . . . for me? For now?"

Q pointed to a high window. The girls inched back farther into the shadows of the trees.

A girl sat by her window up there. Elbows on the sill. Looking down into the Yard.

"Now," B said.

"Hang on," K said.

"*Now*."

Then K felt two hands upon her shoulders as B and Q dragged her back into the pines.

Without speaking, they ran, using the light from the second Turret to guide them.

And when the light ran out, when they'd passed beyond its range, they used the moon, their new knowledge of the pines, ducking branches and sidestepping trees with more ease than they had on the way there. And when they saw the light of their own tower ahead, they understood clearly how much it looked like the light from the other. How similar it was, approaching their own. How *the same*. As if they'd come from that second tower, seeking to find the meaning of the object upon this one, a mystery K had drawn many times.

They hurried through the light, out onto the Yard, each of them experiencing a sense of nervous-calm for having returned. If they were caught now, they could either tell the Parenthood the truth or simply say they were out in the Yard, bored by the movie, wanted to breathe in the summer night sky. But none of them felt good about it. About any of it. And as they reached the back kitchen door where the staff put out the trash, and slipped back into the darkness of the kitchen, their thoughts remained harpooned to the frightening girls they'd seen in the woods.

The naked backs of the short-haired girls.

The hairy face of the Inspector.

The girl up high in the Turret window, looking out.

Passing through the kitchen, K felt tangled with too many emotions. She couldn't name them. And while she was glad to have had B and Q with her, to verify what she'd seen in the woods, she also wished, in a way, that they hadn't gone with her. That she didn't have to worry about either one telling the Parenthood before she herself came to a conclusion about what it meant.

Stop it, she told herself, moving slow, not wanting to knock a tray of dishes. A cart of pans. *You go in there and you tell your M.O.M. this instant!*

But the inner voice wasn't her own. Not entirely. Rather, it sounded like the Letter Girls sounded, all together, when M.O.M. was about to give a speech, when M.O.M. entered the Body Hall, pausing at the pillars to look up and down the pews, smiling proudly at her girls.

The voice in K's head was her sisters. All of them. At once.

You will tell your M.O.M. this instant!

"Soon," B said, meaning that the movie was ending soon. They'd made it in time.

The girls were huddled, shoulder to shoulder, by the kitchen doors. K looked through one of the circle windows. Saw the faces of her sisters in the pews, lit up by the much larger faces on the big screen.

Some smiled. Most were awed.

"I'm scared," B said.

B. The funniest girl K knew. Scared.

Had they really discovered something so terrible? Oh, if what they'd done tonight were to change things, in any way . . .

"Try not to be," K said. "If we just think about it for—"

But her voice was drowned out by the sudden cheer of the Letter Girls as the film came to an end.

"Now," Q said.

The screen went dark in the Body Hall. K, B, and Q moved through the swinging doors. They slid into their pew, Q first, then K, then B, just as they'd been sitting when the movie began.

When the lights came on, M.O.M. was walking toward the podium, a proud smile on her face. The girls cheered and their voices echoed untamed off the high vaulted ceiling. K looked to B. She didn't want to but she couldn't not. Farther down the pew they saw Q sitting as she always did, her long brown hair obscuring most of her face again.

"Well, I hope you loved it as much I did," M.O.M. said. Her voice full of magnanimity. "We'll discuss it more at tomorrow's Inspections. But for now . . . please head back to your rooms. Study. Relax. Or . . ." She looked directly at K. "Or draw."

The girls in Voices began singing. The full overhead lights came on. The Letter Girls got up at once, chattering about the movie, quoting lines K, B, and Q would never hear for themselves.

And as they began to file out of the Body Hall, K saw the Letter Girls and the tower and all of her life flowing from the lips of one faucet into the open mouth of a drain. As if she'd turned something on she wouldn't be able to turn off. And where would it go from here? Where did the water collect? Where might K find her old life again, the one where she laughed with her sisters on Film Night and did not think about replica towers in the woods, where hairy women did not walk the halls like horrors from a Judith Nancy fantasy?

"Upstairs," B said.

K looked her best friend in the eye. She saw some vestige of humor there. As if, for one moment, they could laugh about it.

But neither did.

Already, K thought, the bond between them felt different. And as they joined the outgoing flow of Letter Girls into the first-floor hall, K knew things would never be the same with B again. How could they be? After what they'd seen?

How could they?

Yet, as B followed close behind her, and as Q slumped her way out the doors ahead, K also knew she'd be going back. With or without B. With or without telling M.O.M. what they'd found.

She'd be going back to that Turret in the woods. Until she was satisfied that she knew where it had come from, who those girls were, and why she hadn't known about them before.

Marilyn

The loft was a nice one, overlooking the river. The constant development on the Water Walk was the only drawback to an otherwise gorgeous view of lapping waves and boats . . . so many boats passing below, day and night, until Marilyn began to invent her own games by the clockwork horns blown below, truth and dare until it became only truth, her soul bared clean and unblemished by the passing of the boats.

She lived alone and she believed she liked it that way. Yet nagging thoughts of her close friends persisted: Most, if not all, had sunk below the surface of relationship mud. Most, if not all, were married. And while Marilyn made the rounds, visiting the closest of these friends as their schedules permitted, even holidays and birthdays were now hard to come by.

Why?

Why did it seem that everyone around her changed so much when paired with another? Take Evelyn, for example. Mean, strong Evelyn Tule. The woman was unrecognizable in her current state: near-housewife to the ridiculous Adam Horn. One day a lioness, the next all giggles and bad television. Is this what she wanted? Is that what she meant when she'd say, *I'm no settler*? What was worse, to Marilyn, was that she didn't think she'd ever seen Evelyn Tule quite so . . . happy. As if the bliss of her marital status had cleaned her troubled consciousness of the cobwebs where the deeper thinking got stuck.

It didn't add up and Marilyn didn't like it. She didn't like the way Tracy Paul quit writing. How Mary Tudor-Johns moved across the country. How Anne Horowitz smiled awkwardly at the slightest hint of something she might deem *single-life*. Like a drink, for example. Like staying out an hour later than usual, for example. Like a one-night stand.

It was enough to drive Marilyn mad.

But she had a plan.

A gathering, if her former close friends could stomach calling it that, in which each of them might be reminded how good the good days were before men. A simple, no-frills party in Marilyn's loft overlooking the Water Walk. Hell, they might even take the walk themselves, drinks in hand, tucked in the same brown paper bags winos used all over the city. Yes, Marilyn was looking for, planning for, hoping for, something a little more exciting than a Tupperware party of hysterical former friends. Tonight she wanted to *show* them the people they once were, the nights they were missing, planting seeds of once-familiar liberation into their dizzyingly predictable current states of adulthood.

Anne was the first to arrive. All makeup and ponytail, skirt and heels. *Aren't we partying?* she asked, squinting as she smiled, revealing how long it had been since she used the word. Marilyn told her yes, indeed they were partying, and took note of Anne's glance as it began at Marilyn's own flat shoes before taking the elevator up her pantsuit to her wild, big black hair. Marilyn had no illusions. She knew she looked the part of the crazed feminist, a woman with no man. But she liked the minute concern she saw in her old friend's eyes.

You look . . . like Marilyn, Marilyn.

It was the best Anne could be expected to come up with and Marilyn simply nodded, having decided hours ago not to allow a single small-talk smile to grace her own face. Not tonight. Tonight was about strength, about reinvigorating a boring, once-vibrant clan.

Mary and Tracy arrived together, which registered in Marilyn's gut as a logical extension of being lost-in-marriage: Wives usually went out with wives. It wasn't enough that the men dominated four-fifths of their lives; that last sliver couldn't be faced alone, no no, had to be met hand in hand with a fellow sufferer.

Marilyn! Tracy said, making to kiss both Marilyn's cheeks, a gesture Marilyn didn't see coming. It went awkwardly, but Marilyn did not feel embarrassed. She'd decided, too, hours ago, not to permit herself a single flushed face tonight; the idea was to inspire, not to spread a mood of loathsome inadequacy. Mary assisted in this way, by being as cheerful as ever and even asking jokingly, *What's to drink?*

Marilyn told her she was glad she asked, that Evelyn could let herself in (a purposeful statement, to be sure: THERE ARE A LOT OF THINGS EVELYN MIGHT DO ON HER OWN), and that she hoped the girls were ready for a *night on the town,* even if that town was Marilyn's own loft.

Things started well. Very well. And Evelyn did let herself in. And the five formerly close friends sat on Marilyn's couches and talked about old times and drank a little too much and swore and joked and complained. It was the last bit that led to talk about their home lives, married life, and how distant the past seemed to them now. Marilyn, who had strategically skirted any talk of the past, tried, in vain, to direct the conversation back to the present, reminding the women that they were still young, it had only been five years after all, that any life they wanted still waited for them, that anything could be achieved if the right amount of energy was put into it. These loftier statements, made three drinks deep, didn't do much to stem the tide of domestic topics, and eventually Marilyn found herself feeling downright bad. Here her oldest friends had convened at her behest, here she'd gone out of her way to direct the flow of conversation, here she'd set out to re-liberate these women-turned-girls, and before eight o'clock she'd completely lost them. For Christ's sake, the things Anne and Mary were talking about sounded like the program for a children's show. The way Tracy apologized for ripping Jeff had Stockholm syndrome written all over it. And Evelyn!

Marilyn had to get up. Had to leave the room, take a deep breath, recalibrate, and enter the living room all over again. She had to remind herself of her goal this evening and how far she was from achieving it. What they needed, she knew, was to get out of the fucking loft. They needed to take the Water Walk to the casino, a restaurant, even a dance club. Anything to remind these ladies what independence once felt like.

Standing before the bathroom mirror, eyeing herself in her white pantsuit and wild hair, she had no doubt the eyes her glasses magnified were obvious in their anger. How to drop that? Drunk people could smell anger. Went out of their way to either avoid it or confront it head-on. Marilyn didn't want either to happen. The women were laughing in the living room. This was good. But what were they laughing *at*? Because there was a big difference between finding it funny how the dishwasher always seemed to break at just the wrong time and rediscovering one's self-worth.

A walk, she told herself. *Just get the girls out of the loft.*

Decided, she returned to find a fresh drink for herself on the table. Happy homemaker Mary had made it. Marilyn said thank you and made no attempt to gauge the conversation, where they were at, how deep they were into it, whether or not it was a topic of merit or not. Rather, she split it in two.

You guys wanna go out for a bit?

Oh, the way they reacted, oh, the way they looked at her, then each other, then their watches, the windows, the floor. Could they go out for a bit? *Could* they? Was it in the ledger of things they could see themselves doing these days? Going out? Or was it so entirely outrageous that Marilyn may as well have suggested they eat the plants?

Noises by the front door then. A huskier voice. Marilyn, still standing, looked from the door to Evelyn, just as Evelyn's face broke into a smile.

Adam's here! Evelyn said, rising to answer a door that had not yet been knocked on.

Marilyn looked to the others just as they looked away.

In that moment, she knew. She knew the night was a bust. Knew that her friends were aware of how she felt and what she was trying to do by inviting them out. She hadn't stood a chance from the start. A waste is what it was. Evelyn opened the front door and a murder of drunk men stumbled into the loft.

Trying her best to accept what had happened, that a silly effort to rekindle the independence lost to her old friends had gone belly-up, Marilyn lifted the drink Mary made as Adam and Jim, Tony and Nate, barked ridiculous jokes, knocked a picture off the wall, and barreled into the living room. Each moved to his respective wife, wobbly waters parting, revealing, with them, a fifth man, alone, unclaimed, still walking toward Marilyn herself.

Who was he?

I hate this shit, he said, reaching out a hand to shake hers. She took it. *Every time we go out we end up back in.*

Marilyn, still not over the surprise of the men showing up, still not over having lost what little grip she had on the night, raised her drink.

You want a sip . . . ?

Her few words climbed up into an unfinished question.

Richard, the man said. *And you have no idea how much I do.*

B Scared

Staring out her living room window, sitting upon the ledge, K thought of the girl she'd seen doing the same up high in the Turret in the woods. She tried not to look in the direction of the spire of that tower but found herself doing it anyway. After all, who would notice? B and Q hadn't told M.O.M. about their journey in the morning's Inspections. And K certainly hadn't, either. And with that, the three had done something, indeed: intentionally withheld information from the Parenthood for the first time in their lives.

But that wasn't exactly true. There *were* instances of what Judith Nancy called "white lies" (Nancy had even titled one of her thrilling books *White Lies*) and there wasn't a Letter Girl in the tower who hadn't blamed something she did on someone else, hadn't said she was studying when she wasn't. This, K was partly able to fool herself into believing, was precedent, proof, that lying wasn't the end-all, wasn't evil, and certainly wasn't reason to be sent to the Corner. Never mind that pretending to read the mathematics textbook was nothing like finding strange (*horribly strange!*) girls in a second tower in the woods; K *needed* to believe it was okay to do what she'd done.

Drawing what she'd seen was, for her, a kind of therapy, despite knowing that a paper trail could be dangerous.

And B, watching these drawings come to life, as the Boats board lay inert and unplugged between them on the carpet, grew increasingly obsessed with the punitive room in the basement: the Corner; the longtime boogeywoman of the Letter Girls.

"I don't want to be sent away," B said.

"Sent away to where?"

As is often the way with best friends and sisters, they didn't need to voice the conclusion they'd both suddenly arrived at. But B still did it.

"Is the second tower the Corner?"

K nodded. "Maybe."

"Does that mean . . . does that mean *J* is over there?"

"Maybe."

The idea that the second Turret was the place they'd long feared, that it was there that girls were sent when they were spoiled rotten . . .

"That might explain the hair on the face," B said. "Rotts. Placasores. Oh, K . . . we saw *the Corner*!"

"Wait. Hang on. We *might* have seen the Corner. But that doesn't explain how there were so many girls over there."

"So many girls."

They thought about this new theory. They talked about it. They poked holes in it. But both kept returning to it, in its simple, original conceit: *The second tower is the Corner.*

Despite articulating no good explanation for the other girls, despite having no idea how a girl might get from a room in the basement of *this* tower to an eighth-floor window in the other one, the theory simply made too much sense to be wrong. And they needed to be right about something.

"We should ask M.O.M.," B said. The stressed smile on her face revealed more than just the pride of having solved a difficult riddle. K saw relief there. It was killing B, she knew, not to tell M.O.M. what they'd found.

"I don't think so," K said.

B tried to maintain her levity, but it was not easy. "I don't get you, K. We skip out on Film Night, hoping to find a stick in the dirt.

Instead, we find . . . *that* . . . and you want to keep it all to yourself! Why?"

"Well, now I wanna know if J is there."

"There's one very easy way to find out."

"Is there?"

B looked hurt. Not like K had offended her personally but rather had offended every detail of the world B lived in, the world B felt comfortable living in. "What are you saying, K? What exactly are you saying? Because, at first, I was under the impression that you just wanted to think about what we found. Isn't that what you said we should do? And here we've figured it out, that place has to be the Corner, but you *still* want to hide it from M.O.M. Why? Because you suddenly don't . . . trust her? And why not? Because she expressed interest in your drawings?" B looked to the new drawings, the ones of a potbellied Inspector with hair on her face walking the glass hall of the second tower. "I think you're taking this all *way* too personally, K. That's what I think. You don't like that the Parenthood is interested in your drawings for any reason other than they are *good*. That's it, isn't it? You want accolades, not questions. You want a pat on the back without anybody saying, *Hey hey, what's* this *in your drawing?* Do I know you anymore?"

B got up. So did K.

"Wait a minute," K said. She reached out for B's arm, but B pulled it back. "Hey! Aren't you interested in finding out if J is over there? Aren't you interested in *why* she was sent in the first place?"

"Of course," B said. Then, "No. You know what? No. I'm sorry, K. But this is a matter for M.O.M., and every minute we hide it from her is another minute of us falling deeper into this craziness! Think about it, K. Do *you* want to be sent over there? Do *you* want to live in that second tower with all those . . . those . . . *terrible girls*?"

K looked to the window, to give herself a second. If she stared too long into B's eyes she'd either cave or say something she'd regret.

She thought fast. Because she had to. It had never been something she prided herself on, thinking fast, being more quick-witted than her sisters, but now she simply had to be. And as the words came pouring, smooth, out of her mouth, she began to question her own motives, for when had she ever sounded so . . . convincing? And was this sudden ability to convince B born of genuine concern for what was out there (and why the Letter Girls had never been told about it) or was it simply a matter of wanting to be right?

"B, I'm thinking this way to protect M.O.M. Truly. You've seen how much work she's doing lately . . . do you think she needs to be burdened by our silly trip into the pines? And besides, what exactly happened out there? How was your Inspection this morning? Did they say you have Rotts? Did they say you have Vees?"

"No. I was declared clean."

"Of course you were. So, there you have it. We did this *terrible* thing, right? We skipped out on Film Night. We went out on our own and we saw a second tower. But we both passed our Inspections today, too. I don't see any reason in the world to drop this on M.O.M.'s lap. The poor woman has enough going on as it is."

B's eyes grew distant and K knew she had her. For now anyway. Whatever she'd said, it was working. And with B, once a thing started working, in the end it worked.

"Fine," B said.

"Okay?"

"Yes. Okay. Fine, K. I get it." She looked to the window. "Kind of."

K took her arm, and this time B let her. K led her to the window. "Come here," she said.

"What?"

"I wanna show you something."

"What?"

At the glass, K pointed. "You see that Yard? You see those pines? All still here. So is the room we're standing in. And so is your body and your mind. We didn't break anything, B. We didn't ruin something. And we were both declared clean today. We're not spoiled rotten."

B smiled. "You're right." She looked down at the Yard. "It was fun, wasn't it? I mean . . . it was completely . . . *crazy.*"

B laughed, and it sounded so good to K. K said, "We'll figure out more about it. But until we absolutely have to, I don't see any reason to bother M.O.M. Like the Judith Nancy books: Some adventures should be for the young girls alone."

B looked her friend, her sister, in the eye. A last beat, an unspoken agreement. For now. Then she made for the door. Halfway, she said, "How, K?"

"How what?"

"How are we going to find out more about it?"

K silently chided herself for having said it the way she did. "The same way we find out more about everything . . . by using our *limitless minds*!"

K laughed at her own imitation of Professor Hjortsberg's sluggish speech.

"Okay, K. See you later tonight."

"Okay."

B left. K turned to the glass again.

Staring into the pines, she saw herself there, not using her mind at all but rather her hands, her feet, and her eyes.

Going Back

Moonlight again. The pines again. But this time K was alone. Fleeing the Turret was simple. The Letter Girls hardly ever left their floors after sundown, and K, having mastered the art of taking the stairs quietly (including, of course, the opening and closing of the stairwell doors), relied on her routine as she arrived first at the ground floor, then waited for Inspector Rivers to make her rounds—not once, not twice, but three times—before slipping out of the stairwell, hurrying to the Body Hall, and stealing out through the kitchen again. The Turret floodlights illuminated all of the Yard but K took the shortest distance across, from the back door to the pines bordering the Orchard entrance, just as she had done with B and Q. Wearing her black slacks and turtleneck, she sank easily into the shadows and marveled at her own opacity; her hands seemed to be free-floating in the darkness. Safe at the border of pines, she turned to study the tower in full. Once she was satisfied nobody had seen her, not even a sister, she waited another minute more. Then, using her compass, she headed out for the second tower.

She thought about J on the way.

It'd never been hard to recognize the stronger attributes of her sisters. Indeed, the Parenthood stressed looking for such things. And while all the girls were intelligent, J was bright in a different way; she was what M.O.M. called *optimistic*. When the other Letter Girls (K included) fretted over their exams, J used to say, *I know as much as I know until I know more.*

"I know as much as I know until I know more," K said now, trekking through the pines, alone. The compass declared her direction true, and her watch let her know she was already halfway there.

Would someone find her missing back home? Inspector Rivers, perhaps, checking the bedrooms? And if so, would B tell her where K probably was?

K couldn't worry about that now. She'd reached the lights of the second tower (the Corner?) and she could see the tips of her black boots on the forest floor. She stepped fully into the new light and used the trees to hide, one by one. The memories of what she'd seen last time out were impossible to ignore: the naked backs, the short hair, the plodding Inspector.

At the edge of the pines, the second Yard stretching so far in front of her until it reached the sidewalks and the brick base of the second Turret, K crouched. She watched. And she heard a sound behind her.

"Oh!" she said, turning quick, expecting to see B, perhaps, or Q.

Or maybe the lumbering Inspector.

She didn't want to use her voice, didn't want to talk at all so close to this tower. But she spoke all the same.

"Is someone there?"

Yes, her eyes told her. Someone only half-hidden by a tree.

K wasted no time. Rather than remain frozen-still like her mind told her to do, K bolted toward the very tree that hid someone. She gripped the bark and spun around it, then around it again, then once more, before being convinced that nobody was there.

Yet . . .

"Yet . . . you're scared silly," she said. She scanned the woods as best she could. The considerable light from the tower helped. She listened.

When she faced the tower again, she saw figures through the glass of the first-floor hall. Three short-haired girls, taller, it seemed, than the Letter Girls back home. K had to consciously stop herself from stepping out from the pines, crossing the Yard, pressing her face to the glass. Knocking.

Seeing life in this tower for the second time was no less astonishing than it had been the first.

She wished she had the means by which to view them closer. A magnifying glass like the ones used by the Inspectors every morning of her life.

The girls in the hall laughed. It was the sort of communal laughter that, no matter how K or B might spin it, indicated legitimate happiness. The Letter Girls learned about happiness in Professor Hjortsberg's class. Learned about innocence and sorrow, too. What K was seeing, the large smiles, the cocked-back heads, the hands to their chests: It was all incompatible with the idea of the place being the Corner. Surely girls sent to the Corner didn't *enjoy* being there . . .

. . . right?

"It's not the Corner," she told herself. But she wasn't sure. Not yet.

From a window above, K heard a voice cry out a single name, a single letter, that broke her heart.

"J!"

J. The very name she sought. Proof that the lost Letter Girl was here after all.

K stepped out of the pines, onto the grass of the enormous Yard.

She wanted to be, *had* to be, closer to the window on the eighth floor, where she'd heard the name shouted, where she now saw four girls by the window. Two of them had their backs to the frame; the other two faced them. K didn't recognize J at all. None of these girls had J's blond hair, her lithe build, her way of standing, of sitting, of moving.

None of them had the face that K once drew.

If that was J up there (and it *had* to be, it had to be!), what had this place done to her that she'd changed so much?

K stepped back into the cover of the pines. The first floor looked vacant now. No girls. No Inspector. Nobody.

Up in the window, the girls talked. And their voices carried.

"It was his idea!" one said. One with glasses.

His. K guessed *His* was a name.

"It was not!" said another. This one with short curly hair.

"He didn't mean it that way," another said.

He. Another name?

"Oh, he most certainly did." The one with glasses. "J always means what he says."

J always means what he says.

Too many words for K to process. She had to get closer. She wanted to see them up close. Wanted to hear them up close. Wanted to be able to draw them, wanted to be able to—

An alarm sounded. A sound so familiar to K that, at first, she mistook it to mean she was home.

It was the bedtime bell. The gentle sound of a wooden horn, blown by the night Inspector on duty. K looked to the first-floor hall. Saw nobody. Looked up. Saw the girls stepping away from the window. One of them (the one they called J? *J always means what he says*) closed the window and waved to the others.

Bedtime.

Just like at home.

K looked into the pines. Had the same bell sounded back home?

"It's not the Corner," she repeated, eyeing the tower again, still trying to process the words, the names, the gibberish she'd over-heard.

One by one, lights went off in the mysterious tower. And just like at home, girls shouted good night to one another through the walls of their bedrooms, through the floors and ceilings, too.

But what voices they had. The girls in this tower spoke in a different register.

"Good night, Q!"

"Good night, L!"

"Good night, D!"

"Good night, J!"

Good night, J.

His.

He.

When the last light in the tower went out, K thought of the same happening back home.

K checked her watch. She looked once more to the dark windows going up and down the Turret.

Then she ran home. Through the pines, carrying so much new information, so many confusing words and images.

And feelings, too. Yes. K was experiencing so much at once that she couldn't be sure if she was excited, scared, or if she'd somehow discovered new emotions out there in the pines.

But she remembered how to run. Run home. Yet, the closer she got, the less like *home* it felt. For if there was a place just like your own, only three miles out in the woods, a place with the same windows and walls, the same Yard and pines, the same bedtime bell . . . who was to say what home was anymore?

Live Like You're in a
Judith Nancy Book

At the next morning's Inspection, Krantz and Rivers spent a lot of time examining a scratch on K's neck. M.O.M. asked where she'd gotten it. K said she didn't know. Which, in its way, was true. K might've known it was from a branch, but *which*?

She was declared clean, but nothing about the day following was ordinary, and K understood that it was possible no day would ever be again.

She didn't mind it. She had an objective now. A puzzle. A legitimate problem to solve.

First, eyes and ears. K needed better of both if she was going to observe the second tower from so far away.

"You're talking about *super glasses,*" Q said. "And I know what you want them for."

"Super glasses," K echoed. They stood in the Hall of Classes before the day's lessons had begun.

"I've actually considered this before," Q said. She raised and lowered her own glasses, as if to prove to K that she had indeed thought of this before. "You think I don't want to be able to see better?"

"Shh," K said. Then she wished she hadn't shushed her. It could make Q nervous.

Why so much secrecy, K?

"Numerous lenses," Q whispered. "Obviously."

"Girls?" Professor Hatch was peering out the physics door at them. "Now."

As the tardy Letter Girls hurried into the classroom, Hatch eyed the space they'd just occupied in the hall. As if she might see a trace of what they were talking about.

"MICROPHONES," Q SAID, later that same week, as K and Q treaded water in the shallow end during Free Swim. B was attempting dives off the high dive, but K saw her watching them talk. "Obviously."

"But could you do it without the cords?" K asked.

"Probably," Q said. "But we'd have to think hard on that one."

"Well, then let's."

B LAUNCHED HERSELF from the ten-foot board, split the water nicely. When she came up for air, the other Letter Girls applauded. B looked to K and Q in the shallow end. Saw they hadn't seen the dive. Saw they were still talking quietly like they had been for a week now.

"IF I HAD to change one thing about myself," Y said, sitting in the front seat of the far-left row in Professor Hjortsberg's class, "it would be to become more . . . heroic."

"Heroic?" Hjortsberg asked, setting her glasses on the desk by the chalkboard. The Letter Girls liked when she did this, because it meant she was interested in a topic and didn't plan to read from her books for a minute or two. Y had struck a chord.

"Yes. I often find myself keeping quiet when I would rather speak up."

"But here you are . . . speaking up in class."

The Letter Girls laughed at this. Y said, "Well, I've got a new theory."

"Oh?" Hjortsberg said. "Please . . . out with it, then."

Y breathed deep. She looked over her shoulders at her sisters.

"Well, it's like this," Y finally said. "I think Judith Nancy is . . . the *best*." The Letter Girls cheered behind her. "And if you line up all fifteen of her books, if you read them back to back, and you really pay attention to the *pattern* that carries over from one book to the next . . ."

"Yes?"

"Well, you begin to see that *all* of Nancy's characters research a problem until it's solved. They don't let pesky bad thoughts and doubts get in the way. If the star of a Nancy book wants to get to the bottom of something . . . she does it."

"She does indeed."

"And so . . . my new theory is . . . my *mantra* . . ."

"We're waiting, Y."

Y practically shouted it. "If you want to get something done, you need to *live like you're in a Judith Nancy book.*"

Professor Hjortsberg smiled. The Letter Girls laughed and cheered. All but K, who sank back into her seat, relieved, as if Y had just handed her the answers to all her newfound and borderline unfathomable questions.

Live like you're in a Judith Nancy book. Right. What other way was there to be? And what would K do if she were in a Judith Nancy book? Where would she start in trying to get more details about a tower she'd discovered that so resembled her own?

She'd start by studying her own.

The thought came so powerful, so loud, that K looked around the room, half-expecting her sisters to be staring in confusion. But Professor Hjortsberg was already debating the merits of Judith Nancy characters and how fiction is not the same thing as real life. The Letter Girls all had their hands up with something to say. K raised hers, just so she would fit in, just so Hjortsberg wouldn't wonder what she was thinking.

Hjortsberg called on her first.

"K? Add something?"

K slowly lowered her arm as the class went silent. She wasn't exactly sure what to say, but she knew enough of what everyone was excited about to say something. Anything. Yet she was fearful lest the words that came out of her mouth reveal her true thoughts. As if her lips held back the reality of her two sojourns through the pines, the images of the frightening Inspector out there. The growing evidence of the place J may have been sent to.

"I just wanted to say that, um," she stammered, tried to compose herself. Then, just as she was about to let anything pour forth, anything that might be accepted as a classroom contribution, K realized she wanted to say something real instead. She stood up. "Y is right, of course. We should all live like we're in a Judith Nancy book. But since we're *not,* we need to take stock of what makes a hero in *our* world. In the Parenthood. The real Parenthood." Hjortsberg nodded acknowledgment and made to reach for her glasses, as though K was done speaking. But K was not. "And the most heroic thing any of us Letter Girls can do, the absolute most important thing in our lives and what we must devote our lives to . . . is the defense of one another." Hjortsberg raised an eyebrow. K's sisters were silent. "If one of us falls, the rest of us must pick her up. If one of us gets ill, the rest of us must discover a cure for her illness. And if one of us should go missing . . ." She thought the name J. She heard it as it had been hollered from the eighth-floor window of the Turret in the pines. "The rest of us should never stop trying to find her until she's found."

K sat again. The room was very quiet. Her sisters turned to face Professor Hjortsberg, who, glasses already on, said, "Back to the textbooks, girls. The ones that count."

IT WAS PARENTHOOD law that no Letter Girl was allowed below and, until now, that was good enough for K. There might be Rotts down there. Vees. The diseases the Parenthood Inspected for daily.

Besides, as far as being tempted to see the basement, the staff offices, Judith Nancy's office, the Corner ... there simply was no known *door*.

Jogging the indoor track that made an oval around the Yellow Ball court, it struck K how unbelievable it was that she'd never thought to seek out the basement before. The place had played such a large part in the Letter Girls' lives. Their favorite books were written down there. The Corner was (allegedly) down there. The good and the bad of the tower seemed to rise up from that subterranean lair, and never, not once, had K thought to see what it looked like.

Why?

"Are you going to go out there again?" B asked, jogging beside her.

The question felt too sudden. Here B asked about going out and K was thinking about going farther in.

"I don't know yet," she said.

"Well, I don't think you should."

"I know you don't."

"Isn't two times enough, K? Come on. I can't believe you're turning me into this kind of a girl."

"What kind?"

They went quiet as they jogged the front straightaway, as they passed Coach Leslie.

"You're *making* me say no," B said. "When I'm the kind of girl who always says yes."

"Then say yes," K said.

"You know how I feel. Two times is enough. Now you can talk to M.O.M. about it."

"Not yet. I wanna check something out first."

"K?"

"What?"

"You're acting insane. If I was in charge? I'd send you to the Corner."

It was partially funny because B said it. But mention of the Corner was never entirely funny.

"It's interesting you mention that," K said.

"Oh? Why? You thinking of checking out the Corner next?"

K was silent.

"K? Please tell me you're not."

K was silent. For the duration of the jog she was silent.

"WELL, M.O.M. GOES down there all the time," Q said, the two of them in line for dinner. Both dressed in black, but Q seemed extra-hidden by her hair. K felt exposed. Q had whispered but K spoke even quieter.

"Right. So . . . how does she do it?"

"How do they all do it?" Q asked back. Then she nodded toward Professor Ullman. Ullman had long been a Letter Girl favorite. With her big worried eyes magnified behind her big worried glasses and the way she stammered through every lecture. Always nervous, always fearful, might Ullman tell them where the door was? Even by . . . accident?

Once K was seated and eating, Ullman was all she could think about. The meek math teacher ate with three more professors at the table closest to the window. K needed her alone. How? And if she got her . . . what would she say?

"Exams in two days," Y said, splitting a dinner roll in two. "Are you all ready?"

"Of course we are," B said. But she looked to K as though questioning whether her best friend was.

"I'm ready," V said.

"So am I," K said. But was she? She didn't feel ready. In fact, she hadn't studied nearly enough for what lay ahead. No Letter Girl had ever failed an exam, just like no Letter Girl had ever failed an Inspection.

Could the others tell how unprepared she was?

Across the room, two of the professors seated with Ullman

dabbed their lips with napkins, got up from their chairs, and left the cafeteria.

"I can help if you're behind," B said. The way she said it, K felt like B had just shouted across the hall, *K hasn't studied, everyone! She's been too busy THINKING ABOUT A SECOND TOWER!*

A table away, Q got up and slouched her way to the two remaining professors still seated by the window. Hjortsberg and Ullman. K watched closely as Q tapped Hjortsberg on the shoulder. At K's table, B, Y, and V discussed physics and engineering. Exams.

"K?" B asked. "Aren't you gonna even say thanks?"

K didn't hear her. Q had gotten Hjortsberg to get up from the table and join her at the dry-erase board, where the daily meals were written in marker. There, Q wrote a quote in black. Hjortsberg immediately explained it to her.

"Know who can help me most of all?" K said, staring at Ullman alone.

"Anyone but me?" B asked.

"*Her*," K said. "Excuse me, girls."

She got up and crossed the cafeteria. Professor Ullman looked especially vulnerable, hunched at her table, nibbling on bread, seen from standing above her.

"Professor Ullman?"

Ullman turned quickly. In her eyes, seen so close, K saw sadness. "Yes? What is it?"

"Do you mind if I sit down?"

Ullman's wiry hair was pulled so far back from her face it appeared to stretch her cheeks and chin with it. The professor looked skeletal, her teeth bared, her eyes darting about the big, noisy room. "Go ahead," she finally said. "I can't stop you."

Not *How can I help you, K?*

"It's the textbook, Professor," K said, adopting a voice that was still new to her. One that was comfortable with lying.

When Ullman frowned, her entire face tightened. "The *textbook*? What's wrong with the book?"

K feigned disappointment. "It's the print. We can hardly read some of the formulas. The print is . . . too small."

Ullman eyed the girl suspiciously. One eye got very small as the other, the closer, seemed to grow twice as large. "No girl has ever complained about the *book* before."

She's scared, K thought. And with the thought, a brick came loose in the Turret of her mind.

Did Ullman know of the second tower? Did all the staff?

"Well, it's not easy," K said. "And it's getting harder."

"Maybe your eyes need checking?"

K laughed. Ullman did, too, then quickly stopped. As if she hadn't expected to express positivity at all. "But I have no problem with any of the other books! And it's not so much the letters, the words—it's the *numbers,* Professor Ullman. And what is math without . . . numbers?"

Ullman grunted. "What would you have me do, girl?"

"I'm not sure. What *can* be done?"

"Are you suggesting we print new books on your behalf?" Her voice seemed to be growing smaller, weaker. Up close and one-on-one, Professor Ullman was what Professor Hjortsberg might've called *shell-shocked.*

K could relate.

"Not on *my* behalf," K said. "On everybody's." She leaned closer to the teacher. "I'm not the only one who has . . . *said so.*"

Ullman fanned a dismissive hand. "I'm sorry. But I'm not taking a perfectly good book to the printer and asking for larger numbers. You'll simply have to use a magnifying glass."

K smiled. "I'll do it."

"You'll do what?"

"I'll take it to the printer. Where is it?"

K looked over her shoulder as if she might find books being run off there in the cafeteria.

"Don't say that," Ullman snapped. But the fear in her voice didn't transfer to K. K wanted to know how to get down there.

"Why? Where's the printer? I can talk to them. You don't have to do a thing."

"In the *basement*," Ullman said, gripping her shawl with one bony hand and pointing to the cafeteria floor with the other. "And there's no way a Letter Girl is going down there!"

"Ah," K said. But she left just enough in the one syllable to suggest she didn't buy it.

"You're not even allowed in the staff bathroom, let alone the basement!"

Ullman closed her mouth fast. The staff bathroom?

Why'd she say that?

"You're one hundred percent right," K said.

"The answer is simply no," Ullman persisted. "Do you understand?"

"Yes. I get it."

"Good. Now, go find a magnifying glass. Or talk to Nurse Simon about a pair of glasses, for heaven's sake!"

"Heaven's?" K asked. She'd never heard the word.

Ullman's anxious anger fell from her face. In its stead was something much more severe. K had read a word that described the teacher's expression in a Judith Nancy book before.

The word was *horror.*

"That's enough," Ullman said. She got up from her chair. "Now, shoo. Back to studying. Back to work."

Ullman hurried away just as Hjortsberg returned.

"Hello, K," Professor Hjortsberg said. "What were you and Miss Ullman discussing?"

But K was still watching the thin, frightened math professor leave the cafeteria.

"K?"

"Oh, sorry, Professor. We were talking about textbooks. The math book specifically. I can't read the numbers."

Hjortsberg frowned. "Hmm. I've always thought the print

could be a bit more legible in most of the textbooks. Good for you for saying so."

The alarm announcing the end of dinner rang, and the Letter Girls gathered their trash and carried their trays to the cans along the windowed wall. K and Q made eye contact as K dumped her empty milk carton into the plastic bag. In that brief exchange, hardly long enough for two girls to do more than acknowledge each other's existence, time slowed for K, stretched from one end of the cafeteria to the other, and she saw herself walking the first-floor hall, taking the staff hall to the staff bathroom, entering, walking past stalls, finding at the far end there another door, a darker one, one marked BASEMENT.

She shivered as she imagined opening that basement door, then the Corner door, too, finding a tunnel there . . . one that led under the pines . . . all the way to—

Q nodded. She curtsied as if to say, *You're welcome.* It looked as though K had communicated something after all, as a dark shadow seemed to come over the cafeteria, as her bones grew cold, as she imagined herself doing all the things she'd been taught not to do.

How far was she willing to go? How far would the discovery in the woods force her to go?

Live like you're in a Judith Nancy book.

K tried to smile at this idea, tried to smile back to Q. But she couldn't. And she knew that her inability to express joviality, even feigned, communicated something, too.

The Woman Wore Red, All Red

B didn't like any of it. Not one bit.

"The staff *bathroom*?"

Both girls had just completed their morning Inspections. Both declared clean. For K, it was empowering, the way she could go places she wasn't supposed to, think things the Parenthood would have found abhorrent, even lie, all without repercussion.

There was a power to it. At only eleven years old, she felt all of it.

"You should come with me," she said, untangling wires on the bookshelf in her living room.

"No way."

K turned to face her friend, because she knew B very well and the way B said *no way* sounded close to *some way*.

"B?" She left the wires alone, stepped to her sister on the couch. "You wanna come?"

B looked to the window. K could see the warring emotions on her face, as if guilt and adventure stood on either cheek, tugging her nose between them.

"I don't *want to*. No. But . . ."

"But what?"

"But I don't think you should do it alone."

K wanted to squeal. But what she was planning to do didn't warrant it.

The Corner was down there, after all. Or so they'd been taught.

"There's gonna be staff down there," B said.

"We'll go at night."

"What if someone catches us?"

"Then we get caught. We play dumb. We play curious."

"I'm scared."

K sat beside her and put her arm around her. "So am I. But I can't stop thinking about what we found out there and I—"

"I can't, either. How could I?"

"—and I think it's our duty to look into it. All of it. For the Letter Girls."

"You make it sound like the Letter Girls aren't a part of the Parenthood."

K removed her arm, got up, went back to the bookshelf. She toyed with the wires, making sure they were connected well. Q had delivered the device earlier the same day. *A third ear,* she'd called it. *You hook it over one of your two existing ears and you can hear the trees grow.* She warned K that it could be disorienting, could make her dizzy, could also make her think someone was closer than they were.

And the problem with that is, Q said, delighted by her own invention, *what if they're not as far away as you think?*

K tried it on.

"Go ahead and talk," she told B.

"Hello, my name is B."

K reached up quick and took the device from her ear. "Ow!" she cried. "That was *loud*!"

"Can you turn it down?"

K shook her head. "Q hasn't figured out how to do that. Hey . . . go out in the hall."

"Me?"

"Yeah. Go stand by the Check-Up room door."

"Then what?"

"Then talk to me. I wanna see how far this goes."

K put it back on. She could hear B's shoes on the carpet. Beyond that, she heard V and Y discussing exams.

"Hello. My name is B."

K looked around the living room. It sounded like B was standing right next to her. Sounded like B hadn't left at all.

"Wow."

"Hello, my big bad name is B."

K laughed.

"And I think my friend K has lost her mind. Can you help her? Can you help her find it?"

K walked to the couch, sat down.

"My name is B. And now I'm whispering. *My friend K is crazy.*"

The *thud thud thud* of B's shoes in the hall, and K removed the earpiece just before her friend opened the door.

"So?" B asked. "Does it work?"

"Here," K said. "Try it."

AT NIGHTFALL, B returned to K's rooms. The sisters were dressed in their Body Hall best: black slacks, black turtleneck shirts. But this time, black gloves, too.

"You ready?" K whispered.

"Yeah. Don't ask me that again or I'll say no."

They stepped out into the hall.

"Okay," K whispered. "We can do this."

"One thing," B said.

"What?"

"If we discover anything really bad down there . . . I'm telling you right now I'm going to tell M.O.M., and I think you should do the same. At some point, enough is enough."

K nodded. "Agreed."

But as they walked the carpeted hall to the stairs K had taken at least twice a day for most of her life, she wondered how bad it might get.

The door wasn't past a row of stalls, after all.

It was *in* one of the stalls.

"This is insane," B said, the two of them yet to enter the stall. There was no toilet in this one. Only a door.

"What if it's locked?" B asked.

K held up a hand quick. She'd placed the third ear on one of her own, and B's voice was deafening. She stepped into the stall, listening for anything beyond the door. Anything at all.

She removed Q's device and tried the knob. It turned easily. The door opened.

They looked at one another for a few seconds before moving. And in those few seconds they seemed to age. As if the experience, from their first trip through the pines to now, had done something irrevocable to them. Forget the lying and hiding, the clandestine missions at night.

In that moment K and B felt as if they'd grown up. A little bit. A lot. Together.

"Okay," K said. "To the basement."

But they both heard it as *To the Corner*.

TAKING THE STAIRS was as nerve-racking as discovering the second tower. Despite living their entire lives in the Turret, the girls had never been upon these stone steps, never felt the sensation of descending from the first floor. They were different from the stairs above. As though the women who built them had stopped halfway. And below, the basement was lit by loose flickering light.

At the foot of the stairs they paused, looking both ways down long cobblestone corridors where, far off on both sides, paper signs were taped to the walls.

K tugged gently on B's sleeve and led her to the left. They walked the length of the hall very slow. The weak light reflected in their eyes as they read the first paper sign they came to:

REMEMBER TO KEEP THE LANTERNS LIT:

A DARK HALL IS AN UNSAFE HALL

K tugged B's sleeve again and the sisters walked even slower around the first turn, then down the length of a second hall. A closed door broke the monotony of cobblestones on their right.

"The Corner?" B whispered.

K shone her flashlight on the door.

BATTERIES, TYPEWRITER RIBBON, OFFICE SUPPLIES

Typewriter ribbon. Both girls thought of Judith Nancy.

She wrote the books of their lifetime down *here*?

Now B took K by the sleeve and the two girls advanced, gripping each other's arms. K thought of the second tower. She thought of J in there. Is this the way she went? Through these halls, then the Corner door, underground, only to emerge with different hair, a different body, a different voice, in a second tower in the pines?

She imagined the overweight Inspector from that second Turret rounding the hall corner ahead. The hair on her face down to her knees.

"Come on," B said. B suddenly in charge. Hjortsberg had talked about this sort of behavior; she'd called it *overcompensating*.

When someone is afraid, very scared, they often react by being overly brave.

Whatever it was, K was happy for it.

They continued, taking a second turn, this one to the right, where many doors broke up the cobblestone walls. There were more lanterns in this hall and the doors varied in sizes, and the Letter Girls paused to look. K put on Q's third ear. She could hear the flames flickering. A bottle opening? Yes, the twisting of a cap. The unmistakable sound of a struck match coming to life. The sound of someone drinking.

K grabbed B's hand.

The match. Someone lighting the lanterns? Someone to check all the lanterns?

A dark hall is an unsafe hall . . .

K moved fast, pulling B with her into the shadowed cover of a depressed doorway.

Suddenly the idea of being caught in the basement, with Q's third ear, felt like a very bad idea, indeed. She worried about B. Worried about Q. Worried about herself.

She was doing this not only for the knowledge but for her sisters.

Was she doing it the right way?

It felt like she was. It felt like they should continue. Like it or not, there were answers down here.

K removed the earpiece.

"You hear anything?" she asked.

"Let's go back upstairs," B said. "I think we've seen enough."

"Maybe."

They stepped out of the doorway, looked down the hall. Saw another paper sign taped to the wall at the far end.

"Let's read that," K said. "Then we can head back."

But the length of hall looked very long to B. "I'll wait here."

"What? No. We go together."

B inhaled deep. "You owe me so much for this, K."

"I know."

The two stepped out of the doorway and advanced arm in arm. They passed one, two, four doors, each with a name and an occupation. K thought of the staff bathroom upstairs. A door in a stall. More doors in a dingy dark hall. The Parenthood didn't shine quite so bright from this angle.

There was a door marked PRINTING. A door marked ACCOUNTING. Some included the names of women they'd seen upstairs. As if the staff of the Parenthood were no more than the trolls from Judith Nancy's *Under Things*.

"We're *under things* now," B said.

When they reached the white sign taped to the stone wall, neither understood what it said.

GLASGOW TUNNEL:

ONLY TO BE USED BY MARILYN

"Who's Marilyn?" B asked.

But K was thinking only of the word tunnel.

"The second tower," she said. "If we take that tunnel . . . we may come up into—"

"*Into* the tower?"

"We have to at least check the tunnel. We don't have to take it."

"No. We don't." B pressed a finger against the paper. "*Marilyn's* the only one who can use it."

"We're not supposed to be down here at all. Why would we suddenly listen to the rules?"

"See? That's exactly what I was worried about. There's no end, is there?"

"I think there is."

K made to move, but B grabbed her arm.

"If you can tell me right now what the end is, what it could be, I'll keep going."

"J," K said. A crack in her voice was audible in its echo. "Come on. We've come this far. There are answers down here."

"Yeah? Well, maybe I don't want them."

K eyed the length of hall. The entrance to the tunnel was visible, a dark oval amid the cobblestones.

"You do," K said. "But if you wanna wait here, that's all right."

"I'm too *scared* to wait here."

"Then hold on to me. Nobody's gonna get us. I promise."

"You can't promise that."

"No. I can't."

With B clinging, K walked faster, past more doors. They reached the black hole sooner than either wanted to. Above it, just evident in the glow from the flames, the letters, poorly painted, spelled: GLASGOW TUNNEL.

K shone her light into the tunnel. Dirt walls and a dirt floor. No end in immediate sight.

"Turn off your light," B said.

"Why?"

"Someone might see us coming."

They both looked to where K's light faded.

K turned off the light.

They entered the dark of the tunnel with only each other. Through the third ear, K heard their shoes again. She thought of the three miles it took to get to the second tower. Thought of the time that took, too. If this tunnel really went there, they'd be walking in this dark for forty-five minutes. That was too long. Each minute felt too long. What if someone were to come from the other direction? Someone with a flashlight?

Someone in the dark?

Still, the girls advanced. Soon K was leading B faster, the fingertips of one hand sliding along the left wall for guidance.

"K," B whispered.

K removed the earpiece. "What?"

"I heard something."

"I didn't. And I was wearing the third ear."

"Well, I definitely did."

"What did you hear?"

"I heard footsteps. Something. I don't know."

The girls waited. They listened. K raised her flashlight, made to turn it on, but . . .

Someone else's light beat her to it.

Ahead.

Someone had turned on lights not far from where the Letter Girls stood.

Neither girl moved, not even to the wall.

In the light they saw a partition, a glass divider, separating this side of the tunnel from the other.

K knew that if B hadn't heard what she'd heard, if B hadn't come, K might've been all the way to that glass wall by now. She might have been feeling her way along that divider when the lights came on.

And the unfathomable woman on the other side of the glass would have seen her.

The girls gripped hands.

The woman wore all red. Red gloves and a red jacket, red pants and boots. The hair on her face was much darker than that of the Inspector they'd seen in the first-floor hall of the second Turret. So was the hair on her head. Her features were so sharp, so harsh, K couldn't help but imagine drawing a face so unreal, as if by re-creating it exactly as it was she might rise to a new level of artistry. But whoever this was, K didn't want to get any closer.

The woman slid open a glass drawer on her side of the transparent divider. She placed a stack of papers inside it.

K and B thought of Judith Nancy's *The Hut,* in which a young girl, Miranda, discovers a witch living in the Orchard behind the Turret.

The witch slipped secret notes to the Letter Girls in their sleep. Was this woman slipping secret notes, too? Pages and pages of them?

She was tall. So tall. Wide at the shoulders. K had never seen a woman exude such physical strength before. As if, here in the Glasgow Tunnel, lived a woman strong enough to crush a girl.

Was this what lived in the Corner?

It got out, M.O.M. once said. *And it took everything we had to get it back inside again.*

The woman grunted, slid the partition drawer closed, scratched the hair on her face, reached for a knob on the wall, and the lights went out.

The Letter Girls didn't move. Not even as the sound of the woman's red boots echoed into the dark distance of the tunnel's other side.

"Those pages," K said.

"Back," B said. "Now."

K turned on the flashlight and, without waiting to debate it with B, rushed to the glass partition. She opened the drawer from her side and took out the pages.

As she hurried back, it struck her that, if someone were to catch them now, the papers would crush any already-thin excuse they had.

"Okay," she said. "Let's go."

B didn't argue. They moved fast toward the light at the open end of the tunnel. They stuck to the wall, they held hands, they hurried.

A few feet shy of the entrance, B pulled hard on K's wrist, stopping her.

"Are we okay?" B asked.

K thought of Rotts. Of Vees. They both did.

"I don't know."

Out the entrance, they scurried back the way they'd come. One hall, then another. The hall with many doors.

The girls had taken two steps when one of those doors opened.

B froze. K quickly set the pages on the ground, stood up straight again.

A face peered out of the doorway, turned fully toward them.

It was a woman with large glasses, curly gray hair high upon her head. Smoke rose from a cigarette between her fingers, obscuring the collared off-white blouse she wore. K thought of the match she'd heard struck on the way to the Glasgow Tunnel. Despite seeing her out of context, the girls knew who this woman was.

This was Judith Nancy.

"Well, holy shit," Nancy said, her voice hoarse and wise. "Holy *shit*."

The girls had seen Judith Nancy many times before. She always entered the cafeteria with a smile, her wrinkled hands cutting the air as if made of the same silk as the handkerchiefs around her neck. She'd always looked regal to K. Unapproachable. And like someone who had possibly been crying, but who had come to a hopeful conclusion just prior to stepping out in public.

To K and B, Judith Nancy was exactly what a writer looked like.

The only one they knew of.

"Please don't tell," B said. The words blurted out of her mouth like she'd thrown up. K wanted to grab those words before they reached Judith Nancy. They made the moment real, proving that, yes, they'd been caught in the basement, doing something they shouldn't.

"Tell?" Judith Nancy said. She stepped out full into the hall. She wore a long skirt that almost reached scuffed heels. She had a bottle in her other hand.

B looked at K, K who had gotten her into this, K who started the snooping.

"M.O.M.," K finally said. "Please don't tell her."

Nancy leaned a shoulder against the wall. She lifted the bottle to her lips, took a drink, puckered her face, and lowered it again.

"You two," she said. "I'm so drunk, come tomorrow morning I'll question whether or not this happened at all."

The girls didn't know what to say. So they said nothing.

"Come in?" Nancy asked, stepping aside, making room at her office door.

"Into your office?" K asked.

Nancy smiled. "And why not? We'll want to be quiet, of course." She looked up. "But I think we could all use a good expunging talk."

Still a Place You've Never Seen

"Why tonight?" Nancy asked. Her now-shoeless feet were up on the desk beside what both girls recognized as a typewriter. Beside the old machine was a stack of pages. The ink on top looked fresh. Dark black.

"What do you mean?" B asked. Her voice continued to betray her horror at having been caught, invited in or not. But K knew what Nancy meant.

"I learned that the basement door was in the staff bathroom," K said. "And we wanted to see it."

"Ah," Nancy said. The way she eyed K suggested she believed some of what K said but not all of it. Still, it was enough, it seemed. Or, rather, it seemed she believed the right parts. "That's the way to be. You have an idea to do something, you *do* it."

Judith Nancy took another drink from the bottle. The Letter Girls could smell it from across the desk. The matching chairs they sat in creaked as they leaned forward, together, to read the label.

"It's called bourbon, girls, and it's one of life's many pleasures."

"Does it taste good?" K asked.

Nancy laughed. "Absolutely not. But aren't some things more about how they feel than how they taste?" She waved a dismissive hand at the two blank stares that followed. "The answer to that is *yes*. Always yes. Life must be about the three *S*s. Do you know what they are? Can you guess?"

K and B exchanged glances. They were in Judith Nancy's office. Judith Nancy just asked them a question. How to answer? K tried.

"Study, sacrifice, and . . . stamina?"

Nancy removed her feet from the desk. Leaned toward them.

"No," she said. "Jesus. No." She lit a second cigarette, pointed it at the two Letter Girls. "Sensation. Suspension. Spirit. Sensation because you must savor every meal, every syllable of laughter, every second you smile. Suspension because you must be able to suspend your disbelief in all walks of life. And spirit because . . . well . . . your spirit drives the whole car, now, doesn't it?"

"Yes," K said. "It does."

"If I can teach you girls one thing, if I can reveal one tiny aspect of this life that you might not already know . . ." K spotted distance in the woman's eyes. Nancy wanted to say more than she was. She wanted to talk all day. K was struck by an image of the author crawling across the desk, gripping the girls by their wrists, leading them out into the pines. *Let me show you something, girls. Let me show you another . . . tower.* "It's that you must question authority. You must trust your instincts. And you must do the very thing you're doing right now."

"What are we doing right now?" B asked.

Nancy laughed. But K heard deep sorrow in it. "You're questioning *everything.*"

K felt something like an electric current inside. Leave it to Judith Nancy to articulate what she could not.

"We found a—" B started to say, but K elbowed her. Nancy looked from one girl to the other. Then she looked to the door.

"Whatever it is, don't tell me," Nancy said. "The point of bringing you two in here was most decidedly *not* to unearth what you've learned but to play the role of a character you meet along your journey throughout life, and certainly over the course of your sojourn down here to the basement. Think of me as—"

"As Rosalyn from *Over and Over*," K said. Her voice betrayed her sudden excitement. She was talking Judith Nancy with Judith Nancy.

"Yes," Nancy said. She half lit up, half went into shadow. As if her own book was something to be both proud and ashamed of. "Like Rosalyn, indeed. What purpose would you say she served for little Candace P?" Nancy raised her eyebrows, waiting for a response. Then her eyebrows dropped back to the level of her large glasses. "Forget I asked that. I also do *not* plan to give you a pop quiz. Certainly not on the books *I* write."

"We love the books you write," B said.

Nancy brought a hand to her mouth. Both Letter Girls saw the bottoms of the author's eyes well up wet. Nancy looked down. It took her several seconds to regain her composure. "I suppose I should thank you," she said. "And so . . . K and B, thank you."

"You know our names?" K asked.

"Of course I know your names. It's the writer's job to observe, is it not? And there are only so many of us in this tower to begin with. How hard is it to commit so few to memory?"

K and B exchanged a glance. Was Nancy alluding to the second tower? Other people?

A sound out in the hall and K turned so fast it hurt her neck. When she looked back at Nancy, she saw that the writer looked as frightened as B. Worse: Judith Nancy looked like she'd seen her own death, just like little Candace P in *Over and Over*.

"If they enter this room," Nancy whispered, her magnified eyes on the doorknob, "I will lie. I will tell them you entered on your own. That you forced me to speak."

"What?" B asked.

Another sound in the hall. Nancy held up a hand swiftly.

They waited. All six eyes on the office door, here in the last place in the world Judith Nancy should tell a story.

"A mouse," Nancy said.

"A mouse?" B asked. "In here? In the Parenthood?"

Nancy took a drink from her bottle. "This is the *basement,* girls. Where the shadows play." She paused. "But I suppose they play everywhere in this place."

"Do they?" K asked.

The writer studied K close. "You," she said. "You started all this, didn't you."

B nodded. "It was her."

"It was my idea to come down here," K said. "Yes."

"But not just *that,*" Nancy said. "Again, I have no interest in scolding you. My God, even I refuse to sink that low."

"Your God?" K asked.

Nancy's face changed abruptly again. She looked to the bottle. "My goodness," she corrected herself. "Tell me, girls. Do you know what *misinformation* is?" Then, "Of course you do. I'm writing books for postgrad reading levels."

"Postgrad?" K asked.

Nancy shook her head. "My, you *are* sharp, aren't you?"

"We know what misinformation means," K said, not wanting to let the thread go.

"It's when someone tells you something that just isn't true," Nancy said anyway. She looked to the door again. "With the intention of you believing it."

K felt the hair on her arms rise. Was Nancy about to reveal something? Tell a secret?

"Like a lie," B said.

"Oh, much worse than *that,*" Nancy said. "A lie might be used to get yourself out of trouble. A lie can make somebody feel good. A lie can even be *fun*. But misinformation—there's no fun in that one."

K thought of the frightening woman in the Glasgow Tunnel. She thought of the papers she'd left outside in the hall. Was the mouse eating them? Was it a mouse?

"You're doing the right thing," Nancy said. She leaned back in her chair, slurred certain words. Smoke rose to a vent above her.

Her skin looked especially pale, off-white, close to the color of her blouse. She attempted to lift her feet up onto the desk but fell short. She leaned forward suddenly, recovering from the mistake, and sat with her legs apart, her elbows on the arms of the chair. K noticed that most of the liquid in the bottle was gone. When Nancy spoke again, it was with more enthusiasm. But of a dark variety. "You are doing the right thing with your *suspicions.*"

"We're inspired by your books," K said. She did not say, *Suspicions?* She did not want Nancy to stop talking.

Nancy looked at her and it seemed, to K, that she was looking over her shoulder, then her other shoulder, then vaguely in her eye. "Don't say that to me," she said. "Don't you ever say that again. I have *nothing* to do with the fact that you're seeking answers . . . looking for justice . . . engaging your . . . your . . ."

The girls waited for her to finish what she'd started to say.

"Are you okay, Judith Nancy?" B asked.

Nancy looked quick to B.

"This is why I asked you in," she said. "This . . ." She fanned both occupied hands to the greater part of the office. "You've never been in a basement like this before. And you've never been in an office like this, either. And while it's not much to look at, I'd like you to look at it all the same." She paused, giving the Letter Girls a chance to look around. They did. "Because, even if the barren walls elicit no excitement, even if the dank air momentarily suffocates you, even if the space itself feels something like a casket built too small, this is still a place you've never seen. And, girls, those places are the most important places to see in all the world."

"In all the world," B echoed.

"Now," Nancy said, "scram."

"Scram?" K asked.

Nancy nodded. "Let's be grateful that was only a mouse."

K and B were slow to rise, but they rose. Nancy was lighting another cigarette as they reached the door. Taking another drink from her bottle.

"Thank you, Judith," K said. She wanted to say so much more. Ask so much more.

"It's Vivian," Nancy said, "Vivian Kleinplotz. But who would read a book written by *her*?"

K and B smiled awkwardly, not understanding what the author meant.

They left then and shut the door quietly behind them. The type-writer erupted to life beyond the wood.

K went quick to the pile of pages on the hall floor. Still there.

The girls took the same halls back. But how different they looked this time.

"I can't tell if I feel better or worse," B said at the foot of the stairs that led to the staff bathroom above.

"About what?"

"About lying."

"B, I think we can agree there's more going on here than—"

"I mean, here I was, *so* worried about lying to M.O.M., the Parenthood, everybody. But did you hear her? *Judith Nancy?* She said she would lie, too. Told us right to our faces. Said she'd lie to the Parenthood, tell them we forced her to talk."

K looked up the stairs.

"I guess we're not the only ones with secrets."

"No," B said. "We're not. And if Judith Nancy would lie . . . who else would?"

The girls climbed the stone steps. At the top, K put Q's third ear back in place. She listened.

It felt, to her, like she'd answered B's question without speaking.

Everybody, she hadn't said. *Everybody would lie.*

Over and Over

K returned to the second tower every night for two weeks. By now, thanks to the pages she'd stolen from the Glasgow Tunnel, she knew it was referred to as *the boys' tower*. She had no idea what the word *boys* meant, but she had an idea it had something to do with the variety of women who lived there. Some had hairy faces. All had flat chests. Some were abnormally strong or overweight. All spoke in a different timbre, a tone she'd never heard around her own. She didn't ask B to come with her, because she didn't want to force that on her friend. B had flip-flopped many times on whether or not to tell the Parenthood, but it'd been days since she'd said they should, and K wanted to keep it that way.

Q helped with the super glasses, just as she'd helped with the third ear. By way of a series of lenses (some of them upside down), K was able to easily observe the girls in the second tower from under cover of the pines at the edge of the second Yard. She took notes. She made lists.

She drew.

She drew J a lot. And while she no longer thought this J was the same J that had been taken from home, her fascination with this short-haired, flat-chested girl seemed to have no bounds. By the end of the first week of spying, she had ten drawings of J, photographic quality, most of them by the view through Q's super glasses.

But one or two came from much closer.

As summer became autumn, K had begun sneaking *into* the second tower.

The similarities between the two Turrets would've occupied more of her thinking had not the horror of being inside a place she did not belong occupy so much space. The second tower smelled different. Start there. Smelled . . . deeper, if such a thing were possible. Smelled darker, too. Not in a moody way . . . but in a physical assault to the senses. K found herself on high alert the first time she entered the building. Not just because she was justifiably concerned with getting caught, but because the actual smell of the place scared her. It smelled more . . . violent. As if the women who walked these halls, took these stairs, entered these rooms, were partial to different methods from the Letter Girls back home.

She learned a lot from the pages she'd stolen. *Boys* wasn't the only word. Lengthy descriptions of the girls in the second tower always included the gibberish words she'd heard in the second Yard: *his* and *he*. More than once the girls were referred to as *the Alphabet Boys,* and K was intelligent enough to note the similarity between that appellation and *the Letter Girls* at home.

She'd read many paragraphs depicting each of the inhabitants of the second tower, their likes and dislikes, inclinations and sensitivities, a behavior report of sorts. But something was missing.

Exactly *what* was a boy?

Until K knew that, they would be girls.

There was no mention of the stolen papers at home. No professor mentioned it in class. M.O.M. did not ask about it in the morning Inspections. The daily *Turret Times* made no mention at all and certainly didn't allude to any meeting between K, B, and Judith Nancy.

Judith Nancy. Wow. *That* conversation played out in K's head just like the title of one of her favorite Nancy books, *Over and Over.* Never before had K partaken in a discussion she felt necessary to dissect every letter of. Nancy's wet eyes, her scratchy voice, her delivery, and her three Ss . . .

It all inspired K to reread all the Nancy books on her shelf.

Maybe the secrets Nancy didn't want to tell were hidden in those pages.

B noticed the books. Said she tried reading one, too, but struggled. Couldn't stop hearing the slurred words. Couldn't stop thinking that Judith Nancy was a sad person. That's how she put it. A liar, too.

K's investigation of the second tower, the odd and still-frightening women and girls, the *Alphabet Boys,* seemed to be pitted against the clock, the tick-tocking of B's back-and-forth regarding whether or not to tell M.O.M. all they'd done and seen. Things may have toned down for the time being, but B looked and sounded like a Jill-in-the-Box about ready to explode in a loud and startling way.

K didn't want to think about B at all. The nightly treks weren't only an enduring unraveling of her former reality; they were also eating into her sleep. She was running on four, four and a half hours a night, and Inspectors Krantz and Rivers had begun asking her about it.

Bad dreams, K?

No.

Insomnia?

No.

Then why the dark eyes? Why the yawns?

I'm a bad morning girl. Always have been.

Mercifully, this was true. A thing K never dreamed she'd use to her advantage. M.O.M. was curious as well, but, as was her style, she observed silently from across the Check-Up room, her arms folded across her chest, her thin frame in a formfitting white pant-suit, her dark glasses obscuring most of her face.

Did she know? Could she tell K went out at night? Could she tell K observed the second tower through super glasses, that K had read pages delivered through a glass wall in a dark tunnel she wasn't supposed to be in? Did she know those pages employed gibberish, code language perhaps, when they inexplicably called it *the boys' tower*?

Did she know?

Could she tell K had found it easier than expected to cross the Yard over there, to sneak in through the same garbage door she, B, and Q had used on their first journey from this tower? Could she tell K had been *inside* that tower and had smelled things and heard things and seen things no other Letter Girl had ever imagined? Could she tell K used the stairs in the boys' tower like she did in her own and that she took those stairs to the eighth floor, where a girl named J still existed, a girl that was not *her* J but a J all the same? Could M.O.M. tell that K was experiencing feelings she'd never felt before for this second J?

Did M.O.M. sense that K had entered this J's rooms and silently crossed her quarters until she'd snuck inside her bedroom and stood beside her bed and watched her sleep for many minutes at a time?

Could M.O.M. tell K liked drawing J? Liked the shape of her face? The look in her eye? The look on her face when she slept?

Did she know?

Could she tell?

M.O.M. hadn't given a sign that she knew a thing, and each Inspection had ended with a *clean*. K thought long on this in her rooms, long after the morning Inspections had passed. Time she once devoted to studying was now divvied up between Judith Nancy books and heavy thought, as K tried to make sense of the fact that, though she'd lied, and though she'd hidden so much, and though she'd been inside places she should never be, she was passing each and every Inspection like she always had.

What did a Letter Girl need to do to fail one?

Could one be failed?

With each *clean* conclusion, K smiled at M.O.M. on her way out of the Check-Up room, wondering if the woman had any idea that her Letter Girl could deliver a detailed drawing of the kitchen of the second tower in the pines.

And J's weren't the only rooms she'd seen.

The crazed woman K and B saw delivering the papers in the tunnel slept fitfully most nights and, despite the tossing and turning, was easy to draw. The black hair on her face, the strong shoulders, the sense of aggression, all brought K to draw her from farther away, employing the super glasses from across the room as she worked. The woman snored and snorted, whimpered and howled. K drew it all. Even the open mouth that sometimes cried the names A and Z in her sleep.

It was in this woman's living room that K found a bottle that smelled like the one Judith Nancy drank from. It was in this room, by way of many documents, that K determined that this woman was the M.O.M. of the second tower. And it was in this room that K opened a desk drawer and removed a thing called *The Burt Report,* dated *November 1, 2019.* And it was in the pages of that report that K found the thing she'd been missing, the missing link, enough of an explanation for the two things that had eluded her so far:

First, the girls in the second tower were not girls at all. They were *boys.* And while this seemed a simple deduction, given the name of the second Turret, it still confused K deeply. She understood that she'd been resisting a core reality to the situation she'd been studying.

A different species? She wasn't sure. Something they called *the opposite sex.*

The second thing was much more important and when K read it, the sleeping woman sat up in her bed. Shirtless, her short dark hair ruffled, she stared into the darkness of her doorway for a long time. K, flat to the wall behind the desk, did not move. Except her mind moved, processing what she'd just read.

The Parenthood had hidden the Letter Girls from the Alphabet

Boys. And vice versa. Intentionally. For purposes K hadn't quite uncovered . . .

Listening to the woman (man?), D.A.D., breathe hard following another bad dream, it was the first time K saw her own tower and the second as equals. One as badly treated as the other.

D.A.D. finally lay back in bed and K, still unmoving, held back tears of embarrassment, tears of rage, held back, too, the desire to rush screaming across the room, to attack the lying thing in its sleep.

Did M.O.M. know? Could she tell K had smelled *men* when Inspector Krantz brought her magnifying glass up to K's naked body?

As she slipped out of D.A.D.'s room, K was crying. Not for having been scared and not even for the brutal shock of this new information.

K cried because it was sad. What had been done to the girls. To the boys. To fifty-two minds that had no way of knowing better.

Article One of the Constitution of the Parenthood: Genius Is Distracted by the Opposite Sex

The Burt Report's mention of castration could only mean neutering the boys in the same way Professor Langan tasked the Letter Girls with neutering cells to stop them from multiplying.

Boys and girls.

Multiplying.

Reproduction.

K thought of the naked parts she'd seen through the windows. The parts of her own body, too.

She thought of the Living Trees in the Orchard and how not one Letter Girl had ever seen one in person.

She thought of lies.

As she snuck out the garbage door, as she hurried across the Yard to the miles of pines that separated the boys' tower from her own, K could not stop crying, believing she understood what had been done to her, to the Letter Girls, to the Alphabet Boys, to them all. And while it was impossible for her to say she understood it, she believed she understood enough.

Halfway home, she again imagined herself rushing across the rooms of the man they called Richard. D.A.D. She saw herself striking him. Stabbing him with a knife from the kitchen. Castrating him like the Burt Report suggested he do to his boys.

She imagined blood on her hands. Blood on her clothes. Blood on her boots.

She did not run through the pines toward home. Rather, she walked slowly, her head in her hands, her hands wet, leaving a trail of tears as obvious as the breadcrumbs in Judith Nancy's *This Way to Home*. She imagined breadcrumbs of blood. Blood of the man they called Richard. She thought of the Letter Girls. She thought of the Alphabet Boys.

She thought of the responsibility she now had.

And she thought, too, of the feelings she had for J. Of the way he made her feel. The things he liked. His worries. His laugh. His voice. His eyes.

She paused in the pines, infused suddenly with what could only be called inspiration.

And she wondered, aloud, what kind of cruel people could consider such feelings a distraction.

Marilyn and Richard

*I*t can't be a prison, Richard said. He'd been adamant about this point from the start. When the conversations changed from flippant talk to serious planning. They'd both been overwhelmed throughout the process. Inspired, too. Oh, so inspired.

Surveillance does not a prison make, Marilyn countered. They'd had this argument before. Had many.

They ate sandwiches in Glasgow's, a restaurant downtown, a place where they often met at the end of another distracted day. They ate well, tipped well, and were often seated without a wait. Marilyn was particularly refined, and Max Lowe, Glasgow's young owner, wanted her there as often as possible. This meant he also wanted her seen just as often. Richard and Marilyn were seated at a table for two in the center of the dark dining room. Always.

The acoustics, garbled and dim as the lanterns, allowed them privacy despite center stage.

If we do our job, Richard said, *they won't want to search the woods.*

The woods was a vague idea then. Two towers in . . . *the woods.*

While I agree, Marilyn said, *there may come a day when practicality outweighs philosophy.*

The idea is to prove that an undistracted mind will focus on its own. If we force that focus, via cameras and babysitters . . . what are we proving?

Richard sucked down a third of his sandwich. Drank some scotch.

Nothing. You're right.

Marilyn's eyes were partially obscured by her large-framed glasses. The lower half of Richard's face by his beard. The two had changed much in the fifteen years they'd been married.

Ex-cons, she said. This had all been discussed before.

Yes.

And we buy the babies.

Richard didn't look over his shoulders. Didn't look to the greater part of the restaurant. Who would believe it if they heard it?

Yes.

A dozen or so each.

Maybe more.

Why more?

How many chances are we going to have to attempt an experiment like this one?

One.

So maybe more.

Marilyn sipped red wine, leaned back in her chair. The waiter came quickly from the restaurant shadows, a towel over one arm.

Would you two like another round?

The answer to that, Richard said, *is always yes.*

Alone again, Marilyn said, *I've found the towers.*

Richard perked up. *Where?*

She made the shape of the state with her hand. *Here.*

A school? A hospital?

Neither. She pulled her purse from her chair back onto her lap. From it she removed a photograph. She handed it to him across the table.

Richard was expecting an aerial shot, and that's what he got. Two squares embedded deep in tall pines. The scale told him there wasn't another building for twenty-six miles north or south, twenty east. Lake Michigan was thirty west.

Forestry, Marilyn said. *A failed experiment of its own.*

Who owns it, then? The state?

Marilyn nodded.

No, Richard said. *We can't involve the state. Can't let them know we're there.*

Nobody's going to question what we're doing . . . as we'll buy it from the people who might question us in the first place.

Marilyn turned and smiled at a couple seated in a booth. Richard recognized the man who smiled back as Senator Evans.

Marilyn.

He thinks we're looking to buy land for a hunting camp. We're first in line for the sale.

Richard studied the photo. *It's gorgeous,* he said.

It's perfect.

The waiter brought their drinks. Set them down. Richard reached for his quick. He raised it.

Cheers, he said. *To ex-cons and babies.*

And to Inspections, Marilyn said.

Inspections? I'm intrigued.

To make sure our little ones haven't crossed paths.

And if they do?

Marilyn shrugged. *Then we do what all parents and teachers do. We ground them. We send them to the corner.*

The Corner

A month.
No return.
No pines.

No further information about the boys' tower. Or her own.

A month.

To think. To consider. To weigh. To grow agitated, to grow nervous. To feel free. To feel trapped. For knowing what she now knew. Some days the tower walls felt thicker. As if the actual space of her rooms was shrinking.

A month.

To playact. To attend class and to study. To endure what she now believed were phony Inspections. Phony because everything the Parenthood did was phony. Lies. Misinformation. Judith Nancy called it that. Remember that? When K and B sat across the author's desk in her basement office? As the writer sucked on a bottle and sank deeper and deeper into her chair? That wasn't a fond memory anymore. K was able to retroactively make sense of a lot that Nancy said. Once a broken reality. Rewritten in the right way. The memory of Nancy was as monstrous to K as the bearded man they called D.A.D.

A month.

To swim in the tower pool, to play Boats with her sisters, to avoid extended eye contact with B. No matter what subject they pretended to talk about, both knew what they were really talking about. Always. And the longer they looked one another in the eye, the longer that quasi-buried, that not-so-hidden truth looked back at them both.

A month.

Of being alone. Whether she was physically with her sisters or not, in the Check-Up room or the cafeteria, K was absolutely alone. Q kept to herself. B tried. K tried, too. At moments, it felt like the Parenthood hadn't changed at all. Inspections in the morning, mealtime to follow, the occasional speech by M.O.M. Class. Study. Winter in the Yard. The Orchard. At times it felt like K could turn her back on the whole thing, everything she'd unearthed. Like she could one day smile for real, talk for real, swim without thinking of what J was doing in his tower and how he *needed* to know he'd been lied to. So that he could tell the Alphabet Boys. So that everybody knew. So that the Parenthood knew that everybody knew. Sometimes it felt close, the ability to reestablish this false narrative. Sometimes she even stopped thinking of J.

But something nagged. A big something. A place she hadn't seen yet. The one room she hadn't entered in either tower.

The Letter Girls had been raised to fear the Corner like no other place in their world.

She wanted to see it.

A month.

To get up the nerve. To plan. To lose the nerve. To find it again. K had read the word *deprogramming* in a Nancy book in which the main character, Ursula Ochs, told her sister that she needed to *deprogram* herself out of so much self-loathing. The word, the phrase, had stuck with K.

The Corner. That was the big one. The image K held in her mind, the door itself, seemed to come to her at terrible times. While laughing with her sisters. While waiting in line for breakfast. While bundling up to head out to the Yard. And always as she took the stairs down to the first floor. Every time.

Sometimes K worried that her feet were going to keep going no matter what she told them to do. That she was going to step out onto the first floor and walk directly to that staff bathroom, to that false stall, to the basement below.

A month.

The Effigy Meet came and went. K thought a lot about her inadvertent spotting of the second tower. The day she rode B's ice slide around the Turret to the snowy Yard below. In that year she'd also gone from unknowing to knowing and she believed the latter could be seen in every mirror she passed. She tried to give her all to the Effigy Meet. To play the part of a Letter Girl doing good. But she just wasn't doing good.

K wanted to go to the Corner.

Taped to the bottom of her Boats board were drawings, veritable blueprints of both towers and all they had inside. She'd been everywhere, seen it all, taken photos with her memory and mind.

The Corner.

Could she do it?

She felt like she had to do it. Had to know.

A few days following the Effigy Meet, the afternoon following an Inspection in which M.O.M. asked after the poor quality *(lacking vision, dear)* of her sculpture, K decided the walls of the Parenthood had gotten too thick, too tight. The space she'd enjoyed for so many years wasn't close to big enough anymore. It had become harder to breathe, juggling her anxiety, her bravery, and her desire to tell her sisters the truth.

They lied to us.

About what?

About everything.

But K understood clearly that before she could reveal to her sisters what the Parenthood had taken lunatic pains to withhold, she had to know what the punishment for knowing the truth might be.

Spoiled. Spoiled rotten.

K had no illusions. If ever a Letter Girl was spoiled rotten, it was her.

The Corner. It had to be. That night. Which meant she had to endure her classes, dinner, study time, Yellow Ball with her sisters, a regular day in the Turret.

All while silently planning what she'd bring with her to the Corner.

The unfathomability of her *desiring* to go to that room of all rooms was not lost on her at all. Oh, how things had changed.

Was the Corner cold? She'd bring her winter coat. Was it dark? A flashlight. Would she die upon entering the room? Would she turn to ice, turn to ash, turn to stone?

She played poorly in her one game of Yellow Ball. Though she tried. Tried to look as though she was engaged. Hid from her sisters the fact that tonight she was going to the Corner.

Voluntarily.

And when night fell upon the tower, as the cold outside gripped the sculptures in the Yard, as one by one the Letter Girls fell asleep, K sat on the edge of her mattress in the dark of her bedroom, trying hard to resist the fear of that door in the basement. The painted letters rose so high in her mind that she could hardly imagine herself capable of turning the knob, pushing open the wood.

Entering.

She already wore a backpack full of her drawings. Drawings of the Letter Girls, the second tower, everything. Not because she feared the drawings would be found while she was gone, but because if she were to be caught, if she were to be declared *unclean,* she wanted her life's work with her.

The backpack straps were comfortable on her shoulders. She hardly felt the light weight of the pages within. But she saw the drawings, her world, as if the pages were all suspended before her eyes.

The Parenthood mapped out. Detailed.

Revealed.

"Okay," she said. "Remember when B said you can't be brave unless you're afraid of the thing you're facing?" She closed her eyes, breathed deep, opened them again. "Go be brave."

But by the time she was in the staff bathroom, it was as if she were lucid dreaming, willingly traveling through a nightmare. Her mind told her feet, *Yes yes, advance, this is how we, yes yes, go.* She knew she had to be aware of the things she always had to be aware of when she snuck out of her room. But this night was different. This night K was piqued to a level she couldn't have fathomed prior to discovering the second tower in the pines, and even then, *even then,* she did not experience the depth of fear she felt now, opening the basement door in the false stall and closing it behind her.

She didn't have to do this. She didn't have to take the stairs down to the basement and willingly seek out the Corner. But that's what her brain told her feet to do. And so they listened, as K's eyes and ears floated above her body, seemingly disconnected, and mantras were the only thing to glue her sanity to her self.

This is right.

This is righteous.

This has to happen now.

B and Q were sleeping in their rooms high above her. Did either of them dream of the Corner? Did any Letter Girl dream of the rotting wooden door . . . the purple letters . . . the letters they'd all believed were written in blood? J's blood? And if one of her sisters did dream, did they see K walking the cobblestoned hall, her legs like the noodles in the cafeteria soup? Could a dreaming sister see the fear emanating off twelve-year-old K as she rounded one hall, then another, her hands involuntarily reaching behind her as if she were trying to grasp on to the way back?

The lanterns did not flicker. The hum of the boiler did not rise and fall. Nothing moved in the shadows, and no doorknobs turned.

No footsteps could be heard, and K wondered if the beating of her heart had done something to her head, had made it so she was incapable of experiencing anything but fear.

Her brain told her feet to move.

So they moved.

They moved again.

And they moved again.

Until K was standing a hall's length from what must be the door to the Corner.

The purple letters were difficult to read, but she could see enough of them to know this was it. She had arrived.

Walk one hall. Twist one knob. Enter one room.

That's all she had left to do.

She turned around. Then she turned around again so that she was facing it once more. She half-expected to find it partially open, as if whatever beast waited within had smelled her coming.

But the Corner door was closed. And when K's brain told her feet to move, this time they did not.

She stayed in place but she did not remain still. Her knees shook, and for this her legs felt useless.

She didn't have to do this. Not at all. She knew enough about the Parenthood and the second tower. She could turn right around, go back up, tell her sisters everything. She could put on her winter clothes and brave the freezing cold outside, hurry to the boys' tower, wake up J, wake them all up, gather them together, tell them what she knew, tell them their entire lives were lies. With twenty-five girls and twenty-four boys, surely they could protect themselves, *defend* themselves, from . . . from . . .

K shook her head. Had it come to this? Was she now imagining the Letter Girls waging war with the Parenthood?

She turned and left the hall, flattened her back, and the backpack of drawings, to the stones of a new one. The Corner door was out of sight and K tried to pull herself together. This was too much. All of it. She should plan it out, whatever *it* was. She should go back to her room and sleep. Tomorrow she could find Q and B and talk to them and really figure out what they thought the next move should be. It was simply too big a task: pulling aside the veil alone, unearthing reality for all her sisters, all those boys in the pines, too.

Too much!

K slipped down the wall until she was sitting, then lying, on the floor. She cried.

And though she had many reasons to cry, she only cried now for how daunting the job really was. Why her? Why was she down in the basement when she should be resting, should be preparing what she'd say to her sisters? Why was she digging deeper when she'd already found so much buried in the dirt?

K cried for what felt like too long a time. Then she got up and, heart hammering, looked back the way she'd come. Wouldn't be hard. Had to be a lot easier to walk back down that hall, turn, turn, take the stairs, leave, leave. Had to be a lot easier on her mind, her feet, her heart. How long would it take? Minutes. That's all. Then in bed. Then juggling a manageable amount of anxiety. Not manageable. But still. This. This was blind panic. This was scarlet mad. This was—

K rounded the hall and ran. Ran for the Corner door.

She wanted to scream, to let it out, to shout at the door, to tell it she was going to open it, she was going in.

Instead, her lips pulled back as though taped to her ears, the whites of her eyes bright as the lanterns, K rushed in silence, even her boots making no sound, so little time spent touching the dirt floor.

When she reached the door, she used both hands to stop her forward momentum but slid into it, palms out, hands against the splintered wood, the faintly painted letters, the exact description of the Corner door she and her sisters had grown up with, had been raised to fear.

LIES!

The word shot through her head from a cannon, lighting up her mind's sky with terrible colors as the door gave way under the power of her little hands and swung to, inward, the mouth of a sleeping man with a beard opening to release a nightmarish scream as he tossed and turned in his bed.

K stopped herself at the threshold, heard the long groaning creak of the hinges, as the door did not swing back, did not return to smack her in the hands, the face, the spirit. It took her eyes a moment to adjust to the darkness, and from her pack she removed a flashlight, cutting the darkness down.

K saw something, didn't know what it was, opened her mouth to scream.

But the face she saw before her was made up entirely of rolls of toilet paper on four shelves against the wall.

She shone the light on the door, on the letters. She read:

DON'T FORGET TO RESTOCK TP ALWAYS

Not the Corner. Not the Corner at all.

She grunted a sound she didn't know she had it in her to make. The sound of defeat and relief sharing space. Confusion, too, and the distant suspicion that she had been fooled. She'd seen the words on the door from down the hall. She'd *seen* them!

Lies.

Stepping out of the supply closet, K closed the door and turned to face a new hall. She took it. Took another. Took another. The tip of a pen trying to solve a maze. A small marble rolling along the tracks of B's inventive labyrinth, built for shop class, the fascination of every Letter Girl two springs past.

K kept silent and close to the walls. She traced the mortar between cobblestones with a fingertip, as if touching the solid surface would keep her grounded, keep her from turning to dust, to dirt, to be walked upon by the Parenthood staff come morning.

Then, having passed Judith Nancy's office and the Glasgow

Tunnel, numerous supply closets, the printing press, a room for sewing, and a room of old textbooks, she gave up.

She walked slower now, partly unafraid of getting caught. She was only a girl, after all, curious about the basement of the building she lived in. The underbelly of her world. And anyway, it wasn't like she'd found the Corner or was inside the Corner or had to explain herself at all to anybody who might find her standing outside—

"The Corner," she said out loud.

She was pointing at the door that made her say it.

At the end of an otherwise door-less hall, the sight of solid steel had caught her eye. Not because it was unmarked, though it was. And not because she felt something cold emanated from where it stood, though she did. If it was a door, it was the strangest door she'd ever seen, forming a solid right angle where two cobblestoned walls met, creating a tall metal—

"Corner," she said again.

There was no knob.

K went to it this time without preamble. She put her shoulder against the right side and pushed. Both steel partitions moved; the one she'd pushed went in as the other came out, the corner of a hallway rotating, a revolving door like the one she'd read about in Judith Nancy's *Us Heroes*.

K shone her light into the darkness. Concrete. Shelves. A drain.

She entered and the Corner door closed softly behind her.

If she was scared before, as she raced toward the supply closet so many hallways ago, she was positively changed now. Colder inside than out, K studied the concrete room. She heard a distant dripping and shone the light on the drain. Along one wall was a wood bench and along the other were shelves, upon which rested metal objects K had never seen before, never studied, never known.

She picked one up. It was clear which part was the handle, but K couldn't be sure exactly what it did.

Ahead, an archway, indistinct, with flaking paint framing the passage, seemed to ask her to *come on, come in.* K set down the metal tool and entered a much larger room, where the walls were bare, the ceiling stone, and the floor, all of it, dirt.

A single marker in the far left corner and a single letter upon that marker caused her to speak, to say, *No,* to almost drop the flashlight to the floor.

J

She approached the marker, slow but shaking. She knelt in the dirt and touched the single letter, the name of her lost sister.

J in the Corner. This was the Corner. This was J.

Nothing in the dirt told her how wide the grave was, what space J took up, where exactly she was buried. K shone the light around the room, realizing for the first time how low the ceiling was, how cold the smell.

She cried and her tears landed in the dirt, making mud around the base of the simple wooden marker, no more than the size of a ruler.

J

Her end. Here. In the Corner.

Why? What had she done? What had she seen? What had the Parenthood discovered? Where had they caught her? In the pines? At the second tower?

Spoiled rotten.

Because she'd been taught to fear Vees her entire life, because she'd been raised to believe in Rotts, K covered her mouth with the neck of her black turtleneck.

But she knew better. She'd read the Burt Report. The papers in D.A.D.'s desk.

There was no Rotts. There was no Vees.

There was only the separation of the girls and the boys. And to learn of each other's existence was to become spoiled.

Spoiled rotten.

K jammed her fingers, then her full hands, into the dirt. She dug, crying, her mouth forming a rectangle of anger, the face of rage. She pulled the dirt aside, thinking of the scene in Judith Nancy's *Us Heroes* when Charlotte had to bury her sister after she'd died of Rotts.

"Die, Judith Nancy," K said, hardly able to see her own hands through the wet wall of tears.

She dug and she dug until her elbows were level with the floor. She had a vision of Inspector Krantz examining those nails through a magnifying glass.

UNCLEAN

She didn't care. She dug. She dug. She spoke gibberish, a train of words that, to her, made all the sense in the world. And the words were the only thing connecting her to her new reality, sanity, keeping her from flying away, from burying herself, too, here by J's meek marker.

The Parenthood killed J.

M.O.M. ordered a Letter Girl dead.

She thought of the tool on the shelf in the other room and she understood it was a weapon.

K understood a lot. J was not spoiled. None of them were. None of them *could* be.

She brought her hands up and pounded down into the dirt, striking not a box like Charlotte used in Nancy's story but a soft layer of clothing over something much harder than clothing. K pulled her hands quick out of the grave. She sat up straight. She shone the flashlight into the hole she'd made.

The hole the Parenthood made.

A once-black shirt? Hard to tell. It felt like one. Felt like the very one she was wearing.

K dug more, single-handed, lighting her way with the other, brushing the dirt away so fast that her fingers were a blur and the face (*face*) that emerged did so as if in a series of drawings, as if K had drawn J many times this way, over and over, a little less dirt upon her with each page.

She did not shriek when the sunken small head was fully revealed. The near-naked skull wrapped only in sandpaper flesh, the small teeth bared, the eyes but two smears of off-white in the large bone sockets.

K got up. She shone the light upon her dead sister's face and she thought of how stupid she'd been, how stupid all the Letter Girls had been, to believe anything the Parenthood ever told them.

"I'm sorry, J," K said. Sorry that she'd uncovered the truth too late.

Not only was the Corner not scary to her then, it was less than suitable: a drab, low-ceilinged, undecorated grave for a girl who didn't belong here.

For a horrid moment, K wondered if it were possible to carry J out of here, in her backpack, up through the Turret, out to the Yard, to be buried in a place that received sunlight.

In the end, she covered J up again. Then she was out of the dirt room, past the shelf with the weapon she would not look at, and out the Corner door.

She moved fast through the halls, her spirit trembling with the horror she had seen in the dirt.

K ran a hand across her own face, not thinking about what the dirt might reveal upstairs, only needing to touch something alive, living, a breathing Letter Girl who might avenge her sister.

Past the supply closet she'd mistaken for the Corner. Past the entrance to the Glasgow Tunnel. At Judith Nancy's door she spit. She did not stop as she vomited on the floor, the wall, her shirt. She only nodded, thinking, yes yes, she could do this, yes yes, she could appear to be normal, yes yes, she could hide this from Krantz from Rivers from the Parenthood from M.O.M. for as long as it took to put together a plan.

Couldn't she?

She reached the door to the stairs much faster than she had planned, and it scared her. Everything was moving too fast. Had she missed something? Had she missed the white vomit on her black shirt, the dirt under her nails, the tears in her eyes, the horror so obviously evident in her mind?

No, she'd accounted for it all and done nothing to remove it.

She opened the door and climbed quickly, pausing in the false stall because she heard voices out in the hall. So many voices. Too many voices. As if she'd spent the night in the basement. As if she'd lost track of all time as she knelt by her sister's grave, as she dug up the body of a dead Letter Girl.

She shook her head no. No no. It was still night. Not yet morning. She hadn't missed an Inspection, no no. Couldn't be.

But the voices, the voices in the hall, all her sisters in the hall, the staff . . . M.O.M.?

They're looking for you, she thought. *And the last place they expect you to be is here, HERE, in the stall to the basement. Because nobody expects you to be spoiled, K. Nobody would ever think that you, of all girls, could ever be SPOILED ROTTEN.*

No Nancy book had ever described madness the way K felt it now. She'd never been taught anything like this from Hjortsberg.

So, trembling, shaking her head, *yes, you're fine, you look fine, nobody will know, nobody will tell the difference, they know you, they love you, nobody suspects,* K left the stall and, sick to her stomach, exited the staff bathroom.

The voices were coming from down by the Body Hall.

K followed them, wanting so badly to fit in. Wanting so badly to slip right into the crowd of Letter Girls as if she'd never set out through the pines, as if she'd never questioned the reality that had, for so long, kept her warm.

And she did join her sisters. Wild-eyed and impossibly on edge, she was swallowed by the crowd of them, gathered by the entrance to the Body Hall. Some of the girls were crying, and the staff (in their pajamas, all of them, still night) consoled them. Crazily, K thought they must be crying for J.

V was the first to see her, the first to wipe tears from her eyes as her face contorted from concerned to confused.

"K?" she asked, her voice buried (*J's buried, too*) beneath the clamor of the others, chaos in the hall. "Are you okay?"

K nodded and smiled, but her smile did not work and the face she made hurt her. V's eyebrows came together. She was asking her something, something else, but K was moving past her, having heard the reason for the commotion, having heard enough scattered words to piece the moment together, to understand why everyone was awake, why everyone was so scared and crying.

"B is being sent to the Corner."

Who said that?

"B *might* be sent to the Corner. M.O.M. is deciding."

Who said that? B to the Corner? Everyone was asking why. Why oh why?

"She told M.O.M. she saw something she shouldn't have in the pines."

The other words didn't matter. K heard them all as if she'd drawn each one, one upon the other, until the color on the paper was black.

"Rotts."

"Vees."

"Placasores."

Confessed, confessed, confessed . . .

"B may be sent to the Corner! We'll know soon."

"M.O.M. is deciding."

"Tomorrow."

"The next day."

"Soon."

K tried to speak, but nothing, no part of her, worked. She only shook, a trembling centerpiece to the circle of Letter Girls in the hall.

Then K made to run for M.O.M.'s office. She needed to speak to the staff. She needed to tell them B did nothing wrong. She needed to do something *now*.

But a last vestige of rationality, sanity's fingertips, turned her around.

You'll be sent, too. Don't do it alone. You need an army. YOU'LL BE SENT, TOO.

Before she could decide to do it, K was walking through the Body Hall unnoticed, through the kitchen doors and out the garbage door to the Yard. She was not dressed for this. She was not in the right state of mind for this.

But the name J spurred her on. The name J and the second tower, where twenty-four more twelve-year-olds kept in the dark might help, might be able to do something.

Might make an army.

Eye Contact

Rushing through the pines, the backpack tight to her body, K knocked a shoulder against a tree. Then another. She fell once. She fell again. And with each strike, with each fall, she cried out, then reached for the sound of her own agonized voice, as if she might silence it, silence the agony within her.

She thought of B, she tried not to think of B. She moved, she went, she ran.

She had a hard time believing her own thoughts. Couldn't trust them. Couldn't believe her life had come to this moment, that all her drawings and studies, her laughter and worries, all the times M.O.M. and the Parenthood had picked her up when she felt scared or sad, all of it had led to her running toward a second tower, hoping for help there, needing it.

K came to a sliding halt at the boys' Yard's icy edge. The lights were off in their tower. Twenty-four ice sculptures stood between herself and the back door. Snow fell in fat flakes. Her black clothes were dotted with it. Her face and hands were as red as the gloves and jacket she'd seen on the desk of the man they called D.A.D. J's room (his new room, third floor now, K knew this) looked particularly dark. As if he'd moved out or been buried in a room in the basement.

Ahead, the big Inspector she'd first seen appeared in the hall. He spent some time looking through the glass, more time than K was used to.

Had they heard about B? Of course they had.

M.O.M. told D.A.D.

It was all so close to being impossible to believe. Yet K had seen enough tonight alone to alter her understanding of the world. Her world. Any world. And while something like madness lurked inside her young mind, she ultimately resisted it. Instinctually she understood that there had to be a way out, a solution to what was happening around her. Perhaps that was the great mistake the Parenthood had made, she thought. Teaching the Letter Girls that there was a solution, a way out of everything.

Even the Parenthood.

The Inspector took two steps, wiped frost from the window, put his nose to it.

A second Inspector appeared at the far end of the hall. He, too, looked through the glass.

K looked to the upper windows. No lights. Did the boys know?

No longer in motion, she got colder. Started to feel like a part of the Effigy Meet herself.

Back on the first floor, neither man made to move. A first-floor window lit up. D.A.D.? Another Inspector?

K imagined the Corner in the basement of this tower. She imagined two rulers stuck in the dirt. One marked A. The other Z.

She suddenly wished she hadn't come. The boys' tower was crawling with staff. Her own tower was in chaos at the news of B's confession. Wouldn't M.O.M. give an emergency speech? Wouldn't the staff count the Letter Girls? Wouldn't they know she was missing back home while she was useless to her sisters all the way over here?

K fell to her knees in the snow. She shook her head no. It was too much. Too loud. Too big.

When she looked up, a third Inspector was crossing the glass hall. All of them so much larger than Krantz back home. All of them with some variety of hair on their faces. All of them staring through the glass. Studying the Yard. On guard.

K sank deeper into the shadows of the pines and eyed the sculptures in the Yard.

A room, a cart beyond it, a statue of D.A.D. himself.

She looked to the hall. Yes, infested with Inspectors. Back to the Yard.

A large book. The name LUXLEY in big blocks of ice. A chair.

K silently cried for the life she'd led before accidentally spotting the spire in the pines. Back when her greatest concern was getting details on paper. Drawing in the Yard. Drawing in her bedroom. Her bedroom, where the walls were covered in portraits of her sisters. Where even J once hung, until M.O.M. asked that she take the drawing down, *too sad*, she'd said, as if J might grow younger there, as the other Letter Girls grew up around her, as if J was stuck in

(dirt)

ice.

K saw J as she was now. Imagined herself drawing the translucent skin that barely covered the bones of her face. She could easily recall the exact dimensions of the dirt that framed her face and neck, as her body seemed to melt into the ground, like when a candle burned to its finale, the wick jutting out of the wax. She shuddered at the thought of J's chest. Her feet, her hands, her fingers. With this last thought, she recalled Q's joke about the spire being one long finger sticking up from a grave in the pines.

K made to fight back tears but in the end didn't need to. A harsh wind crossed the Yard, and beyond the frozen cart that would no doubt provide cover, the rungs of a ladder were revealed.

One of the Alphabet Boys had built a ladder.

K eyed the glass hall. Three Inspectors still. All staring out.

She thought of the pages in her backpack. The details. The Parenthood revealed.

She broke for the room made of ice, slipped through the small doorway on her belly, crouched inside. She was breathing hard and her bones felt cold. The turtleneck and slacks weren't close to enough in this weather. Would it kill her?

Across the room was a second small opening. She knelt by it. Looked to the cart.

Crawling to the cart was hard. More space than she'd accounted for. Was she casting a shadow? She paused, out in the open, on her stomach in the frozen Yard. Her shadow was tight to her body. No, they couldn't see it. But did they sense her? People did that. The Letter Girls did that. K had done it her whole life. The feeling of someone at the door. Turn to the door. There's B.

B

K made it to the cart and sat with her back to the big wheel. She stretched her fingers out, moved them, tried to find more feeling in them.

The ladder was off to the side of the cart. How far? The Inspectors would be able to see her if she went for it. Could they see the ladder? She didn't think so. She looked.

What she saw was enough to freeze her already chilled bones. Six adult men in the glass hall. Three Inspectors. Three in different dress. Clothes she hadn't seen before. She hid quick behind the cart again. What to do? Go home? Yes, she should go home.

K breathed deep the winter air. She looked again.

They still faced the glass. The Inspectors. The others were talking. One of them wrote things down on a pad. K imagined the warmth of that hall. She imagined the warmth, too, of being buried under so much dirt in a basement.

Above her, jutting from the body of the cart, she saw the fringed end of a blanket. Upon it, more ice.

K rose carefully, sure to keep her head down. So scared. She heard alarms that hadn't gone off. Saw large men running from the boys' tower door, men that weren't there.

In the cart . . . ice apples. Upon a blanket. Removable.

K reached for the cluster of apples, all stuck together. Would the men see her taking the apples? Could they? They squinted through the glass the way people do when they can't see the whole picture. Was the cluster of apples part of the whole picture?

Was it?

K's fingers and palms nearly froze as she slid the apples from the blanket down along the side of the cart beside her. It was big enough. Yes. Tall enough. Yes. And there were spaces to hold on to, places to grip.

Crouching, using the cluster like a shield, holding it in front of her, K inched out from the side of the cart. She waited. The wind howled against the apples and against her body on this side of them, too. She inched another step. Another.

No alarms. No sudden muffled voices. She wouldn't peek around the ice, wouldn't look to see if they'd spotted her. Instead, she advanced. Advanced again. Some more.

More.

By the time she reached the ladder, she knew she was out of their range of sight. She couldn't see them anymore. She wrapped the ends of her black sleeves around her hands and dug her hands under the ladder. She could do it. She could move it.

She moved it.

Lifting the thing above her head, she was easily able to place it against the third-floor window. J's new quarters.

With images of a sister decayed, another sister in the hands of the Parenthood, K planted a foot on the bottom rung and almost screamed when it snapped in half.

The other rungs didn't look any stronger, but K had no choice. She lifted her leg high to reach the second one. She pulled herself up onto it.

It held. Good enough. From there she moved fast, up the rungs, past a dark second-floor window (M's room, she knew), until she reached the height of the ladder, reached the third-floor window.

Through the glass she saw a light come on. A bathroom light? Was J awake?

She knocked on the glass.

She waited.

She knocked on the glass.

J entered the living room, shirtless, pajama pants, messy hair. He looked warm. So warm.

He saw her.

He hid.

The eye contact they made was the first contact K had made with any boy or man in the second tower. The thrill of it briefly superseded the horrors of the moment. The horrors back home. The urgency. Despite the overwhelming fear, K grasped the power of the moment.

Contact.

J still hid in the hall.

She spoke to him. As the harsh wind tore at her face and hands, as even the parts of her body that were covered felt dangerously, threateningly cold, she told J she needed to be let in. She needed his help.

At a grueling pace, J emerged from the hall, ducked back into it, then finally approached the window.

Frozen tears on her face, knowing that numbers were needed, she asked for help. The Letter Girls needed the Alphabet Boys. And the boys needed to know.

What happened was what she thought would happen. What she *needed* to happen. Rather than running to tell D.A.D. there was something monstrous at his window, rather than pulling the drapes closed, J acted, in the end, in the moment, how K believed he would.

Oh, K knew there had been such a slim margin for error. But didn't everything exist now in a slim margin? And wasn't the space between information and misinformation only wide enough to fit one who knew the difference?

J opened the window. J let her in.

Frozen Truth

Snow and icy wind poured into his room, and with it, the thing at his window. First a black boot, then a black pant leg. Whatever it was, it wore clothes.

J thought of the Luxley book *It Came from the Land of Snow.* How could he not? In the book, a creature rose from the Yard, six arms and six legs. Just stood up as if J had carved it himself. Ran around the snow howling, clawing at the bricks of the Turret. Some of the Alphabet Boys couldn't finish reading it. Some, like L, had nightmares.

"My hands," the thing said. And its voice was different than J's own.

It waved a hand and J understood it was telling him that it couldn't use it. Too cold. He reached out and touched it. Touched the hand of the thing crawling through his window into his room.

A second pant leg. A black turtleneck. Just like his own.

"Help me shove the ladder," it said.

J stared at it dumbly. Fixed with fear.

"If the Inspectors on the first floor see the ladder, they'll know someone came to your window. Help me shove it back down. I can barely move my fingers."

Its face was red from the wind and cold. Its long hair wet with snow. It carried a backpack.

What was inside it?

"Now!" it said. The voice much higher than his own. Like when he was younger. Before he started questioning the Parenthood.

Side by side with it, J gripped the top of the ladder and they shoved it from his window together. They watched it thud to the white ground below. The thing placed a freezing hand over J's mouth. They watched the Yard together, eyes wide.

"Okay," it finally said. "Close the window."

As J did what it said, he thought again of the words from Warren Bratt's incredible book. *Her. She.*

Woman.

He had no way of knowing what the character's voice sounded like, the long-haired character on the stool who Robert wanted so badly to confess to.

"Who—" J began. But the thing from outside cut him off.

"My name is K," it said. "I'm a Letter Girl."

J made to speak again but couldn't.

"I'm a girl," it repeated. "You're a boy. The Parenthood has been lying to us."

The Parenthood has been lying to us. Even then, despite all recent events, J felt a rush of anger. Had he ever heard someone say those words before? Had anybody ever said them? Yet here this impossible person was verifying what he'd been suspicious of.

J thought, *This is what Warren Bratt was trying to tell you.*

"We live in a second tower. Three miles through the pines. There are twenty-five of us. We lost J. Our J. To the Corner. And tonight B confessed that she'd seen your tower. I don't think she said I was with her. But this isn't good. I saw inside the Corner. I saw J's grave."

J's grave. The Corner.

"Hey," J finally said, stepping away from her. "I don't know why you're saying all this, but you're scaring me."

Tears welled in K's eyes. Her face scrunched as she tried to stop them from coming.

"I'm sorry," she said. "I get it. But I didn't know where else to go. M.O.M. might send B to the Corner, too." Then, "We have to act now. Tomorrow."

"M.O.M.," J echoed. He felt like he was going to faint. K stepped to him, placed her cold hands on his shoulders. He wanted to shrink from her, but he didn't.

"You're going to feel betrayed, lost, confused," she said. "Feel it all. I've been watching you for a year."

Now J did step from her. He looked out the window. "You've been hiding behind Mister Tree. I saw you!"

K looked out the window.

"Mister Tree?"

J pointed. "That one. Where the Orchard begins!"

K shook her head. "No. I've never hidden behind that tree. I mean it. You saw someone there?" She didn't wait for an answer. "We need to tell the rest of the boys and the rest of the girls what we know."

"I don't know what I know!"

K grabbed his arm. "*The Parenthood has been lying to us.* You must believe this. Now. We don't have time for me to convince you."

J understood that, whatever she was, she was not threatening.

"I read those words," J said. "*She* and *her*. In a book."

Now K looked confused.

"Where? What book?"

"A book by a man named Warren Bratt. The Parenthood took them from us."

K considered this. "That's your leisure writer? Warren Bratt?"

"No. Lawrence Luxley. I don't know who Warren Bratt is. None of us do. But we woke up to a book in our rooms. It described . . . Are you a woman?"

"No. Yes. Not yet."

"I still don't—"

"And you won't. Neither will I. We learned that in psychology. That it takes a long time for certain things, new things, to sink in. Things that you didn't think were true but are. But who knows . . . maybe that was all a lie, too."

J sat on the couch. He couldn't stand anymore. K took off her backpack. Set it on the carpet.

"*You* have to go," he said. "They'll send me to the Corner if they find you. They'll send us both. We'll get Vees, Placasores, Moldus . . ."

"Lies," K said. "We won't. I've been in your rooms many times. I've been in many rooms in your tower."

J got up again. "You've been in *here* before?"

"Yes."

"That's not . . . right!"

"I watched you sleep. I went through your things, all the Alphabet Boys' things. That's why I'm here. That's why I knocked on your window."

"What do you mean?"

"Because I like the way you think. You think like me."

J tilted his head, stunned momentarily silent. "Me?"

"Yeah. You."

K went to him, knelt before him on the couch. "We have to tell everyone."

"Why?"

"If everyone knows . . . then everyone's spoiled rotten. They can't send us all to the Corner . . . can they?"

J got up. Moved farther away from her. "I don't want that for me. For any of the Alphabet Boys!"

"You think I do? But what are you going to do . . . now that you know what you know? Now that you read that book . . . now that you met me?"

J made to speak, but nothing he thought to say made sense. "Why did they hide us from each other?" he finally asked.

K went to him. "From what I read . . . it's because we distract one another."

"What does that mean?"

"When you should be studying . . . you'd be thinking of me instead."

J hadn't expected this answer. "Is that true?"

"Ever wonder how you came into being?"

"No," J said. "We come from the Orchard. The Living Trees."

"Ever seen one? Ever seen a new boy growing on a Living Tree?"

"No."

K nodded. She didn't hesitate when she took off her boots. Undid her pants. Took them off.

J could tell she'd planned this. But it was no less shocking for that.

"What are you doing?"

"Look," K said. "*Look.*"

J looked. He couldn't not. And what he saw scared him.

"Did they do this to you?"

"Who?"

"The Parenthood."

"No. This is what a girl looks like. Yours"—she pointed—"and mine . . . that's how we reproduce. No Living Trees, J. No Orchard." She looked down at his penis. "Can I see that?"

J shook his head no. "You have to go. I can't . . . this is . . . too much."

But K's expression didn't change.

Before he could talk himself out of it, J pulled off his pajama bottoms. He stood quiet, blushing, before her.

"What do I look like to you?" he asked.

K stared. "Like a weird Letter Girl."

They laughed briefly, insanely, and in that laughter J heard harsh angles.

Suddenly he felt some measure of the responsibility that had come with her through the window.

"Is this how we fail Inspections?" he asked.

"Yes," K said. "I think they've been inspecting us to find out if we've met."

J looked to the window, as if the glass had always separated him from reality.

"Listen," she said. "It's bad. It's so bad. But we have to be strong. And we can do this. We can make sense of this. Think of it as an equation. Haven't you ever thought something was too complicated for you to solve? And then you solved it?"

"Yes."

"This is no different. We have to be smart right now. We have to plan."

"How can you be so . . . composed?"

"I'm as scared as you are."

She went to him.

She kissed him.

J felt his lips part, felt her teeth against his. Her tongue against his. It was a blur, a rushed confusion. When K pulled away she was not smiling. She only stared at his mouth. Then his body.

"What was that?" he asked.

"I don't know." She kissed him again, then pulled away. "I once read a Nancy book where a girl was taken prisoner for ten years. She finally escaped, using lessons we'd seen her master."

"Luxley had a book like that."

He saw anger flare in K's eyes. Color had returned to her cheeks. She moved her fingers freely. J felt his lips with his own hand. Thought of her lips against them.

"The thing is," she said, "the girl in the story missed out on ten years of being with her sisters. And in those ten years her sisters changed a lot."

"Sisters," J repeated.

"And when she came back, when she saw them again, she didn't relate anymore."

"Sisters."

"That's happened to us, J."

"But we're not—"

"Something very important was stolen from us. We've been prisoners for twelve years. And you know what's worse? We didn't even know there was freedom to miss."

J thought of Q. He wanted to wake him. Wake them all.

K took his hand. "Whatever they took, J, let's take it back."

J brought his mouth to hers. He wanted to taste her again, to smell her so close.

They kissed once more, now with confidence. After, K walked the hall to J's bedroom.

"Where are you going?"

But J followed. And when he entered his bedroom he saw she was already lying down on his bed.

He felt like his body was bigger than his rooms. Bigger than the Turret.

He lay down beside her.

"You get it," she said. "You're not telling me to leave. You're not calling D.A.D. You get it." Then, "I don't know if I'm supposed to go back home now or not. I don't know what to do."

"Stay a little longer," J said. But he thought of her M.O.M. Would she be looking for her?

Would she come looking for her here?

J held her without thinking.

Then K cried for a very long time. J, overwhelmed by her body, her voice, her smell, *her*, imagined all she'd been through before arriving at his window. The cold. The fear. The knowledge that her friend might be in trouble.

Eventually her tears became broken sobs. Convulsions that shook her body until she fell still again. J cried, too. He trembled as he held her. Then K started speaking in what sounded, at first, like gibberish. Impossible plans.

"We can kill them," she said. "Every one of them."

The phrases were too big for J to process. And they came too fast.

There's more of us than them.

We're strong. We're young. They're old.

We have to do it soon. Before they change how they do things. Before they make it harder for us to get to them.

We have to send M.O.M. to the Corner.

We have to send D.A.D. to the Corner.

We have to kill them.

Kill them all.

"K," he said.

"What?"

"Stop."

"No, J. This is really happening."

She fell asleep in his arms. But J wondered how deep it could be.

It struck him then that he wanted to help her. Whatever it was she wanted to do. He wanted to help her.

He had to.

And with the thought came the first vestige of serenity he'd experienced since seeing her at his window.

He got up and went to the window. Below, Inspectors walked between the ice sculptures, checking the Yard for . . .

. . . for what?

J looked to the lip of the Orchard. Mister Tree. The place K said she hadn't been. But if not her . . . who?

"We can't both fall asleep," K said, almost as if she'd talked in her sleep. "We both have to make it to our . . . Inspections . . ."

J thought of her tears on him. Thought of them four times larger under the magnifying glasses of Inspectors Collins and Jeffrey.

"We'll make it," J said.

But they did both sleep. As J slunk back from the silhouettes of the Inspectors down in the Yard, as they studied what might have been prints, mostly covered by more fallen snow, as they signaled one another, as they brought their glasses to the cart, the room, the ladder.

J and K slept. As their worlds crumbled to dirt around them, as the dirt left marks upon their bodies, their minds, enough dirt to be declared unclean in any world.

They slept.

Together.

And J woke in the moonlight to see her still in his rooms.

K. Standing against the wall. Watching him.

J sat up fast. Was he dreaming? Had to be.

K stepped from the wall, a small stack of papers in her hands. She came to the bed and sat beside him. She didn't speak. Not yet.

She set the pages between them. J saw they were drawings. He knew they'd come from her backpack. They looked like photos, as if K had taken pictures in and out of both towers. It was the first time J saw the inside of the girls' Turret. And while it was similar to his own, there were differences.

The Letter Girls, for one.

So many drawings of other girls. Faces and hairstyles J had to remind himself were real. An Inspector without a beard. M.O.M.

With this last one, J felt cold. The large glasses obscured most of the woman's face. The bones of that face were proud, strong, and her lips looked like they were made to say words like *the Corner.* Is this what D.A.D. looked like to K? Did he wield the same power? The same mystery? The same fear?

She showed him a picture of himself. It was a perfect portrait, as if the artist, K, knew him better than he did. His features, warm and sincere, emerged from a dark background, the black turtleneck that reached his chin. And despite K's intent, J was embarrassed to look into his own brainwashed eyes.

She placed a drawing on top of it. A tunnel. A barrier splitting that tunnel in two.

"Meet me here," she said. "Tomorrow night. After dark. The tunnel will be safer at night. The Turrets could be crawling with staff during the day." She paused, considering. "And who knows what they've gotten B to say."

But J had never been below before. The thought did more than scare him. It momentarily made him want to turn her in.

"Why the tunnel?"

"I'm going to tell the girls everything. Tomorrow. You're going to tell the boys."

"Me?"

"And we'll meet when the sun goes down. And we'll plan. And we'll act on that plan."

Before he could ask her how he was supposed to tell his brothers, when, and how to get to the tunnel, K produced more drawings that, by way of images, explained the way. The door, J saw, was in the staff bathroom. Stairs then. Halls. Doorways. The Corner?

A paper sign telling him where the tunnel was. Telling him that *Richard* was the only one allowed to use it.

"That's your D.A.D.," she said. "His real name."

The letters looked impossible to J. Written by someone who made everything up and wanted everyone to believe it, too.

"Even his name," he said.

J looked to his bedroom door. As if he could see all the Alphabet Boys there, as if he could see himself telling them.

More drawings then, pictures that elaborated on K's vague plan. J had to turn away from some, couldn't from others. Faces he had seen for the first time only minutes ago, now distorted with rage, pain, and horror.

J understood. All of it. He would go to his morning's Inspection. Talk to the boys. Meet K in the tunnel.

Then . . .

"I don't know if I can do this," he said. He looked to a drawing of a Letter Girl carrying an ax through what looked like the hall outside his rooms. "I just don't—"

"It doesn't matter if you can," K said. "You have to. And also . . ." She touched his face. "You can."

Distorted by his own folded reality, kept sane by her presence, J touched her face back. They kissed. They ran their hands through each other's hair. They cried.

K set the drawings aside, as if by this small ceremony, the plan had been agreed upon, the plan had already begun.

Tomorrow.

K crawled back into bed beside him and the two held one another beneath the blankets. Outside, winter had yet to relent. The world, it seemed, was frozen, all of the world, all of reality, except for the small warm space they made together, slowly, a red circumference expanding, melting away all the ice they'd found themselves in. Twelve years of frozen truth, finally, now emerging.

They kissed. They touched. They wanted to laugh, they knew they *should* be able to laugh, but neither did. The Turret was silent as K and J took the final hours of night to explore, to love, to heat. And while neither thought it wise to fall asleep, both did, stupefied by the feelings, despite the unfathomable danger that lurked. J did not wake until he heard that familiar word, that Turret rooster's cry, three syllables cracking from the silver box in the hall outside his rooms.

"INSPECTION."

He opened his eyes. Looked to his bed, saw K was gone.

In her stead was a note that read: *Boats.*

He got up quick, even as he heard the doors of his floor mates' rooms opening and closing, even as he heard the command for the second and final time in the hall.

"INSPECTION!"

He went to his Boats board and touched the unmoving waters. Felt beneath the board and found K's drawings taped there, in full.

No dream.

Wide awake now.

And, J realized, as he put on his pajamas, as he rushed for his living room door, as he entered the hall and the line outside the Check-Up room door, no time for a shower, either.

But even if he'd washed her from his body, would they find her on his mind?

M.O.M. and D.A.D.

*A**nd if they ever revolt?* Marilyn asked, eyeing the first of the two towers deep in the northern Michigan woods. *If they should ever all be spoiled rotten at once?*

Richard shook his head no. *You said yourself, if we raise them right . . .*

But Marilyn's expression didn't change, and Richard knew this to mean her mind hadn't, either.

The cabin, she said, nodding beyond the Orchard behind the first tower.

What of it?

A cavalry of cons, if you will.

Richard understood. Revolt was one thing; needing backup to keep that revolution down was another.

Marilyn went on. *A stash of armed Inspectors. They might be on call for twenty years. And they might never be needed at all. We'll pay them double. Who wouldn't do it?*

Oh, someone would do it, Richard said, grabbing the rake and beginning the arduous task of clearing the lawn of what they'd already decided would be the girls' tower, *but I just don't think it's necessary.*

Fifty-two twenty-year-olds, Richard. Angry as hell. And by then . . . us, twenty years older. Our staff, too. One day we may be very grateful we secured protection from our own experiment.

Silence between them. Richard raked. Marilyn stepped to the

sidewalk, then to the front door of what they hadn't yet come to call the Turret.

Richard knew what she was doing. Where she was going. The inner office was already equipped well enough for work. Marilyn was going to make some phone calls. Set up some meetings. Late-night interviews with men and women who had reasons, perhaps, for dropping out of society, who might like to hide for two decades or more.

As was her way, always, she'd immediately put into practice what she'd preached.

Marilyn was on the phone.

Offering protection.

Hiring the same.

PART FOUR

SPOILED ROTTEN

Inspection

The voices in the hall just echoes . . . J's thoughts already in the Tunnel . . .

Isn't she amazing?

Yes.

Isn't she?

Yes.

Even now, in line for the Check-Up room, two Inspectors only a metal door away from bringing their magnifying glasses to his tired body, J was soothed by the wonder of the Letter Girl K in his rooms.

Lies, she'd said about Vees, Rotts, Moldus. She'd been in his rooms, all over the Turret. She'd been declared clean for a year while behaving decidedly unclean.

He brought his hand to his chest and lightly touched it . . .

Just moments ago her body was pressed against yours . . . her lips touched yours, too . . . her legs . . . can you still see her legs?

Yes.

Don't forget her legs.

Ahead in line, F made a joke.

We lost J, she'd said. *Our J. To the Corner.*

X laughed at it.

Her eyes are brighter than any of your brothers'. Her hair smells like the Orchard.

F looked at J. *Did you get my joke? Didja?*

Even if they don't find any physical sign of her, they're gonna smell her on you.

The Check-Up room door opened. G walked out, sleepy-eyed.

"Next," Inspector Collins huffed from the cold, angular shadows of the doorway.

X was next.

Inspection

Her body, her touch, her smell . . .

X entered. The door closed behind him.

Inspection

(the dogs, J, the dogs)

Can you still see her lips? Tell me. Do you remember her lips? Tell me. Can you describe them?

Wet.

(dogs)

Wet like water?

No.

Tell me.

Wet like sweat.

Tell me.

Don't forget. Relive her. Relive her. Relive.

(even if the Inspectors don'—)

Tell me.

She smells like the Orchard.

Tell me. Relive.

(even if the Inspectors don'—)

"Hey, J," F said. "Who said bark to the tree?"

Can you still feel her skin?

Yes.

The feel of it under your fingers?

(even if the Inspectors don't smell it—)

yes yes yes yes yes

"Come on, J. Who said bark to the tree?"

She came from the planet of snow. She knocked on my window.
I let her in. We met, we spoke, we touched.

Tell me. Because I want you to remember every detail.

There's more of us than them.

Every detail.

We're strong. We're young. They're old.

Tell me.

We have to do it soon. Before they change how they do things.
Before they make it harder for us to get to them.

Describe her . . .

We have to send M.O.M. to the Corner.

We have to send D.A.D. to the Corner.

Tell me . . .

We have to kill them.

Her nose was smaller than mine . . . her shoulders curved, be-
came her arms, sooner than mine . . . her chest was soft, soft as her
legs . . .

Kill them all.

(even if the Inspectors don't smell it on you—)

"A dog," F said. "Come on, J. Wake up."

(even if the Inspectors don't smell it on you, the dogs will)

The Check-Up room door opened. X walked out.

"Next."

F walked in. The door closed.

J alone in line now. Alone in the hall.

Run?

But no. The drawings. The blueprints. K. The plan.

The tunnel in the basement.

This might be our only chance, she'd whispered at some point
in the vague, overwhelming night.

Do you believe in her?

Yes.

Why?

Because she's truth.

Truth? Look at you. K is dripping from your fingertips. You're drenched in her . . . SHE. You feel the muck of her? The Parenthood protects you, J. The Parenthood protects you from the likes of HER. The Parenthood lied to you because her'll make you sick. Her'll make you mad. And here you've brought her with you to the Check-Up room door.

He heard the word *clean* through the closed door. Any second now.

Excellent Inspection, J.

(CLEAN!)

Wonderful Inspection, J.

(CLEAN!)

We love you, J.

(CLEAN!)

Wait. What's that smell, J?

J smelled his wrists. Smelled her on him.

The Check-Up room door opened. F came out. A big-toothed smile across his face.

"Wake up, pal. You're up."

Collins stood in the doorway. "Next."

"Need me to slap you?" F said.

Drawings of a second Turret.

(I'm a girl)

It doesn't matter what they're looking for . . . it's worth it.

The Parenthood is here to protect you, J.

It doesn't matter what they're looking for . . . it's worth it.

They're gonna smell it on you. I can smell it on you right now.

(there are twenty-five of us Letter Girls)

The Parenthood is here to protect you.

From?

From . . .

From?

From Vees.

No.

Rotts.

No.

Moldus.

LIES!

From K.

(I'm a girl)

The Parenthood is here to protect you.

I've changed.

You're wrong.

I'm scared.

You've always been scared.

Have I?

Yes.

I have.

Yes.

There are no Placasores, J.

No.

D.A.D. is your disease.

EXCELLENT INSPECTION, J!

Collins cleared his throat. J stepped into the room. The door closed behind him.

Under the lights he thought he could see her handprints on his. Disrobing, he could see her everywhere.

The two Inspectors looked from his feet to his face.

They know.

"Ready?" he asked. His voice was not his own. Changed.

The Parenthood is here to protect you.

"Begin." A voice from behind him. Also changed. Different now.

D.A.D.

His name is Richard.

Don't say his name.

Inspector Collins brought his magnifying glass to J's chest.

Could he see K with it? She was so big. She was everywhere.

Collins leaned forward, smelled the air around J. The dogs whined behind him.

"D.A.D.?" Collins said.

J felt the tunnel receding. It didn't matter to him then that what Collins was about to say to D.A.D. might result in his death. He wanted to see K in that tunnel. It's all he wanted. Ever again.

To see K.

Collins pointed to J's fingers. J hadn't even noticed the Inspector examining his hands.

D.A.D., beside him now, lifted J's left hand to his eyes.

"Charcoal," he said. Then, without looking J in the eye, as if J were already gone, unclean, removed from the Parenthood, "Been drawing pictures lately, J?"

The mood in the Check-Up room was horribly different from Inspections of old. J noticed it now. And not just because D.A.D. had found charcoal on his fingertips. If the Inspectors were to pull a two-foot worm from J's ear, he'd say he understood the mood; now the mood made sense. If they peeled the flesh from his face with their fingers, he'd understand the apprehensive look in their eyes as they examined him, head to toe, magnifying glasses in hand.

"Some of the ink in the textbooks runs," J said.

"Yeah?" D.A.D. asked. His voice different now. J thought maybe it was changed forever. "Which book?"

"Most of them."

"Which one were you reading last night?"

J tried to think quick, but it wasn't easy. Exams were coming up. Which exams?

"Math," he said.

Outright lying. No way to rationalize it. Not now.

D.A.D. did not respond, and in the steel wall J saw a distorted reflection of the Check-Up room at large. Himself made extra thin, D.A.D. and the Inspectors so big.

Collins and Jeffrey exchanged a glance. Did they know J saw them? Did they know he saw the unknown in their eyes?

No boy had ever failed an Inspection.

Would he today?

"Raise your arms, J."

D.A.D. in the reflection. D.A.D. taking the glass from Collins. D.A.D. wielding the magnifying glass himself.

J had never seen him do that before.

"Arms, J."

J raised his arms and felt the cold metal rim against his skin. Then his ears, his nostrils, his lips.

D.A.D. paused at his lips.

He sniffed the air so close to J's face, it felt like he was sucking the air from J's lungs.

Did the Inspectors know about girls? Had they ever done what J did last night?

Had D.A.D.?

J heard dark wind out in the hall, heavy breathing through the silver square speaker high on the Turret wall.

But no. Just the dogs behind the glass.

The Inspectors moved nervously, their reflection betraying much weaker men than the ones J had believed to be so strong.

Why hadn't he noticed all this before?

The cold magnifying glass pressed to his penis.

J closed his eyes and saw the drawings taped to the bottom of his Boats board. Drawings of the two Turrets, the halls and the bathroom stalls, the basements, the tunnel.

Meet me in the tunnel after dark.

Yes, J thought. *I'll be there.*

The glass came quick to his face again. J didn't want to open his mouth, but D.A.D. forced the thing against his teeth and his lips parted. The Inspectors moved in closer.

Could they see a kiss in there? Did they know how good it felt? How true?

The Parenthood has been lying to us.

Oh yes, indeed.

A puppy will turn on its master, D.A.D. once said, *once it thinks it knows what's best. But the master always arrives at what's best* first.

The dogs scratched against the door that kept them in.

The Parenthood protects you.

"Anything you want to tell me?" D.A.D. asked.

J's mind's eye saw a figure crouched behind Mister Tree. Saw D reading all of Warren Bratt's insane book. Saw K at his window, her fingers numb with winter. Saw her drawings of other Letter Girls, patrolling a second Turret's hallways with rusty tools in their hands. Saw K's M.O.M. Heard the name *Richard.*

Anything you want to tell me?

Yet, despite this unfathomable wash of confusion and new information, despite the fact that he trusted K, entirely, and believed the reality-cracking tales she'd told him, there was only one thing in the world he felt he could still hold on to. One buoy in the scarlet-mad waters of this new worldview.

D.A.D.'s ever-caring face.

And how those eyes had watched over J and the other Alphabet Boys all their lives.

Madly, J found he was able to wholly believe what K had told him while trusting the Parenthood in full.

Still.

Tears pooled in a tunnel in the basement of his eyes.

Yes, there was something he wanted to tell, D.A.D. Something he wanted so badly to say.

"I saw a girl out my window."

The words seemed to crawl out of his mouth, fingers first, a new J emerging into the Check-Up room. A boy he didn't recognize at all. The beginning of a much bigger story, only a piece of what felt like a huge truth. But he felt great relief for having cracked that truth open for his D.A.D.

"Say that again," D.A.D. said.

Behind the man, the eyes of the Inspectors seemed to grow too wide for their faces.

J smiled nervously. Surely D.A.D. was already thinking how to protect the boys from another visit from another girl. Right? Surely D.A.D. was employing all his powers of protection, summoning answers from places J would never have to fathom for himself.

The Parenthood protects you.

Right?

"What?" J asked, attempting, insanely, to make light of a mood he'd added one thousand pounds to with a single sentence. "I saw a girl outside my window."

J saw something colder than winter in D.A.D.'s eyes. As if, for a flash, the man were made of ice, standing forever still in the Yard below. Then, a second flash, horrible life, followed by a question J wasn't prepared for.

"How do you know the word for what you saw?"

"Oh no," J said. Because they were the first words that came to mind. Because he hadn't realized he'd told more of the truth by only telling part of it.

What else might he accidentally reveal?

Despite wanting to say her name, wanting to hear himself speak it, he felt like he was sinking, like the Check-Up room had always been an elevator, descending now to the Corner.

Don't say her name.

No, don't say anything else at all.

"You told me you didn't start that naughty little book, J. How do you know the word for what you saw?"

When had D.A.D. moved closer? J hadn't seen it happen. But there he was, gripping J's shoulders, spitting crazed words in his face.

"HOW DO YOU KNOW THE WORD GIRL?"

The impossible balancing act almost broke then; J was momentarily incapable of seeing D.A.D. in both the light by which he'd always viewed him and the new illumination cast by . . .

He couldn't even think her name. Didn't even want to use a word that contained her letter. As if he might put her in the Check-Up room, *her*, magnified by the glass D.A.D. gripped so hard.

But hadn't D.A.D. given him a way out? A lie?

"I read some of the book," J said. "I read the word *girl*."

D.A.D. turned so fast, his reflection in the wall looked like a man with a permanently blurred face, no longer definable at all.

"Unclean," he said. The two syllables like knives suddenly stabbing the soles of J's feet, telling him to run. *Run. RUN.*

But he only shook, glued, it seemed, to the rubber mats.

The Inspectors looked to each other, then to the floor. They didn't know what to do with the word any more than J did.

"Help me," J pleaded to the Inspectors. Then he cried, as his mind seemed to catch fire.

He turned to D.A.D. just in time to see him gesture to Collins and Jeffrey in a way J didn't recognize.

Then J was being dragged, naked, yelling, from the Check-Up room, dragged down the hall, as doors opened, as his brothers looked, as visions of K weaved about his body and mind, unable to protect him. He and K were still side by side, in his bed, discussing their stolen lives. As he passed F's confused face, J thought of K's lips upon his own, her body in his hands, and how smart she had been for figuring it all out first.

As the elevator doors closed, as he saw the twin silver walls meet beyond a veil of horrid misinformation, as he tried to resist the Inspectors but discovered instead the difference in strength between a man and a boy, J saw the entrance of a tunnel caving in, blocking off his last chance to ever see K again.

Because that's all that mattered. Life, death, truth, lies . . . seeing K again was everything.

Yes, J thought, as the elevator doors closed, as he struggled to free himself, as he cried, naked, in the grips of the Turret Inspectors, seeing K again, just seeing her face again, meant more to him than getting out of this building alive.

Cheers to a New Beginning

He hadn't been out of the shelter for two days. Hadn't stepped foot outside the actual building itself. It was funny, in a way, because here he'd gone from one building he hardly left to another. And here he was trying to get away from that. *Had* gotten away from that. But now, always within the same four walls, the two sets of bunk beds his entire world for two days. The other three mattresses were occupied by a total of eight different men already. Men. Always men. No women. Not yet. Despite ten years of limited contact with women, here he'd chosen a hideout that had to, by law, separate the men and the women. A homeless shelter couldn't allow for men to have access to where the women slept. It was funny, sort of, the way the real world was the answer to the one he'd fled. Back there they studied who the separation benefited more. Out here there was no doubt it was the women.

Was two days long enough? He wasn't sure. He'd showered twice, which was something, and used the laundry in the basement. He had no other clothes on him—he'd left in a hurry—and so he'd had to stand by the washer and dryer wearing only a towel. Nobody came down to the basement during that time, and after a while it began to feel like its own liberation. Standing by a washing machine in a towel. Just one of ten thousand little things he hadn't done in what felt like ten thousand years.

So what to do after two days? He'd eaten slop in line with the other homeless men. Ate three times a day. Even when he wasn't hungry. And he didn't have much on him. Not much of anything. And there was no way he was going to remove any amount of money from his account. An account that had over a million dollars in it. Was the money still there? Did it matter? Did he want that kind of money anymore? Blood money or false money or money earned by lying to two dozen boys for a decade?

No, he didn't have much. A couple hundred dollars. A wet pair of shoes. A stained T-shirt. A jacket.

What he did have was needs. Not the book. Not even that.

He needed safety. Anonymity. Money. Clothes. A place to stay. A vehicle to keep moving. A friend? Possibly. A phone? Possibly. A new name?

He laughed at this last one, though the laugh was more like an aging cough. A new name. After using a pseudonym for ten years.

He sat alone in the room of bunk beds. He considered his next move. He had to keep moving because he wanted to keep moving, but he wasn't sure that was the right thing to do. Would they know to look for him here? Would it be easier to find him if he visited more places? More dots on the map? Back in the Parenthood (that word, so ugly to him now, had been ugly for a long time), Richard wielded endless power. But out here? How far was Richard's reach? How far could Marilyn see? How willing were they to step into the light, to be seen themselves?

Institutionalized, he thought. The word was especially ugly when applied to himself. He'd probably used it in a book before but couldn't remember it ever sounding so scary. *Institutionalized* didn't only mean a man was so used to his environs that he ended up needing them. It also meant that man was *changed*. And the problem with *changed* was that he might not be able to change back to the man he was before.

For the first time in a long time, he realized he liked a little of the man he was before. Before the Parenthood. Yes, he saw that man now in a much different way. He'd hated that man so much that he'd agreed to live in a tower, write books for boys who were lied to, lie to the boys himself, all for a pile of money that didn't look quite as big once he got to sit on it.

Still, he wasn't sitting on it at all. No. The money was locked up in his not-so-private account the Parenthood had access to. Could they remove the money? Breach of contract? What kind of lawyer would take their case?

Your honor, Warren Bratt broke his contract with the Parenthood. We believe we should be reimbursed the funds allocated him to lie to two dozen boys in the woods. Boys we bought from desperate, often drugged, mothers.

The door to the bunk room opened and Warren looked up quick. He gripped the handle to his mostly empty suitcase.

"This one taken?"

An old man. Once-blond hair. Who knew his actual age? So hard to tell in a place like this. Everybody looked dehumanized. Yet, in a way, they all looked better than Warren. While some had secrets and all had histories, it was unlikely any of them had sold their souls in full.

"Here," Warren said, rising from one of the lower bunks. "Take mine. I'm checking out."

"Yeah? Where you going?"

Warren studied the man's eyes. Why did he want to know?

"Greece."

The man laughed the way most men laughed in this place: true but harsh. Warren picked up his case and coat and exited the room. Then the shelter soon after.

It was evening. He hadn't noticed. Hadn't been outside in two days. With the money he had on him he could take a bus to Florida. Take a bus to Wyoming. Hop a train somewhere, anywhere. Get a job at a local paper. Get a job flipping grilled cheese.

But first . . .

He'd seen the bar the morning he arrived at the shelter. And oh what a morning that was. Drenched and cold, out of breath and invigorated, righteous and free. But still caged, too. Institutionalized. He'd wanted to enter the bar, but even if it was open, he couldn't. He simply didn't have the nerve. Couldn't find it.

Now he believed he did.

He looked up and down the street. To the windows of the apartments across the street. To the alleys. He wasn't exactly sure what he was worried he might see. Richard crouching in red? Marilyn hiding behind a lamppost? Back when he was offered the job, there wasn't any mention of how he might be tracked down if he ever wrote a book about women, printed it off himself, and left a copy for each of the Alphabet Boys. Nope. No word on that front. So . . . what? What might he see and how would they come after him?

Warren shuffled up the sidewalk. A homeless man, indeed. As he slipped inside the bar, he gave the street, the buildings, the windows, the roofs, one last look.

Inside, warmer, he cleaned the fog from his glasses and eyed the small room. Two unoccupied booths to his left. Two unoccupied booths to his right. Two women sitting at the bar, their backs to him. A young man behind the bar. My God did the young man look clean. Uncluttered. Happy.

"What can I get you, sir?" the guy asked.

Warren took an open stool. "Bourbon," he said. "Please."

The word *please* escaped him in such a genuine way that he almost felt like crying.

It had been a long time.

The bartender served him. Warren sipped. He looked down the bar. Of the two women, the one facing him smiled.

At him.

It had been a long time for that, too.

The woman was close to what he once would've called his type. Smart eyes behind kitschy big glasses. Brown hair. An old-school dress. Was this what people considered hip these days? He wouldn't know. He'd been away for a decade.

Institutionalized.

Warren finished his drink. Considered his next move. Out of the country? It was probably the right thing to do. Leave. Get out entirely. Shave his head. Grow a beard. Devote his life to helping young people know the real ways of the world.

He ordered a second bourbon. The two women down the bar cracked up laughing, and Warren thought what a great sound it was. Oh, how many great sounds had he missed back when all he cared about was being the big fish in whatever body of water he swam in. Oh, what trouble that angry ego had gotten him into. Oh, how distorted the last ten years had been.

Oh boy.

He sipped. He thought of heading south. East. West. Anywhere but back north. Right? Yes. Anywhere but back north.

Yet . . .

The boys. They were going to need help. Weren't they? How many of them were spoiled rotten by his book by now? How many young lives had he taken by deciding for them what they should and should not know?

Why hadn't he pulled each aside? Why hadn't he talked to the boys directly? He could've told them the truth, then told them to be quiet.

Why hadn't he taken them with him?

Surely, given his state of mind, Warren could've killed an Inspector or two. Whoever was on duty that night. It made sound moral sense in hindsight. The murder of an ex-con hiding in the woods, in the name of rescuing two dozen boys from a life of slavery.

He sipped. The women erupted again and Warren looked over at them. Tried to get into the jolly mood. As if he might siphon some of what they were feeling.

Good God, these women. They had no idea what the man down the bar had been capable of. No more so than if he'd been a cult leader. A doctor who prescribed unnecessary medicine. A false prophet, a false author. Here to hurt, not help.

The woman smiled at him again, and Warren understood then

that if he was going to begin a life outside the Parenthood, he was going to have to eventually tell someone what he'd done. Probably. Or . . . if he could just erase the ten previous years, start from there, pick up where he left off . . .

Could he?

As he smiled back at the woman and raised his glass, as she raised hers in return then blushed for the silliness of it, Warren understood that he couldn't erase his part in what went on. Not only because a man wasn't able to turn back time but because the man he had been then was the man who had decided to end up where he was now.

The two women got up and put their coats on, and Warren ordered a third drink and wished he could erase every year he'd lived, erase them all. Start the whole thing over. Identify with being an overly kind person this time around. Eschew a life of darkness. Bury the intellectually superior cloak he'd worn for so many years before agreeing to toss any and all of his soul into a fiery pit for profit.

The women had gone. Warren thought of the roads he'd taken once he fled the Parenthood. Imagined himself taking them again. In the opposite direction. Saw himself approaching the tower with a rifle in hand. Saw Inspectors falling in pools of blood, ex-cons shot in the back. Richard with a barrel to his chest.

The bartender looked over Warren's shoulder.

Who's there?

The one woman had come back. Just sat down right next to Warren. Her drunk eyes were huge behind her big frames. Like she was holding two magnifying glasses up to her face. Warren, trying hard to fit into the old world, the real world, ordered a round for them both. They talked, they laughed. Warren caught himself slipping back into old Warren: curt and snobbish. How? How was it possible any vestige of his former persona remained? He saw himself rounding up the Alphabet Boys. He'd answer their questions about the book. He'd tell them everything. They'd learn the truth of the world as the soles of their shoes soaked in Richard's blood.

Warren was paying his tab suddenly, then leaving the bar with the woman, arm in arm.

It was cold outside, freezing, and she said, *Don't worry, we can go to my place.* Warren smiled but he couldn't stop thinking about the boys. Yes, this was good. A woman. A place to stay. But the Parenthood went on. Did it not? And if the base rule of the constitution was broken . . . wouldn't all the boys be sent to the Corner?

And hadn't he made that happen?

And had it happened already?

He climbed old stairs with the woman. The woman was clearly drunk, laughing, hanging on to him, as Warren held her up, held himself up, too. He hadn't been quite this drunk in a decade. Good feeling, bad feeling, both. Oh, the boys the boys the boys.

The woman fumbled with her key and Warren helped her. He imagined Richard at the podium in the Body Hall, hands raised, crying out defiantly before his boys. Demanding they tell him who'd read what and how many pages. Surely Richard had to know that much. A simple game of Boats? Surely. The woman half-fell into her apartment and Warren stumbled after her. She turned on the lights and said, *This way, more booze.* Warren, torn up inside, aware that it was far too soon to make any attempt at lowering himself back into the real world, followed. More booze sounded good. So good.

Nice place, he said. But he didn't feel nice. Didn't feel like a good guy at all and definitely didn't feel like he deserved to be having a good night with, of all things, a woman. And she was holding his hand, leading him through the apartment, through the living room, into the kitchen, by a stove. She was getting glasses from the cupboard. The bottle was already on the counter. She said how much she liked whiskey and the smell of whiskey and she didn't care what it did to her and suddenly Warren just wanted to leave.

Go. This was way too soon. There were two dozen boys whose lives were no doubt in jeopardy because they weren't even allowed to read about a woman, and here Warren was in a woman's apartment, getting drunk, doing the exact thing any one of those boys should be able to do. And here she was talking and pouring the drinks and here Warren, his mind a muddle, his soul torn in so many pieces, some of which were irretrievable, already blown by the black winds that circulated through the basement of the Turret, the breath of the Parenthood, and his fleeing the tower, too, didn't deserve this. Didn't deserve this at all.

"Cheers," the woman said, handing him a glass, clinking it with her own. Her eyes looked great. So big and funny. Warren hadn't seen eyes like this in so long. It was almost as if the woman looked like an odd man to him, a man in costume, a man who had pulled cheerful features from a Halloween bag and slapped them together before heading to the bar. Warren sipped his drink. Thought of the boys drinking milk in the cafeteria, Richard drinking scotch in his office. Could the boys smell it on him? Surely. How could they not? Warren could smell it on the woman, on himself, on the apartment, too. The woman talked about town, about failed relationships, as Warren, nodding along, eyed the counter behind her, the refrigerator, the archway to the kitchen, the living room beyond, the couch and the pair of shoes behind the couch. The ankles in those shoes, too.

"Hey," he said, trying to smile, not even sure why. "Who's that hiding behind the couch?"

The woman mock-frowned and looked to the living room. Then she cracked up laughing, but Warren didn't join her. No no. Because the moment after he asked it, he saw the full-bodied reflection in the glass of the balcony door as clear as his own thoughts were not.

Warren grabbed the woman's wrist.

"What's going on here?"

The cold he felt then was much deeper than the winds that had resisted him as he ran from the Turret, ran through the pines, took the roads he hadn't seen in years.

"Hey," the woman said. "You're hurting me."

Warren let go. He made for the living room. Behind him the woman said, "What do you wanna cheer? Inspections?"

Warren moved quick through the living room as a man rose from behind the couch and a second one stepped out from a doorway Warren hadn't noticed at all. A third man came through the apartment's front door. When Warren looked back to the woman, she had no glass in her hand, and her eyes were no longer funny.

"You were easier to find than a deer at a salt lick. A homeless shelter? A bar? A woman? The Parenthood expected more from their creative writer."

Warren moved for the front door, despite the man who stood in his way. Something sudden and solid happened at the back of his head, and he fell to the carpeted floor.

Dizzy, fading, he noticed there was hardly any furniture, no pictures on the walls. But he hadn't seen any of this on his way in. His mind had been on the boys. On possibly, insanely, returning to the Parenthood.

And so, he thought, as the four figures crouched around him, he was. He was heading back to the Parenthood.

Heading back to the boys.

Kill 'Em All

One drink. As the Inspectors held J in quarantine. An hour or two. Two drinks. However long it took to prep himself, to make certain he was asking the right questions when the time came to ask them.

Boats, of course. The Parenthood's only form of surveillance. You couldn't win Boats without telling the truth.

A lie detector disguised as a game.

J had seen B from his window. Okay. This had happened. He'd recognized the girl *as* a girl from Warren Bratt's description in his insane fucking book. Okay. This had happened. B might not have seen him. Didn't matter. The girl had to go. J had to go.

Who else? Who had J told? Who knew?

Richard stood by his desk, eyeing the living room table he'd soon sit at. He saw the event before it happened, himself in one chair, J in the other; man and boy; father and son; a good old-fashioned game of Boats.

Gray area. The expanse between the rules he and Marilyn had made long ago and how many of those rules had been broken now. Had someone asked him ten years ago what he'd do with a boy who read all of Warren Bratt's sneaky fucking book, Richard would've of course said the boy was no good. Spoiled. He'd have sent him to the Corner, no questions asked. Because he'd have to. Because the Parenthood and the rules he and Marilyn established were more important than the number of boys and girls. If through the years Richard had been responsible for sending every boy but one to the Corner, and if, in the end, that one boy rose to become the brightest, most focused, assuredly original scientist, then so be it. The experiment would be a success. Proof that the mind is capable of unfathomable heights once the elements of distraction are removed. But now, three kids, two Alphabet Boys and one Letter Girl, all in quarantine . . . but all spoiled rotten?

Take D . . .

Richard read the book, too. He seethed with each paragraph, growing angrier as the letters played across the pages like passengers on a train coming to destroy a man's lifework. A lot of bad shit in there. Oh, were there slights at Richard; oh, were there innuendos that implied only a monster could do what the Parenthood had done.

Many.

Yet . . . the mention of a woman . . . early in the book the woman at the bar . . . later, during the gruelingly long monologue, in which Warren spelled out the Parenthood's mission as though it were imagined by a fool . . . might not it all come off as science fiction to a boy like D? To a boy who not only hadn't ever heard the word *woman*, a boy who had come to expect whimsy and the fantastical in his leisure books, what could it mean? What was the difference between Warren Bratt's *Needs* and Lawrence Luxley's *One Big Ollie in the Orchard*?

Gray area. So much of it. Higher than the Turret, wider than the Yard. Longer, too, than the winding roads through the pines, the four hundred curves that Warren himself must have taken on foot to reach the first sign of civilization, the tackle shop at the corner of county roads 12 and 13.

Richard smiled, but it did not feel good. He wanted very badly to know what Warren did when he got there. Who he talked to. What he said.

He'd get those answers tonight.

Gray area . . .

Take B . . .

The girl confessed to crossing the pines and discovering the second tower. She said she was alone. Said she didn't see anyone inside the tower. Didn't make contact with anyone at all. Asked if it was used for storage. Why would the girl tell the truth about one thing and not another? She'd been crying during her confession, trembling and unable to get sentences out without a lot of obvious effort.

Burt cited many reasons the girl might tell only a partial truth.

Covering up for a sister?

Ashamed for having seen something she wasn't supposed to?

Scared for having seen a boy named J?

But how would B know to be afraid?

Gray area.

So much of it.

Marilyn had a game of Boats scheduled with B in quarantine. If there was a bottom to this fathomless fall, Marilyn would get to it.

Richard, still standing, his red jacket upon the carpet before his desk, shirtless and angry, tried to assure himself that the problem, the disease, the ruination, had been quarantined indeed. But how could he know how many Letter Girls B spoke to? Or how many were with her on her journey through the pines?

Marilyn said it was out of character. B wasn't the type to explore.

Was she the type to lie? To hide? To shatter a psychological masterwork?

And how many boys had read Warren's book? And who had J told about the *girl* out his window? And what other boy looked out his own window as well?

Oh, the word *girl* sounded so rancid out of J's mouth. So foreign. As if Richard hadn't heard it himself in so long that he'd forgetten it existed.

Boats.

Already on his third drink, Richard imagined knowledge

spreading through the towers like Rotts, like Vees, like Placasores. For five hallucinatory minutes, he imagined that these diseases were real and not made up by the Parenthood to explain the Inspections. Staring glassy-eyed, he shuddered, imagining those never defined (and certainly never photographed) Placasores spreading from one Alphabet Boy to another until they fanned out into the Yard, where the Letter Girl B picked them up and carried them with her back to the second tower. He imagined Warren loosening the lid on a jar Richard once thought impossible to open. He imagined bugs, millions, scurrying about the Turrets, hiding in cracks, under pillows, in the windows and walls.

He absently brought a hand to his bare arm, swiped at the Moldus crawling there, plucked Vees from his knuckles.

"Kill 'em all," he whispered.

If this was what the end looked like, he refused to be embarrassed by it. So long as one boy was still clean (and there were many, right?), the experiment was without stain.

He tried to imagine a clean boy in all that gray area. Tried to recall his magnificent Alphabet Boys only a week back, before Warren Bratt betrayed him.

He crossed to his desk, picked up his phone, and pressed the number 1. He and Marilyn had their limited time together, by appointment, in the Glasgow Tunnel, an effort to respect the philosophy of their own experiment. A Plexiglas wall to separate even themselves from each other.

But sometimes a woman's touch was crucial.

"No," Marilyn said when she answered the phone.

"No?"

"I will not abort."

"We could begin anew."

"A new what, Richard?"

Richard didn't have an answer for this. In the beginning it was easy to contemplate attempting the experiment more than once. But twelve years deep, it was clear this was their only shot.

"Do you feel it, Marilyn?"

"Feel what?"

"Revolt."

Some silence. But Marilyn rarely allowed silences to grow. "I think it's time to do a little parenting, Richard."

"Speaking of parenting . . ."

"Yes. The man we found in the Orchard is in your Corner now."

"How many times has he come?"

"Does it matter?"

"To me. It does."

"He'd been watching your Turret for many months. It appears 'Mister Tree' makes for a reasonable hiding spot."

"Do we know which one he is?"

"He made no effort to hide it. Told us right from the very beginning who he was here to see."

"Which one?"

"He's J's father, dear. Come to assuage the guilt for having sold him."

Richard stared into his drink. Believed he could see the ice melting.

"J," he said. He didn't like that two controversies surrounded one boy. The odds didn't feel right.

"You'll get your answers from him by way of Boats."

"Oh, Marilyn . . . to hear him use the word *girl*."

"Did he?"

"I told you. He saw B outside his window."

"But did he use the word *girl*?"

"Yes. I told you, he—"

"No. You did not." Some silence. A shuffling of papers. "In Warren Bratt's book titled *Needs,* he used the word *woman* seven hundred times. *Her* four hundred and fifty. *She* about the same. But *girl* . . ."

Richard brought his drink to his lips, already knowing what

Marilyn was about to say, already feeling the bricks of the Turret loosen a little more.

"Not once, Richard. He didn't use the word once."

"Oh God."

"Where did J learn the word?"

"Oh God."

"Who told him the word, Richard? Who knows it other than . . . my girls?"

Boats

Richard was seven drinks deep by the time the game got under way. The sky was not dark beyond the windows of his first-floor quarters, nor would it be by the conclusion of any average game of Boats.

But this was no average game.

I saw a girl outside my window.

GIRL

Richard knew what questions to ask. Knew he'd have to answer some along the way. But what did it matter, telling the truth to a dead boy walking?

They had all day. After all, no parent was coming to pick up the boy.

"How about a game of Boats?" Richard asked.

UNDER DIFFERENT CIRCUMSTANCES J would have marveled at D.A.D.'s rooms. His private quarters, the place to which the man retired to privately improve the Parenthood. On a different day J would have been proud to be shown this inner sanctum.

But now J only saw D.A.D.'s lips opening and closing, opening and closing, repeating the one unfathomable word:

UNCLEAN

He's going to explain to you why you're okay. He's going to make you better.

Even now he turned to the Parenthood for comfort. J was the one who had failed. Not them.

"Comfortable?" D.A.D. asked.

D.A.D. did not look at him as he spoke. He arranged the Boats on the board, the muscles in his arms slinking under his skin like a buried reality. His voice as icy as Q's ladder.

"I'm fine," J said. The Inspectors stood by the door, blocking J's view of it.

A woman stood against the wall.

M.O.M.? J didn't think so. But whoever she was, he couldn't stop looking at her, over D.A.D.'s shoulder, until, visibly uneasy, she crossed out of view, behind him.

"Need anything to drink, J?"

D.A.D. smelled like he'd drunk a bottle of medicine before sitting down. But J didn't want anything himself. Felt too nervous to lift a glass of water.

"No, thank you."

Water

D.A.D.'s board was nicer than the ones the boys used. The water on the surface was much bluer and the individual waves were as detailed as if K had drawn them. The boats, made of metal, shone, just polished perhaps, and looked so real they could be carrying passengers, students of the game, here to watch them play.

To J, the deeper waters at the center of the board looked real enough to drown in.

"You like Boats, J?"

"Yes, of course. I love Boats."

J hardly recognized his own voice. Sounded younger than he was when Z was sent to the Corner.

"You hear that, Burt?" D.A.D. said, acknowledging the woman

standing behind J. "He loves Boats." Then, looking J in the eye without humor, without fatherhood, "Let's connect the nodes."

They both did, man and boy, sticking the small rubber ovals to their necks, their chests, their wrists.

D.A.D. gripped the line switch. The board hummed to rattling life.

"How did you learn the word *girl*, J?" D.A.D. asked calmly, sipping from a glass J hadn't noticed was on the table. "You can't win a game of telling the truth if you don't talk."

J knew the rules well enough. If you lied, your boat did not advance. And if your boat did not advance, everyone in the room knew you lied.

"The girl outside my window . . ."

"Yes?"

"Her told me the word."

"*She* told you the word."

J's boat moved forward. Its wake a white mist. Actual droplets descended to the tabletop.

The water in D.A.D.'s board, J realized, was real.

"Thank you," D.A.D. said. It was clear he was already waiting for his next turn. But J had turns of his own.

"What's a girl?"

D.A.D. answered without hesitation. "A girl is the opposite sex of a boy. She is necessary in procreation, being the one who carries the baby."

Ever seen a new boy growing on a Living Tree?

It was D.A.D.'s turn.

"Where did she tell you the word?"

"In my rooms."

J's voice trembled as his boat advanced. As a small yellow light turned on outside the captain's cabin, illuminating the darker waters ahead.

At first, D.A.D. said nothing. Only stared. As if whatever he'd been sipping had turned him to stone. Then, "Your turn."

J saw red rising in D.A.D.'s face.

"Have you always known what a girl is?"

D.A.D. smiled, but there was nothing happy about it. "Yes. How'd she get in your rooms?"

D.A.D.'s boat advanced. Its light came on, too. J tried to process what D.A.D. had just said. Yes, he'd always known. Then why hadn't J?

The Parenthood has been lying to us.

Boats had a way of making an Alphabet Boy want to tell the truth, if only to pull it from his opponent sooner.

"She climbed Q's ice ladder. She came to my window."

D.A.D. leaned back in his chair. He let out a single clipped syllable of angry laughter.

J's boat advanced.

"I have so many questions," J said. "I can barely—"

"Your turn, J."

J's mind reeled. A wheel of worries. He took hold of the closest one. "Am I sick?"

D.A.D. did not look him in the eye. "No," he said. "You're not sick."

"But I—"

"One question per turn, J."

D.A.D.'s boat moved forward, rocking upon bigger waves.

"Which of the other boys did you talk to about her?"

J was still trying to make sense of the last answer. Not sick? Yet . . . unclean?

Lies. K's voice in his bedroom in the dark.

"Boats is so much more than a game," D.A.D. said, a spark of pride in his eye. He ran a finger along the tabletop, the space between himself and the board. When he lifted it, water glistened. "It's what's known in the real world as a lie detector. I'll ask you again. Which of the other boys did you talk to about her?"

The real world, J thought. And what was his own?

"None of them."

J's boat moved forward, approaching the increasingly rocky middle of the board.

"Why did you hide the second Turret from us?"

"Because I didn't want you to know what's in it."

D.A.D's boat advanced. J knew he'd asked a bad question. It was one of the tricks of Boats: asking a question that could be answered halfway.

"How long have you known, J?"

"How long have I known?"

"Play the fucking game, J!"

J leaned back in his seat. His entire body felt bright with panic.

"Her came last night."

His boat advanced.

"Why did you hide girls from us?"

"I wanted to breed great thinkers, J. The opposite sex gets in the way of this happening. Men waste their lives chasing women."

D.A.D.'s boat didn't move. The woman cleared her throat behind J.

D.A.D. said, "I felt my life was a failure. In precisely this way."

His boat advanced.

"How was your life a failure?"

D.A.D. slammed a closed fist on the table.

"One question!"

D.A.D.'s face went as red as his coat, which hung on the back of his chair. He gulped from his glass. He said, "You say you didn't mention it to your brothers—"

"No, I didn't—"

"Do *not* interrupt me, you little *shit*."

J's mouth snapped shut.

"You say you didn't mention it to your brothers, but did any of them *see* the girl?"

J shook his head no.

"Answer the fucking question out loud, J."

"Not that I know of, no."

J's boat reached the rough waters at the middle of the board. He felt water upon his face. The boat sank, momentarily, before rising again.

How deep did D.A.D.'s board go?

"Ask me a question, J."

"Were you raised, side by side, with girls?"

"Yes."

D.A.D.'s boat advanced, dipped, stayed down long enough for J to think it had fallen to the floor below, then rose again, level with J's at center-board.

"How?" J asked. "How did you pass your Inspections growing up?"

"One question, J."

"But how did you pass?"

D.A.D. rose and slammed both palms on the table. Cold water from the board splashed onto J's hands.

"The Parenthood is an *isolated community,* J. In the real world there are *millions* of children raised without Inspections. You were given the opportunity of a lifetime. And you blew it."

J only stared.

Millions.

D.A.D. sat again. The table shook. He said, "Did you write down what you know?"

"No."

J's boat advanced, but not much. The water pushed back past center-board. Only big truths could deliver a boy to the end.

"Your move."

"Is my whole life a lie?"

This time D.A.D. did hesitate. He stared long at the two pieces bobbing between them. He sipped his drink. Then, "Do you know there are twenty-year-olds reading at the same level as you *right now*? That you could pass a university mathematics course? If you're asking if you've been lied to your whole life, the answer is yes. Things have been hidden from you. Many things. But if you're asking me if the person you are is not real because of this, then I would answer with an emphatic no. I would argue that you and your brothers are more *truth* than any boy ever was."

J watched as D.A.D.'s boat advanced. It moved farther than his own had.

"There are no Living Trees?" he asked.

"No," D.A.D. said, ignoring the double question. "You were created by a weak father and a murdering mother."

J wiped water from his face. Boats?

Tears?

"What's her name, J?"

J shook his head no.

"What's her name, J?"

"I won't tell you."

"You know that I'd never hurt her, right?"

J looked to D.A.D.'s troubled face. The man looked as pained as he felt himself. It sounded so true, those few words. Sounded so much like the man J knew D.A.D. to be.

"You wouldn't?"

Of course not, J! The Parenthood protects!

"Never."

"I can't." Crying now. Unable to make out anybody in the room. Unable to make out the room.

Even the action on the board was a blur.

"What's her name? Was it B? I don't think it was."

"I can't, I—"

J wiped his eyes and D.A.D. was beside him. The board shifted as the wires connecting the nodes to D.A.D. were pulled.

"Richard!" the woman behind J yelled.

But it was too late. Through the foggy wall of tears, an open hand. J didn't realize he was falling until he hit the floor.

"You want Vees, J? You want *Placasores*? TELL ME HER NAME OR I WILL GIVE YOU ROTTS!"

J didn't want to get up. Didn't want to open his eyes. Didn't want to hear D.A.D.'s voice ever again like he'd just heard it.

And, despite K's words, despite what he believed to be the truth, that Vees and Placasores did not exist . . . he thought then that maybe they did.

And that maybe D.A.D. meant it when he said he could give them to him.

"K," he said quietly. "Her name is K."

Even then, under unfathomable conditions, speaking her name felt good.

Telling D.A.D. the truth did, too.

And his boat advanced. Far.

"Good move, J." D.A.D. was seated again, removing the nodes from his body. J sat halfway up, saw water spilling over the edges of the table. "Saving the heavy truth for rocky waters. Gives you more distance. You might have won this game after all." D.A.D. took his coat from his chair back. "But we're done here."

As D.A.D. put his arms into his red jacket, J saw it as blood, *real* blood. As though K's ax-wielding girls walking the Turret halls had already been to this room.

"D.A.D.?"

But D.A.D. was lifting the black receiver on his desk.

"What's going to happen to her?" J asked.

The Inspectors stepped to the table. The woman to D.A.D.'s side.

"J is spoiled rotten," D.A.D. said into the phone. "Your K is, too. No surprise there. K and B. Thick as thieves."

He hung up.

"D.A.D.?"

D.A.D. was heading for the door.

"Like cockroaches, you fucking kids. I save you from death before you're even born and somehow *I'm* the bad man."

"You said you wouldn't hurt her," J said, up now, stumbling toward D.A.D.

The Inspectors were on him fast.

"You ask what's going to happen to her," D.A.D. said, "but you never stop to think what's going to happen to *me*."

The Inspectors dragged J to the door. D.A.D. opened it, then bent until his nose was touching J's.

"You ever pay attention to the bread in the cafeteria, J?"

J only stared. Only thought, *K*.

Meet me in the tunnel after dark.

Beyond the windows of D.A.D.'s quarters, dark was near.

"You ever seen bread when it sours?"

We have to do it soon. Before they change how they do things.

"It grows mold, J. It rots."

K.

"You've *gone bad*. And the only thing to do with boys who have gone bad is to throw them out."

D.A.D. gestured, and the Inspectors dragged J out the door.

Meet me in the tunnel . . .

K would be in the tunnel, too.

. . . after dark.

Her voice like a door of its own. Not closing. Opening.

J was on his way.

As the Inspectors took him, as he clawed to get loose, as he imagined a wood door with melting blood-red letters, the names of boys and girls, *T-H-E C-O-R-N-E-R* dripping to the floor, J thought, yes, he would meet her in the basement after dark.

It wasn't until they were in the staff bathroom, caged momentarily in a nightmare acoustic box, that J accepted the high-pitched wailing that had accompanied them from D.A.D.'s quarters as his own.

"Show Us What You Would Do"

It smelled bad below, something dead, something wet. Having spent his entire life in the clean Turret and the fresh air of the Yard and Orchard, J had nothing to relate it to. The closest association he made was his wet winter clothes on the heater in his rooms, but this thinking didn't last long, as his reality was unspooling by the second.

The rumbling hum of the boiler brought him to dig his nails into the arms that dragged him through the cobblestoned halls. The Inspectors didn't seem to mind. Either J's strength was insignificant or, as he had fleetingly seen in the storm of blurred terror, the men felt too guilty to swat his small fingers aside.

J was certain every door they passed was the Corner, until he could actually read the nameplates, the stencils, the pieces of paper. With his mind's eye (piqued, cleaved) he saw blood-black letters, the blood of the child, the blood of dead brothers and the Letter Girl J. In his mind's eye the letters were uneven, the word getting smaller as it was spelled, as though the man responsible for labeling the door did so in a rush to get away from it.

THE CORNER

You ever pay attention to the bread in the cafeteria, J?

He heard breathing from up the hall, from behind him, from either side. The Inspectors? It sounded more like the halls themselves were breathing. As if the basement had begun the process of swallowing him.

"Turn around!" he called. "I haven't done anything wrong! You'll feel . . ." He thought of the book *Needs* and how perfectly Warren Bratt had titled it. "You'll feel *contrite*!"

"Easy, J," Collins mumbled. "This isn't any easier for us."

How *human* the Inspectors looked to him now! How unlike men and like grown-up boys instead!

These men had protected him his entire life. These men had loved him. He'd loved these men!

Let me show you how to tie your shoe, J.

Let me help you with those gloves, J.

I hear you're doing well with your studies, J. Tell an old man, what's your secret?

"*You're* the ones with secrets!" J yelled as Collins tugged him around a corner and Jeffrey attempted to quiet him with a hand over his mouth.

Luxley once wrote of a *gothic castle,* and J now believed he'd modeled it after the basement of the Turret. Lanterns high on the walls. Wet stones. Sweat stones? *Funereal* was a word J had to look up in the Parenthood Dictionary. He loved that word. Dreamed of that word many times. Even tried to use it in an essay in grammar class. But now, here, it was much too real. *He* was the focus of the funeral, dead soon, the shrieking, bleeding boy.

He reached for the stones in the walls, to put a stop to this forward motion, but the stones were sharp, damp, without pattern, and his fingertips bled like the letters on the door they took him to.

With every supply closet they passed, J thought he heard a smacking, big lips hidden here in the basement, the world beneath his own.

J imagined faces as worried as his own in one office they passed.

"*YOU'RE ALL SO SCARED!*" he screamed.

Then, swiftly, the fresh clacking of newly arrived boots ahead. A slash of red in the black heart of the basement.

"A perfect match," D.A.D. said, leading now, his back to J and to the Inspectors that dragged him. "Let them play together in the Corner."

Was K already there? In the Corner?

"Jesus," Jeffrey said. "Look at his toes!"

J's feet were bleeding badly. The big toe on his right foot was almost shredded to the bone. Yet he tried to find purchase with his feet. Tried to slow down the funeral, *his* funeral, the end to his book of needs.

Where was Q? L and D? Did they know he'd been sent to the Corner? Did they cry? Did they think he deserved it because the Parenthood said so?

"You don't have to do this!" J yelled to the Inspectors. "If he lies to us, he lies to you!"

D.A.D. stopped. Turned to face J. In the lantern light his face looked more like a stranger's than it had yesterday morning, when he discovered Warren Bratt's brilliant book.

"What did you just say, J?"

The Inspectors stopped, too.

J, naked, hanging in the arms of the Inspectors, looked up to Collins. "You don't have to do this."

Collins looked away and in doing so revealed, behind him on the wall, an arrow painted as red as D.A.D.'s gloves.

J felt hope.

GLASGOW TUNNEL:

RICHARD ONLY

Oh, K, oh, K, oh, K.

And just beyond D.A.D., J saw the tunnel entrance itself. A gap in the wall. Something too dark to be a closet, too wide for an office door.

"Let him go," D.A.D. said.

Collins and Jeffrey only stared. Had D.A.D. changed his mind?

"You mean it?" Collins asked.

"I always mean it."

The Inspectors let J go.

J rubbed his shoulders and his armpits where they'd been holding him.

"And what would you do," D.A.D. asked him, "if you didn't listen to me, if you could make up your own mind? Hmm? Where would you go?"

D.A.D. spread his arms out, mocking J with false options.

J looked to Inspector Collins. Inspector Jeffrey. How different they looked without the dogs behind them. How different they looked, slouched, guilty, against the walls in the basement.

"Show us," D.A.D. said. "Show us what you would do."

J stood up straight, inhaled deep.

Then he ran.

Past D.A.D. as the man reached down to stop him.

J turned right, entered the darkness of the tunnel, felt free momentarily, invisible to both D.A.D. and the Inspectors, undetectable by the Parenthood, *gone*. Behind, already far behind, he heard the echoes of shoes on gravel.

"K!" J called.

His voice came back to him, swallowed then repeated by the throat of the tunnel.

K! . . . K! . . . K! . . . K! . . . K! . . . K!

The steps behind him were losing speed, losing volume.

K! . . . K! . . . K! . . . K! . . . K!

He was almost free, it seemed, free now in the darkness.

K! . . . K! . . . K! . . . K! . . .

Meet me in the tunnel after dark.

"K! I'm here!"

D.A.D.'s laughter behind, the huffing of the Inspectors. Were they close again?

"K!" he cried.

And K responded. K's voice in the tunnel. *Here.*

But it was too late for him to recognize it as a warning.

"J, STOP!"

His nose struck the Plexiglas first, the impact crushing it to the side of his face. The rest of him followed. His teeth, cheeks, and chin flattened to the divider.

K screamed his name again as J was thrown back from the wall and fell hard to the tunnel's dirt floor.

Lights came on.

On his back now, J brought a hand to his bleeding nose. Through watery eyes he saw what he'd hit. He saw K on the other side of it. And beyond her, a mirror of the blackness he'd run through.

As the blood poured from his nose and outlined his lips, J smiled.

Meet me . . .

But K was pointing behind him, telling him to get up, GET UP, *GET UP!*

There was blood on K, too. All over her face and hair. On her hands and arms.

"What happened to you?" J said, trying to stand.

But K was shaking her head no. *No no. Turn around. Don't think of me. Don't be distracted by* me.

The Inspectors tackled him to the floor, his teeth smashing a second time.

K pounded on the glass.

Don't worry, he tried to say. *Don't worry, K!*

A hand went over his mouth, then his eyes. Then he was being dragged again. Back.

Between fingers he saw the color red rushing to the glass divider. Saw D.A.D. pointing at K. Saw K reach for the tunnel's dirt side. Heard D.A.D. yelling at her.

The lights went off. He swiped the hand from his mouth.

"LET ME GO!" J yelled.

But they pulled him from the tunnel, back into the cobblestoned halls. Then deeper into the basement.

J, blind and bleeding, remembered D.A.D. as he'd looked just before the lights in the tunnel went off. Saw the fear and confusion on the man's face.

He looked more afraid than K did.

When Collins finally removed his hand from J's eyes, someone tugged hard on his hair.

D.A.D. again. He brought his nose to J's broken face.

"How does it feel to know the one decision you made on your own was a bad one?"

But D.A.D. didn't wait for an answer. He looked quick down the hall, back toward the tunnel.

J heard a creaking behind him. Jeffrey opening a door. He craned his neck enough to see something he didn't think even Lawrence Luxley could've imagined: A spot where two basement walls met was revolving, opening to a hidden room.

It didn't matter that the door looked nothing like the one he'd been raised to fear. It didn't matter that there was no label on it at all.

It was the Corner, no matter what J said it was.

"I'm sorry," Collins said.

J fell as he was shoved hard into the room. There he saw scant light from a distance, felt a concrete floor beneath his scratched palms, and heard harsh wheezing from only a few feet away.

"K?" he asked. But he knew she wasn't in here with him.

As D.A.D. yelled for the Inspectors to follow him, the door swung closed.

"No," a voice answered. "I'm not K."

J was too weak to be afraid of it.

"Who's in here?" he asked.

A man leaned forward on what J's eyes now told him was a wooden bench. The man wore cracked glasses, and his face and arms looked as battered as J's own.

"Lawrence Luxley," the man said. "We've met." J's eyes hadn't adjusted enough to see the sad smile. "But you can call me Warren."

Two Markers in the Dark

"**J**esus Christ," Warren said. "They didn't even let you get dressed?" Then, "Come on, sit down."

His voice was hoarse. As if he'd been yelling.

"I don't belong in here," J said.

"If there's one person who knows you don't belong here, it's me."

In the dim light of the second room, J saw two markers in the dirt.

"Sit down," Warren said.

J did, feeling the cool metal lockers against his back, relief in his bleeding feet.

"I think they went after K."

"Where is he?"

"Her," J said.

Warren was quiet. Then he chuckled. "My God," he said. "Things have changed quickly around here."

"She came to my rooms. She figured it all out. Everything you were trying to tell us."

"So you read the book?"

"Some of it." Then J gave Warren the most exhausted, the most meaningful and meaningless compliment he'd ever received. "It's the best book in the world."

"Thank you," Warren said, holding back many emotions. "You don't seem very surprised to discover Lawrence Luxley is also Warren Bratt."

J stared into the darkness, his eyes still adjusting.

"I'm just worried about K."

"I understand. But worry about us, too. We've got probably ten minutes to live."

Some silence then.

"What's going to happen to us?" J asked.

"I can't say for sure. But it can't be worse than what's upstairs."

J understood.

"Are we going to die in here?"

"Yes."

J looked to the scant light emanating from the second, deeper room. It stretched into this one, curling over a concrete lip like a piece of yellow fabric. At the very extent of its reach, J saw the soles of two shoes.

He sat up quick.

"That's a person!" he said. "Who is that?"

He hurried to the body on the floor. As he rolled it over, he saw it was a man. Old enough to be an Inspector. Old enough to be D.A.D.

He inched away from the dried blood upon the man's chest.

Warren said, "I think it's one of your fathers."

"What does that mean?"

"One of your *real* fathers. Here to see if his son was okay." Then, "Hasn't been dead long, I don't think. Minutes, maybe, before I arrived."

J inched toward the body again, touched the man's head, his shoulders. He opened the dead eyes with his thumbs. Closed them again.

He thought of a figure crouched behind Mister Tree far below his eighth-floor window.

"We're gonna die like him," J said. "Just like this."

"Well," Warren said, "I should know more about this than I do. But what I believe will happen is that door we came through is going to open. Someone is going to come through it. And, yes, they're going to kill us."

J stood up quick.

"So let's not let them!"

A cracking sound from out in the hall and J and Warren froze.

"It's the Parenthood," Warren whispered. "Still breathing."

They stared at the door a long time.

"We have to try to get out of here," J said. "When they come. When the door opens."

Warren shook his head. "Go ahead and try. And my God I hope you succeed. But me? I don't deserve to get out of here. I'm one of the monsters who lied to you."

"But you tried to help!"

"A little too late."

J stepped to him in the dark, thinking instinctively that he needed this man to help him, that he couldn't make it out of this room without the help of an adult, a man, a member of the Parenthood.

Still looking for the Parenthood to protect him.

But the Corner door opened before he reached him.

J turned fast, squinting at the light from the hall. Warren spoke first, and the fear in his voice scared J more than the hooded figure that entered.

"Couldn't look us in the eye, you coward? Had to wear a hood?"

"You," the figure said, pointing a tool at Warren. "Go stand in the corner."

J recognized the tool from one of K's drawings. But he didn't know what it could do.

He inched away from it, toward the corner of the room.

"Not you."

Warren stood up. "You're gonna have to kill me standing as I am. I'm not standing in the fucking corner." Then, "Who are you? Collins? Jeffrey?"

The figure raised the tool level with Warren's head.

"No!" J hollered. "Please! He tried to help me! He tried to *help*!"

"That's the *last* thing they wanna hear right now," Warren cried. He gritted his teeth and closed his eyes. "Go on! Do it!"

But the figure lowered the tool and turned its hooded head to J. As it did, J smelled something sweet enough to break through the despair.

He had no way of knowing the pillowcase was worn the same way Marcia Jones had worn it in Judith Nancy's *White Lies*. But he could've picked that smell out of a forest.

"K?"

"No," the voice said. The unmistakable voice of a girl. "I'm Q."

She removed the pillowcase, revealing only the third woman J had ever seen in his life.

Warren opened his eyes.

"Is K okay?" J asked, astonished, breathless.

"Who is he?" She nodded toward Warren.

J saw that Q's face was streaked with as much blood as K's had been on the other side of the wall in the tunnel. He understood she'd already killed today. Maybe many.

"This is Warren Bratt," he said. "He's on our side."

She stared at Warren. "Can you get us out of here?"

"You mean can I get you to the real world?" Warren asked.

"Yes."

"Yes. I can do that."

"All right," Q said. She lowered the tool. "Get us out of here, then."

Warren went to the Corner door.

"Where's Richard now?" he asked her. And the way he asked it, J understood that Warren planned to kill today, too. Maybe many.

"We have a plan," she said.

"We?"

Q nodded. "We got everyone else."

Revolt

Earlier that morning, as J still slept the troubled sleep of knowledge, K slipped quietly out of his rooms. She was not worried about encountering any of the staff. If someone saw her, she would kill him.

She got the chance before leaving the building.

Passing through the Body Hall, through the swinging kitchen door, she stopped and stood motionless, facing a man holding a plate, water filling a sink behind him.

"Whoa," the man said. "What are you doing here?"

K walked toward him, a direct line, as if there was nothing he could do to frighten her.

She saw the way his eyes shifted from one side of the kitchen to the other, perhaps looking for help.

She saw the way his lips parted, as though ready to call out, to announce the arrival of a girl in the boys' Turret.

And she saw, too, as she slashed his neck with a knife from a magnetic rack less than a foot from where he stood, the way the skin of his neck split easily.

He fell to his knees.

K took hold of him by the back of his white shirt, dragged him out through the garbage door and into the Yard. It wasn't until she had him buried in pine needles and snow that she allowed herself to think, *You've killed your first adult.*

She was grateful for the man in the kitchen. For teaching her how easily it could be done.

She was ready, she knew, to do more.

Within two hours of returning to her Turret, she knew that most of the Letter Girls were, too.

Some girls refused to believe what they were hearing. Some believed but wouldn't partake. In total, four decided to stay in W's bedroom until it was over. G stood guard to make sure none of them attempted to reach M.O.M.

E was especially hysterical. The news went against her nature in more ways than one; she'd modeled her entire self-image after M.O.M. Down to how she responded to the insane information.

"K," she said, attempting to maintain a civil smile. "You are *scaring* me."

K didn't have time to convince. Rather, pressing the point of her knife to E's back, she forced her sister into the dog area of the fifth-floor Check-Up room. She didn't say anything encouraging upon exiting, didn't try to calm her.

There was simply no time.

Q helped a lot. Including removing B from quarantine, which consisted of unlocking a first-floor room and letting B out. B, finding it difficult to let go of her former life, despite siding with K and Q, said she had a game of Boats scheduled with M.O.M.

"Not anymore," Q said. "Never again."

They started in the basement of their Turret. At first, some of the girls ran from what K and Q did. But the bloodletting revealed more than the colors running through the veins of the Parenthood staff; with each office they entered, the Letter Girls saw more and more evidence of the lies K, B, and Q were convinced of. A thing called a "Burt Report" removed more doubt. And the paltry marker for their sister J (in the Corner!) took the rest.

With the other Letter Girls on board, the job of killing the adults went much faster. But it wasn't without its emotional repercussions.

Crying, Q and P slit the throats of two women who worked in a room labeled PRINTING. In ACCOUNTING, F and H held down a much older woman as B stabbed her repeatedly in the chest. A whistling janitor was clubbed in the nose by a shrieking R. Z strangled a nurse with her bare hands. Then shook for the five minutes following.

They chanted as they worked, unified by a mantra K had given them, their voices marred by terror:

"Take . . . it . . . back."

The three words could be heard in almost every hall of the basement, as the staff was swarmed by Letter Girls armed with everything from knives to paperweights.

Blood erupted in the offices, the women who were yet unaware that the Parenthood had been sliced open. Blood on the cobblestone walls. Blood on the supply-closet doors. Bloody handprints on every door.

On Floor 1, they slaughtered the cooks, the teachers, the cleaners. B gutted a nurse with a billhook. Q half-beheaded Professor Ullman with a spade. They spent a lot of time hiding. Waiting in the shadows of the halls. Hiding in the corners of doorways. Listening to the otherwise everyday movements and motions of the Parenthood.

They searched, too.

K found Inspector Krantz in the same staff bathroom they'd passed through on their way up from the basement.

She recognized the boots under the stall door and didn't hesitate to kick that door in. The flat metal cracked the Inspector's nose, bringing K the immediate satisfaction of immediate blood. As Krantz brought her hands to her face, K shattered her skull with a hammer. Then she shattered it again. And again. Until the woman had completely fallen to the side of the toilet, squeezed between it and the stall wall.

Q slammed Inspector Rivers's head in a classroom door until Rivers stopped crying out for help.

K used a saw on Judith Nancy.

The leisure writer was asleep in a bedroom not far from M.O.M.'s quarters. She woke to a prickling sensation, then all-out pain, as K broke the skin on her belly, the saw going back and forth, digging, digging.

"What's *going on*?" Nancy cried. Then, "You."

As if, even under unfathomable duress, she'd admitted to having seen this moment coming.

B and Q stabbed Nancy in the eyes. The ears. The mouth. K broke her fingers and, crying, said, "You'll never write again!" But the woman was already dead by then.

So much killing done, the Letter Girls congregated outside the Body Hall. For the first time in their lives, they felt the power of numbers. K sent B to release E. To tell G to let the other four out of W's room. There was nobody left for the Letter Girls who weren't involved to warn.

Let M.O.M. know. Let her come looking for K.

Twenty minutes later, just as the first slash of gray interrupted the sky and sent word through the glass hallway that the sun was on its way down, M.O.M. exited her quarters to find a band of Letter Girls, armed and bloody, their eyes unfathomably without innocence. But Marilyn knew better. Her girls were looking at her, for the first time, out the *front of their eyes*, having been shown the light by someone, someone who had unearthed the truth of their lives.

She didn't need Richard to have told her it was K. That was clear when K spoke to her first.

"Upstairs," K said.

M.O.M., twelve years used to giving commands, twelve years used to molding their minds how she deemed fit, did not make to move. Rather, she made to scold.

"Who do you think you are?" she said. "Conduct yourself like a lady this instant." Then, perhaps because nothing changed in the eyes of the girls, and certainly not in K's, she made to turn back to her office, but B sliced her hand to the bone with a tool Marilyn recognized as being used often in the Yard. As the blood spilled to splash the outfit she'd picked for a game of Boats with the very girl who'd cut her, she screamed. A brief and horrible sound the girls never expected to hear from her lips.

"Upstairs," K repeated.

THE SEVERITY OF the situation was self-evident, but Marilyn was still thinking of her hand. Thinking of B, who had cut it. B, who should have been in quarantine. B, who should have been sent to the Corner last night, when she confessed. Had she and Richard lost their minds? Had they been blinded by the very children they'd worked so hard to raise?

"A," K said, addressing her sister that had the most mature voice. "You stay in the office. If the phone on the desk rings, pick it up. Pretend to be M.O.M. Okay?"

"Okay."

A, covered in blood, entered M.O.M.'s office and, after a moment's hesitation, sat in a big chair at a big desk. Some of the other girls stared into M.O.M.'s quarters—still, even now, awed.

Then K had a knife to M.O.M.'s back. Marilyn didn't need to be told again. She let the girls lead her to the elevator. Q pressed the button. When the doors opened, M.O.M. removed her glasses and turned to smile at her girls. Her eyes looked much older than even the last time they'd seen them.

"What's upstairs?" she asked.

"We can lie to you," K said. "For twelve years if you'd like. We can make up something that's up there. We can hide words from you and pretend we're not going to do what we're going to do. Or you can get in now and get it over with."

M.O.M. scowled. "And who do you think is responsible for you being so smart, K? Who made it so you can plan at all? Your mother, your *real* mother, was prepared to butcher you."

V held the elevator doors open.

"In," K said. "To the roof."

"The roof?" M.O.M. asked. More than one girl gasped at the fear in her eyes. L even pointed at it. "And why the roof, dear?"

B slashed at her belly. Blood rose to the surface of her white pantsuit. M.O.M., still gripping her hand, screamed again.

Then many girls shoved her into the elevator at once. But only K, B, and Q rode up with her.

As the doors closed, the remaining girls' stoic expressions vanished and Marilyn knew this had all been planned. Even this. The three girls and herself. Riding up.

"It's been a long time since you've been in an elevator," she said to K.

An eleventh-hour attempt at diplomacy?

It was Q who had pressed the highest floor and it was Q who got out first, holding a long blade to M.O.M.'s chest as K and B forced her out of the elevator.

"Upstairs," K said, acknowledging the ladder at the end of the hall.

"The roof," M.O.M. repeated.

"You can see the Placasores from there," B said.

"Don't get cute with—"

Q slashed M.O.M.'s ankle with the blade. M.O.M. cried out.

"Upstairs," K repeated.

Marilyn attempted to walk with dignity, her shoulders square, her chin level with the floor. But her ankle, her wrist, her belly, all brought her to stumble.

B climbed the ladder first.

"I want you to think very hard about what you're doing," M.O.M. said. Q made to slash her again, and she slapped the girl's hand away. "I'm going. *I'm going.*"

K and Q followed her up.

On the roof, the sun's descent was even more evident. K thought, *Meet me in the tunnel after dark.*

"To the edge," she said.

"No," M.O.M. said, her chin higher than level now.

Q slashed her thigh.

Marilyn fell to the roof floor. She tried to grip her leg with both hands, but the one B had cut simply wouldn't work. She cried out, eyes to the sky, as Q slashed her chest.

Then, perhaps born of an instinct greater than her breeding, Marilyn tried to crawl for her life. The girls did not marvel at her will to live. Rather, they nodded as she got closer to the very place they wanted her to be.

Once there, M.O.M. seemed to recognize, distantly, that she'd reached the furthest point she could. She smiled. It was perhaps the warmest expression the girls had ever seen on her face.

She had crawled to the Corner.

"Spoiled rotten," Q said. The other girls did not laugh. Below, however, voices could be heard, some more lively than others.

When M.O.M. looked over the edge of the Turret, her one good hand gripping the corner where the two ridges of concrete met, she saw the faces of the other Letter Girls staring up. They were standing around a hole in the ground, a big one, and her first thought was, *Would you please look into this, Krantz?*

But it was M.O.M. who looked into it, as some life remained in her head, even after K had severed it from her body with an ax.

She could almost count the bricks of the Turret as her head fell down to the Yard.

The last thing she saw was a makeshift marker in the hand of one of the girls—which girl she could no longer tell. It was certainly an unworthy tombstone for a woman such as herself. The marker had three lowercase letters and no more upon it:

m.o.m.

She had just enough time remaining to attempt an understanding, to sound the three letters out, before the life finally left her, her brain run dry, and her head landed with a wet thud in the dirt. Had she one more half minute of thought, she might have noted the perfect arc of the fall, the precise depth of the grave.

All a perfectly executed experiment, conducted by her brilliant, precocious, and undistracted Letter Girls.

Revenge

After J was shoved into the Corner, Richard, flanked by both Inspectors, returned to the tunnel's entrance, where the phone was set in the stone wall.

The Letter Girl K had been on the other side of the glass in the tunnel. Covered in blood.

Whose?

This is not a mutiny, he told himself. *It's an isolated incident and J has been dealt with. Now K will be dealt with, too.*

The other boys were on lockdown. Confined to their rooms. J's telling him that nobody else had seen the girl wasn't good enough. Even if it did register as honest with the game. J might not have known who saw what. Richard would find out.

But first, why wasn't Marilyn answering her phone?

He considered aborting the whole experiment. Considered rounding up all the Alphabet Boys, lining them up against the Turret bricks, shooting them one by one.

Should he panic?

He hung up the phone. He didn't *want* to panic. J was in the Corner. Surely K had escaped her own Corner. Surely she'd been put back in by now.

He considered sending the Inspectors to the second Turret. But no. That would jeopardize all of Marilyn's girls.

What else to do but go up? Call Marilyn again from his office?

"Watch the Corner," he told Collins and Jeffrey.

He'd already put together an explanation for J's absence by the time he reached the first floor. He refined it in the elevator to the third. J simply didn't fit in. He was sent to a new Parenthood, where boys like him might thrive. Life was about overcoming sadness, boys, my boys. Lose and live. Live and learn.

He wouldn't tell them about J in the Corner. Not yet. He needed more information from the others before he froze them with living nightmares.

No man can withstand this much guilt.

Warren had said that to him earlier, as Richard walked him from quarantine to the Corner. But it was something else the fat troll had said that really irked him.

Women don't distract, Richard. They inspire.

As the elevator rose, Richard reminded himself that he was indeed a big thinker. He cited the speeches he'd given, the events he'd planned, the boys he'd raised.

Oh, how the staff must revere him! All he'd done for them! All they'd seen him do.

He had no way of knowing that both Collins and Jeffrey were killed by the Letter Girls Q and B outside the Corner that harbored Warren and J.

He had no way of knowing Gordon had a garden fork in his belly, that he lay flat on the white carpet of the Body Hall.

You can't consider yourself remarkable, Richard thought, *without being disappointed by the people around you.*

And, ah, what a disappointment J was in the end.

When the number 3 lit up and the bell announced his arrival, Richard had convinced himself the Parenthood would be stable once again. Perhaps it would even grow stronger for this.

He stepped off the elevator and entered the hall.

He paused.

The hall looked the same. The doors and the floors.

So what was different?

Richard sniffed the air. Possibly it was the floor shift, boxes of belongings moved about, strange scents rising.

He waited. He didn't like it. Whatever it was. He didn't like it.

He went first to F's door and opened it. Inside, F the boy and F the girl stood side by side, facing him.

They held knives.

A vision as impossible as A and Z, risen from the dead.

An Alphabet Boy and a Letter Girl.

Together.

"Hi, Richard," F said. He wagged the knife.

Richard fled the room. Went to X's, opened it.

X the boy and X the girl.

Holding knives.

Do not panic. Do NOT panic. If one boy is secure, JUST ONE BOY . . .

Richard moved to G's door and kicked it open. Before he could register that G the boy and G the girl were walking toward him, carrying axes, the door to the stairs opened down the hall.

W the boy holding hands with W the girl.

D the boy and D the girl.

"D," Richard said, the authority in his voice irrevocably lost, "you have been a *bad boy*!"

Ruined, Richard. Every one of them.

No . . . just this floor . . . just this floor . . .

What are you going to do? Start again?

"Unclean! You're all unclean!" he cried, inching back toward the Check-Up room door. "You all have Placasores! Are you happy, F? *STOP SMILING! STOP SMILING AT ME!*"

Richard charged and F stuck him with a knife.

Gaping at the blood from his gut, the blood on his fingers, Richard looked to Q, his Q. When had Q arrived?

"My boy . . ."

When had they *all* arrived? The floor was full of them. And only more were coming through the stairwell door.

"Inspection," B the girl said.

Richard looked to her.

She's covered in blood. Where's Marilyn?

"Inspection."

They were all saying it. All the boys and girls.

"What do you mean to do?" he said.

"INSPECTION!" they yelled.

From the far end of the hall, the elevator doors opened. When had it gone back down?

In it, J. The Letter Girls K and Q.

Warren Bratt.

"Warren," Richard said. "No no. You can't be a part of this. This is ... this is *murder*, Warren. You did not sign up for this! Think of your life! You're throwing your life away!"

"INSPECTION!" the boys and girls yelled.

Forty-nine of them.

"Get in the Check-Up room," B the girl said. But it might have been any one of them.

"Marilyn predicted you'd revolt at age twenty," Richard said, trembling, one hand on the Check-Up room door. "But here you've done it at twelve." Then, a smile. "See how advanced you are? My boys ... ?"

The kids stepped toward him. Armed. All of them.

He opened the Check-Up room door and stared down at the handle.

"This door has never opened from the outside," he said. "Who reversed the locks?"

From the crowd of them, nobody raised a hand.

Tears in his eyes, Richard nodded.

"That's my boys."

He entered the room. He turned to face them.

"What will you do without me?" he asked.

But they gave him no response.

And J closed the door. And K locked it.

Out

Two days after locking Richard in the third-floor Check-Up room, Warren and the forty-nine kids discovered a shack a mile through the pines behind the girls' Turret. Inside, they found three sleeping men. The cabin smelled of alcohol and smoke. Warren recognized them as classic Parenthood employees: ex-cons with a real need to hide.

He woke them as the kids stood outside the cabin door. He told them their employers had been killed, that they would want to pack up and leave if they didn't want to meet the same end.

The only question they asked was how to get their money out of their individual accounts. Warren told them how. Then, with only a bag of clothes each, they left the cabin, the pines, and the Parenthood.

The boys and girls spent a month in the two Turrets. Warren told them they had to. Had to eat. Pack. Plan. They couldn't just leave this world and enter the next one. They needed some guidance. Some wisdom. They needed to know the rules of the real world, no matter how unreal it was going to feel.

They all read *Needs*. Cover to cover. Boys and girls.

Most avoided the third floor of the boys' Turret, but not all. In the early days of their stay, some enjoyed listening to the starving man moaning on the other side of the metal door. And when those moans became weak utterances, a few boys and a few girls snuck inside. Just to see.

"He's still dressed in red."

"Thin as a blue notebook."

"His hair is longer; his nails are longer."

"He looks like a statue. Stuck that way."

"Reaching."

"Reaching for a magnifying glass on the floor."

Warren didn't need to see this, though he understood why the boys and girls did. Their accounts grew more ghastly and, in direct proportion, a sense of justice expanded.

K and J did not avoid the third-floor Check-Up room. Just like they didn't avoid the feelings they were experiencing for one another. In a way, it was easy to pinpoint: Their having met was the catalyst for the freedom they were all preparing themselves to enjoy. But in another, it was hard to make sense of the urges, the soft smiles, the endless desire to kiss one another's lips, to hold hands in the Orchard, to lie beside one another at night.

Nobody was as scared for the real world as K and J. But if there was one thing the end of the Parenthood taught them, it was that a boy and a girl couldn't be brave unless they were scared of something to begin with.

The others noticed this. Their sisters and brothers came to them for reassurance. And K and J tried their best to give it.

Yet, despite a man slowly perishing in one of the two buildings they temporarily still called home, despite the unfathomable and sudden responsibility of forty-nine twelve-year-olds, Warren Bratt was much more worried about a word that kept coming up.

And that word was not *Inspection*.

"You guys keep saying that," he'd say to the Alphabet Boys and the Letter Girls. "But you realize we can go anywhere, right? Anywhere in the world?"

"Yes," they'd say. "We know," they'd say.

"So why?" Warren would ask. Over and over he'd ask, "Why do you want to go there? Of all places . . . Why *there*?"

"Because," they'd say. "Your book," they'd say.

And they continued to say it until the incredible day came that they left the Turrets behind.

They even said it on that very day.

"We want to go to Milwaukee."

Barbara Burt, M.D.
65 West Collier Street
Laramie, WY

Michael Stowe—

Thank you again for giving me a chance to represent myself via letter, as I don't believe I come off quite the same way over the phone and, besides, it's by the written word that I'd be working with you, if I'm so honored with the chance.

I'm interested in what you're doing in Michigan. I have an extensive history with the area, though I've been west for a year now, and, as you know, I have over a decade of experience with what we both like to call "Elevated Experiments." I'll stop shy of evaluating you here, in a letter aimed at getting me a job, but allow me to say how impressed I am with the fact that you want a personal psychiatrist in the first place. I think it's a very healthy sign. Perhaps it means you'll go far. And while the baggage I come with is mostly full of wisdom, there are also warnings in the suitcases I carry.

For starters: It's important to allow your vision to grow organically, as the people in your flock will invariably change throughout the years.

Secondly, it's wise to incorporate yourself, but I'd avoid anything religious in the process. "Small" religions are guaranteed to elicit the dreaded C word, and where there are cults, authorities will follow.

If you're interested in a much lengthier list of wisdoms and warnings, I'd be thrilled to send some along. Simply send me your tenets, in writing, so that I might go through each one, not only revealing my take on how your flock will most likely react to each one but so that I might enlighten you as to why you've chosen these particular ideals.

Finally, on the phone you implied you are single. If I may, I'd advise you to retain that status until you at least get this thing off the ground. In my experience, couples seem to get in one another's way, each with their own agenda, even when presenting a unified front.

I witnessed the failure of a very large undertaking that could have easily been avoided had either the man or the woman simply let the other work alone.

For no matter how large the vision, no matter how big the eyes to see it, relationships, it seems, make the rules and grow in places no seeds were planted at all.

Thank you and I hope to hear from you very, very soon.

BARBARA BURT, M.D.

Acknowledgments

I met the editor of this book for the first time in person at a bar. It was fitting for a number of reasons. For starters, the setting was loose. The music was loud. We were surrounded by book people: writers and agents, editors and more. And just before signing with Del Rey, I'd confided in a friend that the feeling I was looking for in a publishing house was the metaphorical equivalent of an intellectual clubhouse. That I could almost hear, in the distance, the group of people I ought to be working with, as they caroused in a wooden pub, as someone played a live, and sloppy, guitar, as the conversation rose and ebbed on the waves of electric art. It wasn't until I was actually standing beside Tricia Narwani, discussing (at the time) *Unbury Carol* and New York City's Lower East Side, that I realized I'd signed with the editor of my imaginings, a woman whom I could not only talk shop with, but talk anything, truly, at all. *Carol* was an incredible experience, but the process was surely intensified with *Inspection*. Tricia's notes weren't simply *good ideas*. They were (and are) observations that encouraged me to give the book another round, and another, to reach for a higher level of performance. All while retaining the joy of the impetus it took to begin with.

Tricia, thank you so.

And Allison . . .

A quick story here: I was a week out from wrapping the rewrite of *Inspection*. I got up from my desk with a mind to take our dog,

Valo, for a walk. As I was latching the leash to her collar, Allison, from the couch, asked if I'd considered a certain something happening in the book and didn't I think the book would be better if I did? I brushed the suggestion off, told her it was a good idea but it was also a 150-page idea, and, you know, darling, I'm a week away from finishing this thing. I took Valo outside and made it half a block before I stopped. Valo tugged but I didn't give because I realized then that I couldn't turn my back on the idea that was just presented to me. I rushed back inside, told Allison she was a genius (a cruel one at that; the work I had to do!) and phoned my manager, Ryan Lewis, to tell him her idea. He said the same thing I'd thought outside. *You gotta do it.* And so I did, and so *Inspection* became richer in a way that almost frightens me now, when I consider what the book was close to being if Allison hadn't said a word.

Allison, thank you.

And thank you to Kristin Nelson, my superagent, who had a feeling Del Rey would be a good home for me. Kristin's "feelings" are closer to psychic phenomena, as her instincts are the stuff of legend.

Thanks to Wayne Alexander, who read *Inspection*'s rough draft. I can't imagine a more fascinating lawyer than Wayne, nor one so full of stories of his own.

Thank you to my bandmates in the High Strung who listened to me go on about a megalomaniac who believed genius was distracted by the opposite sex. I can guess how weird this one sounded in its earliest stages.

Matt Sekedat, thank you.

David Moench, Mary Moates, Julie Leung, and the rest of the Del Rey crew, thank you. You make the business of publishing books look as exciting as the act of writing them.

Dave Stevenson, thank you for a cover that made me leap from my office chair.

Kathy Lord, you're the copy editor I wish was there in my office every time I sit down to write. Your assistance with the timeline and so many other things . . . thank you.

My mom, Debbie Sullivan, and her husband, Dave, thank you for reading the books when they were just printouts, unindented and all.

Candace Lake, thank you so.

And Ryan Lewis: when I tell people my manager is one of my best friends, they justifiably guess Ryan and I had been friends before my books started getting published. But that wasn't the case. While working together—under what sometimes has felt like arctic-expedition conditions—Ryan and I have reached that spot where we've extracted bona fide friendship from a notoriously intense dynamic: the artist and manager. It's like we've traveled two arcs, concurrently, one of work, one of play.

We're still traveling them now.

And Dave Simmer, always and ever, thank you for getting this engine started to begin with.

ABOUT THE AUTHOR

Josh Malerman is an internationally bestselling, Bram Stoker Award–nominated American author and one of two singer/songwriters for the rock band The High Strung. His debut novel *Bird Box* was published in the United Kingdom and United States in 2014 to much critical acclaim. His latest novel, *Unbury Carol,* was published in April 2018. He lives in Ferndale, Michigan, with his best friend/soul mate Allison Laakko and their pets Frankie, Valo, Dewey, Marty, and the fish.

joshmalerman.com
Facebook.com/JoshMalerman
Twitter: @JoshMalerman
Instagram: @joshmalerman

ABOUT THE TYPE

This book was set in Sabon, a typeface designed by the well-known German typographer Jan Tschichold (1902–74). Sabon's design is based upon the original letter forms of sixteenth-century French type designer Claude Garamond and was created specifically to be used for three sources: foundry type for hand composition, Linotype, and Monotype. Tschichold named his typeface for the famous Frankfurt type-founder Jacques Sabon (c. 1520–80).